th
SECRET
HEIRESS

A TALE OF DARK SHADOWS
AND EXTRAORDINARY DECEPTION

LUKE DEVENISH

SIMON &
SCHUSTER

London · New York · Sydney · Toronto · New Delhi

A CBS COMPANY

THE SECRET HEIRESS
First published in Australia in 2016 by
Simon & Schuster (Australia) Pty Limited
Suite 19A, Level 1, 450 Miller Street, Cammeray, NSW 2062
This edition published in 2017

10 9 8 7 6 5 4 3

A CBS Company
Sydney New York London Toronto New Delhi
Visit our website at www.simonandschuster.com.au

National Library of Australia Cataloguing-in-Publication entry
Creator: Devenish, Luke, 1966- author.
Title: The secret heiress/Luke Devenish.
ISBN: 9781922052162 (paperback)
             9781922052179 (ebook)
Subjects: Historical fiction.
Dewey Number: A823.4

Cover design: Blue Cork
Cover image: Joana Kruse/Arcangel
Typeset by Midland Typesetters, Australia
Printed and bound in Australia by Griffin Press

The paper this book is printed on is certified
against the Forest Stewardship Council®
Standards. Griffin Press holds FSC chain
of custody certification SGS-COC-005088.
FSC promotes environmentally responsible,
socially beneficial and economically viable
management of the world's forests.

For my grandmothers, Ethel and Bea

IDA

DECEMBER 1886

1

The tall, strikingly handsome and beautifully dressed gentleman with fair, curling hair, olive skin, impressive moustache, and the deepest, kindest, cornflower-blue eyes was quite the most good-looking gentleman sixteen-year-old Ida Garfield had ever seen in her life. He looked to be about twenty, not much more, and his name, Ida already knew, was Mr Samuel Hackett, and he seemed to be keenly looking for someone among the mourners, Ida thought from her unworldly, never-once-left-the-farm perspective. She harboured a fantasy that he was actually looking for her. Mr Hackett lived at Summersby, after all, where he was employed as a secretary; Ida knew that much about him, if little else. Town gossip had given her those details before she'd even seen him in the flesh here at the funeral.

Summersby was the fabled house with a magical name from where, just two short weeks before, a beautiful lady called Miss Matilda Gregory had emerged to journey to Ida's mother's farm where she held a conversation that had ended with Ida offered employment as a maid. Ida had thought she would never again know as much excitement as the prospect of working at Summersby had given her, until, shockingly, everything came crashing down. The news arrived just one week later that Miss Matilda Gregory was dead. Ida hadn't even started work.

Ida's mother was very disappointed, but Ida refused to accept that the tragedy spelled the end of her Summersby prospects. How could something bestowed upon her so miraculously be taken away from her so fast? No official word had come from the great house that she was no longer wanted, and just because a person died did it mean the floors would start cleaning themselves? Ida knew that it didn't. She stared at the handsome Mr Hackett again, and clung anew to her conviction that employment in the same lovely house where he worked could somehow still be hers. Perhaps he'd been charged with collecting her in comfort and style, she fantasised, today being the very December day that Miss Gregory had told her she was to commence her work? That was why she had come to the funeral. She had even brought her little canvas bag along, in which she'd packed a maid's black dress. Somehow everything could still come good, she had said to anyone who'd listen. Ida's mother hadn't stopped her from going, although she'd made her take her sister Evie along for company. It would have been improper to attend a funeral on her own.

The late Miss Matilda Gregory had asked Ida very few questions when she'd come to the farm, so few that Ida had forgotten what most of them were. She had been too dazzled by Miss Gregory's beauty and elegance. Yet one question stood out in memory: was Ida a very bright girl? Her mother had unthinkingly answered for her: sadly no, Ida was not very bright. Her younger sister Evie had got all the brains, Ida got by with the scraps. Ida had shrunk with the humiliation of this, even though she knew it was true because everyone was always telling her as much. Her mother realised then that the opportunity to make something of her unpromising daughter was in danger of receding, because she insisted next that what Ida lacked in brains she made up for with inquisitiveness; so inquisitive was Ida, in fact, that her endless asking of questions was enough to wear a person down, her mother declared; people in town talked of it; in short, Ida was inquisitive to a fault. Ida had squirmed with further embarrassment to hear what were apparently words of praise, yet Miss Gregory had not been dismayed, quite the opposite. To Ida, it seemed that Miss Gregory had almost been pleased by this answer. But that meant little now.

Given Ida was ill-dressed for a funeral, and trying to seem as if she wasn't officially there, it was no surprise Mr Hackett was having trouble spotting her, she thought. Perhaps, Ida supposed, as she paid more attention to the handsome young man than she did to the funeral itself, the crush of townspeople, staff and neighbours made his getting a clear view of those keeping their distance difficult. And yet it was to the periphery that Mr Samuel Hackett still stared, to the very area where Ida stood, and while doing so he gave off the air of someone used to the effect of his good looks upon others.

Ida turned to her sister Evie, christened Evangeline, who, being three years younger, was even smaller than she. Evie had not only heard little, she'd seen little, too. The funeral had bored her and she'd switched off her mind to it. 'Do you see that gentleman, the one with the lovely hair?' Ida asked.

Her sister rubbed her nose. 'No.'

Ida winked. 'I'm going to marry him. Just you wait and see.'

Evie looked rightly sceptical.

'When I'm older,' Ida added. 'When he's seen me for the beautiful girl I really am.'

'You should read a better class of novels,' Evie pronounced.

The coffin containing the late Miss Matilda Gregory's remains was placed beneath soil, and Ida continued to watch as Mr Samuel Hackett made his way towards his waiting carriage, accepting condolences as he went from those mourners who had not managed to utter them earlier. These were mostly Castlemaine District men and women who knew him, Ida supposed.

'Very sudden it was, for a woman so young.' An older lady nearby, sheltering beneath a red parasol, seemed to be talking to no one in particular. 'Terrible shock when the news got out. She was gone before a thing could be done by the doctor.'

Ida looked around to see if there was anyone else to whom the lady might be addressing these remarks, and seeing that there wasn't, she braved a reply. 'It was very sudden. Miss Gregory must have been ill. I met her, you know—'

The lady cut in before Ida could establish her credentials. 'The valet took care of it all. No one could bear to see the body. So how would we know she'd been ill then? Nothing's been said of it. The Coronial Magistrate barely gave it a blink. They're a law unto themselves up at Summersby.'

'Are they?' Evie piped up next to Ida, interested now.

Ida kept her eyes on tall Mr Hackett's face, high above the heads of those who surrounded him.

'No one can keep track of who's living up there and who's not, anymore,' said the parasol lady. 'That's why we need more police constables, love.'

Intrigued, both Ida and Evie waited for what else might be said.

'Who *is* she?' Evie whispered in Ida's ear.

Ida didn't know.

'Makes me remember when old Mr Gregory died two years back and it was weeks before anyone else knew of it,' the lady added, after a moment of watching the crowd. She repositioned her parasol against the sun's glare and brought a hand to pat at the back of her hair. 'And then when we *did* get told, well, we heard that Miss Matilda was engaged to the gent from England, didn't we?'

Ida took her eyes from Samuel Hackett. 'She had an intended?'

The older woman had spotted someone she knew and was preparing to make her leave. 'That's him up there.' She nudged her parasol in Mr Hackett's direction.

Ida was startled. 'But isn't that Mr Hackett? He's the secretary.' She felt her heart melt for him now, seeing his dignified grief for what it was. He'd buried his beloved.

'Quite a rise in the world, wouldn't you say?' The woman looked cynically weary and Ida had a sudden dread they'd been standing conversing with a person of ill repute. She saw now that the lady was actually wearing cosmetics beneath her veil. 'Still, they say he was always a toff to begin with,' the woman said airily as she went off.

Ida and Evie just looked at each other, in equal parts thrilled and mystified.

'Was she what Mum would call a tart?' Evie wondered.

'She had rouge on her cheeks,' said Ida, nodding, wide-eyed.

In the centre of the mourners, Samuel Hackett mounted his carriage with people still waiting to speak to him. He took his seat as if the throng had already dispersed. Ida watched, enthralled, as he again raked all eyes, landing finally on her own. Thrown, she tried to appeal her sympathy in the look she returned him, along with outage on his behalf that Fate could be so cruel as to take his betrothed, and then she offered reassurance that she would serve Summersby loyally, devotedly until the end of her days. This was rather more than a single look could convey.

Samuel Hackett's voice rolled out, a smooth and lovely tenor, as polished as a piece of wedding silver. 'I say, over there, are you Ida?'

It was like the graveyard had opened, spitting up all of the dead. Ida was too shocked to speak.

He smiled at her, amused, realising he'd awed her. 'You, over there, yes, you.' He was waving at her now, friendly. 'Are you, by any chance, Miss Ida Garfield?'

Ida opened her mouth and shut it again, useless.

'Yes, she is!' piped up Evie. 'She's my big sister!'

Ida found herself sitting high and comfortable on a padded leather seat inside Mr Hackett's open-topped carriage. Standing outside where she'd been left to wait, mouth gaping in amazement, Evie stared at Ida inside the glamorous carriage as if she'd just seen her married into royalty.

Samuel sat forward in the padded seat opposite Ida, next to another man of about the same age, being no more than twenty.

But Ida only had eyes for Samuel. 'I must introduce myself,' he told her, presenting a hand, 'I'm Hackett – Samuel Hackett – from Summersby, you know.'

'Yes, I do know,' said Ida, finding something like her voice at last.

'You do?'

'Oh yes,' said Ida, and she was just about to tell him how greatly discussed he was in Castlemaine for his fine looks and lovely voice when she thought the better of it.

'Oh, very good.' He indicated the man next to him. 'And this is my man, Barker. A very loyal chap, been with me for years.'

The other man offered a grunt by way of acknowledgment, his hands scraping back thick, black hair from his forehead. Struck by the startling contrast he made next to Samuel, Ida supposed the other man possessed what might be called sinister good looks, being extremely lithe and dark, with his shock of a mane hiding piercing black eyes. She realised she'd already known of Barker's name in Castlemaine, just as she'd already known of Samuel's, although she hadn't guessed they were connected. Barker was famous, too, or was that infamous? People spoke about him in whispers, bewitched by his baleful appearance. It was thought he had a secret lover, stashed away somewhere surprising. Ida couldn't imagine how a story like that might have started.

'Now then, Ida,' Samuel started to say, 'indeed this is a very sad day—'

'I'm so sorry for it, Mr Hackett,' Ida leapt in, 'it's a terrible loss you've suffered, and I'm so very sorry for it, I really am. Your fiancée, Miss Matilda, was the loveliest young lady I ever met, I swear she was—'

The surprise of seeing the cynical smirk that appeared on Barker's face stopped her.

'You are very kind to say it,' said Samuel, oblivious to the other man. 'As I said, it is a very sad day and we must be forgiven if we let emotions get the better of us.'

'I do understand it if there's no position for me now in the great house, sir,' Ida told him. 'It was Miss Gregory who hired me and now that she's gone . . .'

Samuel looked surprised. 'No position?'

'Dirty floors don't clean themselves, I know that, too, sir, but still, it was poor Miss Gregory who came for me, and those she loved and left behind must have very different plans now, I'm sure—'

The man Barker seemed to be stifling a laugh as he watched her.

'But you have the offer of a position still,' said Samuel.

'I'm sorry?'

'Of course you're still wanted,' he clarified, 'we have very great need of a maid. We would be pleased to see you at Summersby. My late fiancée praised you highly.'

'But?' This struck Ida as wrong. With a sinking heart she knew she had no option but to explain his misapprehension. 'Mr Hackett, I met Miss Gregory for the very first time and the very last time just a fortnight ago, when she came to our farm and had a talk with my mum. She couldn't have praised me – she didn't know me.'

This news was clearly unexpected. 'That is not how my fiancée perceived it. She spoke of you as an upstanding girl. That was why she wished to hire you.'

Humbled, Ida brought a hand to her heart. 'I've been raised right, sir, my mum is always strict yet fair, but perhaps there was some mistake?' Now that Ida actually thought about it all, excitement aside, she remembered that her mother had been just as astonished as Ida was to host the beautiful Miss Matilda Gregory in their home at all, and then to receive an offer of employment from her, what's more. To the best of Ida's knowledge, which wasn't extensive, admittedly, her mother had never met the elegant visitor before either. She was so keen to seize opportunity for Ida that she hadn't asked questions. Miss Gregory's credibility had sat with her name. 'Is it possible Miss Gregory just got me mixed up with someone else?' Ida asked.

Samuel shook his head, beaming at her. The effect was

uplifting; Ida thought she could live forever in such a smile. 'If bringing you to Summersby was what my fiancée wished for then I wish only to honour it. We have need of you, Ida.' He looked at his man again. 'We have need of a *friend*.'

She felt her heart skip a little at the word.

'What is important is that you say yes.' His eyes moved to the little canvas bag that Ida had brought with her to the funeral.

Ida blushed. 'I must confess, Mr Hackett, I wouldn't let myself give up hope about the position – I wanted to work at Summersby more than anything else in the world when Miss Gregory asked me to.' She patted the bag. 'Today is the day she told me I'd be starting. I brought my things along, you see, just in case.'

Ida hadn't expected to be sniffing back tears when she'd stepped down from the carriage in order to say goodbye. 'I'd best be on my way then, Evie,' she told her sister where they stood by the grave-yard gate, a little distance from the carriage, the canvas bag tight in her hand. 'Tell Mum it all worked out wonderfully, just like we prayed it would, and I'll write to her every week.'

If she hoped for Evie's own tears at the perfect turn the day had taken, she didn't get them. Evie was pleased. 'How soon until you're properly earning then?'

'How should I know?' said Ida. 'He didn't tell me that.'

Evie didn't much appreciate this answer. 'Fortnightly? Monthly? When will they pay you your wages?'

'I'll find all that out when I get there, won't I?' Ida said. She was excited beyond measure at the prospect.

Evie frowned. 'I've got schoolbooks to buy, remember. That's what Mum wanted you to go to work for.'

'I know.' Ida kissed her and held her tight. 'I'll not forget it; you're a real champ at that school, Evie, the smartest kid I know.' She wiped a happy tear from where it had adhered to Evie's cheek. 'But until you get the books just keep on going to the Mechanics' Institute, all right?'

Evie nodded. 'Just you remember not to annoy everyone by asking questions. You do that, you know. *A lot*. People talk about it.'

Ida snorted. 'I'm not a twit. I know how to mind my Ps and Qs.'

She took her leave from her sister then, picking her way through the last of the departing mourners to where her new friend, the handsome Mr Samuel Hackett and his man Barker waited patiently in the transport.

Ida told herself she would remember it always, that she'd etch it onto her brain somehow, her first ever look at Summersby. She snatched tempting glimpses of it to begin with, the great mansion half-seen through the canopy of elms and kurrajongs, as they made their way in the carriage past the wrought-iron gate and the Osage orange hedge, and up the long, sweeping drive that led to the house. The carriage trundled and squeaked for hours it felt like, but probably not that long, Ida's canvas bag in her hand all the way, containing a shiny new uniform. She caught new glimpses, different glimpses of her destination as the drive snaked its way through the park, until suddenly Summersby presented itself in entirety, out in the open on the crest of a hill, skirted by wide, green lawn, and bathed in sunshine with not a soul to be seen. As Ida sat there staring, she told herself she would remember forever Summersby's grand, *Italianate* style (for she already knew that this was the name for it), built from Harcourt granite in two long wings that met at an angle. She would recall its full three storeys until the day she expired, she declared to herself, and recall the magnificent tower placed, it was true, somewhat eccentrically so that it rose from the middle of the eastern wing; an affront to some in town for its lack of symmetry but never to her, not now that she'd seen it up close. She would remember the tower's elegant, rounded windows, and remember it topped with a pole flying proudly the flag of Her Majesty's Colony of Victoria. Ida knew she would see forever in her mind the great house ringed by its loggia and above it the encircling balcony giving views. She told herself that she would see the many

French windows, open to the breeze and giving peeks inside on the day she lay down on her death bed, and she would see them just as clearly as she saw them now. She would remember her first look at Summersby better than anything else that had ever happened to her because the fabled home of the Gregorys was to be her home, too.

As Ida came to a halt behind Barker in the upper hallway, she let herself peer up at the strange servant she was expected to treat as her superior.

'How long you been here then, Mr Barker?' Ida asked, keen on making conversation.

Barker's look suggested that such a question was a personal insult. *'A while.'*

She nodded. 'How long you been with Mr Hackett?'

'A while more.' He decided to grace her with chips of information. 'Found him on the Melbourne docks, I did, when he was just off the boat. Pathetic he looked. He needed me.'

Ida didn't much like his words, which struck her as being extremely disrespectful. 'What do you do for him, then? What's your position?'

He seemed to be noting her fresh-scrubbed features with distaste. Unfazed, Ida wouldn't let herself care about that. Other people said she was pretty. 'Valet,' Barker told her.

Ida didn't know what that was but didn't say so. 'Who else lives here? Who else is there in the Gregory family?'

'No one else.'

'No one?'

'The old bloke carked it before my time.'

Ida tried to recall any town gossip she'd been privy to, but found it was hazy in her memory. 'But wasn't there some other girl once, a sister?'

'None of your business if there was.'

'So there are only servants here?'

Barker chuckled. 'I'll tell His Lordship that one.'

Ida caught herself. 'I didn't mean to call Mr Hackett a servant.'

'Call him what you fancy, he gets his pay just like the rest of us – he's the one who does the paying, being the secretary.' He sniffed derisively. 'Bone idle otherwise, but.'

'How much am I getting paid, then?' Ida asked, going straight to the most important matter at hand.

'Twenty pounds per annum, the standard rate.'

'"Per annum"?' she baulked. 'You putting funny stuff in the bread?'

The man did a double take. 'Per year, you fool.'

Ida grinned. 'That means I'm not temporary then, does it? A year guaranteed?'

Barker offered a grunt by way of reply, hands scraping back his hair.

Twenty pounds really wasn't very much, Ida thought. Still, it was better than what she'd earned before, which was precisely nothing. 'I'll take it,' she said, as if she'd been contemplating flouncing off home.

Barker grunted again. 'You'll get your bed and board on top of it.' He unconsciously jangled the keys he carried on a big brass ring.

Ida marvelled at the number of them. 'How can you remember what opens what?' she asked.

Barker ignored her. He twisted the knob of a narrow door. Beyond was a plainly furnished room containing a little iron bed with a quilted coverlet; an old and faded armchair that looked quite inviting all the same; a small wardrobe; a pine tallboy with six good drawers; and a little table upon which stood a washbasin. It was a simple yet comfortable room, filled with light streaming through the lace curtains.

'Hope this suits,' said Barker. He cleared a wad of phlegm from his throat, an ugly sound. 'Hard cheese if it don't.'

Ida didn't have to lie. 'It will suit me very nicely, Mr Barker, thank you,' she told him. She laid her hand on the bed quilt. It was thick and soft.

*

Barker flung aside the damask drapes of the dining room windows, letting the glare of the afternoon sun bounce inside the room. He undid the first window catch and yanked the bottom pane upwards on its sash, letting the clean air of the garden to do its work on the fug.

Ida peered at him from the door.

'What's the matter with you?' said Barker, as if only now remembering she was still there at all.

'I'm not going in,' said Ida, firm.

He blinked at her under his mass of hair. 'You'll do as you're bloody well told.' This earned him one of Ida's best blank stares. 'You'll do as we pay you for.'

'She *died* in there, didn't she?'

The valet glared. 'Who told you that?'

'No one. It's obvious,' said Ida. 'The room's been shut up for a week. There's still breakfast things on the table.'

He crinkled his lips, no doubt wrestling with how best to force her. Short of being beaten into doing it, Ida intended to set her boundaries down as soon as she could. She'd willingly take orders from Mr Hackett because he was a gentleman and nice, and he wanted to be her friend, but his man Mr Barker was another matter.

'All right, she died in here,' Barker conceded. 'Haven't you seen a place where someone's died before?'

Ida blanched. 'I should think not.'

'Ever been inside a hospital?'

'I saw my mum at the Benevolent Asylum in Castlemaine when she went there after having our Frank,' Ida told him. 'He tore her insides.'

Barker was unfazed by this image. 'Did your poor mum cark it?'

'*No.* She pulled through.'

'Saw her lying in a bed, then, did you?'

Ida looked at him like he was a simpleton.

'She was lucky then,' said Barker, 'but somebody before her wasn't; more than one, more like. That's what happens in hospital beds, people cark it in 'em. People cark it in dining rooms, too. It's a fact of life. Now clean this room before I clout you for it.'

The threat of violence, if that's what it was, had negligible effect on Ida. She stayed where she was at the door. 'How did poor Miss Gregory die then? Nobody seems to say.'

The seams of Barker's coat complained, too tight across his back. 'She had a turn.'

'What's that even mean?'

Barker's temper snapped properly. 'Get in here and start sweeping now!'

This worked. Ida scuttled inside, clanging her dustpan, and began to address the floor. Hawkish, Barker watched her for a minute, satisfying himself she was cowed. He departed, leaving her to the chores.

Ida continued as she'd started for a little while longer before she stopped and looked sadly about the room. People died of unknown things all the time, Ida knew, especially here on the goldfields, and especially women. Still, Summersby's beautiful mistress was gone too soon and this was a terrible sorrow. Ida would never know the honour of serving such an elegant person. She wondered where in the room Miss Gregory had breathed her last. Had she been seated or standing? Had she fallen to the floor? What signs were there that someone had even died in here at all?

The gleam of something blue caught her eye where the folds of the window dressings spilled to the floor to form a dust trap. Ida tried to tell what it was from the distance. The object was something hard, brightly blue and shiny, and not very large. It was glass. Curiosity overcame her and Ida stole to the window, lifting the drapes to see. It was a pretty vial, rather like a perfume bottle. Ida picked it up and held it to the light; there was liquid inside. She shook it and the contents moved about, but not as water might. This was definitely scent, Ida thought, or something like it. The vial's neck was secured with a stopper and Ida felt a compulsion to open it. She tentatively tried but found it was tight. She could have forced it, she supposed, but another impulse took her, equally as strong, that she should leave well alone. Ida contemplated putting the vial back where she found it, but feared Barker coming across the thing later and thinking she hadn't cleaned.

The room had grown less spooky. Ida resumed the cleaning, which was mostly a token effort, but an effort all the same. She placed the vial on the dining table, keeping an eye upon it as she went about gathering the week-old breakfast things onto a tray. Cold tea, milk that had turned into lumps, hard, stale slices of toast.

She was grateful to pull the doors shut behind her when she finished, with enough grit and lint in her pan to act as evidence of her labour. Balancing the tray she made her way beyond the stairs to the green baize door and into the kitchen, hoping there'd be someone else about to chat to. She walked in to find the same cosmetics-wearing woman from the funeral.

'Oh!' she said in surprise.

The woman turned around from where she was throwing ingredients into a pot of vegetable soup. 'So he found you then, love?'

'Yes. I mean . . .' Ida was thrown to find her here. Nothing of what the woman had said at the graveyard had suggested she was a servant at Summersby. She'd spoken like an outside observer.

The woman seemed to appreciate Ida's confusion. 'I'm Mrs Jack,' she told her, winking. Ida saw with dismay that her face was still heavy with rouge, which had run a little from bending over the stove. 'I cook here from time to time, in emergencies like, and only then if I can be bothered with it, which between you and me, is less and less. Mrs Jack's well jack of it,' she laughed.

Ida didn't know what to say.

Mrs Jack pulled her apron off and tossed it onto a chair. She was still wearing her funeral clothes. 'Anyway, that's me done and dusted. Keep an eye on the soup, will you, love. Keep it low and covered, then take it off after an hour. That'll do you all for your supper. If you don't see me again, good luck to you.'

She plucked her folded red parasol from an umbrella stand near the dresser and made for the door to the garden.

'But where are you going?' Ida called after her.

'Home, love. You didn't think I actually lived here, did you? Not likely!'

She was gone.

Perplexed by this, Ida sat on a kitchen stool and wondered what to do next. It occurred to her that although there'd been a funeral, there'd not been a wake. While this seemed rather miserly, perhaps it was best. Who would have done the cooking for it, she wondered? Clearly not Mrs Jack. The grand house seemed to have a skeleton staff. The thought of the word 'skeleton' vaguely spooked Ida once more and she was reminded of the perfume vial inside her apron pocket. She took it out and looked at it again. It was really quite lovely, but she didn't dare risk keeping it and being branded a thief on her first day on the job.

Ida needed her maid's wages dearly, or rather, her sister Evie did. A pact had been made between Ida's mother and her maiden aunts that would see Evangeline given respectable schooling. Ida's sister was considered to be bright, far brighter than Ida, and the whole family accepted it and hoped one day to benefit. Ida's own schooling had ended three years ago, at age thirteen, but not so Evie's, who was thirteen now. Ida's maid's wage would now help ensure Evie did the Garfield family proud. It was why Ida's mother had been so happy when Miss Gregory had offered employment. It was why Evie herself had not shed a tear at losing Ida.

Something stuck in Ida's inquisitive mind. The late Miss Gregory had specifically asked about Ida's brightness, and when told that Ida was not much known for being bright but was inquisitive at least, she had not been put off. Ida was sure she had not imagined this. Miss Gregory had been open to there being something good about her.

Ida tucked the pretty glass vial inside her apron again, planning to do whatever was appropriate with it later. She had just given up on sitting alone and was pushing through the green baize door once more when she felt the hair on her forearms prickle. It was an unpleasant sensation and she rubbed at her skin, which then became goose pimpled under her fingers. Shivers ran up her back as if a cold, dead hand was clamped to her, shoving her into the entrance hall. Ida stood startled for a moment and compulsively looked behind her. No one was there.

She heard a tapping sound from somewhere very close; a sound both unexpected and yet familiar. It took a moment to place it. 'Dog's nails,' Ida said when she recognised it. She listened again, it was unmistakable. It was the sound of a dog's claws trotting up the stairs overhead.

Delighted that Summersby housed pets, Ida ran to the great staircase to see what sort of animal it was. Looking up, she could see no sign. 'Here, girl!' she called out, hopefully; all dogs being girls on account of Daisy, the beloved Garfield farm dog.

Ida ran up the stairs to the first landing, and when that revealed no sign of the animal, she went all the way to the next floor, peering up and down the hallway. She listened again. The tapping was still there somewhere, only further away now, and then it was gone entirely.

Ida was perplexed. There was no sign of a blessed dog anywhere.

'Mr Hargreaves Cooper from Kyneton is here,' Ida announced to the drawing room in a voice little suited to the task. Two days had passed since the funeral. The men within reacted as one to her squeak and Ida thought it best to fetch brandy, but in doing so she forgot about the guest, leaving him abandoned in the hall. Hargreaves Cooper made his own way inside, approaching Samuel Hackett.

'Hargreaves.' Blond, handsome Samuel shook the greying solicitor's broad hand. 'You must be very parched,' he said, 'you've ridden a long distance.'

'It's a sad business. My condolences, Hackett,' Cooper replied.

Watching them both, and watching Ida, too, the valet Barker scraped the hair from his eyes. Perhaps it was the light, but

Barker was looking happier today, it seemed to Ida. She supposed that his demons – if that's what he had – were not troubling him quite as much. He was looking somehow fuller in his tight, black garb; more physically imposing with his black eyes glinting at her from beneath his net of hair. Still, he was nothing in comparison to Samuel Hackett, by far the most handsome man Ida had met, or would ever likely meet, she thought. The sight of him alone still sent Ida slightly giddy. The few occasions in the last two days when he had spoken to her – there'd been three so far – would be cherished always, Ida told herself. Already she had found herself dreaming of him at night.

Ida had on a different uniform than when she'd been hired, and now wore an official housemaid's black crepe frock and bustle. She'd received a promotion after only one day, and although she feared that Summersby – or Mr Hackett at least – might have wished for a better class of domestic than herself, she was not going to question good fortune. As her mother had so often told her, girls of small intelligence were lucky to know what day it was, let alone the month and the year. Ida knew she had been given the one opportunity she was ever likely to get in her life and she'd not be found poking holes in it.

She delivered Samuel and the visiting solicitor a brandy bottle on a tray, having remembered to include glasses. Cooper had already seated himself in an armchair, and Samuel began to pour them both a glass once he realised that Ida lacked the wit to do it for him.

'All death is a sad business,' Samuel said to Cooper, 'but I think in this instance we both know I was forewarned.'

The solicitor cradled his glass and raised an eyebrow.

'Well, don't we?' Samuel asked.

Ida looked around for Barker only to realise he had already gone. She made her way to the room's great double doors and pulled them almost shut behind her as she left the room. But some perversity made her remain on the other side. She knew it was wrong, yet she did it anyway. The people of Summersby fascinated her, all the more because none of them much took the time to talk to her. Robbed of the pleasure of speaking, Ida felt she had no choice but to take new comfort from listening. She looked behind her into the grand entrance hall for any sign of the valet but could see nothing of him. She pressed her eye to the crack between the doors.

'Miss Gregory was the embodiment of good health when you declared your engagement, Samuel,' Cooper was saying from inside the room.

'I have a doctor's report to attest to it,' said Samuel.

'Foal is a fine Castlemaine physician.'

'Who sadly writes worthless reports,' Samuel said. 'My fiancée, as I'm sure you now see, was anything but well and I am all the more a dupe for ever believing otherwise. Very gratifying to see Foal change his tune for the Coroner's benefit, at least.'

Ida had left the doors not quite closed, and through the crack she could actually tell that Samuel was pleased to see the solicitor show discomfort at this remark, although as to what it all quite meant she had no idea. The implication seemed to be that Miss Gregory had in some way been unwell, but not in a way that the doctor had been able to diagnose.

'Her ailments, if that's what she had, were not physical,' Cooper reminded him.

Samuel said nothing.

'Blame cannot be cast upon Foal. Physically Miss Gregory was very sound.'

'I am not blaming Foal,' said Samuel, 'I am blaming myself.'

'Why, for heaven's sake?'

'For loving her.'

Ida's heart broke. 'Poor man,' she whispered to herself.

Cooper looked further embarrassed, perhaps he was wary of tears, Ida wondered. 'For a man to love his intended is not shameful,' said Cooper.

Samuel signalled an end to this path of discourse. 'You are here about my late fiancée's will, an unpleasant formality, but one for which I appreciate you making the journey, Hargreaves.'

Cooper placed his brandy down. Ida realised too late she'd not given any coasters.

'I'm sure matters could have waited another week or so,' said Samuel, 'until I felt fit to attend you at your office at least, but as I say, I appreciate your professionalism. When my fiancée and I signed our wills with you last year, your professionalism then put us both very much at ease.'

Ida vaguely wondered why a Kyneton solicitor might have been preferred over a local man.

'There is a later will,' the solicitor said.

Samuel looked up from his brandy. 'There are the wills Matilda and I signed in your presence.'

'There are. And there is a further will Miss Gregory asked my late colleague Herbert Walsh to draw up for her to sign some days later.'

Without quite knowing why, yet knowing that she was privy to something interesting, Ida bit her tongue. Through the crack in the door, the look she saw upon Samuel's face was one of absolute astonishment. 'My fiancée had you prepare another will? Further to the one she just signed upon our engagement?'

'Not me, Walsh,' said Cooper. 'She made an appointment to see him of her own accord, I gather, and she instructed Walsh to draw up another will – a will that post-dates the other.'

Samuel became disbelieving. 'But why didn't she tell me of this?'

Cooper could provide no answer.

'Why didn't you tell me?'

'I didn't know of it.'

'But you and Walsh shared offices?'

The solicitor seemed to be sweating. Ida felt under her own arms and realised she was perspiring a little, too. 'Shared rooms and furniture, yes,' Cooper told Samuel, 'but not confidences. I had no idea of it, Hackett. I only learned of the will's existence when Walsh died in June. His files came to me.'

Samuel's temper rose. 'Still you didn't tell me?'

Cooper seemed to be resisting the urge to hook a finger under his tight, high collar. 'You praise my professionalism, so I'm sure you see I was in something of a bind,' he said. 'Miss Gregory was very much alive when I discovered it. It was not my right to inform you she had made another will with my departed colleague. It was her right to inform you and hers alone. If, as it seems, she chose not to do so . . .' The solicitor trailed off.

'Please show it to me,' said Samuel.

Cooper withdrew a stamped, sealed document from a case at his feet as Ida strained to see it properly through the crack. She couldn't quite. 'It is one of two copies,' Cooper said, 'the other remains in my chambers. I have read neither document, of course, and have no idea of the contents.'

Samuel took the document, examining it closely for a moment, before lifting the wax seal and opening it. He took his time in reading what was there. Once finished he refolded the document but did not return it to the solicitor.

'As I said, the sealed copy remains in my chambers,' said Cooper when it seemed likely to him that Samuel would not speak first. 'I shall open it upon my return and commence the executor's duties formerly assigned to Walsh.'

Samuel still said nothing, but now gave all the appearance of wrestling with some internal force. 'Barker!' He suddenly stood up, making Cooper jump. 'Barker, I want you!'

Ida lost her footing and tumbled into the room, barrelling into Samuel's armchair.

'Ida?' he said, surprised.

She blushed to the roots of her hair. 'I . . . I'm so sorry, Mr Hackett . . . I must have tripped in the hall.'

He placed a reassuring hand on her shoulder. 'No harm done. I am afraid that Mr Cooper has been the bearer of unexpected news, that is all, nothing of concern.'

But the look on his face told Ida that he was very concerned.

'Where is Barker?'

Ida was still blushing. 'I don't know.'

Samuel looked annoyed but was making an effort not to speak harshly in front of her.

'What is it, Mr Hackett?' Ida asked, pulling self-consciously at her ill-fitting apron. It had belonged to a girl who had recently given notice.

'It is quite all right, like I said, you mustn't be concerned.' He guided her towards the hall. 'And try to remember to close the doors behind you when you leave a room. Has Barker given you any instruction?'

'I'd be lucky if he gave me the time of day,' Ida exclaimed before she thought, then saw the error in it and wanted to kick herself.

She assaulted the drawing room doors on her way out, making a clamour of the task until she had them properly shut.

Ida waited on the other side again, knowing herself to be mad for the risk she was taking, yet compelled to hear more all the same. By pressing her ear to the closed doors she could still make out the conversation.

Cooper said, 'Again, let me express my sadness and condolences, Hackett.'

It was some seconds before Samuel answered. 'Matilda's money . . .' His voice sounded weary and strained. 'I am not the beneficiary of her estate. This second will nullifies me as her heir.'

The solicitor was evidently shocked. 'Has she named another?'

'Yes.' Samuel paused for another moment, as if he was giving what would come next due weight. 'She names *Matilda Gregory*.'

There was a further pause, until Cooper said. 'But your fiancée had no other legal family.'

'She still has no other legal family,' Samuel said. 'She is still the last of her line.'

'Hackett, this is not making sense,' Cooper protested. 'Your late betrothed has willed her estate to *herself*?'

Ida heard Samuel pass the document to him. 'It seems my late fiancée was not, as she had me believe, Matilda Gregory at all. According to this will, she was *Margaret* Gregory, her twin sister, and she makes the deception clear.'

Ida's eyes bulged in her head.

'It's not possible,' said Cooper.

Samuel went on. 'It would seem that she wished for the world – and for me in particular – to believe that she was Matilda, and in this she was successful while she breathed. But she says in this will that she was not Matilda at all, she was Margaret . . . and I'm sure you now appreciate the somewhat alarming implications here, Hargreaves.'

In the pause that followed Ida wondered if the solicitor had now gone rather pale.

'Allow me a moment to read the document, Hackett.'

Ida waited, ready to spring away in an instant at the slightest sound of anyone approaching the doors from within.

But neither man rose from his chair and Cooper began to read aloud from the will: '. . . *in the months before my father died I discovered a provision in his will stating that I, Margaret Gregory, was not to inherit any portion of his fortune. This fortune would instead be bequeathed to my twin sister, Matilda. Furthermore, as willed by my father, I was to leave Summersby upon his death and move to Constantine Hall, there to receive a small income from a trust, unless I chose to leave, in which event I would be left completely penniless and destitute. In short, Summersby was never to be mine nor the wealth and position that came with it.*'

Ida tried to get her head around what she was discovering. She thought she grasped it, but the notion of wills and counter wills was all very new.

'*I believed this provision in my father's will to be unnecessarily cruel,*' Cooper continued to read aloud, '*it was ample evidence of his lack of love for me and his relentless obsession with controlling my heart and happiness. Moreover, the prospect of leaving beloved Summersby was intolerable, and so, in the days of his last illness, I committed a deception I had committed many times before: I exchanged places with my sister, who is identical to me in appearance. She is also, regretfully, an impressionable and vulnerable person, extremely naïve in her being, and she agreed to the trick, just as she had so often done before in our childish games, but this time she did not know the real reason for it. At my insistence, the deception was maintained up to and beyond my father's death, and Matilda, very wrongfully, was subsequently removed from our home under the false belief of others that she was I.'*

There was another pause and Ida tensed to flee again, ears strained to hear the slightest creak of a footfall on the floor. But the solicitor returned to reading the will.

'I have carried this dark secret into my engagement but I cannot carry it to my grave. Although I love my fiancé dearly, I pray that he some day comes to understand my reasons for willing Summersby, along with all my wealth and property, not to him, as it should be, and would be if we wed, but to Matilda, from whom it was so shamefully gained . . .'

There was a further pause, and then Samuel said, 'The real Matilda Gregory is very much alive.'

'But this beggars' belief,' Cooper told him, 'it's an appalling deception, and that it has somehow been allowed to continue undiscovered for this long – it's almost inconceivable. Where and what is this Constantine Hall?'

'That's the best part, Hargreaves,' Samuel said, 'the part you'll enjoy the most—'

'Hackett, I am finding this bewildering enough,' Cooper interjected. 'Is it one of the great houses along the Bellarine?'

'There's very little great about it,' said Samuel, 'Constantine Hall is a genteel institution for the well-to-do insane.'

Ida gasped, appalled.

Inside the room Samuel delivered a *coup de grâce*. 'The real Matilda Gregory is confined to a mad house.'

Her eyes wide, Ida's real fear of discovery at last outweighed her need for scandal. She tore herself away only to run little more than a yard into the entrance hall before she saw Barker at the end of it with his arms crossed, glaring at her. The shock of this proved short lasting.

'You can scold me or even sack me, but if you've got any sense at all you'll not do neither, Mr Barker, and you'll ask me what I heard instead,' Ida declared.

The valet regarded her through flinty eyes.

'Well?' she wondered.

Barker took a single step towards her. 'I've worked with some muck-common types in my time,' he told her, 'but a scrap like you would make a flophouse look respectable.'

Ida bit her lip at that but chose to brazen it out. 'The sack then, is it? Your loss, Mr Barker, and a crying shame, too. You wouldn't believe what I just heard.' She made to walk past him, head high and aloof, but failed to note the boot he stuck out in front of her. Ida tripped and fell sprawling to the floor. Stunned, she flipped inelegantly on to her backside, fearing he'd now give her a kicking, but when he didn't she just blinked at him from the floor in dismay.

'No one's giving you the sack,' said Barker, eyes glinting beneath his hair, 'unless . . .'

'Unless what?' Ida shot back.

'Unless what you tell me proves to be as miserable as you look right now.'

She told him.

While Ida waited for Barker's response to the news she saw the ghost of a smile appear and disappear on his lips in the space of a heartbeat; long enough for her to tell that the news had actually *pleased* him. Ida guessed she'd not be getting her marching orders yet. She took a chance on climbing to her feet again and was further relieved when he didn't do anything else to humiliate her. 'What do you think of it, then, Mr Barker?'

'I think many things,' said Barker, enigmatically.

Ida found this not very illuminating. 'But Miss Matilda wasn't even Miss Matilda,' she ventured, amazed. 'The real one's locked up in a nut house!'

Barker just crinkled his lips, still as a statue, saying nothing.

'Don't you even find this a shock?' she harped.

'Nothing shocks me when it comes to those twins,' he said, flatly.

Ida couldn't fathom his non-response. 'But to have changed places – to have had everyone fooled!'

He shrugged his bony shoulders. 'They spent their girlhoods doing it, so I've heard. Things got to the point where no one could have told you who was who anyway, even if they cared, which I hear no one much did. They were a pair of minxes both and best handled with thick gloves. Should be no surprise it came to this. Just desserts by the sounds of it.'

Ida looked even more startled. 'Well, I never . . .'

The valet suddenly lurched from inactivity like stalled clock-work thumped free. She gaped after him as he loped down the hall towards the baize door to the kitchen. 'Well, Mr Barker?' she called after him.

He stopped at the door, craning his long neck to look back at her. 'Put your head to getting the bedrooms made nice.'

'Why? Will the real Miss Matilda be coming to stay?'

'It's no business of a muck-common scrap like you if she is. Get on with it.'

The one bad thing about being at Summersby, Ida had decided, was the company she had to keep, or rather, the lack of it. The work itself was drudgery, but that was no better or worse than what she would have suffered if she'd been kept on at home, yet the company was decidedly poor, and it was this that threatened to get her spirits down. Aside from handsome Mr Hackett there was no one else to help make the days go faster.

Ida had almost made a friend of Ruby, the kitchenmaid, when she'd first arrived, but that was over before it was barely begun when Ida came downstairs in the morning to be informed by Barker that Ruby had given notice and was just then being driven off to town in the trap. Ida had rushed outside to see Ruby in a Sunday bonnet, perched high in the seat, vanishing in swirls of dust. Not even a goodbye.

In Ruby's wake Ida had looked around to see who else might be a source of fun but had found the pickings grim. Summersby's official cook had already departed before Ida had even been hired and the household was making do with Mrs Jack, who displayed little interest in the grand estate and even less in the staff. Worse, Ida feared Mrs Jack was of an indeterminate foreign persuasion, and Ida's mother had warned her about the unwashed ways of Continentals. On most days Mrs Jack didn't bother showing up, which was when the rest of them had to forage for something to eat from the kitchen stores, and from this somehow scratch up a meal for Mr Hackett. When Ida referred to 'the rest of them', she meant herself and Barker. The one or two outside staff that tended Summersby's grounds had nothing whatsoever to do with those who worked indoors, looking after themselves in their own little cottage. Ida had no hope of friendships beyond Summersby's walls. She lamented this the most when alone in her cot at night.

'How long are you and me supposed to manage all by ourselves then?' Ida complained to him one morning over the porridge.

'None of your business,' said the valet.

'It is my business when I spend all day doing the work of hundreds.'

Barker seemed to be eyeing the bumps of her breasts beneath the dull crepe uniform. Ida shifted awkwardly in her seat, self-conscious of her womanhood. 'If you're handing in your notice you'll want to make a head start on it,' he shot. 'It's a long walk to town.'

'You sent Ruby home in the trap!' Ida protested.

Barker's mouthful of porridge went down the wrong way and he coughed and spluttered it across the tabletop. 'You can use Shank's pony,' he told her when he'd recovered himself. He took another mouthful.

Ida sulked at this insult, but declined to quit. 'Won't we ever be getting some more new staff then?'

'That's nothing to do with me,' said Barker.

Ida wiped his porridge mess up with a rag. 'You're the valet,' she said, 'don't you have a say?'

Barker's lack of comment on that gave Ida the further impression he was very happy for arrangements to stay as they were, though she couldn't conceive why.

'But a house this size – I can't keep up with it, Mr Barker.'

The porridge tried to stick in his throat again until he forced it south. 'You're keeping up well enough,' Barker said.

This took Ida by surprise. Had she been complimented on her work? She decided she had been and shot a smile at him.

He groped for his mug of tea. 'His Lordship's going away soon,' Barker announced, 'and me with him. Things will be sorted, one way or another, upon return.'

Ida took some heart from this. 'Oh, it'll be nice to have someone else to talk to!'

'You'll not be talking to anyone,' Barker told her, slurping at his tea.

The heart fled as quickly as it had come. She felt depressed. Contemplating yet more days and weeks of unrelieved loneliness, save the occasional snatches of chat with Samuel, it was almost as much as Ida could get her head around without crying. She thought of her sister Evie so happy and loved in the little Castlemaine school, the apple of the teacher's eye, praised to the skies by her mother and all her maiden aunts, and herself sent packing to a life of domestic drudgery without so much as a word of gratitude from any of them. Ida felt abandoned.

'I heard the dog again,' she whispered. 'It was wandering around when I was trying to clean.'

Barker looked up sharply from his cup.

'I heard the clip of its nails on the floorboards.'

Barker slammed his cup on the table 'What bloody dog?'

'The dog that lives here,' said Ida. 'She wouldn't let me pat her, she wouldn't let me find her even. I wish she would, she'd be a bit of company.' She felt a sob catch at her throat. 'At home we have a dog called Daisy.'

Barker stared at her through night-black eyes a moment. 'Summersby doesn't have any dog.'

Ida took a sip of her own tea. 'Yes it does. I heard her.' The tea had grown cool.

'It has a *dead* dog,' said Barker.

Ida blanched. 'Don't you try to hurt her!' she said, clutching her cup. 'Poor thing's not doing any harm. She doesn't even do her mess inside!'

Barker was chilly. 'It's already dead, you little idiot. Carked it the same day as the mistress did.'

Ida blinked at him. 'They died *together?*'

Barker just sniffed.

'But, but I've been *hearing* it, Mr Barker.'

He mocked her. 'What you've been hearing is the sound of your own bloody cretinism.'

Ida fell back as if struck.

'And what sort of dog kennel will I find those bedrooms looking like when I kick open the doors in two minutes?' he wondered.

Ida squirmed and knocked back her last mouthful of cold tea. 'Which bedrooms?'

'Don't know yet,' said Barker, toying with her. 'I'll decide that on the run.'

'They all look spick and span, I swear they do!' Ida protested, mentally counting off those rooms she'd cleaned and those she'd merely 'tidied'.

'I'll be the judge of that,' said Barker, 'and I judge *hard.*'

Ida was off from the table before he'd shifted a muscle.

Once it became apparent that Barker's threatened inspection would likely not be happening anytime soon, Ida ceased her panic somewhat and set her mind towards putting what she termed 'finishing touches' to the bedrooms she'd been assigned. Of the six or seven rooms that had fallen to her care the one she liked best was the one she called the 'Chinese Room', on account of its Chinoiserie screen of pagodas and dragons. Ida very much saw it as a lady's bedroom, even though it wasn't typically feminine. She put all her efforts into making it as attractive and comfortable as she imagined a fine lady would require it. It was Ida's belief that a lady would be gracing the room before long. The extraordinary confession from beyond the grave had seared itself into her mind. A poor, hapless woman, the *real* Miss Matilda Gregory, had been shut up in a madhouse by her own twin's lie. Ida was very shocked to think that the now-dead sister, the one who had come to Ida's mother's farm so elegantly dressed and seeming so nice, had in fact caused such a thing to happen. And yet *how* had it happened? To Ida it raised far more questions than it answered, and her mind went back to something she had felt so sure about on her very first day at Summersby: the late Miss Gregory had hired her *because* she asked questions. The late Miss Gregory had been pretending to be her own sister so as not to be shut away, committing a deception that was certainly despicable, yet all the same, she was still the one who had hired Ida. So, questions she would ask.

Surely the wronged Miss Matilda would be given her liberty soon?

To this end Ida had already placed inside the room a number of items she had found in other locations that she felt would give pleasure to a woman of exacting tastes: a ruby vase, slightly chipped at the base; a German shepherdess figurine; and a small, flat and rather fetching ivory inlaid box, quite empty, yet decorated in a Moorish style, on which someone had inked inside the lid, 'Remember Box'. That Ida had never actually had exposure to a person of exacting tastes accounted for these eclectic choices – choices driven by impressions gained from ladies she'd read about in novels.

Ida placed the blue perfume vial among some other ornamental bits and pieces on the dressing table. Having kept it hidden in her apron pocket for far too many days, it was with some relief that Ida decided that the Chinese Room was the only possible place for such a lovely piece of glass.

As she arranged it on the tabletop, regarding it before she shifted it another inch or so to the right, she was seized again by the impulse to open it. Ida picked up the vial and held the glass to the window light. She shook it a little and the liquid sloshed about inside. Before Ida knew it she had gripped the stopper with her apron and was struggling to pry the thing loose. It came free with a little pop. Ida brought the vial to her nose and gave a sniff.

It was rosemary oil.

Slightly mystified by this, as if she'd been expecting something different, even though she couldn't have said what that might have been, Ida dabbed a little on her wrist and sniffed it again. It was unmistakably rosemary.

She turned with a start to see Barker at the door. He saw the vial in her hand but made no comment on it. 'The room is as clean as a shiny new pin, Mr Barker, I swear it!' she exclaimed. She quickly put the stopper in again and placed the thing back on the dressing table.

But Barker had apparently forgotten any threat he'd made of inspections. 'You're coming with us,' he told her, 'His Lordship and me, first thing in the morning, to Melbourne.'

Ida's jaw dropped in amazement. 'I . . . I've never even been as far as Bendigo.'

He laughed. 'Then don't make a tit of yourself. City types sniff out a hayseed like you by the dung in their hair.' He inhaled through his long, sharp noise, smirking, as if to show her how it would be.

Rightly offended, she self-consciously smelled the air around her. The scent of rosemary remained. 'Are we going to find the real Miss Matilda, then?'

He was paused to leave the room again, but held back for another moment. 'We're doing more than that. We're bringing her home.'

Ida was thrilled. 'Poor lady. She'll be so happy.'

Barker just shrugged.

'And Mr Hackett's so kind.' An unfortunate oversight occurred to her. 'I haven't told him how sorry I am to have heard what happened!' she cried.

'What you heard by spying at doors?'

Ida felt awkward. 'It wasn't like that.'

'A sackable act was what it was like,' said Barker, enjoying this. 'You should be thanking me for not telling him myself.'

Ida thought is wise to change the subject. 'What does he think will happen when she comes here?'

Barker looked suspiciously at her. 'What do you mean "happen"?'

'Well . . .' Ida didn't know quite what she meant. She looked around her. 'Will she like this room?'

Barker seemed to take in her decorating efforts for the first time. He frowned. 'It's not to my taste.'

'It's meant for a lady!'

He dismissed this. 'You can bung her in a barrel for all it means to me.'

Ida was finding these conversations very trying. 'Mr Barker, you do see that this new Miss Matilda is our mistress now, don't you? Shouldn't you speak with respect?'

She watched as he apparently contemplated the idea. Then he smirked again and let the net of black hair fall across his eyes, hiding them from view.

It was incredible to Ida that a single house could have so many rooms – and so many hallways and windows and long flights of stairs into the bargain – all of which a person was somehow expected to keep clean. Ida closed one door on a sparkling room only to open another on a room that was filthy. Or at least it felt that way, struggling with her mop and pail, her broom and pan, her duster, her rags and her vinegar. Ida tried to tell herself it would all be worthwhile, if not for herself, sacrificing her best years so selflessly, but for her sister Evie, to whom Ida would be able to turn, broken and prematurely aged by her hard labours, to duly fall upon as a favour returned.

Ida daydreamed at length about this imagined future indolence.

She constructed images of herself, reclining on cushions, happily fat and immobile, calling for honey-spread bread, sliced thick as her arm, served on good willow pattern china by her ever-grateful sister, who would succumb to hot tears of gratitude at the life Ida had so lovingly provided for her. As to what this life for Evie might actually be, Ida was vague. She found it hard to conceive of what the opportunities might be for girls who got schooling. She knew of no other girl who had been schooled beyond thirteen. She'd read in a novel once of a girl who'd worked in a big house as a governess. The job seemed to have brought the girl very few moments of happiness, but at least it was a job and better than beating rugs.

Another room cleaned to her diminishing standards, Ida hefted her things into the hallway and pulled the door closed behind her. About to congratulate herself on having completed the entire third floor's worth of rooms in record time, Ida was on the point of returning to the stairs when she realised there was a door she had overlooked. Different than all the others, it was disguised to match the walls, being papered halfway up, with the bottom half covered by a dado. But it was still a door – it had a handle and hinges – and Ida worried that she had hitherto missed it.

'Gawd knows the state of things in there . . .' she said to herself, anticipating Barker's words should he learn of her mistake. She turned the handle. It was locked. Ida twisted it harder, pushing her weight against the door. It wouldn't shift.

Apprehensive, she looked up and down the hallway, feeling as if the dark valet was somewhere, watching her from a shadow. 'But how can I clean a room I can't even get into, Mr Barker?' she whined, rehearsing the moment he would spring out and catch her.

She peered at the ceiling above and then back towards the stairs again and tried to work out from the map of the house she carried in her head what the room beyond the door might be. 'Is it the door to the tower?' she wondered to herself.

Ida gave up. The door was locked fast; the one door in the whole of Summersby to be so. She pressed an ear to it. From somewhere beyond she almost thought she heard the tap of dog's claws upon boards. She sprang back before her mind played any more tricks upon her.

'Not falling for that again,' she said aloud.

Barker stretched out his black-clad limbs as he settled inside the carriage, the last one to enter, forcing Samuel to make more space for him.

'Do take care,' said Samuel, wincing.

Already squeezed into a corner of her own, Ida watched both men, eager to make the most of the opportunity that being confined with them gave. She was primed for conversation, but thought it best to wait for overtures from Samuel first. She attempted to gauge his mood.

Dressed splendidly for the metropolis, Samuel shifted in his seat as the carriage lurched into motion, pulling away from the great house. A fat, buzzing blowfly was trapped inside the space with them. Samuel looked fixedly outside, watching the stately kurrajongs pass the window. The fly crawled across the windowpane.

'So, then. What's the plan now?' Barker asked, breaking the ice.

Ida was startled. Was he addressing the question to her?

Samuel answered without looking at the other man. 'You are well aware of what is ahead.'

'I don't mean that,' said Barker. 'We're going to Melbourne, ain't we? Be a shame to miss the pleasures of Gomorrah.'

Samuel shot him a glare. 'We are *not* visiting bordellos.'

Ida felt herself growing hot.

Samuel remembered her then and was mortified. 'I am so sorry, Ida.' He turned to the window again, before looking back at her for a second glance. 'How attractive you look. You have chosen your clothes with care today.'

She beamed. 'Thank you, Mr Hackett.'

'Who says we're not?' Barker shot back, not having dropped his topic.

Samuel frowned. 'Need I remind you that I am a man of position?' he asked, incredulous. The fly took off again, buzzing at his face.

'A secretary?' Barker chortled. 'What position's that in the footer field?'

Samuel smiled apologetically at Ida.

Barker frowned in the direction of Samuel's trousers. 'What's the trouble? Doesn't your tackle work no more? Sounds like the old mistress had a lucky escape, then.' He laughed at his own coarse humour.

Ida couldn't believe her ears at what he was saying.

Samuel seemed to be using every ounce of his will not to speak his mind. Ida wished the carriage seat would open up and swallow Barker whole for speaking so insolently. Then she and Samuel might be left alone to conduct a civilised conversation. So badly she wanted to ask him about his broken heart and his fiancée's dreadful lies.

'Don't worry, I'm sure it all works like clockwork,' said Barker. The fly alighted on the seat gap between him and Ida and he crushed it under the heel of his hand.

Silence fell between all three of them as the carriage left the Summersby grounds through the great wrought-iron gates, joining the gravelled road that led to Castlemaine. Barker seemed to be eyeing the travelling jacket Samuel wore. He reached over and plucked a cigar from the inside pocket.

'Got a light?' Barker asked him.

Samuel visibly bit back his anger, fumbling in his pocket for a box of Cricket matches. Barker lit the cigar himself, retaining the box. 'Fair enough,' he said. 'No cat-houses then. Not if you're squeamish about catching a dose.'

Samuel was icy. 'Might I remind you, Barker, you promised to aid me in this journey?'

'That I did,' said Barker, puffing on the cigar. It had failed to catch and he fumbled for the matches again. 'Found a prime grade idiot for you in Ida.'

Ida felt the words like a blow to the face. If he'd said them back in the house, when it was just the two of them, then she wouldn't have cared, but to be called a fool in front of Mr Hackett was crushing. 'You did not *find* me, Mr Barker,' she said with dignity, 'the late Miss Gregory did. And I think you're being horribly rude to Mr Hackett.'

Barker leant forward, relighting the cigar. 'She reckons she hears the dog when she cleans.' He tapped the side of his head with a long finger. 'Prime grade idiot.'

Samuel cast another look at her; it didn't hold pity, there was only kindness in it. 'I apologise again for my man, Ida,' he said. 'You are already my friend, a friend I value, and you deserve no such rudeness.' He cleared his throat, evaluating the valet. 'Barker is my friend, too, and he is very loyal to me, as I am to him, but at times I wonder if perhaps we are each too loyal.'

Barker was chuckling now, waiting for what might come next.

'. . . Some have remarked that our closeness bonds us like brothers. And like brothers we sometimes squabble and disagree more than we should. Barker can be a moody fellow, as you can see.'

Ida looked condemningly at Barker. The valet puffed on his cigar.

Ida took the opportunity to take the lead. 'Mr Barker told me he became your man when you first arrived from England, Mr Hackett?'

'That is true,' said Samuel. 'I was very grateful to find him. Perhaps we both were?' He gave Barker a measured look.

'Been here very long, then?' Ida wondered.

'I've been in the colony just a little under four years. I was not long turned sixteen when I disembarked – your age, Ida. Seems a lifetime ago now. Did you know Barker and I share the same birth year?'

The valet kept the cigar clamped in his teeth, eyes out the window now, bored by Samuel's story.

'Do you miss your old home?' Ida asked next.

Samuel considered this, and if he arrived at an answer, Ida got the distinct impression that it wasn't one he was prepared to share. 'Australia is a very lucky place,' he told her. 'Opportunities exist here that one might never encounter at home.'

'What opportunities?'

'Well, ah . . .' He blinked at her for a moment, before covering this reaction with his luminescent smile. Again Ida wished that she might never leave the warmth of it, so lovely was it to see. He patted her, his gloved hand resting upon hers, the second time in her life he had touched her; the sensation of it was intoxicating. 'There are opportunities to converse with bright young ladies like yourself, for example,' he told her.

Ida felt like swooning that he should consider her 'bright'.

'At home in England such things never occur,' he said. 'People are that much freer here, one's class means nothing. Everyone is able to make of themselves whatever they wish.'

'But aren't you a gentleman?' she wondered.

'Well, yes,' said Samuel. 'I suppose that is what I am.'

'Doesn't a gentleman find opportunity wherever he might live?' Ida suggested to him. 'He doesn't have to come all the way to the colonies for it.'

Samuel's smile lessened a degree and he took away his hand. 'What happened to Billy's body?' he asked, turning back to the valet.

'Tossed it on the rubbish heap,' said Barker, still looking out the window. 'Crow feed.'

The image this placed in Ida's mind was a very unpleasant one. 'Was that the little dog's name?'

'Shut it,' Barker growled at her. But when the valet was looking out the window again, Samuel nodded to her, confirming what she'd asked.

'My fiancée adored her little pet,' Samuel whispered. 'She couldn't bear to be parted from those that she loved . . . *Couldn't bear it.*'

There was a heartbreakingly unsaid aspect to the statement, Ida thought. Had Miss Gregory loved her fiancée?

The two men lapsed into silence as the carriage continued on its way to Castlemaine, from where they would board the Melbourne train. In her mind Ida returned to the Summersby dining room and there summoned up a spot on the carpet where she imagined Miss Gregory might have expired. It was still a real shock to think that both mistress and pet had died together. Someday, Ida decided, when she was sure that Mr Hackett thought only the very best of her, and she was certain that his smile was heartfelt and not something he put on just to please a person, she would ask him about the details of those two deaths. Even she could tell that it would not be appropriate to ask of it now.

Barker gave the appearance of snoozing, sprawled across the seat where he and Ida sat. 'Think she'll remember?' he asked, with his eyes shut and his arms folded across his chest.

Ida started. 'Remember what?'

A slap rang out like rifle fire and Ida saw Barker clutching his cheek. The carriage lurched on its springs as Samuel threw himself at the lanky man and gripped him by his collar. 'Do you think I am completely your subordinate in this venture?' he demanded.

The valet was very shocked. 'No.'

'No what?'

Samuel waited, hands clenched at the valet's throat.

'No what?' he repeated.

'No, Mr Hackett.'

Samuel shook him until Barker's collar tore.

'No, *sir*,' Barker said.

Following a loaded moment while the two men held each other's look over the sounds of the labouring horse's hooves, Samuel let go of Barker's ruined collar and sat down again. 'Better,' he said.

The valet shifted uncomfortably. 'My mistake,' he rasped, after another minute, 'why would she remember anything?'

He saw shocked Ida staring at him and gave her a wide, white grin.

Ida said nothing else for the rest of the journey. It seemed very sensible. But in her inquisitive mind new questions suggested themselves.

One. Mr Hackett put up with outrageous liberties from his valet. How did he find this acceptable? What stopped him being rid of this man? Whatever the reason was, it outweighed everything else. Was he bound to Barker by it?

Two. What on earth was it she might remember?

It occurred to Ida that much of her working life could be spent profitably listening to others if she chose it to be – and she chose it now. It was wrong to condemn eavesdropping as maliciousness, Ida told herself in justification. How else was a person who was otherwise denied basic facts supposed to get by? Eavesdropping was the one bit of usefulness a person such as herself might have in her efforts to make good.

Ida waited outside a door, one that was firmly closed to her presence; a large and polished door of oak, very respectable, and bearing the lettering *H.P. Clarkenwell Esq., Director*. As lunatic asylums went, Constantine Hall was quite disappointing. Ida had anticipated a foreboding place with moaning wretches chained to walls. Instead, she had found a large, well-appointed, upper-crust house, much like Summersby. There wasn't a wretch to be seen. She wasn't even certain there were patients.

Inside the room a man and a woman held a tense discourse; the woman, a servant of this establishment, Ida had glimpsed just briefly before she entered the room as Ida nodded at her respectfully. The woman was a little older, twenty-five perhaps, and a little stout, though not displeasingly. Her name was Aggie Marshall and Ida had already determined that she was employed at Constantine Hall as a lady's maid. The man with her was Mr Clarkenwell, evidently her employer – or was he? This was slightly unclear. Ida had glimpsed him as the lady's maid went inside: he was short, fat, bug-eyed, and as is so often the case with men of his stature, pompous. Ida stood as near to the door as she dared should anyone walk past and catch her. Having already spoken to Mr Clarkenwell at length, Samuel Hackett was now waiting outside in the garden with Barker, having given Ida orders that she was to emerge with Miss Matilda, her new charge, when the lady was ready. Ida hoped she would not be kept too much longer in this task.

Inside the room, Aggie Marshall the lady's maid was clearly reacting with shock as Mr Clarkenwell reached the crux of the news that Samuel had given him. Listening, Ida considered her own response, given she'd had rather more time than the lady's maid had to digest it. Ida had initially thought it unbelievable, until all of a sudden it wasn't so unbelievable at all, but typical; the deception, the sheer injustice of what had been done to a hapless woman felt very believable to Ida's sixteen-year-old ears. It was sickening confirmation to her that this was how things could be in this world if you were young and female with no one to look out for you.

'And what's she supposed to do now, sir?' she heard the lady's maid demanding to know from inside the room.

Mr Clarkenwell evidently disliked her tone. 'Remember your place here, Miss Marshall,' he told her, his swivelling chair issuing complaints beneath him, 'if we are to continue.'

'I've worked here four months now, Mr Clarkenwell, and I think I know it well enough – and Miss Gregory does, too. Or she'll think she did until today. When you break this news to her she'll be left not knowing anything at all.'

Ida liked to think she was becoming adept at reading uncomfortable pauses, and one followed now. Mr Clarkenwell cleared his throat in the vacuum and Ida imagined lady's maid Aggie reading his look.

'Oh. Now I see things even *more* clearly,' Aggie said, cynicism in her voice.

'Again, I remind you of your place and the tone of your voice when addressing a superior,' Mr Clarkenwell warned her.

'My place is as a lady's maid, sir, nothing more,' Aggie replied.

Ida now pictured Clarkenwell forming his fat, grey fingers into a steeple as he waited behind his desk.

'But you want *me* to be the one to tell her, don't you?'

Evidently Mr Clarkenwell did. His chair complained in a different way and Ida wondered if he was leaning back in it. It occurred to her that telling Miss Gregory the news about her wrongful confinement should be a joyful task to receive. Why was Mr Clarkenwell so keen to delegate it?

'You're a coward,' said Aggie.

Ida smiled, liking her spirit.

'Very well,' Aggie went on, 'I will inform Miss Gregory of what you have just informed me.'

'There must be no scandal,' he warned from inside the room.

'Really? And why is that?' said Aggie. 'Worried you'll go to court? Well, from what you've told me I'd say you're right to be worried.'

Ida heard a drawer being pulled open in the deep, mahogany desk and she wondered what was being withdrawn.

'Please don't insult me,' Aggie said flatly from within.

'Ten guineas,' said Mr Clarkenwell.

Ida thrilled. Was the lady's maid being bribed?

'That much?' Aggie mused. 'I'll buy myself something very pretty with that, I'm sure.'

There was another pause, during which Ida heard Mr Clarkenwell wheezing. Was he writing out a cheque, Ida wondered?

'Here,' Mr Clarkenwell said.

There followed the distinct sound of something being torn up. Ida heard Mr Clarkenwell choke and stand, shoving his chair.

'You can eat your money,' declared Aggie. 'I work for Miss Gregory, not you, and she's where my loyalty lies.'

'The Hall pays your wages . . .' Mr Clarkenwell started to say.

'Miss Gregory's late father's estate pays them, actually,' said Aggie, 'and as for scandal, there'll be none, provided you show her the decency you've obviously never shown her before. She's not even the same person that everyone's been telling her she is since she came here!' The lady's maid was furious now and clearly didn't care how it sounded.

Loving Aggie's gall, Ida imagined Mr Clarkenwell fighting back his spite; fat, sweaty fists balled on his desk top. 'Let me remind you that her late father believed her to be ill,' he said, also getting heated now, 'which is why he willed her care to the Hall!'

'Believed *Margaret* Gregory to be ill, perhaps,' Aggie spat back at him, 'but she's not Margaret now, is she, Mr Clarkenwell? She's *Matilda*, and she was all the time she's been here. Margaret is dead. Matilda is the heiress to a fortune.'

Ida hoped the strain was showing itself on Clarkenwell's fleshy face; deep lines scoring his flabby skin. 'The situation is . . . very irregular,' he conceded from the other side of the door. Ida visualised him pulling a handkerchief from his coat and scraping it across his brow.

'Especially for my mistress, who's been shut in here under a falsehood,' said Aggie.

'Under her late father's legacy,' he tried to remind her.

'Which you not only corrupted but milked all you could,' she said. 'Because that's the nub of the scandal, isn't it, sir? The cost is very dear to be a resident here at the Hall, but the late Mr Gregory could afford it. The only trouble was, we now see, is that because he was dead there was no one to confirm we were taking the correct daughter. I suppose it suited your pockets not to make sure.'

A sudden movement at Ida's feet outside the door made her start. A little white terrier had appeared from nowhere and was looking up at her, wagging its tail. Ida's eyes almost fell out of her head. The dog showed a flash of uncertainty at this reaction, before doubling its efforts to be friendly. She tentatively reached out to pat the little animal. Apparently pleased by this, the dog licked her fingers, before sitting on its hindquarters near her feet, content to share her company.

Inside the room Mr Clarkenwell was saying, 'When you inform Miss Gregory of what has been learned from Mr Samuel Hackett, you will tell her she is now discharged.'

'That's all I ask,' said Aggie Marshall, 'all that is *decent*.'

Ida realised the lady's maid was about to pull open the door. She leapt back a pace so that it wouldn't look like she'd been listening. When Aggie emerged, the white terrier dashed forward, whipping its tail.

'Yip, you little scallywag,' Aggie whispered, stooping down to kiss the animal, 'have you been eavesdropping?'

Ida blushed.

The white terrier thumped its tail on the floor and licked Aggie's chin. 'Get off!' she complained, but she kissed and hugged the dog harder. 'Good girl. Good girl.' She looked up and addressed Ida. 'Yip was a stray. She wandered into the garden one day and just seemed to make herself part of the household.'

'That's nice,' said Ida, smiling, for want of something better to reply with.

'Her meals were pot luck to begin with until I took them in hand,' said Aggie, standing up. 'Now she thinks of me as her mistress.'

Ida smiled again, before lapsing into self consciousness when she realised the other servant was looking at her not altogether appraisingly. A city servant, Aggie looked rather smarter than Ida in appearance

'I'm very new in service,' Ida said, by way of explanation. 'Still in training.'

'New at the great house?'

'New at Summersby, that's right.'

Aggie sniffed and nodded, accepting her. 'So, I suppose you know all about what I've just been told inside.'

Ida wasn't sure how to answer that without revealing she'd eavesdropped on not only one, but two conversations. 'I know I'm here to help fetch Miss Gregory,' she offered, 'to whom a grave injustice has been done.'

Aggie frowned, but not at Ida, and looked to Yip. 'And what's to become of us now, that's the question.'

'You're Miss Gregory's lady's maid?'

Aggie nodded.

'Won't you be wanted at Summersby?'

The other servant seemed to consider that for the first time. 'What's it like there?'

Ida told her in the truest way she could, aware that the other woman was her best ever chance for gaining a friend. If she could just convince Aggie to come then there'd be no more loneliness. She tried to explain a household she barely understood herself. Aggie fixed on details that struck her as irregular, in particular the paucity of fellow servants. 'How on earth do you do it all?' she gasped.

Ida didn't think her answer satisfied Aggie, who clearly had higher standards.

'I suppose you've got family here in Melbourne,' Ida asked, suspecting she'd failed to entice Aggie.

But the other servant shook her head. 'Just me,' she said. 'And I'm from Beechworth, not Melbourne. My people have all passed on. I've been serving Miss Gregory for the last four months, since her first woman, a Miss Haines, left her.'

'Oh,' said Ida, taking hope. 'Why did the first maid leave?'

Aggie looked at her as if that was a pointless thing to ask. 'I've been in service all up since I was fifteen,' she said, 'that's nearly ten years. Made my way from the kitchens to become a lady's maid, although what I've got for it apart from ruined looks and abandoned hopes, I don't know.'

Ida must have looked shocked as well as crestfallen, because Aggie was quick to counter this with a smile. 'Not really,' she said. 'Nothing's ever so bad that a walk outside on a bright sunny day won't fix it.'

'There are some lovely long walks at Summersby,' Ida offered. 'You should see the grounds.'

Aggie now seemed to reach a resolve. 'A terrible thing has been done to my mistress.'

Ida agreed.

'She deserves decency, don't you think?'

'That why I'm here.'

Aggie looked at her oddly.

'With Mr Samuel Hackett and his man, Mr Barker,' Ida qualified. 'They are waiting outside. We're all here to make better the terrible thing that's been done to Miss Gregory and bring her home – most particularly Mr Hackett, who is the nicest, most handsome gentleman I've ever met. Just you wait and see.'

Aggie raised her eyebrow at that and Ida felt a shot of embarrassment that she'd given her feelings away. 'I've not met many gentlemen,' she added quickly, 'although I promise you won't find him disappointing.'

Aggie looked into the little dog's eyes. 'I told myself once I'd stay to the end of the world with a mistress who was kind to me,' she muttered.

'And is Miss Gregory kind?' Ida wondered.

Aggie considered. 'She's the kindest mistress I've ever known.'

Ida's heart lifted. 'She's also heiress to a grand house and a fortune.'

While Aggie patted the little dog, Ida watched as she made up her mind. Aggie would claim her own fair share of any decency going, and what's more, her beloved little Yip would have a piece of decency, too.

Observing from near the door to Miss Gregory's bedroom Ida saw the emotion welling up inside Aggie as she studied her mistress's reflection in the mirror. 'You are lovely, miss, just lovely,' Aggie told her.

Something about the beautiful Matilda Gregory's fragility clearly made Aggie feel protective towards her, Ida noted. Nineteen years old, the Summersby heiress had an otherworldly quality, as if she were merely visiting this plane and would at some time soon of her choosing elect to ascend to the clouds. Having met the dead woman she now knew was actually Margaret Gregory, Ida was struck by how identical Matilda was in every

way to her twin – in physical appearance at least. In manner it was
apparent they couldn't have been more unalike.

Outfit complete, Matilda beamed; her rich, dark hair arranged
to perfection beneath her hat, framing her olive-skinned face, her
deep brown eyes. Aggie glanced at her own reflection in the glass,
where she saw a woman mousy and plain; Matilda's looks placed
her squarely in the shade.

'Are we ready then?' Aggie asked.

Confusion seemed to come to the young woman's eyes, but
Aggie spoke before her mistress could give voice to it. 'We are
leaving the Hall,' she reminded, 'and here is Ida to help us.'

Matilda glanced at Ida and nodded. 'That's right, of course
we are, and I am very well presented for it. Thank you, Marshall.'
She stood, taking a final glance at herself in the glass. 'I do like this
yellow dress.'

'Well, soon we'll be buying you some new dresses, I'm sure,'
Aggie suggested, glancing at Ida herself, who smiled at her in turn.
'All different colours for the season, too. Won't that be nice?'

'When do we leave?'

'Once we're out and about in the world again,' said Aggie,
giving Matilda's gloved hand a little squeeze. 'Won't that be nice?'

'What time will we return here?' Matilda asked.

Aggie was patient. 'We will not return. These are our last
moments ever at the Hall, miss.'

It seemed to Ida that Matilda now digested this information
as if hearing it afresh. It struck her then that Matilda was more
than otherworldly – she was *odd*. 'Then I must farewell dear
Mr Clarkenwell.'

Clearly Aggie intended having none of that. 'Already done,'
she claimed, signalling Ida to open the door to the hallway. Ida
did so.

'I said goodbye to Mr Clarkenwell?' Matilda's confusion
re-bubbled.

Puzzled by what she was witnessing, Ida stood aside as Aggie
eased her mistress into the polished hallway that led towards the

stairs. Ida went to close the door behind them, but Aggie shook her head, so Ida left it, following in their wake. 'It was a moment of little importance,' Aggie continued the fib, 'barely worth recalling. Mr Clarkenwell congratulated you on becoming so well.' She smiled and nodded encouragingly.

Matilda smiled and nodded too, clearly now seeing the scene in her mind as if it was a memory. 'That's right. He did. And I do feel well, Marshall. Better than I have felt since . . . goodness.'

Aggie nipped the fresh confusion at the bud. 'Since a very long time,' she suggested. 'I think you look radiant. Your relative will remark upon it, too, I have no doubt.' She placed Matilda's hand upon the banister and encouraged her to begin the descent. Ida trailed behind, transfixed by the strangeness of it all.

'My relative . . .' Matilda pondered this somehow extraordinary concept. 'Yes, I have a relative.'

'For want of another word, miss, yes,' said Aggie. 'Ida says he's a very pleasant gentleman, quite young in years, but by no means a boy. Ida came here with him. Do you remember what I told you that she said?'

Matilda thought that she did. 'His manners. Did Ida remark upon his manners, Marshall?'

'She did,' said Aggie, smiling approvingly over her shoulder at Ida.

'She said they were very fine. I remember now. A gentleman's manners, she said.'

'Exemplary,' said Aggie.

'And his style of dress? She said I'd like that.'

'She did,' said Aggie. 'Very well attired, Ida promised us he was. Very fine clothes.'

Matilda smiled. 'I feel as if perhaps I shall like him already.'

They all reached the landing together, bathed in the glow from a stained glass window above them. 'I feel it, too,' Aggie said, directing her mistress to the last flight of stairs.

'And now he waits for me?'

'He is just outside,' said Aggie, 'isn't he, Ida?'

The beautiful young woman looked to Ida, who in turn indicated the ornate front door in the entrance hall at the base of the stairs. 'He has come such a long way to meet you, miss,' she said. 'He is anxious that he should make a good impression upon you.'

Matilda stopped short. 'Why?' Suspicion filled her face. 'Why should he care?'

Ida faltered, not sure of what to say. Aggie pressed her hand to Matilda's back, encouraging her to continue the descent, but the young woman stayed where she was, clutching the banister.

'What is all this about, Marshall?' she asked, immune to pressing hands. 'Tell me, please, and if I dislike what you say, I shall return to my room and no more will I allow the matter talked of.'

Horrified that she'd somehow been responsible for this change of heart, Ida watched as Aggie answered with tact, evidently used to Matilda's changeability. 'He worries on what you might think of him only because he understands his responsibility,' Aggie told her. 'Or rather, he would like to acquire this responsibility and he wishes to ask you for it.' She let this sink in a moment.

Ida chipped in. 'He knows you won't grant it should you fail to like him, miss. Therefore he is anxious. Do you see?' Ida glanced at Aggie to see if she approved of her contribution, but Aggie was so focused on her mistress she couldn't tell.

Matilda's suspicion melted to become confusion again and Aggie used the moment to coax her down the remaining stairs. They reached the tessellated floor of the entrance hall where another array of stained glass lit the impressive front door.

'But what is this responsibility he imagines I will grant him?' Matilda wondered, finding a thread of the conversation again.

Aggie kept the momentum going, propelling her forward. Ida saw the parlour door snap shut and guessed that Mr Clarkenwell hid behind it, a coward to the end. Yip was waiting patiently near the hallstand. Aggie slipped the rope she obviously used for walks around Yip's neck and the little dog at once became keen to be off somewhere.

'The responsibility is that of your wellbeing, miss,' Aggie went on, the polished brass of the front door knob almost within reach, 'the responsibility is that of your health and happiness and care.' She slipped the front door key from her dress pocket, no doubt intending to cast the thing and all it represented aside forever, Ida thought, once the door was wide open.

Matilda stopped short again and Ida's heart sank at the fear she would fall at the final hurdle. 'No, I don't like it,' Matilda said. 'I'm going back to my room.'

Aggie's look suggested she would not be releasing her grip on the hope of escape while she still had a fight in her. 'But what is it you don't like, miss? Tell me.'

Matilda fluttered, ready to run. 'The pressure, the expectation upon me . . .'

'What pressure is there in stepping into sunshine on such a nice day, in such a nice yellow dress, with your hair so lovely, in your very best hat?'

Matilda's fingers rested on the curls that Aggie had laboured hard in perfecting with the irons. 'You say he is my relative?' she whispered, her huge, round eyes threatening tears.

Aggie turned the key and twisted the brass knob of the front door, letting a stream of sunlight fall upon them all as Yip ran out and stretched the rope to its end, impatient to pull them outside with her.

'He is the man who was betrothed to your twin sister, your poor Miss Margaret, the one who died.' Aggie took her mistress by the hand and stepped onto the portico first.

Matilda beheld a strikingly handsome man her own age, expensively dressed, with the summer sun striking the gold of his hair and skin and moustache. Samuel looked briefly askance at Yip before stepping forward with a greeting smile, his grey gloved hand outstretched.

'That makes him like your brother-in-law.' Aggie slipped her mistress's hand inside Samuel's, then stepped aside, restraining Yip.

'Mr Samuel Hackett of Summersby . . .' Beaming Ida introduced him.

Matilda stepped fully into the light and was clearly dazzled for a moment by the way it struck and glittered and bounced upon Samuel's blond hair, upon his smooth, tanned skin, upon his lips, and upon the gold of his cufflinks and waistcoat buttons. With her untaken hand she tried to shield herself from this light but he gently turned her from the glare so that the sun was behind her and she could see him wholly and clearly as he was.

Samuel brought her lace-gloved hand to his lips and kissed it.

'This is Miss Gregory, Mr Hackett,' Ida was telling him. 'Miss *Matilda* Gregory, that is, our new mistress.'

Ida watched as Matilda seemed utterly struck by Samuel's beauty, and this only caused Ida herself to look at him anew. His features were perfectly symmetrical and so highly pleasing, like a face from a painting. A girl could learn to love such a face, Ida already knew.

'Miss Gregory, we meet in and are united by the saddest of circumstances,' said Samuel, releasing Matilda's hand. 'I am sure you are as heartbroken to lose a cherished sister as am I to lose so beloved a fiancée.'

Matilda glanced at Aggie and was aware that some form of reply was expected of her. 'I wish she had come to visit me,' she offered, before glancing at Aggie again to see if this meant with the maid's approval. It didn't. 'She never came once, or at least . . . I don't remember her doing so,' Matilda continued, apparently unable to choose a new course. 'Why do you think she stayed away from me? She so hates being parted.'

Samuel responded with no disapproval of his own. Rather, his face showed only the deepest sympathy – and movingly for Ida – shame. 'I wish only that I could offer you an explanation for your sister's actions,' he offered, 'but I have none.' He cleared his throat and regarded Matilda with an expression that was earnest and humble. 'A great injustice was done against you, Miss Gregory. I don't know why or really how, but it was done all the same.'

Matilda seemed to lose herself in his cornflower blue eyes.

Ida became aware of Barker, dark and brooding, watching the exchange from where he slouched at their hired carriage, in the leafy street beyond the wrought-iron gate. He was intensely focused upon Samuel from beneath his unruly hair.

'It is my sister who is ill?' Matilda asked, tentative.

Aggie stepped in. 'That's right, miss, as I told you before. No one thinks an illness lies with you. Not anymore. Isn't that right, Mr Hackett?' she asked, turning to Samuel.

Samuel answered without taking his eyes from Matilda. 'It was my fiancée who was unsound in her mind,' he said, with a catch in his voice.

Ida saw Barker step through the gate and onto the front path.

Samuel seemed to recover himself. 'You were kept here wrongfully, Miss Gregory. I don't know how it was done, as I said, but it could only have happened before I began courting Matilda . . .' He corrected himself. 'Margaret, I mean – before I even courted Margaret and knew your dear, late father.'

Ida listened intently. There was so much about the situation that remained mysterious to her mind. Samuel seemed to become aware of her attention just as Barker appeared at his elbow. A look passed between the two of them that Ida was unable to read.

'I must confess I had no knowledge of your existence until I read my late fiancée's will,' Samuel said to Matilda, ending whatever further explanation he had seemed about to provide. 'Had I known of the truth, I assure you I would have done my utmost to expose and amend the situation.'

Ida blinked, digesting this, as Barker gave a cough. Samuel seemed reluctant to introduce him. 'Oh – this is my valet, Barker, Miss Gregory,' he told her, with lessened interest, indicating the black-clad man beside him. 'He is an indispensible man.'

Barker displayed hard, white teeth as he grinned. Ida averted her eyes from the display. 'It will be my pleasure to direct the mistress's comfort,' he said in his rough accent.

'You were not a valet then,' Matilda said, squinting at him.

Barker's grin froze.

'You were something else. Not a valet. We didn't have a valet. Did you work in the stables?'

Barker cast a sideways glance at Samuel. 'Miss Gregory is right, I'm sure. My memory ain't what it was.'

Aggie stepped in. 'Miss Gregory's own memory sometimes plays tricks,' she said, tactfully.

Samuel smiled, apologetic. 'Like myself Mr Barker is not originally from Summersby. Perhaps he resembles another servant you know?'

Matilda studied Barker again, before smiling knowingly at him. 'You were so madly in love . . .'

Ida saw a vivid blush sweep up Barker's throat from his collar, before he stepped back with a negligible bow.

Samuel held out his arm for Matilda and she accepted it naturally, as if she had known him for months, not minutes. 'Let me show you to the carriage,' he said, 'I do so look forward to having you as my guest at Summersby while you decide what your future holds, Miss Gregory.'

Ida started in surprise. 'Doesn't Summersby belong to Miss Gregory now?' she asked without thinking.

Samuel and Matilda stopped.

'Well, yes, of course,' said Samuel. He gave Ida a smile that told her he was grateful for being shown the oversight. 'Under my late fiancée's will, or rather, under her late father's will, Miss Gregory of course owns Summersby entirely.' He turned to Matilda again. 'It is your home and I am the guest.'

Ida looked pleased she'd not spoken out of turn – or revealed the extent of her eavesdropping – until she saw the look on Barker's face, which plainly said otherwise.

Matilda looked confused. 'Summersby. Is it where I once lived?'

Aggie nodded at her, reassuringly.

'I do believe it was,' said Samuel.

Ida watched them walk down the path towards the carriage beyond, and prepared to follow them. Aggie realised Barker was frowning at Yip, still straining at the rope in her hand. 'Is that your mistress's animal?' he asked.

'Oh, no, Mr Barker,' Aggie said, 'I mean, not really, you see—'

'Good,' said Barker, cutting her off. 'Summersby's no place for lapdogs.' He began to slope off after Samuel along the path.

Aggie looked at Ida in confusion. 'But ... Mr Barker?' she called after him.

The valet turned, his piercing black eyes lacking all warmth.

'But I'm to come, too ...' Aggie began. 'What will my mistress do without me if I don't?'

'No care of mine either way,' said Barker. 'If you're coming, then be quick about it, woman, but the dog's got no place, understand?'

Ida felt she'd experienced more than enough of Barker's ill humour for one day. 'Why shouldn't she bring the dog, then? What's a little mutt like that going to harm?'

Barker turned around fully and then strode all the way back to where they stood. 'You arguing with me, Ida?'

Ida stood firm. 'It's a big house and as good as empty. Aggie's Yip won't get under your big flat feet, so stop being such a misery.'

Barker bunched his hands into fists. 'No.'

Ida thought of the poor little dog that had died. 'But there's been a pet before.'

'And it was the *last*.' His face was murderous.

'You rotten old—'

Aggie put a hand on her arm, stopping her. 'It's all right, Ida,' she whispered. 'I wouldn't want to upset Mr Barker, not when I'm only new. Yip will be safe and sound here at the Hall.'

Taking her seat in the second, lesser carriage that Samuel had provided for the luggage, Ida cast a last look back at the bewildered dog, tethered to the door of the Hall and wondering where the walk had gone. Her heart broke at the cruelty of it. She knew that Aggie's own heart had already snapped in two. Ida willed herself to think only of the new mistress now, who was going,

Ida knew, to a life of happiness at last, and Aggie with her. Surely, someone at the Hall would continue feeding Yip, Ida told herself.

When the carriages pulled away, Ida tried to block her ears to the sound of Yip's barking but found that nothing would quell the noise. She tried listing in her mind the things that had struck her as interesting about the day.

One. Samuel had known the sisters' father, the late Mr Gregory. Ida had not thought to ask when it was exactly that Samuel had come to Summersby, but now she had the likely answer – it was when Mr Gregory was still alive. And yet he had not met Matilda before today.

Two. Matilda had mistaken Barker for a servant she had known in the past, a man who held a different position than valet, and yet as Ida had watched Matilda it had seemed equally possible that Matilda had *recognised* Barker as much as mistake him for someone else. The man she remembered had been in love. In love with who?

Three. Barker had been adamant that Yip would not accompany them. Had he been so devoted to the late Miss Gregory's dog that he simply could not contemplate another taking its place? Ida thought this unlikely. Barker hadn't even bothered to give poor Billy a burial. All he'd done was toss the little animal onto a rubbish heap.

The late Miss Gregory had hired Ida because she was inquisitive. Deceitful the lady may have been, and dead she now sadly was, but neither was reason in Ida's view to warrant her being let down. Miss Gregory had seen the potential in Ida when so few others had, her own mother included.

This was potential that Ida greatly intended to reach.

BIDDY

DECEMBER 1903

2

*B*iddy MacBryde was cheery, pretty, lately sixteen, and employed as the Reverend's first kitchenmaid, and the story she spun on the way to the Bridge Road shops with her best friend Queenie, fifteen, the Reverend's second kitchenmaid, was this: Biddy was engaged in a clandestine romance with Tom, the handsome grocer's boy at Topp's General Store. Good-looking Tom could appreciate a beauty when he clocked one, Biddy's story went, no matter how soot-stained the rags that lessened her, and he and Biddy were in love as a consequence, but no one must ever know of it.

'You don't say,' said Queenie, in flat response to this preposterousness.

Biddy was hoping for rather more investment in this fantasy as they made their way by foot in the hot summer sun up the Lennox Street hill. 'I've been so tormented by the burden,' she added, encouragingly. 'You can't picture what it's been like for me, with a near-bursting heart. Being in love is wonderful, just like they say it is in stories, but the pressure it places on your emotions, well, it's like being laid up in bed. It's a relief to tell you everything at last.'

Queenie looked in danger of being bored.

Biddy had loved spinning stories for as long as Queenie had been her best friend, which was a year and a half now, and as long as they'd worked together as kitchenmaids for the Reverend Archibald Flowers. Some of the stories she came out with were so outrageous they sent Queenie into fits, but today Queenie seemed not quite herself and Biddy feared she knew why.

In the week just past, Biddy and Queenie had together over-heard talk in the front parlour between Reverend Flowers and Mrs Rattray, the stern Scotch housekeeper who was their superior. The talk concerned the need to find an 'upstairs' maid for the Manse and the difficulties this involved given the deplorable standard of domestic servants in Melbourne. Mrs Rattray had proposed that Biddy or Queenie be elevated with the help of additional training to become a quarter-way capable 'above-stairs girl', which would still be preferable, Mrs Rattray had said, to the flotsam the Reverend would end up with if he advertised in a newspaper. Reverend Flowers had seen the good sense in this and agreed, even though his Manse had neither upstairs nor down, being built on the one storey. But any thrill of excitement Biddy and Queenie might have felt at the prospect of advancement was cut short. Having to choose between the two kitchen maids, Mrs Rattray had told the Reverend that she was rather more inclined to consider Biddy suitable for uplifting, given she was so much more pleasing to the eye.

Eavesdropping with Biddy on the other side of the parlour door, Queenie had felt this slight like a dagger though her heart, turning to Biddy with tears in her eyes. Mortified by Queenie's deep hurt, Biddy had found herself lost for words, and the subject had not been mentioned by either of them since. Biddy had told herself she would refuse the promotion if offered. Far better to retain a friend. But the moment had not yet come where she might make this intended sacrifice known to Queenie. If she so much as skirted near the sensitive topic Queenie threatened to turn on the waterworks again. The romance story was a refuge. It gave Biddy something to say while she thought on how best to broach the thing that most needed saying.

The two girls reached the top of Lennox Street and paused in the hot December glare to dab their faces with hankies and adjust their broad-brimmed straw hats against the sun.

Queenie turned to her. 'What shall I do when we go inside the store, then?' she asked. 'Now that you've told me the big secret, I feel like I might burst with it as well.'

Biddy was pleased her friend had decided to pick up the romance story after all. 'Any hint of what I've told you on your face and old Topp will be onto us! He disapproves, you see.'

'But what about Tom? How can I treat him the same way now that I *know everything*?'

Biddy caught an odd look in Queenie's eye, a look she couldn't quite name. 'I told you everything because I thought you could be trusted,' she said, wringing the melodrama and happy that Queenie was now playing along.

They turned to the right and began strolling along dusty Bridge Road, grateful for the shade from the row of shops' verandas. 'It's just that I'm not as worldly when it comes to secret romances,' Queenie said. 'I don't know what I might do or say under the pressure of containing it.'

Biddy slapped down a perfect trump card. 'Turn around and go back to the Manse right now!'

'What?'

'Now. Off!' Biddy snatched the basket from Queenie's arm with a flourish and hooked it over her own.

'Biddy . . .'

'You'll bring about my ruin. I can see it!' Biddy raised a quivering finger and placed it against her lips, before moistening her eyes in sorrow, the finger at her lips becoming a hand that vainly halted a choked sob. Biddy turned on her toes and rushed into the front door of Topp's General Store as if she'd just drawn the first act of her play to curtain.

*

Finding herself the only customer inside the cool interior of the store, Biddy allowed her eyes to adjust for a minute, inventing Act Two in her head. She glanced through the glass, saw Queenie still lingering outside and wondered how long it would be before her friend followed her inside to continue the fun.

'Afternoon, Biddy,' said a knowing voice from behind her. 'You two playing silly games again?'

Biddy spun around to meet the smile of Tom himself, tall and lean, and certainly handsome. As with many of Biddy's stories, the embroidery that was the 'secret romance' had needed a scrap of truthfulness to stitch itself to. Biddy and Tom, when the store wasn't busy and no one was at them to get back to work, quite enjoyed talking to each other. The conversations they had, while by no means highbrow, weren't exactly street level either. They discussed interesting things; things they saw in *The Argus* newspaper; things they'd learned from a book; opinions they'd gathered about the world and the interesting people in it.

'Don't know what the matter is with Queenie today,' said Biddy, approaching the counter, 'she can't seem to stay in the same mood for more than a minute. Must be the heat.'

'The heat's something terrible,' Tom agreed. 'I've even rolled my shirtsleeves up.' Biddy pretended she hadn't already noticed the rare sight of Tom's sinewy forearms. 'But it's not so bad in here,' said Tom. 'The mercury says it's only eighty-five. Be twice that on the tram tracks.'

Biddy had been fanning herself but stopped. 'It's like a Coolgardie safe in here, it's so reviving,' she claimed, knowing that it could have been hot enough to boil a sheep on her head and still she would have called the store cool, for Tom's sake.

Tom filled a glass with water from a jug kept upon the counter and passed it over to her, their fingers touching for just an instant as she took it from him, holding his smile as she sipped it. 'Thank you. That's kind,' said Biddy.

'So then, something for the Reverend's supper?' Tom enquired.

'Yes, for starters,' said Biddy, taking her eyes from his face long enough to peer at Mrs Rattray's list. She glanced out the window again and spotted Queenie still there, now engaged in conversation with a stooped and elderly figure in widow's weeds. Biddy frowned, feeling inexplicably uneasy. It was Old Mrs Daws, whom Biddy knew was blind, or near enough to it, given how much she talked about the trials of being sightless. Biddy thought Mrs Daws was a whingeing old wowser and she wondered what Queenie would ever have to talk to her about. The contents of the old woman's basket were upended on the ground. She realised that Queenie must have somehow bumped into her.

Biddy turned to handsome Tom again. 'I suppose I'll be lucky if you've got any decent loaves left,' she said.

He reached for one, handing it to her. 'This one's decent.'

'It's brown,' said Biddy with disdain. 'Everyone knows brown bread leaves you hungry again sooner. Haven't you got any proper white ones, or am I expected to walk all the way to the baker's?'

'These are from the baker's, you twit, got them fresh just for you.' Tom reached for a more expensive white loaf and handed it to Biddy.

She sniffed it. 'I smell alum.'

Tom rolled his eyes. 'There's no alum in that bread. It's a proper white loaf made with good flour.'

'Give me a hot knife and I'll be the judge of it.'

'You will not stick a hot knife in that loaf!'

'How else can I be sure?' asked Biddy, enjoying teasing him. 'If there is any alum it'll stick to the blade and then we'll all know what law breakers you and Topp are for selling suspect goods.'

'Just put the bloody thing in your basket,' said Tom.

Biddy did so. She glanced out the window again but could now see no sign of Queenie or the widow. She wondered where they might have got to.

Once Mrs Rattray's list was traversed, the moment came when it looked as if other topics of conversation would not, for once, arise between them, owing to the stifling effects of the heat. But the moment was gone before Biddy could even feel anxious about it when Tom launched a salvo regarding an editorial he'd read that morning in *The Argus*, which he thought Biddy would appreciate.

'Go on then,' said Biddy, in no hurry to leave.

'Your situation might turn you against me for repeating it,' Tom warned.

'Not likely,' Biddy scoffed.

Tom let her have it, unfolding the thin broadsheet to read aloud. 'Christianity,' he quoted, 'is no longer desired to be preached nowadays, except at a very safe distance by missionaries.'

Biddy took a second to process this and then gasped. Tom laughed again at the look on her face.

'The paper says *that*?'

'Says that and more,' said Tom, enjoying the blasphemy of sharing it with her. 'Nobody wants to hear the word of God anymore, says *The Argus*, not when it runs counter to all that the toffs in Hawthorn and Kew hold dear.'

'The toffs in Kew don't believe in the scriptures?'

'Well, *they'd* reckon they do, of course, and say as much on Sundays, but ask them to live as a Christian should and not one of them will do it, Biddy, because the only things they believe in are Making Money and Survival of the Fittest – the Fittest being them and bad luck for the rest of us.'

Biddy's jaw dropped again and Tom remained straight-faced for another moment, before giving her his wink. 'Wonder if the Reverend read his paper this morning?' he mused.

Biddy burst out giggling with the outrageousness of it. Then she crinkled her eyes, appraising him in his rolled-up shirtsleeves, before she offered him a titbit from her own reading. 'It's no surprise people have given up going to churches,' she said. 'Have you heard about the Reverend J. Beer from East Melbourne parish?'

'No. Who's he?'

'You mean you've never heard what the good Reverend Beer did that sent his whole congregation into shame?' marvelled Biddy.

'So tell me,' said Tom.

Biddy leant closer to him across the counter, lowering her voice. 'Got his cook in the family way and then bribed a man from Lilydale to marry her.'

'Ha!' roared Tom.

'Then he sold off all his furniture and skipped to California. Disgusting! But that's nothing compared to what "Demon Hughes", the Reverend from Ballarat did.'

Tom loved Biddy's tales, be they invented or not. 'What was his trouble then?'

'Invited four little girls to his luxurious manse where he plied them with ether and had his wicked way with them. When he let them go afterwards the doctor discovered all four girls had come down with incurable syphilis.'

Tom roared anew.

'It's the fact that these stories appear in trusted newspapers that makes people sit up straight with their eyes open,' said Biddy. 'Did you hear about Reverend Booth, the Methodist minister from Wangaratta, and what he did to that poor dog?'

At some point during their laughter, and well before they'd finished trading stories of lurid clerics, they heard the front door's bell tinkle, meaning a customer was coming in. Tom clocked the new arrival, nodded, but did no more than that because the customer fell heavily into a seat and started fanning themselves, content with resting without need for further service for now. Biddy didn't bother turning around to see who it was, too busy in stitches, and as the talk went on she forgot there was anyone else there at all.

'Then there was Reverend Taylor from the Baptist Church in Collins Street,' said Biddy, reaching a crescendo in scandal mongering. 'You must have heard about *him*, Tom. They say he had to resign for moral offences so grave that no torture on earth would ever draw a word from him about it!'

The shout of horror from behind Biddy's back brought her down to earth with a start. The two of them remembered the heat-affected customer fanning away in a chair. It was Old Mrs Daws.

'You should both be ashamed of yourselves!' cried the old lady, lurching to her feet. 'What disgraceful slanders – and a disgrace to repeat them!'

With a flash of dreadful certainty, Biddy knew that Queenie had somehow sent the old woman in to deliberately catch her.

'Mrs Daws, please let me help you there,' said Tom as he hurriedly came around from the side of the counter.

Biddy had the presence of mind to take the water jug from the counter and pour the old lady a glassful. 'Mrs Daws, here you go, you look done in. Isn't it a horribly hot day?'

'Biddy MacBryde, I knew it was you the second you laughed like an imp,' said Mrs Daws, squinting in condemnation at her.

'Now, Mrs Daws . . .'

'*You*, the Reverend Flowers' girl, daring to say such terrible things about godly men; he took you in from the gutter!'

Biddy went crimson. 'He did not do that!' An older story had come back to bite her. Biddy had once invented a background that was quite Dickensian, complete with a claim of orphanhood.

'You know full well he did, you ungrateful girl,' admonished Mrs Daws, who had fallen for that tale. 'No parents; living in squalor and shame; you had nothing when he hired you and you've gained nothing since.'

Biddy reddened to the roots of her hair.

Tom took control. 'Please forgive us for holding an unsavoury conversation in your earshot, Mrs Daws; I don't know what came over us. We've had our heads turned by inflammatory words in *The Argus*.'

The old lady wasn't having it. 'My poor eyes might be defective but my mind isn't, young man,' said Mrs Daws. 'You two are carrying on with each other like a couple of cursed anarchists.'

'That's not true either!' cried Biddy, 'I've only come in here to do Mrs Rattray's shopping.'

'Carrying on under the noses of your betters; stabbing the

good Reverend Flowers in the back. What a way to repay him for all his decent Christian charity.'

Biddy now spotted Queenie through the window again, her friend wearing a mocking smirk. She knew Queenie had sent the old woman into Topp's store in the hope she'd make trouble. 'Mrs Daws, I beg of you, we didn't mean any of it, it was just a bit of silliness,' Biddy protested.

'Silliness is it, plotting against the Church? That's what anarchists do, and nihilists; scheming to shoot good Christians in their beds.'

'Mrs Daws, can I assist you with any grocery purchases?' asked Tom, taking the most respectful tone he could, and flicking his head towards the door to give Biddy the hint.

'Well, I really don't know after all this. It's been a great shock to me.'

'Of course it has and I apologise again.' His look told Biddy to go, and fast. 'There'll be no more of it. You've put us right and done well to be mad. We had it coming and deserve worse from you again for saying what we did.'

Biddy looked dismayed at this but Tom wanted her gone, so she picked up her basket of groceries and slipped out the door, upset at the way the interlude had ended.

Biddy carefully carved a slice of the fresh, white, alum-free bread at the place of pride it occupied on the board at the end of Mrs Rattray's kitchen table. Loaves were exulted in the Reverend Flower's household and eighteen months of working as his kitchenmaid had given Biddy some much-needed skills. One thing she could now do well was slice the bread. Few things were as insulting to a man of quality as to be handed a slice of too-thick bread. That was what *working men* ate, slathered with dripping, because that was all that their pitiful earnings not thrown away on drink would afford them. A man of quality ate his bread sliced thin, and the slice Biddy placed upon a butter plate before being coated in a spoonful of jam was as thin as seventeen months of careful training could make it.

Biddy handed the plate with a curtsey to the Reverend Flowers, for the want of knowing what else to give him. Supper was still some hours away and he'd already had teacake fifteen minutes before. The Reverend's lofty presence was making Biddy nervous, but she knew he expected an audience for everything and anything he spoke. Today's sermon concerned the Melbourne summer.

'The worst, the very *worst* of it, child, is the deleterious effect it has upon the constitutions of the young,' he droned, scratching his mutton-chop whiskers.

'Yes, Reverend.'

'You agree with me? Well, of course you do, you're a good girl. The Australian heat is so *sapping,* you see, for that's what it does, most especially to the young – it saps their vigour near clean away.'

'Yes, Reverend,' Biddy nodded, her hands clasped in front of her apron.

'And this is why I fear for our new nation so gravely, child,' said the Reverend, biting into the bread, 'this is why I cannot partake of the hope to which our countrymen adhere so readily, so thoughtlessly!'

'Is it, Reverend?' said Biddy, now eyeing the fresh bread herself and wanting a slice of her own, and not a thin one.

'What hope can there exist for a nation whose young persons are wholly sapped of vigour? Wholly crippled by lethargy? This is a nation depleted by the heat!' He now had apricot jam on his whiskers.

'That's very, very true, Reverend,' said Biddy, gripping the bread knife again in such a way as to have an observer believe she had no intention of going near the bread with it. 'I'd never thought about the way the summer sun depletes me, apart from sunburn of course, but I can see what you mean now, and do you know, I very much fear for my health.'

'Oh, I don't mean girls of the working class,' said the Reverend, waving off her attempt at accordance, 'or the working men for that matter. You need not fear; you could pull a dray all summer long with that good, strong back of yours.'

Biddy's brow creased at him. She attacked the bread.

'No, it's the upper-class young who feel it,' said the Reverend, putting the now empty plate aside and stretching out in his chair, 'our nation's future leaders. The havoc this accursed heat plays upon *them*. Each successive generation faces further enfeeblement.'

Biddy took a healthy spoonful of jam and slapped it on the liberated slice. She was about to eat it in front of him when the stern visage of Mrs Rattray appeared from the hall.

'Biddy, that's unacceptably thick. Have you forgotten everything you've been instructed?'

'It's all right, Mrs Rattray,' said the Reverend, taking the bread slice from Biddy's hands, 'this heat has instilled a famine within me, I think; Biddy has done well to provide a larger portion.'

'Very good, Reverend,' said the housekeeper. 'You enjoy your bread and jam and I'll ensure that Biddy tests no more of your patience.'

'I wasn't—' Biddy protested.

But Mrs Rattray cut her short. 'What are your tasks, girl, and what have you still to complete before tea?'

'Festoon the veranda posts in Christmas greenery, if it's arrived on the cart,' said Biddy, beginning to reel off her mental list.

'It has arrived and Queenie's already doing it,' said Mrs Rattray. 'What's next?'

'Check on the goose.'

'I haven't started cooking it yet, that's another day off.'

'Check on the goose where it sits in the ice box, I mean, to ensure it's not gone fowl.'

'Biddy, if that's your attempt at levity then I despair of you,' said Mrs Rattray. 'What's next and stop wasting my time and your own.'

'Boil and scrub the threepenny bits in readiness for the Reverend's plum pudding.'

'Indeed, set to doing so at once.'

'Yes, Mrs Rattray.'

The bell at the front door rang and the housekeeper retired to answer it.

The Reverend Flowers was eyeing the loaf again from his chair, but Biddy pretended not to notice as she twisted the lone tap above the sink to fill the kettle. The pipes behind gave a shudder before issuing sounds like consumptive coughing. Nothing else emerged.

'Oh, for pity's sake,' said Biddy, 'now there's no water for it.'

'This heat . . .' the Reverend muttered.

Biddy was vaguely aware of Mrs Rattray dealing with some kind of consternation at the entrance to the Manse.

'Too much draw upon the supply, I suppose,' said Biddy. 'Always happens, doesn't it, Reverend, just when we want it on a hot day? I'll leave the tap turned on and maybe something will come out of it in time.'

The Reverend expressed discomfort, scratching at his mutton-chops. 'I had been contemplating a cooling bath.'

'Oh dear,' said Biddy, 'that is a shame.'

The housekeeper reappeared from the hall and when Biddy glanced up she saw such an unexpected look upon the older woman's face that she felt a chill from it.

'Mrs Rattray . . . I . . . I can't do anything about the water, there's just too much draw upon the supply,' Biddy told her.

'Be quiet,' said Mrs Rattray.

Reverend Flowers realised that something was amiss. 'What is it? Has something happened?'

Mrs Rattray's eyes were steely. 'There's a parishioner at the door, Reverend, and very put out. I'm mortified to say she's made some disgraceful claims.'

'Claims?' said the Reverend, standing up, 'What sort of claims? What is this about?'

'About ingratitude,' said the housekeeper.

Biddy at once felt the blood leave her face.

'What on earth do you mean? Who is here, Mrs Rattray?'

The older woman stood aside to allow a furious figure in widow's weeds show herself from the hall.

'Mrs Daws!' exclaimed the Reverend, coming forward. 'What is this of ingratitude? Who has been ungrateful?'

The water finally came through after an hour, and then it was only a trickle, and worse, a brown trickle smelling of sulphur.

'The only reason tea is so popular in this country is because it disguises the tone of what so distressingly comes from the taps,' said the Reverend, accepting a cup of sugary brew from Mrs Rattray.

'The very best Ceylon tea improves it quite out of bounds, Reverend,' the housekeeper agreed with him, sipping a cup of her own.

They fell silent, aware that Biddy had finished packing her bag in the little room she shared with Queenie at the rear of the Manse, and was now passing the kitchen door. Biddy stopped and peeped in, still shocked by how quickly things had turned so sour. But the deed had been done and so had the Reverend's decision; there was no shifting it now, after all that had been said, and he wouldn't meet Biddy's eye or in any other way acknowledge her further. Biddy opened her mouth to say something more, but Mrs Rattray's look froze her cold and so Biddy said nothing. The shame of what had happened and the speed with which she'd been punished for it warranted no additional comment from anyone.

The Reverend and his housekeeper remained stock-still in their kitchen chairs until Biddy's footsteps receded and she'd gone out the front door, carrying her little portmanteau.

On the Manse's wide veranda Biddy took in Queenie's handiwork with the Christmas greenery. She'd done a fine job of it, Biddy thought. Large sprigs of eucalyptus leaves freshly cut from the Heidelberg hills and brought into town on a cart. Queenie had threaded them all through the wrought-iron lacework of the veranda posts; they looked extremely festive and smelt lovely, too.

A stab of memory from happy Christmases past brought the threat of tears to Biddy's eyes, but she'd held off crying so far and wasn't prepared to shame herself further by ending her employment with waterworks. She sniffed them back and cleared her throat a little.

Queenie appeared from the side veranda carrying a broom to sweep up stray leaves. Biddy hoped her friend had been too occupied to overhear the dreadful exchange with Old Mrs Daws and the Reverend.

'You've got your good shirtwaist on, Biddy,' noted Queenie, 'did you pull it straight off the line?'

Biddy tried to smooth the wrinkles with her hand, wondering when she'd again get the chance to press an iron to the faded striped cotton that was her only nice garment. The high collar button was loose and Biddy feared it would fall and be lost before she'd have a chance to mend it.

She made up a story. 'I'm just popping out,' she said. 'I shan't be long.'

'Oh yes?' said Queenie.

'Just an errand. For the Reverend.'

'What to get?'

'Claret. From the wine merchant.'

'In your Sunday skirt and hat?'

Biddy nodded in the face of this implausibility and Queenie stared for a full five seconds at the little portmanteau Biddy held in her gloved hand, before adding, 'So, I suppose I'll be doing supper on my own then.'

'No, you won't,' said Biddy, hastily, 'I'll be here to help you, just like I always am. You'll see. I'm only popping out.'

'Oh, well, that's good then,' said Queenie in a tone that was stark with its lack of conviction.

Biddy felt the tears threaten again as she held the eye of her friend. 'Best be off. Don't want Mrs Rattray asking questions about why I'm taking so long.'

The ghost of a victor's smile appeared at Queenie's mouth, and with sickening certainty Biddy realised that the prospect of becoming an 'upstairs' maid had meant far more to Queenie than Biddy herself had. While Queenie couldn't have guessed the course of sending Old Mrs Daws into Topp's Store to make trouble, she was transparently pleased with the outcome. Queenie set to sweeping up the leaves as Biddy stepped off the veranda and walked the garden path. At the little wrought-iron gate she turned and hoped her friend would have a wave for her at least, but Queenie's look was hard. The gate squawked as Biddy pulled it open. She felt a rush of emotion at the thought she'd never hear it again.

'Biddy?' Queenie called out as the gate closed.

Biddy turned with hope in her face.

'Was that just a story? About going to buy claret?'

Biddy drew breath, the hope gone as she saw smirking Queenie for what she really was: no friend at all. She pulled herself upright, her back straight.

'It's the God's honest truth,' Biddy said, and was gone.

As she waited patiently on the other side of Bridge Road from Topp's Store, watching the late afternoon customers come and go, Biddy constructed a Christmas of her own inside her head. In this Christmas she was just a little girl, and her mother, Ida, not much older than a girl herself, led her by the hand in the cool evening air towards a weatherboard hall where inside, Ida promised, Biddy would see a tree more wonderful than any tree she'd seen before. And indeed, once they were through the wooden doors Biddy beheld a very fine tree; one that Ida called a 'mountain pepper', erected proudly upon the stage. But that wasn't why it was special; the tree's foliage was trimmed with wreaths of coloured paper and candles; candles that were lit as the sun went down. Hanging among the decorations were little numbered gifts; dozens and dozens of them. Every child inside the hall was handed a number written on a card, and when all was ready, a nice man called the numbers out and each child came forward in turn to receive a matching gift from the tree. Biddy held number thirty-two; her present was a sweet-faced little doll made from cotton scraps.

The comfort this brought felt, at first, like the comfort that came with fantasy. Yet as Biddy's mind sought out embellishments that were in no way extravagant, but quite ordinary, she had the jolt of awareness that her head was not in fantasy at all, but memory, which was not where she liked to be. Once opened, however, that door wasn't easily closed; the memory showed itself in full. Biddy remembered walking home from that Christmas with her mother, happy and laughing, clutching the doll to her chest. Ida was laughing, too, until all of a sudden she stopped. They had reached a street corner. If they continued along the road they'd been walking on, they'd be home in close to an hour. But if they turned at the corner, they'd make use of a shortcut and easily be safe in their beds in half the time.

'What's wrong, Mum? It's a shortcut,' Biddy had pressed, looking up at Ida.

But Ida had been reluctant to turn, peering anxiously around the bend.

'But it's not got nasty men,' Biddy had protested. Looking down the leafy side street, all she could see were houses; nice ones, big ones with gardens. What could there be to fear down there?

Ida assented and they made the turn, continuing on their way, but the laughter had gone; Ida was silent, gripping Biddy's hand tightly in her own. Biddy felt her mother's apprehension and looked about her wide-eyed, wordlessly questioning every house they passed, every gas-lit window, every well-cut lawn. What could be so wrong here?

'I don't understand why you're being strange,' Biddy had said at last.

But her mother said nothing.

Realisation dawned like a new birthday. 'Is this where you work, Mum?'

Ida stopped dead, staring at Biddy's upturned face in shock.

It was all the answer Biddy needed. 'Hurry up,' Ida said, dragging Biddy faster along.

Not another word was said between them while they walked the full length of the attractive street. With every step Biddy studied the nice homes, trying to determine for herself which one it was, the place where her mother laboured for a living; the place her mother had always told her she was never to ask about, because she would never be allowed to know.

For a final moment before she blocked it all out, the image of lovely Ida completed the picture, with her milk pale skin and soft brown hair. They were safe at home again and Ida was bending to kiss Biddy in her bed where she held the new doll.

A young Chinese market gardener's boy staggered past Biddy, lost in this memory, while she waited under the shop awnings. He was barefoot in the dust, his wilted wares in buckets suspended from a bamboo pole slung across his shoulders. Glancing at Biddy as he went by he suddenly stopped short with surprise.

'Biddy?'

Recognition jolted her from her thoughts. 'Johnny!'

He couldn't believe he was looking at her. 'But you *missing* – you dead!'

She gave a horrified intake of breath.

'You gone run away from home months back,' said the Chinese boy, pointing at her now, excited. 'All people in Carlton think you dead. Your mum very sad. But here you in Richmond! You alive!'

'Johnny, please,' said Biddy, smiling, trying to rub the anxiousness from her voice. 'I did run away from Carlton, it's true, but that was a year and a half ago – Mum knows where I am now, I told her, you see.' She held her nerve for what was the most barefaced of fibs.

'You sure?'

'Of course I'm sure. I've been working in service. You mustn't be upset.'

He regarded her, thoughtfully, bamboo pole dipping up and down across his shoulders. 'But why you run away? You were happy. What go wrong?'

She straightened herself, dignified. 'I'm afraid that's none of your business . . .'

He considered this. 'You happy now?'

She blinked away all the events at the manse. 'I'm beside myself!'

He smiled. 'You want veggies then, Biddy?'

Biddy laughed and shook her head, looking past him at another customer entering Topp's. 'Not today, Johnny, sorry. Maybe next time you're in Richmond?'

'Why you dressed up? Not even Sunday yet.'

Biddy went to make up another story, and then stopped herself. She just shrugged instead.

The lad wiped a wrist across his brow, tipping his coolie's hat back from his head so that he could see Biddy's features better, scrutinising her. 'It's been too hot,' he commented at last. 'Getting better but. Sun go down. People come out.'

'Yes,' said Biddy. 'It's a little better now.'

She smiled for politeness's sake but gave nothing more, praying he'd go away. Johnny took the hint and ambled on, following the track of the gutter.

'I tell you mum I see you,' he shouted over his shoulder.

'You do that,' she called, then added, 'and Merry Christmas!'

The last customer left Topp's and the store was once again empty for the moment. Lifting her hem to keep the skirt from the dust, Biddy immediately stepped onto the macadamised gravel and dashed across the road, giving space to an ambling horse and carriage, and tripping around the manure piles. Reaching Topp's veranda on the other side, she saw through the windows that Tom was still behind the counter and alone. She beamed with the enormous relief of it and went to let herself inside, ready to announce her unfortunate news, but Tom looked up and saw her doing so. He gave a firm shake of his head, frowning at her, and Biddy was devastated. Her hand froze at the door handle. Tom looked very hard at her for several more seconds, distanced by the window, every drop of warmth in his face gone, before he took his eyes from hers and went back to his newspaper.

The hasty plan Biddy had made about what she was going to do with herself evaporated, given that it had involved the assumed participation of Tom. With it went the fine impression Tom had made across the months of shared words.

Biddy opened her little portmanteau on the footpath and found the last remaining sheet of a packet of writing paper among the things she'd packed. Further rummaging unearthed the blunted stub of a pencil. Biddy leant against the windowpane and wrote a few quick words, knowing that Tom would see what she was doing if he looked up again. When she was done she glanced through the glass and saw his eyes flick back to the newspaper; he'd been watching her. Biddy folded what she'd written in half and popped it into the slot meant for letters.

It was clear that Tom thought she had gone when he came to the front door and took the note from the letterbox. But Biddy had not gone, she'd simply returned to her spot across the road, where she tucked herself into the late afternoon shadows.

She watched him stand there and read it, and she recited in her mind the words she had written.

Please do not worry for me, Tom. I have a brother who is a floor-walker at Alston & Brown. I have gone to visit him now in Collins Street. He will be very pleased to see me and will let me share his accommodation. This is why you mustn't worry. Your loving friend, Biddy.

She saw him look around, as if suspicious of one of her pranks. He could see no sign of her. Then he stared for another long minute at Biddy's note. She hoped her handwriting spoke to him of a girl he had barely known, a girl who had presented only a sliver of her true self, and that sliver disguised by play-acting.

Biddy saw him slip the note inside his pocket and then, before his fingers could even have let go, he slipped the scrap out again, tore it in half, and then another half again, before dropping the pieces into the street.

The woman's name was Miss Evangeline Garfield – Biddy learned that by lingering near the Collins Street doors and overhearing the Alston & Brown store assistants as they greeted the arriving customers – or rather, greeted the arriving customers they knew by name. Miss Evangeline Garfield was greeted warmly. No one greeted Biddy because no one knew her from a bag of salt, but no one stopped her entering the elegant ladies' fashion emporium either, which thronged with shoppers, and after a while it was as if Biddy was invisible.

The tall and slender Miss Garfield was a respected governess of thirty, Biddy further discovered by continuing to eavesdrop on the shop girls while the lady browsed; Miss Garfield was known to have a "weakness" for fashion, or so she had claimed in the past. This flaw, or virtue, depending on personal perspective, manifested itself in visits made irregularly yet memorably to Alston & Brown. Each time she condescended to call Miss Garfield would exclaim that the styles she found within had changed wildly and unrecognisably since the time she visited last. The shop girls thought this hilarious. If this so-called weakness actually made for rather more frequent visits to the establishment Miss Garfield would discover that styles did not really change, from season to season, quite so radically or sweepingly as she supposed. Fashion *evolved*, one of the shop girls stated, in the manner of animal life as so convincingly described in Mr Darwin's theories. It did not burst forth fully formed, wholly and utterly without precedent.

It was the shop girls' belief that Miss Garfield did not know many ladies with a genuine failing for fashion. She had a sole pupil, they believed, a girl of sixteen, who was also fond of clothes, but due to restrictions placed upon this girl's movements was not permitted to acquire items by any means other than mail ordering from catalogues.

Biddy stored all this purloined information in her head. Something about the governess's manner greatly drew Biddy, although she couldn't have explained why, except to say that there was a hint of her own mother's kindness in the expression about her eyes. Miss Garfield looked like a nice person. Biddy made her way towards her, being still invisible to the staff herself.

Miss Garfield was staring at the fashion array around her in bafflement.

'Are you lost?' Biddy offered in a friendly voice behind her.

Miss Garfield turned and found pleasingly featured Biddy smiling at her with her clean, white, evenly spaced teeth from beneath a pair of sparkling brown eyes and a sweep of well-kept, chestnut hair arranged in the Gibson Girl style, upon which a broad straw hat was perched. Biddy was shorter and much younger than Miss Garfield, her serviceably plain Sunday best in uncommon contrast with the lavish clothes on display.

'Perhaps I am a little lost,' said Miss Garfield.

'Let me help you then,' said Biddy, 'I know this place backwards.' And before the governess had quite considered it, Biddy linked her arm in hers and waltzed her towards a display of mannequins. 'See here some very nice new styles in shirtwaists,' said Biddy, hoping the governess would pay little attention to the faded old garment she herself was wearing. 'Look at the tucking in these; clusters in the centre back *and* in the sleeves. Very finely done. And this one has lace insertions alternating with the tucks, which makes it particularly pleasing, especially with the bishop sleeves.'

Miss Garfield agreed.

'Shall we select you some for trying on?' Biddy asked.

'I don't know . . .' said Miss Garfield, even though she was evidently feeling much more comfortable than she had when she'd entered the store.

'But you must try them on, you'll be pleased with how nice they look, and why not combine them with one of these lovely five-gored flared skirts?' Biddy went on, seizing items from display. 'The fabric is summer weight, you'll see, with four gathered ruffles along the hem and an inverted box-plait at the rear.'

'Well . . .' said Miss Garfield, taken aback by Biddy's apparent knowledge and keenness. But she allowed herself to look properly at what was on show and then cast her eyes upon the wardrobe choices she herself had made when getting dressed that very morning. It was clear she didn't much like the comparison. 'I confess I'm feeling somewhat out of date,' she whispered.

Biddy was sympathetic. 'You and me both,' she said. 'The way time moves on, it's dizzying, isn't it? Who can keep up with the rate of changes?'

Miss Garfield blinked at that. 'I really came here to consider new hats.'

'Nice! Lots to choose from. Not all of them with stupid prices attached either.'

Miss Garfield appreciated that. 'Do you know, I may be tempted to purchase rather more than a hat, if my needs are met.'

'I've got every faith they will be,' said Biddy, winningly.

Miss Garfield obviously decided she could trust this shop assistant, despite her unusually familiar manner. Friendliness always went a long way and Biddy knew she was very good at being friendly. 'I've visited this store in the past,' Miss Garfield told her, 'and found things . . . quite unpleasant here.'

Biddy tut-tutted, dismayed.

'I've even walked away without purchasing a single item,' the governess added. 'It's been because of the service I've encountered; almost amounting to contempt, really, and quite uncalled for. It's as if I was offering coins of a foreign currency.'

'That's disgraceful,' said Biddy, meaning it. 'Strikes me that any shop which makes a lady feel small just for trying to buy a dress doesn't deserve to be a shop at all, and most likely won't remain one for very much longer.' She looked around her, accusingly.

'If you see the culprit that offended you last time, point him out to me, won't you, miss? He might have some comeuppance due.'

Miss Garfield took a good, long look at Biddy for a moment, at arm's length. Then she enquired: 'Are you a country girl?'

Biddy hesitated, unsure of what sort of answer might be called for. 'Are you, miss?'

'I was born near Castlemaine.'

'Takes one to know one,' laughed Biddy, ready to concoct another story should more details be required.

'How nice,' said Miss Garfield, feeling ever more at ease in Biddy's presence, 'I live at Summersby now. Have you heard of it?'

For some reason the name rang the very faintest of bells with Biddy, as if it was a half-remembered word from deep in the past that she'd heard spoken of once or twice, perhaps, but not in many years. Hearing it again it had a magical quality, romantic even, which was probably why it had stuck in her head in the first place. Or perhaps she was mistaken and had simply seen it written in a newspaper? 'I think perhaps I may have read of it somewhere . . .' she said, vaguely.

'Most likely,' said Miss Garfield. 'It's a very great house, quite famous in the Castlemaine District. I'm the governess there. Summersby is also the name of the little village that is situated near to the property. Very pretty country.'

Biddy took note of all this although she scarcely knew why.

'I could tell that you were a county girl,' said Miss Garfield. 'It's your manner, you know.'

'Yes?'

'You're very sweet-natured. Country girls are always sweet-natured. Girls from the city so often put on airs quite at odds with any right they might have to do so. So few of them have anything much to justify the entitlements they lay claim to at all, I find.'

Biddy wholly agreed. 'Frauds, the lot of them,' she whispered.

Miss Garfield really had to giggle at that.

Biddy suddenly located her brother. She'd been unobtrusively looking for Gordon from the moment she'd walked in off Collins

Street, but hadn't seen him. Now he appeared across the room, on the other side of the ground floor, and Biddy regarded him discreetly, her mind ticking over, while she continued to explain items to Miss Garfield.

Gordon MacBryde had always been passably good looking, to Biddy's critical eye, apart from his stained teeth. Not quite eighteen but he had the manner of a man somewhat older. Gordon wasn't charming with customers so much as he was oily; which, in salesmanship, amounted to the same thing, Biddy supposed. No other junior floorwalker could slide a chair under a customer's behind with his speed. Few could issue tellings-off to shop girls with his level of sting. When Gordon's roving eye suddenly took in the sight of Miss Garfield gaily trying on skirts, shirtwaists, hats and other garments his thoughts clearly went to determining which of the assistants was actually attending to her. It was then that the penny plainly dropped – none of them were. The person performing such effective attendance upon this spendthrift was not an employee of Alston & Brown at all, but grinning Biddy.

Miss Garfield was furnishing a humorous explanation of the current disastrous state of the Summersby kitchens as Gordon neared with panic alight in his face. Biddy was all ears to Miss Garfield, well aware of her brother's presence.

'Things got so dire that our poor housekeeper, Mrs Marshall, felt she had no other choice but to hire the Chinaman as a cook,' said Miss Garfield. 'Can you imagine?'

'But don't they eat funny food?' wondered Biddy, thinking fondly of Johnny's uncle's delicious chop suey shop in Carlton.

'Ungodly,' said the governess, 'but he swore he could do good English meals and he had a reference from the Shamrock Hotel in Bendigo, so Mrs Marshall, citing Christian charity, gave him a chance.' Miss Garfield drew a deep breath, enjoying herself. '*Well* . . .'

Biddy allowed her eyes, wide with knowing anticipation, to land upon those of her brother.

'Not only did she discover that Ah Sing stoned the pudding

raisins with his teeth,' continued Miss Garfield, 'but his method for moistening dough required him to spit in it.'

Biddy gasped with horrified delight.

'Oh, it's dreadful,' said Miss Garfield. 'Mrs Marshall will be driven to advertise again, if she hasn't done so this morning. No great house of Summersby's standing can possibly continue with such a dismaying betrayal of standards, even if it leaves no other option *but* to advertise, simply to alleviate such horrors.'

Suddenly Gordon was before her. 'Madam is making a very fine selection of purchases, I see?'

Miss Garfield blinked at him, allowing Biddy to fill the void. 'Madam's found some lovely new items,' Biddy informed her brother, presenting him with a beaming smile.

'Perhaps I can carry them to a counter for you, madam, to allow one of our *assistants* to tally and package them?' Gordon wondered.

'No need,' said Miss Garfield, 'your lovely girl Biddy is taking such excellent care of me, and loosening my purse strings no end.'

Gordon laughed, hollowly.

'I intend presenting her with a generous tip.'

Gordon nearly choked. Biddy smiled and blushed, but refrained from adding that such kindness wasn't necessary.

'Please, madam, it's really no trouble for me to begin the boxing process for you,' Gordon insisted, with a murderous glance at Biddy. Employing a movement so quick that the unsuspecting Miss Garfield missed it, he kicked a mannequin at its pedestal, causing the gowned display to teeter. 'Watch yourself, girl,' he said to Biddy.

Biddy looked up in time to see the dummy crashing down upon her. 'Ow!'

Gordon had his hand at Miss Garfield's elbow and was already gliding her away, as Biddy looked helplessly after them. He clicked his fingers at two legitimate assistants to clean up the mess and see to the governess's purchases. Miss Garfield looked worriedly back at Biddy. 'She deserves my tip, she really does . . .'

Gordon was the voice of kindly reassurance. 'Of course she does, madam, and I promise you personally that Biddy will receive exactly what's due to her.'

Biddy's replacement story, the moment it was said, proved to be as tissue thin as the one that preceded it a minute earlier, but this time Gordon laughed in response and Biddy took heart that she'd succeeded in entertaining him at least. The mirth was short lived.

'Bulldust,' said Gordon. 'You've been sacked from whatever rotten job you got yourself when you nicked off from home.'

The truth of her situation delivered as baldly as this left Biddy out of breath.

'What did you do to ruin it then?' he demanded, arms folded condemningly across his ribs. 'No, wait, don't bother telling me, I might spare myself any more of your stories.'

Biddy squirmed upon the tea chest she'd been made to sit on after Gordon had hauled her up the service stairs to the attic store-room where there'd be no further risk of her shaming him.

'I was hoping you might help me, as my brother . . .' Biddy ventured.

'But I'm not your brother.'

She winced. 'Yes, you are – *as good as, anyway.*'

'Biddy,' he began, his smile falsely bright, as if he was talking to a dim-witted child, 'do you remember that day, oh, a year and half or so ago, when a certain gentlemen calling himself Mr Samuel Hackett came to our door?'

Biddy didn't want to remember it but she knew she would never forget. It was the strange visitor's fair hair that had so captured her attention at first – like honey it was, the nicest hair she'd ever seen on a man – but her mother Ida had been very angry to see him turn up at their house, and then he had started speaking of things that he claimed Biddy needed to know. 'Let's not bring all that up again . . .'

'Why not? Sorry, but you don't get to stick your head in the ground with me.'

'Please, Gordon, don't bring it all up!'

But he wouldn't let her off. 'That Mr Samuel Hackett came round to our house and he made some startling pronouncements, didn't he, Biddy, the chief one being that *he*, and not my poor old late dad, was actually your father?'

Biddy wanted to die. 'It wasn't true.'

'Oh, but it was,' said Gordon, 'it was as true as I'm standing here. We knew it was true from the look upon Ida's face. Your mum and my dad had told us a little lie, a lie we'd believed our whole lives, but that's what it was – *a lie*. My dad was never your dad. Your mum was never my mum. That's what Mr Hackett made plain to us. Our family was nothing but big, fat fibs.'

She was miserable. 'But what does any of it matter now?'

He laughed. 'It mattered to you – you ran away! Took off like a shocked rat, you did! But I guess you got a bigger surprise than I did because what else did Mr Samuel Hackett tell us that day, Biddy, do you remember?'

'Don't, Gordon, please don't do this.'

'He told us your mum wasn't even your mum! Neither parent was yours – a double blow!'

She hated him for making her relive this terrible experience.

'Shame Ida kicked that Mr Hackett out before he could finish what he had to tell you, otherwise we might have heard who your mum actually was – you must have been busting to know the truth, given it wasn't Ida at all. All the more so when Ida wouldn't tell you the truth herself. She said she'd take the secret to the grave!' He hooted at the memory. 'No, I can't blame you for bolting. Lies had been told to you by the person you loved most in the world. I suppose you had to run away and make a new life just to be rid of them.' He sniffed. 'So, I shouldn't be surprised, really, that you've turned up lying to me now. The whole sorry experience must have left you with a very strange notion of what "truth" even is.'

Biddy had heard enough of this. 'Ida was always kind to your poor dad!'

'And as well she might have been – she stole his bloody name!'

Biddy cringed. 'It's a fine name, MacBryde.'

'Just not the one you were born with. Wonder what it really is? Guess we'll never know now. I've turned my back on Ida, you see, just like you have, though I bet it hurt you more to do it.'

Biddy blinked back a tear. Eighteen months might have passed but the wound of running away still felt raw.

He spat on the floor with contempt. 'And how much money do you think they pay me here!'

'I don't want money!' Biddy added quickly. 'I'd never ask you for that.'

'What then? Why are you here?'

'Well,' said Biddy, managing what she hoped was an endearing smile, 'while I was serving that lovely lady . . .'

'You were *not* serving.'

'Well, whatever you'd like to call it.'

'What you were doing was immoral; there are laws against it. You were representing this establishment when you had no business doing so. That's fraud.'

'There's no need for any of that,' said Biddy, worriedly. 'If you'd just let me finish what I want to tell you.'

'Finish it then.'

'Like I said, when I was . . . *talking* to that lovely lady, I wasn't doing it to make a fool of you, I swear.'

'Bulldust.'

'I swear it!'

'Pull the other one.'

'I was doing it as an experiment.'

Gordon summoned another wad of spit in the back of his throat.

'To see if I was capable of being an *assistant* here . . .' said Biddy, triumphant.

Gordon abandoned spitting for another crack of laughter that seemed to Biddy to go on for rather too long.

'But that's just it,' said Biddy, 'my experiment worked, didn't it? I sold that lady all those things; skirts and shirtwaists, hats and scarves. She wouldn't have bought none of that stuff without me. She said she hated this place before I got to her; she said the service here was criminal.'

Gordon's mirth died twice. 'What do you want from me?'

'A job?'

'No chance.'

'Gordon, just listen to me . . .'

'You're muck, Biddy; dung from the street.'

She was stung. 'But our dad – *your* dad – really cared for my mum, they were great mates . . .'

'More's the shame of it and I pray to whoever might listen that you'll go to your grave with that knowledge shared with no one else,' said Gordon. 'Thank Christ my old dad's gone to his grave ahead of you.'

'Gordon!'

'Your mum's side of things were a humiliation from the very start. Some people reckoned she worked at a nut house – if so, she should have been locked up in there herself. She dragged my poor dad down to the gutter.'

Biddy flinched at this fresh spike of pain. 'He was already there!'

Gordon pulled himself up to his full height. 'Yeah? Look around you, then, Biddy. Who's managed to make something of themselves despite it, eh? Who's got prospects? Who's stepping out of the muck? And who's got a grimy old tram ticket to the doss house with a detour to the Little Lon knocking shops first?'

Biddy's tears, held off all afternoon, now threatened to spring forth. Gordon volubly spat again in response to her quivering lip. 'Pathetic, you are.'

'I'd never sink to any of that,' Biddy managed to counter.

Gordon said nothing else and offered her nothing to stem her imminent tears either. Biddy fished her old hankie from her skirt pocket and tried to wipe her face with it. 'It's just so unfair,' she began.

Gordon looked away.

Biddy pulled herself together again. 'I have another plan—' she said, but he cut her short.

'Moving in with me?'

'I'll keep a nice house for you,' she vowed, 'I learnt so many good things from Mrs Rattray.'

'Where do you think I live now, Biddy?'

'I don't know. Wasn't it in Fitzroy?'

'You're standing in it,' said Gordon.

Biddy looked around, confused. 'What do you mean?'

'I kip in this room. I work eighteen hours daily. What's the point in paying rent? I've got my head screwed on correctly, haven't I? Saving money, making progress. Not like some.'

Biddy swallowed, now utterly humiliated, her fingers tightening around the little coin purse in her skirt pocket. 'What I said to you before about money, Gordon . . .'

The spectre of the streetwalker, raised by Gordon as it had been in the attic room and presented to Biddy as her likely employ in the future, clung to her all the more portentously as she followed him down the five flights of service stairs, well away from the eyes of any customers, and into the alley where all the rubbish was hurled. Gordon solidified the spectre's presence by handing Biddy a single gold sovereign, wholly in view of the storeroom lads who were puffing their cigarettes. They let out a spray of whistles at the sight of this and Gordon glared at the boys but didn't even bother correcting them. They hushed eventually but kept on snickering into their hands.

'It's too much,' said Biddy in a small voice, meaning the coin that was sitting unexpectedly heavy in her hand; it was the first sovereign she'd ever felt in her life.

'I know it is,' said Gordon, 'but that's how it is with insurance, Biddy. It's comes dear.'

'What insurance?'

Gordon stuck his face in hers, his breath minty. 'That's what I'm paying for, stupid. Insurance that this is the last time I'll ever land eyes on you; insurance that you'll keep away from me for good. This is insurance that will let me forget that you and I were ever "family" and that you were from the rat's arse end of it, what's more. It's insurance that'll let you top yourself for all it matters to me, because I'll never, ever hear of it. Do you understand me? This is my insurance that you're done, Biddy.'

He left her standing there in the trash-choked alley with the sovereign still flat in her palm. Biddy knew then that she understood her 'brother' very well, and it was only because the merest glimmer of her cheerfulness returned in that same instant, microscopically tiny, but there all the same, that she didn't fling the coin to the storeroom boys and let them beat each other's brains out for it in the filth.

Biddy thought of Miss Evangeline Garfield, the kind-hearted governess at Summersby, a magical sounding place in very pretty country somewhere near a town called Castlemaine.

She conceived a new story.

The journey by rail apparently wasn't a long one by country standards, but to Biddy, who had never had reason to ride anywhere on a steam train before, the process seemed impossibly protracted. Her ticket bought, Biddy faced a wait of a number of hours upon the railway platform at Spencer Street, with all the other trains coming and going, and she seemingly marooned because none of them were the train that matched her ticket. For a short time, when the realisation of what she was planning hit her at last, Biddy thought about taking the electric tram to Carlton, which wasn't very far away, and there finding Ida and somehow saying something that would make up for the eighteen months she had let her think she was dead. But then the prospect of doing so paled. Her life with Ida had been a total concoction, and not one with which she'd had any part in making. Biddy had promised herself that all future concoctions would be her own, and if she was ever to have any respect for herself at all she must continue to live by this promise, even if it killed her. But Biddy's thoughts strayed to cherished memories of Ida again and it took her some effort to shake them off and will her cheerfulness to return.

The platform slowly filled up with other passengers who would be taking the same journey, and the time for departure drew near. Most of Biddy's fellow travellers had shopping with them; newly bought things, presents for themselves, surprises for others. Many had baggage with them, too, suggesting they'd been hotel guests while availing themselves of Melbourne's pleasures. Biddy copied the facial expressions of those who waited with her, alternately 'tired' and 'elated', just like they were, and it made her feel as if she was equal to them; a girl with family and friends who had spent the hot December week within the capital, gaily shopping for Christmas and New Year gifts.

When the train arrived at last, Biddy boarded, found her third class seat, regretted at once not forking out for first, and then chastised herself for taking on unwarranted airs. Third would do her until she had money honestly earned. Biddy hoped that someone might sit next to her, so she could pass the evening in company at least, but no one did. She'd not packed any books or even a newspaper, and so she resigned herself to watching whatever passed outside the window. Not much held Biddy's interest, at least, not much she could see once the train left the electricity-lit tracks of Melbourne and found the gaslit tracks of the suburbs to the west. Soon there was nothing to be seen at all once the gaslight had petered out. Biddy tried to close her eyes but couldn't sleep, in terror of missing the stop when it came. There was excitement fuelling her mind, keeping her alert.

Biddy was still wide-awake when the steam engine chugged into the old goldrush town of Castlemaine, though it was very late. Biddy had no watch to tell her the time but a man on the carriage said it was two in the morning before he went back to snoring; an hour so late that Biddy had never before been awake for it. She emerged, stiff-legged, from the train, clutching her portmanteau, while the station master in his ornate uniform blew upon a whistle and supervised the unloading of newspapers, mailbags and luggage from the goods carriage. There were lots of other passengers alighting with her, full of yawns and greetings and complicated arrangements, and then there were rather less of them about and the stationmaster waved his all-clear flag and lantern as the train departed, and then there were no more passengers at all.

Biddy found herself alone, knowing what she needed to accomplish as the next step in her plan, but unsure of any means at her disposal to achieve it. She discovered the dimly lit passage to another platform and from there found the station master's residence. But a sign on the door said 'Asleep', which was cruelty as far as Biddy considered, because she'd only just seen him before. But she didn't risk knocking for fear of creating a scene.

Biddy settled down to wait until daylight, hoping, though she couldn't be sure, that a coach might present itself, which would allow her to complete the journey she'd started. It was just on dawn when her opportunity came. The gentle calls of magpies awoke her first, though she had no memory of falling asleep on the railway bench, and then she heard the clatter of horses' hooves and carriage wheels on gravel. It was a Cobb & Co coach pulling in to the station's forecourt, lit up with swinging kerosene lamps, like little suns in the breaking daylight. Buoyed by the sight, Biddy stood and beamed, waiting for the transport to halt. Some passengers emerged from the interior, and another climbed down from the roof. Biddy told the coachman her destination as the horses ate their grain.

'That's a very nice place to be going to, miss,' he said.

'Oh, I know,' Biddy replied, airily. 'One of the prettiest places there is. It wouldn't surprise me one little bit if someone had penned a poem about it since last I called in.'

The coachman thought she was funny. 'And on my way it is, too. Hop on.'

Biddy still had change enough from the sovereign to take an inside seat, but contemplated the pleasure of perching high on the roof, behind the coachman's spot. The air was already warm, the dawn was making the dew drenched bush glisten; it smelled lovely. Riding atop the coach would be a romantic way to arrive at her brand new adventure, Biddy thought, until she reconsidered it. Perhaps well-mannered girls didn't ride upon a roof when they had a choice in the matter. Biddy paid her fare and stepped inside, the only passenger. Appearances should be adhered to, she told herself, settling in for the ride, even if they were only that.

Biddy almost let those same appearances slip as soon as she got her first, unobstructed view of Summersby House. She'd caught glimpses of it through trees as the Cobb & Co coach entered the long, sweeping drive, through a wrought-iron gateway and Osage orange hedge, and while Biddy could tell that the mansion beyond was impressive, she couldn't quite fathom just how impressive, and so had managed to contain herself. But when the coach fully emerged into sunlight again, having traversed the densely canopied park of Dutch elms and kurrajongs, the great house suddenly presented itself in its breathtaking entirety and Biddy nearly forgot the story she'd told the driver about how she'd been here many times before. Summersby was two long wings that met at a right angle; some three storeys tall and graced with an imposing tower, placed so that it rose from the middle of the eastern wing. The tower was a further two storeys tall again, with elegant, rounded windows, and topped with a pole flying the new flag of the Australian nation. The ground level of the house was graced by a loggia that ran the full perimeter and sheltered the interior reception rooms from the sun. The roof of the loggia formed an encircling balcony for the floor above, offering views of the park and beyond. French windows abounded everywhere, giving Biddy peeks into the sumptuousness within. The windows of the third floor were smaller and were likely those belonging to the rooms of the thousands upon thousands of servants who must surely be required to run such an establishment, Biddy imagined. Yet there wasn't one other person to be seen at the present moment, which was just as well, because it allowed Biddy to gawp at the house unashamedly. The grand entrance to Summersby was situated where the two wings met.

'Knock me over,' she gasped, as she stepped from the coach.

'No place like home, eh?' said the coachman.

'I've never seen anything like it.'

The coachman raised an eyebrow.

'I mean, I've never seen anything like it *this week*,' said Biddy, correcting herself for the story's's sake.

The coachman gave a chuckle. 'Biggest house in the region is Summersby,' he said. 'Course it has its rivals. Chirnside Park is a very good copy they tell me, down Geelong way, and Rupertswood over at Sunbury is also very grand, but neither comes close to what Summersby has, but that's just my opinion.'

'Mine, too,' claimed Biddy. 'Rupertswood's fallen to *very* low standards I think you'll find should you ever have the misfortune to visit there.'

'Is that right, miss?'

'You couldn't pay me to return,' said Biddy.

The coachman just chuckled at her again before stirring his horses to depart. Biddy stood aside, the portmanteau in her hand, as the coach turned in a circle on the drive. Then, so that he wouldn't think of her as someone beneath his own lowly station, she gave the appearance of setting off toward the grand entrance, her dusty boots crunching on the gravel but not with any great speed. When satisfied that she was no longer in the coachman's view, Biddy set off in the opposite direction, making for the rear of the house and the likely entrance for would-be servants.

Biddy's gawping didn't abate as she stood at an open rear door that gave entrance directly to the Summersby kitchen. 'If Mrs Rattray could see me now,' she muttered aloud, before clapping her hand across her mouth. She soon realised that she needn't have feared anyone overhearing her. The kitchen was as deserted as the grounds. There wasn't a soul to be found anywhere. Dazzled by all she could see, Biddy stepped inside the bright, airy room to give herself an even closer look while enjoying the good fortune of being unobserved.

The kitchen was remarkably free of odours, Biddy thought, even though a morning meal had clearly been cooked and consumed there. Biddy put this down to the abundance of windows and the size of the chimney. 'Good drawing power,' she said of it. A large, two-fire iron 'colonial oven', as Biddy knew it was termed, stood under the chimney, with impressive capacity to roast joints, bake bread and do whatever else was needed all at the same time. To the side of it was an equally large boiler with a tap from which, Biddy guessed with amazement, hot water could be drawn when required. 'Pots of tea, washing up, dirty laundry and bathing all made instantaneous,' Biddy marvelled, running her hand over the spout. She didn't quite dare to try it out, however.

Biddy wandered further into the room, taking in the polished slate floor, the French enamelled sink, the dressers full of crockery, the long, scrubbed pine table and eight bentwood chairs, the copper pots and pans suspended from ceiling hooks. Several household storerooms opened from the far end of the kitchen and Biddy realised with a thrill that at least one was unlocked. Pushing the door to it gently to one side, Biddy saw a wall of metal bins protecting bulk supplies of flour, raisins, tea and sugar from the damp. She stopped and listened, but still she was wholly alone, so she lifted the lid of the raisin bin and took a fistful of the sweet, dried fruit, inhaling the delicious scent of them before cramming the whole lot into her mouth. She'd not eaten anything since yesterday's midday dinner. The sound of her own laboured chewing succeeded in blocking her ears to a scratching noise until she had finally swallowed. Only then did she hear the strange commotion coming from the storeroom next door.

Panicking, Biddy darted into the kitchen proper, where the scratching grew louder. Someone – or something – was behind the door to the second of the three storerooms, scratching at the wooden panels furiously.

'Hello? Is someone in there?' Biddy asked as loudly as she dared. She tried the door handle; it was firmly locked. 'Hello?' she asked again.

A plump, mousey, middle-aged woman appeared at a different door, a door padded with dark green baize that Biddy would have noticed properly had she made it further than the storerooms. Carrying a brown paper wrapped parcel, the woman responded to the sight of Biddy with shock, dropping the parcel to the floor.

'Good morning!' Biddy exclaimed, springing at once from where she'd been listening at the storeroom, picking up the dropped parcel, and presenting it along with an outstretched, gloved hand to the woman. 'And isn't it a lovely morning? I hope you don't mind that I'm waiting here. I knocked but nobody answered.'

The woman took the parcel from her, examined it, and then gave Biddy a startled once over before shaking her hand. 'How can I help you?' she asked, coolly. Biddy saw the quick, anxious glance she gave to the locked storeroom door and decided to pretend she'd heard nothing amiss.

'Let's start off on exactly the right footing, shall we?' Biddy beamed. 'I'm Mrs Rattray. Mrs Bridget Rattray.'

'*Mrs?*'

'Widowed,' Biddy nodded in defiance of the truth that she looked far too young to have landed a husband, let alone lost one. 'Married less than a week before the Good Lord gathered him, and all that was left behind for me was his name, sadly. But it hurts me to speak of it now.'

The woman didn't know what to make of this story. 'Why are you here, Mrs Rattray?'

'Please, the right footing. What was your name, if you don't mind me enquiring it of you?'

The woman made a point of looking her sceptically up and down. 'I'm Mrs Agatha Marshall, the housekeeper here,' the woman replied, her eyebrows raised.

'*Mrs?*' said Biddy. In her experience, housekeepers with 'Mrs' in their title were always just plain old 'miss' in reality. There'd certainly been no husband in the real Mrs Rattray's spotless history.

The older woman's eyes flashed as she placed the brown paper parcel on a dresser.

'Of course you are,' said Biddy. 'Oh, we shall be firm friends, I sense it already!'

Mrs Marshall now squinted at Biddy, deep suspicion clearly forming. 'We don't get any casual callers here and my days are extremely full. Is there some matter I can help you with before I bid you good day?'

'Help *me?*' Biddy laughed. 'Well, isn't that kind, but it's not about helping me, Mrs Marshall, it's about helping you!'

'Me?'

'Of course.' Biddy could sense the older woman's temper being tested and decided a more extravagant gesture was needed. 'You see, I'm the very answer to your prayers!'

Mrs Marshall took another long, blank look at Biddy, and then propelled her across the polished slate floor towards the door and made to close it in Biddy's face. But Biddy was quicker than that and slipped her left boot in the doorjamb.

'Really!' exclaimed the Summersby housekeeper.

Biddy backpedalled. 'Please. I'm so sorry. Will you let me begin again?'

'You appear to be a time waster, young woman,' Mrs Marshall told her.

'But I'm not, I'm not at all,' said Biddy through the gap in the door, trying to reassure her while keeping her boot where it was.

'Tell me why you are here immediately or leave.'

'I've come about the position,' Biddy blurted.

The housekeeper was pulled up short. 'The position?'

'I understand the need to keep my mouth shut about it,' Biddy added, 'I really do, and of course no decent household ever wants to advertise because of all the riff-raff you get, so I'm here, Mrs Marshall, to save you any of that by not having to advertise at all. And I'm not riff-raff, I swear it.' She looked at her wedged boot. 'Despite my travelling clothes being soiled from the journey, I grant you—'

Mrs Marshall flushed pink, staring at Biddy in dismay. 'You cannot possibly mean the cook's position?'

'Well, that's exactly what I mean,' cried Biddy, triumphant. 'I'm your new cook!'

The housekeeper looked a picture of mortification. 'Where have you come from?'

'Why, from Melbourne, of course,' said Biddy. 'I've been cooking and keeping house for a Hawthorn Reverend. A very honourable, God-fearing gentleman he is, too, or he was until he died. A dreadful tragedy it was, Mrs Marshall, taken too soon. Sulphur poisoning; it's the deplorable water – and the last thing my poor heart needed after already suffering widowhood.' Biddy contemplated adding tears, but opted against it. 'Still, he's gone to his reward now, just like my husband, and what a reward it must surely be for both of them. But those of us left behind must somehow carry on, don't you agree?'

The door fell abruptly back and Mrs Marshall pulled Biddy inside, knocking her off her balance. When Biddy righted herself, the housekeeper had a warning finger jabbed under her nose. 'Now, you listen here, young woman . . .'

'I have references, naturally,' said Biddy, telling stories hopelessly now.

'I have no interest in references or anything else.'

'But I'm an excellent cook. You'd be amazed by what I can achieve with very little.'

'You've impressed that upon me already, I think.'

Biddy drew herself upright. 'I do hope this isn't your means of telling me there *is* no position,' she said with dignity. 'Not when I've come all this way on a promise.'

Mrs Marshall's eyes nearly popped. '*What promise?* How can you possibly know about the cook's position at all?'

Biddy took a gamble she'd been reluctant to resort to, given the potential it had for backfiring, but she could see little other option with things going the way they presently were. 'My very good friend told me about it,' she claimed, adding with a whisper, 'and about the *Chinaman . . .*'

Mrs Marshall flushed pink for a second time in as many minutes.

'But I haven't told another soul, of course,' Biddy hastened to amend, 'well, it's not the sort of thing that *wants* repeating, is it, and I know for a fact that my friend hasn't breathed a word either.'

'What friend is this?' Mrs Marshall demanded.

Biddy cleared her throat a little, reminded of nothing so much as the feeling that comes when preparing to leap headlong from a pier into the sea. 'My wonderful friend,' she began, knowing at this moment that the only friend she had in the world was indeed this person. Biddy hoped only that she would prove worthy of the honour. 'Her name's Miss Garfield. She's the governess here.'

Further words failed Mrs Marshall as she grappled with news that had clearly astonished her.

Biddy noted the short, stout woman's expression darken in a manner that wasn't easily read, before the look seemed to depart her face just as quickly, leaving her strangely calm in its wake.

'The governess, you say?'

'Yes,' said Biddy, feeling a little more hopeful now, 'Miss Garfield told me all about it – in confidence of course – and did so knowing only that I was in such a fine situation to help you.'

Mrs Marshall was briefly silent again and Biddy was at a loss as to how she might further fill the void, so said nothing, only smiling at the older woman, encouragingly.

'Will you excuse me for a moment?' the housekeeper asked.

Biddy didn't even reply before Mrs Marshall departed the well-appointed Summersby kitchen through the green baize door, headed, Biddy presumed, to the formal rooms of the house. The housekeeper's voice echoed from a distant location, sounding as if she was calling up the stairs. 'Oh, Miss Garfield? Could I trouble you to see me in the kitchen for a moment . . .?'

If there was a reply, it wasn't audible from where Biddy waited on the cool slate floor. Mrs Marshall reappeared shortly and the look she gave Biddy was again somewhat difficult to read. Biddy decided only to take hope from it, and was heartened further when she heard the clip-clop of a woman's heels upon the staircase somewhere above.

Biddy prayed her only friend would see her desperate need without her having to demean herself by even mentioning it. Surely Miss Garfield would remember the fun they had had at snooty Alston & Brown before Gordon had put the moz on it? And surely, although astonished at Biddy turning up like this, Miss Garfield would follow Biddy's lead in what was an inspired story and all would prove wonderfully well?

The governess appeared at the door, the sun from the kitchen windows at that moment striking her in the eyes, so that Biddy was able to see her fully before Miss Garfield even realised there was someone other than Mrs Marshall in the room. Biddy noted with pleasure that the tall, slender woman was dressed in the five-gored flared skirt Biddy had suggested for her and that she looked quite transformed by it, her figure flattered to perfection.

'I'm so sorry for troubling you when you're not long home from your Melbourne excursion, Miss Garfield,' the housekeeper began in a neutral tone, 'but I have here a Mrs . . .'

'Rattray,' said Biddy.

'Yes. Who says you are her friend.'

Miss Garfield shifted so that the sun left her eyes. She saw chestnut-haired Biddy standing upon the floor in dusty, unpolished boots, a wrinkled, sun-bleached shirtwaist and a battered little portmanteau next to her. The recognition that she did indeed know Biddy did not quite come to Miss Garfield for a moment. Clearly she could place Biddy's pleasing face and the less than pleasing clothes, but could not quite recall what the setting had been when last she had encountered Biddy, and so, accordingly, she lacked the vital piece of the puzzle. Then it came to Miss Garfield with a noticeable jolt.

'My goodness, you're Biddy.'

'That's right,' said Biddy, beaming with relief. 'My friends call me Biddy, although I was christened Bridget, of course,' she said, turning to explain to Mrs Marshall.

But the housekeeper showed no sign of relief of her own. 'Your friend has come about the cook's position,' she said to the governess.

Miss Garfield gave a sharp intake of breath.

'Yes. That's right,' said Mrs Marshall, 'The *Chinaman* cook.'

Biddy was thrown to see the eyes of her friend suddenly prick with guilty tears and Mrs Marshall's jaw set into a hard, grim line.

'Oh dear,' said the governess, faintly.

It was a bell that awoke Biddy, clanging consistently, yet irregularly from somewhere near to where she lay. She curled up tighter in the makeshift bed she'd found for herself in the old miner's hut, clinging to sleep while the sky outside was still dark enough to allow it, but the bell kept on sounding, and after a time Biddy's imagination engaged with the noise and she tried to determine just what sort of bell it was that possessed such a ring. It lacked the urgency of a school bell or the excitement of a dinner bell. It was nothing like a church bell, and besides, Biddy already knew for certain that there were no churches near, so she dismissed the possibility. Perhaps it was the bell on a cart? The peal was irregular; if it was a cart, then it was stopping and starting after very small distances. The bell was attached to something else that was mobile. The remaining sleep slipped from her grasp and Biddy found herself awake again and far earlier than she would have liked. It was still as dark as coal beyond the cracked, curtainless window of the dwelling she'd found for herself, and just as dark inside. Her only recourse to stop the fearfulness that had come when dark descended was to try to sleep all the way through it. The bell had put an end to that.

It rang again, nearer now, and Biddy sat upright. She heard a footfall outside; heavy. There was someone there, someone carrying the bell. Biddy knew better than to panic, she, who set store by appearances. Her heart was thumping but she would not give in to it. She debated as to whether lighting the lantern was a sensible thing to do, and then proceeded to do so anyway. Biddy located the box, struck a match against the side of the empty kerosene tin that was her table, and applied it to the stump of candle she'd wedged inside an upturned half bottle. The sputtering light made the darkness flee only as far as the rough bark walls while Biddy crept from the old stretcher she'd been sleeping on, found her boots, slipped them on and then, with her other hand, rummaged among the piles of old rubbish until she found a broken axe handle.

She listened for the bell, heard nothing more for what felt like many minutes, only to leap out of her skin when it rang again.

She rushed to the hut's rickety tin door and flung it open to the night.

'I can hear you out there, you know!' she shouted. 'I've got very good ears! And it's lucky for you that my sleeping husband is as deaf as a post, otherwise it'd be him you'd be dealing with now, not me, and he doesn't need any axe handle to get his point across!'

She waited, tense, to hear what might be said in reply. There was nothing.

Then the bell rang again.

'You lousy bugger, show yourself!'

Biddy lurched into the dark, the lantern making shadows leap and dance around her as she swung wildly with the axe handle at anything and everything. 'Think I'm scared of you? You're the one who'll be scared as soon as I wake my husband up!'

The handle struck something on the backswing; something huge yet yielding, and Biddy spun around with the lantern to see what it was just as the recipient of the blow let out an objecting bellow so loud it knocked her clean off her feet.

'Oh no,' said Biddy, mortified. The handle had connected with a very large bullock foraging in the bush; a bullock with a sheet metal bell around its neck. Girl and beast stared at each other for several seconds, before the bullock registered its objection again with another bellow, equally loud, and then returned to plucking grass as if its assailant was beneath all further attention.

'You stupid twit!' Biddy shouted at it, picking herself up and rescuing the lantern from the dirt. 'What are you doing stumbling around in the dark like that for?'

'I reckon he'll tell you it's because it's a pretty decent hour to get some supper,' said a male voice.

Biddy screamed and dropped the lantern again. This time the candle dislodged itself from the half bottle, coming to rest in dry leaves, the lit wick finding fuel among them before a big leather boot stamped out the flame. A broad, long-fingered hand stooped to pick up the candle stub again, reattaching it inside the half bottle.

'And that's a pretty decent way to start a bush fire.' The boot and the hand belonged to the owner of the voice; someone Biddy could barely make out until the hand produced a matchbox of its own and relit the candle. The sight of the lean, brown face grinning at Biddy in the lantern glow did nothing to bring her voice back any sooner. She could only stare in shock, her mouth hanging open, useless.

'You hit my best bullock. What did you go and do that for?'

'I . . .'

'What's the matter with you? You had plenty of tongue in your head before.'

Biddy remembered the axe handle still in her hand and swung it out in an arc that ended at the grinning man's thigh.

'Ow!'

'You keep away from me!'

'What the bloody hell's wrong with you?'

'Keep away!' Biddy swung the axe handle again and gave him another one in the same spot.

'Jesus Christ almighty!'

'I can keep doing this all night if I have to.'

'Fair enough then, you flaming' harpy, but do you mind if I put this little one out of harm's way first?'

Only then did Biddy realise he was cradling the curled-up form of a puppy inside his shirt. He sprang a couple of buttons and scooped out a melon-sized ball of cream wool that looked to be one half terrier and another half poodle. The puppy yawned, then complained, then sat upon the dirt where its master placed it until it registered Biddy as something new and interesting, and snuffled over to regard her boots.

Biddy found herself speechless again.

'Well? What you waiting for now?' said the dog's master. 'I reckon me other leg needs a bruising just to balance it up.'

Biddy let the axe handle fall to the ground as she knelt down to fondle the pup. When she looked up she was met by the grin again.

'Bruising?' said Biddy, wry. 'You reckon I bruised you, do you? Crikey. Some bloke you are, letting himself get bruised by a girl . . .'

The grinner had more than a puppy on his person; he also had good Ceylon tea in a brown paper bag. Biddy could offer the billy required to turn the leaves into a decent brew, and there was water enough in the rain barrel – though it had a rusty colour – to grant them several mugs of it to drink while the night ebbed away to become dawn. Biddy hadn't enjoyed a mug of tea since she'd left Melbourne, but didn't plan on letting the grinner know of this.

His name was Lewis Fitzwater, she soon learned. He was a roustabout and farm hand, doing jobs here and there, which included finding stray bullocks by their Condamine bells, which is what Biddy had been woken by. He was younger than his voice gave credence to, being just on twenty-one but blessed with a deep baritone that Biddy found rather pleasing. His hair was sand coloured; his eyes were a warm, chocolate brown. He was very tall in the way that Tom had been tall, but taller again and of broader build, being used, Biddy guessed while observing him as he talked, to working long hours out of doors with only his arms and legs to depend on. The sun had browned him almost as dark as a native, but only as far as his face, neck and arms. Lewis's chest peeking through where he'd left his shirt unbuttoned was as white as the woolly white coat on the poodle pup he'd been cradling.

'What are doing with a lady's dog?' Biddy asked him.

'What are you doing out here all alone?'

'Who says I'm alone?'

'Well, *you* didn't. You claimed you had a husband here before.'

'Who says I don't?'

'Well, if you do, he must have a blocked-up nose as well as bung ears because if the noise of us hasn't woke him up yet, you'd think that the smell of the brew would.' He produced a small flat box of tobacco from his person, followed by a packet of Tally-Ho papers, from which he preceded to roll himself a cigarette.

Biddy just narrowed her eyes at him, nursing her tea in the old enamel mug she'd found along with so many other useful things when she'd stumbled across the hut. 'Who says he's not temporarily away?'

'The lack of anything around here that speaks of a man being present at all. Unless he's long dead.'

Biddy dismissed that. 'You didn't answer my question. What are you doing with a lady's dog?'

But Lewis just gave her another grin; like Biddy, he was one to answer questions only when they suited him. 'So, I suppose you're not from around this district then?'

Perhaps because of the early hour Biddy's powers of story-telling weren't fully awake. She found herself revealing the truth, or at least something closer to it, rather more often than she would have ordinarily. It was Lewis's long, brown face that was making her more truthful; a face she liked the look of, much as she'd liked the look of Tom's face once upon a time. But Lewis's was a far nicer face, Biddy felt. 'No,' she answered, 'not from here.'

'I reckon you're not even a country girl.'

'Are you saying I'm not sweet natured?' said Biddy, sticking her chin out.

The young man didn't know why she'd drawn that conclusion. 'I'm saying no country girl would ever consider shifting into this heap of sticks and dust,' he said, meaning the hut. 'But a city girl might; one who's down on her luck and doesn't have much in her experience from which she might pass judgment on a place like this.'

Biddy made to protest, but his nice-looking face knocked the struggle out of her again. 'It's not very decent, is it?' she conceded.

'Least there's lots of rubbish you can use. How'd you come by it?'

'I inherited it.'

Lewis waited, sipping his tea.

'I found it, then,' Biddy admitted.

Lewis nodded. 'No crime in that. It's been sitting empty for donkey's years. Why shouldn't you use it if you've got the need? No one else is.'

Biddy felt a rush of gratitude at this lack of condemnation for her. Lewis was someone to confide in, perhaps, someone who would prove to be a friend.

'I've hit hard times,' Biddy told him in a small voice.

Lewis nodded, screwing his mouth up in sympathy.

'Nothing shameful,' Biddy added quickly, 'not like *that*, it's just, well, it looks like I might have reached a dead end to my prospects. For the time being.'

'Hmmm,' was all he said.

'Something I'd set my heart upon didn't work out.'

'What was that then?'

'A position. I thought it was mine but when I got there it wasn't. They showed me the door. I didn't know what to do or where to go, so I just started walking. I thought I was on a road for a while, but then it seemed to run out and became something else, a track

I suppose you'd call it, and I realised that it wasn't the same road that the coach had taken me on. I got myself lost. I had to sleep in the open the first night. It was horrible. But on the second night I ended up here.'

'Do you even know where you are?' he asked in amazement.

Biddy actually did. 'Knowing that I'd found this place to live in for a while, I retraced my steps and scouted about a bit. I worked out where I was in relation to things; to the little village that's near.'

He was impressed.

'I thought I'd just stay here, at least for a bit. It hasn't been cold and there's a stretcher inside to sleep in and even a bathtub out the back. Whoever lived here left a lot of things behind.' She hoped he wouldn't ask her the difficult question of how she'd been managing to eat.

'What do you do then, Biddy, for a quid? At least, what did you do before you came here from wherever it was you came from?'

'I cooked,' she said, but as soon it was out it felt like a story again. 'I mean, I can cook *some* things, not everything, you understand . . .'

But Lewis had already seized on this, his eyes lighting up. 'You're flash with the tucker?'

'Well, maybe, but not—'

Lewis sprang from the log he'd been sitting on in front of the billy fire. 'I reckon this is your lucky day!'

'How is it?'

'There's a place round here that's damn near desperate for a cook!'

Biddy stood, too. 'There never is?'

'You bet your sweet life, it's the joke of the district!'

'A joke?'

'A mean one, but it's got folks laughing for sure. Oh, crikey, they'll love you as soon as they look at you, Biddy. And don't go splitting hairs that you can't cook "everything" – if you can even cook anything at all they'll be pleased to have you and will pay good money for it.'

Biddy clapped her hands in excitement and the little poodle pup woke up from its snooze and began to watch her again with new interest. 'Lewis, I knew you'd be a friend to me!'

'Eh, what's that . . .?' he said, looking at her askance.

'A true friend, someone who sees this life like I see it: full of reasons to be hopeful!'

'Well, I suppose that's what I do.'

'And that's just what you've given me – hope,' beamed Biddy.

Lewis beamed back and the rising sun hit his grin at that precise moment, causing Biddy to think of him then as something like an angel come to earth, with glowing eyes, teeth and sand-coloured hair. 'I'm so ashamed that I hit you with the axe handle.'

'Don't mention it. There's mozzies that'd do worse damage.'

'And the poor bullock.'

'Something tells me you failed to put him off his feed,' Lewis winked.

He rummaged inside the canvas swag he'd been carrying and pulled out a battered, cardboard bound book from its depths. 'Got something to write with?'

Biddy did, going inside the hut to recover the pencil stub from her little portmanteau. She came back and saw what the book was: bush poems by Mr Paterson. Lewis went to tear out a blank page from the back cover. 'Don't tell the Mechanics' Institute,' he smiled.

'Wait,' said Biddy, 'don't tear up that nice book. I'll find something else to write on.'

She dashed back into the hut and looked around the dusty mess for a piece of paper she could give him, one that had somehow escaped being fed to her billy fire already. She spotted a brown and sorry piece of foolscap, balled up in a corner of the room. She picked it up and smoothed it out, seeing that one side had been written on but that the other was blank. She returned to him with it.

Lewis proceeded to write the details of how to get to the place that was so desperate for a cook, and included the name of the person Biddy was to ask for when she got there. He stopped.

'You can read, can't you?' Biddy nodded that she could read, and Lewis continued pencilling it out.

She found herself so dazzled by the sight of him in the early dawn glow that it seemed like an eternity before she took her eyes from all his appealing aspects and directed them onto what he was writing. When she did she felt her heart sink.

'There you go,' Lewis said, proudly, handing her the scrap.

The hope had gone from Biddy totally, but she wouldn't let him know of it. 'You're a true friend,' she told him, 'you truly are.'

It almost broke her spirit to see him blush.

'I best be off.'

Biddy smiled, nodded and looked down at the devastating details on the paper again, before glancing up suddenly to find his lips upon hers; soft, warm and unexpectedly gentle in the crisp morning air. He broke the kiss and they looked into each other's eyes for a moment, each one finding absolute surprise in there, except that there was no surprise at all and Biddy's imagination had run away with her. There'd been no kiss, just a rush of desire on Biddy's part that a kiss might happen. She blushed that her hope might have been transparent.

'Be seeing you then,' Lewis said, slightly puzzled by all the odd expressions that seemed to grip Biddy's face.

Biddy pressed her fingers to her lips, as if the ghost of Lewis was still engaged there. It was the first time a boy had ever taken such a liberty with her, imagined or not, and now that it was over it didn't seem to Biddy to be half as scandalous as it ought to have been.

'Be seeing you then,' she whispered.

Lewis turned to take the bullock from its tether and lead the beast home.

Once he had disappeared from view Biddy glanced bitterly at the words he had written.

Summersby House. Ask for Mrs Marshall, the housekeeper.

She threw the paper into the billy fire embers, where it landed with its other side exposed, and for the briefest moment Biddy actually read the faded words that had been penned there by an unknown hand at an unknown time in an awkward, ugly hand. There was far more written on the paper than at first she'd realised. Overcome suddenly by an urge to know, Biddy snatched the paper from the embers again just as it started to smoke.

Biddy stamped it into the dirt, to make sure it wasn't smouldering. Then she picked it out and, still standing up, began to read what was there.

Dear Margaret,

At Summersby there was a pair of us, twin sisters, and the father who did love us both, Henry Gregory. We twin girls were identical in all ways – in our clothes and our hair, in our likes and our tastes – identical in all things except this: you suffered a misfortune at birth, dropped so they said. The consequences were felt in your mind. You could remember the things that you'd done, but rarely when you wanted to remember them. Such is the reason for all that I am about to write down for you. It is all for your Remember Box.

As identical twins are wont to do when children, we took delight in confusing others as to who was who. We played this little game in an unusual way. Rather than each of us swapping identities, only one of us would make the change. I, the sister whose mind was whole, would tell the Summersby household that I was really you. You, the twin whose mind was so cruelly damaged, never swapped at all. And so, Summersby would find itself with two girls who were equal in bewilderment – but only I was acting the part. Most of the servants fell for this trickery, but one was never fooled. In the grounds there worked a vile-natured youth, who knew exactly which of us was which. I found his skill of seeing right through us both fascinating and frightening. Even though he knew, he never exposed us. It was because he was in love.

As we girls grew towards our maturity our father grew ill. His decline was a protracted one; it gave him time to make plans for what our future would be without him. Of his two girls it was you, the twin with a broken mind, that our father adored the most. It perhaps seems dreadful that a father might prefer one of us above the other, but he had no doubt in his heart that I, the twin that was whole, would thrive. I am a clever and sparkling young woman. I am also cunning and calculating. You, on the other hand, with your inability to control so much of yourself, will always be at the mercy of those, like me, who are unscrupulous.

And so, our father drew up a will. In this document he left the estate of Summersby and most of his fortune to me, the twin for whom he held no fear. But you were not to be abandoned. To ensure your welfare once he was gone, our father entrusted your care to a lunatic asylum in Hawthorn. You were not to leave that place. You were not to live at Summersby. These measures, our father hoped, would protect you.

Your sister who loves you,
Matilda

Biddy was gripped by what the letter said. There was no date, but it had clearly been written a long time ago, and yet the people and events so coolly described felt almost as if they were happening now. The words themselves were sinister, as if written to worm their way inside a reader's heart and convince them of something outrageous. The letter spoke of desperate times and fearful souls and scoundrels who knew no bounds.

Something about it was almost, but not quite, familiar to Biddy, like a fairytale half-heard once, but only once, and then as good as forgotten.

It was only as she went to sit down again that she realised Lewis had left the pup behind. The shock of suddenly seeing the little animal, fallen asleep again behind the log his master had been sitting on, made Biddy lose grip on the letter. A breeze had come up and before she could save it the paper was blown onto the fanned embers.

It burst into flames and was gone.

The little dog awoke to learn he had been abandoned and he came to Biddy and gently licked her hand.

The discovery of criminality in Summersby's midst surely dismayed everyone inside the great house, Biddy imagined. Not that she brought attention to herself for it; she wasn't that dim, although she was certainly ashamed that she had sunk to the level of thief. Reduced to pinching vegetables from the Summersby kitchen garden and eggs from the fowl house, Biddy was sure that such rare drama as food theft had resulted in fevered imaginations in everyone who was touched by the talons of her crime.

What Biddy imagined was known of her actions was this: the usual culprits were not responsible. Foxes ate eggs occasionally, but not when there were chickens on offer first, and as none of the hens were missing, only their eggs, stray dogs and feral cats had to be ruled out for the same reason as the foxes, along with blue tongue lizards for the lack of tell-tale shells – the greedy things always ate at the scene of the crime. Biddy was convinced that the Summersby household would have quickly worked out that whatever was stealing the eggs wasn't a 'what' at all but a 'whom'.

Biddy feared that a girl she'd seen who lived at Summersby – a girl who looked to be around Biddy's own age – had become transfixed by the shadow of Biddy's evil. The girl's teacher was Miss Garfield, Biddy had seen that too, when pupil and teacher one day took themselves to sit on a rug beneath the shade of an expansive robinia tree, where the girl's eyes stayed fixed on the distant kitchen garden, widening and blinking in rapt fascination while Biddy had tried to hide there, convinced she was caught in the act. Yet, no one had shouted and rushed to apprehend her.

Biddy nevertheless feared she had been glimpsed, and she worried what sort of picture she had made. Surely she looked nothing like an arch-fiend, she hoped, at least as the girl would be able to tell from a distance. Biddy knew that apart from her dreary clothes and a manner of desperation, she would seem little different to the girl who saw her. If she had been glimpsed at all – and Biddy couldn't be sure – she prayed that the girl saw only that they were of a similar age and much the same frame. Biddy's long, dark hair, now worn down, not up, looked near identical to the girl's own. There but for the grace of God.

Biddy finally feared that if the girl now knew of her thieving then she would surely be thinking of her constantly; Biddy would have done the same in the situation. And if the girl was clever she might well work out that Biddy had knowledge of activity in the great house and understood well what time of day she was more likely to succeed in her thievery unobserved. Yet still there was risk and this beggared the question, why not steal at night when no one would be awake to see her? If the girl took a punt she would possibly guess that Biddy disliked the dark. Summersby was isolated; there were no immediate neighbours. To walk to the great house, which Biddy did every two days, involved travelling some distance through bushland with all its unseen nocturnal dangers.

If the girl guessed Biddy had brains, then she might suspect that Biddy wouldn't come back to Summersby at the same time of day as the girl had glimpsed her, through fear of being spotted again. The girl would guess that Biddy would choose another time of day, one that came with lessened risk, yet also precluded having to wander the bush in the dark. It was high summer. The days were long. The sun was up by five in the morning and stayed there until eight at night. To thieve at dawn required walking in darkness to get there, but a theft at dusk, or rather, a theft committed in the space of time immediately *before* dusk, would, if judged correctly, allow Biddy to make her way back to where she came from in the dying light of sunset. Biddy feared the girl was clever enough to work out all of this. She would have done the same. But it didn't stop Biddy coming back to steal again anyway. She was starving.

Hidden at the gate to the kitchen garden, peeking around the wall, Biddy watched as the Summersby girl placed a little sewing basket full of food upon a stone seat that backed against a wall along which apricot and peach trees had been espaliered. Then she seemed to think better of it and placed it beneath the seat, before thinking better again and placing the basket on top once more. Apparently satisfied, the girl then occupied herself with the vexed question of where to wait. Biddy observed, amused, as the girl chose to crouch behind one of the tall, wire pyramids that supported tomato vines. The foliage was so bountiful it would obscure her nicely, she clearly thought.

Something always neglected in mind-imperilling novels where stealthy waiting was involved, Biddy thought, was the dullness of the task. The girl clearly hadn't made allowance for this, perhaps anticipating only breathless excitement while the seconds ticked by. But Biddy allowed the seconds to soon become minutes, and before too long an hour, even though she was dying to scoff whatever the basket held, and so was the pup. The girl waited, her eyes on the basket across the way, but Biddy wouldn't budge. The stone wall radiated heat from a day in the sun and now that the air was cooler and tinged with a breeze, the effect of crouching against the surface behind the tomato pyramid was not unpleasant. The girl fell into a doze.

Carefully splitting the bounty between herself and the little white dog, Biddy was so intent on availing herself of the tasty morsels, that the question, when it came from somewhere in the tomato pyramid behind her, took her off guard.

'Who are you and why have you been stealing from us?' a voice inquired.

Biddy spun round with a mouthful of sandwich to be greeted by – now that she could see her up close – a very welcome sight: the girl was indeed exceedingly pretty and much her own age, wearing quite the loveliest summer clothes Biddy had ever seen on an actual younger person's back and not in a newspaper advertisement. Biddy's eyes drank in the girl's soft linen blouse in coral pink, trimmed with Cluny lace, with an elegant skirt to match, of a slightly darker shade, falling not half an inch from the ground and allowing the toes of the girl's pink silken boots to be seen. Biddy stared, so impressed by this girl, living a life that she could only dream of living, in a Great House with gardens; a life like those wonderful lives lived in ladies' magazine articles and romantic novels and melodramas acted on the stage. 'I'm Biddy – Biddy MacBryde, miss,' she answered at last. 'And I'm sorry for stealing, but I'm just so hungry. And so is the poor little pup.'

The girl regarded her in a manner that was not unfriendly. 'I am Miss Sybil Gregory.'

With food in her belly, Biddy's cheeriness increased markedly, as did the little dog's because he went soundly to sleep at her feet, contented and snoring, while Biddy engaged with her captor. By rights, the well to do Miss Sybil Gregory should have called the Law on Biddy, but the thought of doing anything like that clearly didn't enter her mind, which was too filled up with questions.

'How long have you been coming here?' Sybil asked, wide-eyed, from where they sat together on the stone seat.

Biddy had been right all along that she'd been seen. The girl had been dwelling on her crimes obsessively. 'Near to a week and a half now,' she said, 'although I've lost count of the days a bit. Is it Wednesday?'

'Thursday,' said Sybil. 'And why are you always so neat – patting down the soil around the potatoes and everything?'

Biddy hadn't even realised she'd been doing that. 'Well, it's such a lovely garden, miss. I would hate someone to think I'd been disrespectful of the gardener's good work.'

Sybil gave her a look at this apparently odd concept, but accepted the answer. 'Do you like our food?'

'Very much,' said Biddy, nodding. 'The fruit I eat fresh from the tree, but the vegetables go into my soup.'

'You make soup? But where are you cooking it?'

'In the little hut I've been living in,' said Biddy. 'I can't call it my own; I'm only borrowing it for the time being.' A dreadful thought occurred to her. 'It's not your hut is it, miss?'

Sybil plainly had no idea. 'Where is it?'

Biddy told her, providing rough directions.

Sybil shrugged her shoulders; she'd never heard of the hut and seemed little concerned by it anyway. 'I suppose it's on Summersby land, but nothing's really mine yet.'

Biddy didn't understand what she meant by this and Sybil didn't bother enlightening her. 'I keep a billy fire going with a pot of soup on the go,' said Biddy. 'Anything I get goes into it, so there's always something to eat. But when you spotted me the other day I was scared to come back here again.'

Sybil nodded.

'But I just got too hungry,' said Biddy, ashamed. 'I had no more soup and nowhere else to go to make more.'

'You were so hungry it hurt you, didn't it?' Sybil marvelled.

'Oh, miss, I intend returning everything I stole one day, I truly do – I've made a list, look.' Biddy pulled a scrap of writing paper from her skirt pocket and unfolded it. On it she had written in pencil a detailed list of items purloined.

Sybil was plainly amazed at the sheer volume of food recorded. Biddy had been far lighter-fingered than she knew.

'They won't be the same fruit and vegetables I give back, obviously,' Biddy went on, 'but they'll be ones just like them. The eggs, too – I only stole those for the pup, of course. I'll give back everything when I'm on my feet again, you'll see.'

'That sounds perfectly decent and honourable,' said Sybil, folding up the list again and handing it back to Biddy. 'Am I right that you dislike the dark?'

'I'm not mad about it,' said Biddy, before a look of respect crossed her face that Sybil had guessed this, too.

'And you've studied the household's movements?' Sybil wondered. 'You know when servants are likely to be in the garden and when they're not?'

'I know what chores have to be done and when in any household, if that's what you mean, miss,' said Biddy, respecting her still more.

Sybil grinned, clearly delighted. 'Let me see if I can guess some other things about you!'

'Is this some sort of game?'

'I suppose it is,' said Sybil, 'now don't give me any hints . . .' She stared at Biddy intently, moving from her face and hair, both a little grubby to Biddy's regret, to her faded shirtwaist and skirt that had known better times. Biddy felt self-conscious under the scrutiny.

'You're not very old,' said Sybil, at last.

'All that staring at me just to come out with that?' said Biddy.

'No older than me, or if you are, not by very much.'

'I'm sixteen.'

Sybil held up a silencing hand. 'No hints, I said.' She studied her again. 'I'd say you were roughly sixteen years.'

Biddy laughed.

Sybil held up her hand again. 'Your clothes are poorly laundered.'

'I thank the heavens they're laundered at all. I only manage it because the hut's got an old box bath and there's a creek not far off. No soap flakes though,' Biddy added, embarrassed by the stains.

'You take pride in cleanliness, I can see that clearly now.'

'Well, of course I do! What do you think I am, miss, a sewer rat?'

'You like to clean things?'

'Well, I don't know if cleaning's a chore anyone likes, but we all have to do it, don't we? Otherwise we're no better than savages.'

Sybil went back to studying her. 'You live in the hut all by yourself.'

'Is that a question?'

'A statement. You only take enough to feed one person and a puppy, and then not very well. My suspicion is you have no family to care for – at least, none in the vicinity. No doubt your parents are dead.'

Biddy's eyebrows shot up.

Sybil assessed this reaction, coolly. 'Or if not dead, absent. Or perhaps you have abandoned them? That's presuming you know who they are, of course.'

Biddy's expression may have suggested she was starting to dislike this game, because Sybil withdrew a little. 'We shall speak no more of it then,' she said. 'Family is a painful thing for each of us, I think.'

Biddy didn't disagree and Sybil went on staring for another moment. 'You're definitely not a local girl,' she continued. 'If you were, your circumstances would be known. Someone would be looking out for you; local women would bring you food and dissuade you from stealing. That's what happens, I believe. No, it's quite clear that no one knows of you here at all. You're completely alone and fallen upon difficult and degrading times.'

A sob suddenly welled in Biddy's throat. The girl had assessed her completely.

'I'm sorry, I didn't mean to upset you.'

'At least I have a friend . . .' Biddy said, but emotion strangled the rest of the words. She tried to hide her feelings, bending down to stroke the little dog, which awoke at her touch, looking up at her with loving eyes. 'The pup's my friend,' said Biddy at last. 'So, I'm not alone. He's good company.'

She looked up and was startled to see tears of sympathy in Sybil's eyes.

Sybil blinked them away and there was a moment's silence as they looked at each other anew.

'My turn,' said Biddy. 'Let me guess some things about you.'

Sybil laughed. 'You know Sherlock Holmes as well?'

Biddy didn't. 'I know my own eyes,' she said, enigmatically. 'I reckon I've got the seer's gift.'

'The proof will be in the pudding,' said Sybil, sceptical.

Biddy placed her fingers to her temples, letting her eyelids flutter like a sideshow spiritualist. 'You don't get out much,' she pronounced.

'Nonsense, I come out into the garden all the time.'

'Outside the garden gate, I mean. If this property was mine, miss, I'd know every last inch of it, garden and beyond, and you'd never even heard of the hut before I told you of it, so that says to me you're as good as a shut in.'

Sybil's jaw dropped.

'You also like the fashions,' Biddy went on, indicating Sybil's dress, 'but not the fashions exactly as they are in the shops. You do fashion differently – uniquely.'

Sybil's affront grew. 'I most certainly do not!'

Biddy just shrugged.

'You mean you've never seen styles like these on another girl?' Sybil demanded to know.

'Well, certainly not in those shades of pink, or not in Alston & Brown this season, anyway, but then that's something you should be proud of really, given the rotten standard of their staff.'

Sybil just blinked at her.

'But what you're wearing looks *lovely*, miss, and very expensive,' Biddy said. 'You should let yourself be sketched for the ladies' journals so that other girls might copy you.'

Sybil's face reflected further astonishment.

'This is all more proof that you don't get out much, by the way,' Biddy added.

'For a girl with no knowledge of Mr Holmes, your powers of deduction are quite remarkable,' said Sybil with dignity.

'And you don't have any friends, either,' said Biddy.

It was like the pronouncement had slapped Sybil in the face, so taken by surprise was she by it. Then she seemed to realise too late that Biddy had caught a glimpse of what was clearly her deepest shame. It was her turn to catch at a sob in her throat. 'I have someone . . .' Sybil started to say.

Biddy scooped the little pup from the ground and popped him into Sybil's lap before the dog even knew that his snoozing spot had changed. He cocked an eye open, used it to look around himself, and then close it again, unconcerned.

'So you do,' said Biddy, 'the same friend as me.'

Sybil blinked at the little dog, before bursting into laughter.

Biddy looked up at the red glow colouring the western sky. 'Why don't you mind him for a while?' she suggested, standing up and brushing crumbs from her soiled skirt.

'Mind him?'

'He's your friend, isn't he? He's really no trouble. I think he'd be pleased to eat something other than eggs for his dinner.'

'But where are you going?' asked Sybil.

'You were right when you said I don't like the dark, I don't like it at all, and if I don't get going now I'll find myself down the bottom of a forgotten mine shaft and all because it was too black to see my way around it. Thank you for the lovely food. It was very kind of you.'

Sybil looked acutely disappointed that this meant their conversation was over. 'Please take the little puppy with you, I can't possibly mind him.'

'Of course you can,' said Biddy, 'I'll come and get him again tomorrow. How would that be?'

Sybil beamed. 'Would you? Well, that would be very nice. I shall have another basket of tea things ready.'

'See you then,' said Biddy, and she turned to go, hoping she'd made not even the slightest impression that she planned never returning again.

'Wait!'

Biddy stopped and made to turn a last time.

'You do have another friend, you know.'

'Do I?'

'Me,' said Sybil, smiling, 'I'm your friend, as of right now.'

Biddy was very touched by this declaration. 'You're my friend, too, miss,' she said, after a little moment. 'And already I'm so glad of it.'

Then Biddy turned and was gone for good, she intended.

*

Biddy found herself awake again, hours before the dawn would come, and this time without a Condamine bell to blame for it. She had already reached her conclusion as to what her next plan would be while on the long walk back from Summersby, but had told herself she would sleep on it. Yet she had little slept, the pros and cons playing in her mind. She couldn't return to Summersby. Sybil had been both amusing and perplexing to converse with, but Biddy doubted whether anyone else she might encounter there would prove so diverting, particularly the housekeeper and the governess. Both women already knew Biddy as a fraud, and no amount of scrubbing would remove that stain from her character.

She would return to Melbourne by whatever means she could, and when she got there she would place trust enough in her powers of imagination and cheerfulness to conceive of a wholly new story, her best one yet; a story that would see her good for the rest of her God-given days.

Biddy packed her portmanteau, taking care to include only her own possessions and nothing more. The things from the hut were not hers to remove, Biddy resolved; perhaps some other down-on-their-luck soul would wander by and be glad of what he found there. As the first cracks of light began to show themselves in the eastern sky, Biddy tidied the hut's one room, sweeping the floor, washing the tin plate and spoon, shaking the dusty old blanket and folding it carefully at the end of the stretcher bed.

When dawn had broken fully Biddy felt confident that her way to the road, and from there into Castlemaine, would be as brightly lit as the summer sun would allow it. She emerged from the hut, pulling the battered tin door behind her, when she remembered the pup. Lewis might one day return for it and find no sign of where his pet might be. Biddy opened her portmanteau again and pulled out her final scrap of writing paper and the stub of her blunted pencil. With difficulty, given so little of the pencil lead was left to write with, Biddy composed a message.

Mr Lewis Fitzwater. Your sweet little pup is safe and sound. Inquire of him with Miss Sybil Gregory at Summersby House. She has been taking fine care of him.

Biddy folded the note in half and prepared to place it under a stone on the doorstep, before remembering how she had imagined Lewis's soft lips upon hers and that it had been a heart-stirring thing. She unfolded the note and added an afterword.

I was very grateful for your kindly given advice about the cook's position. I spent some happy weeks engaged there and would remain there still, had not my treasured friend, the Reverend Flowers, taken gravely ill, compelling my return to Melbourne.

It was a story, and a necessary one.

Biddy pondered on what else she might write, and then added:

I think about your kindness very often. It was very nice. With such high regard, Biddy MacBryde.

Biddy placed the note beneath a stone on the old hut's doorstep in the crisp morning air. Her hand stretched out unthinkingly to pat the woolly head of the pup, just as he came snuffling around her knees. Then Biddy realised with a start that the little dog shouldn't have been anywhere near her at all, and Sybil couldn't help but laugh from where she had been watching through the trees.

'Pup!' Biddy exclaimed, standing up. 'But what are you doing here?'

'Being an excellent tracker hound!' cried Sybil in triumph, emerging from the foliage that hid the path that ran beyond. 'He knew the way here exactly, Biddy.'

Biddy went a little pale at having been tracked down and spied upon. 'Miss Gregory . . .'

'You must call me Sybil. Aren't I your friend now?'

'Well, yes, but . . .'

The little pup was pleased to have led Sybil all the way back to the place that he thought of as home, and he jumped at Biddy's legs until she picked him up and nuzzled his face and ears.

'He had lamb's fry for last night's supper,' said Sybil, happily. 'Mrs Marshall was none the wiser. You should have seen how fast he ate it all, and then he looked up at me with those lovely big eyes for some more. Well, of course I gave him some. How could I not? But after that he was very restless. I smuggled him into my bedroom – no easy feat under Miss Garfield's nose, I can tell you, yet she's none the wiser as well – but I couldn't get him to settle. He didn't like my bed at all, and kept running to the door and sniffing at it.'

'Didn't he do his business?'

'I'm afraid that he did,' said Sybil. 'Perhaps I should have seen to that before I took him up to my room, but I didn't want anyone to catch us.'

Biddy almost wanted to laugh. 'Did you clean it up?'

Sybil was shamefaced. 'I didn't really know how to . . . I just threw an old bathing towel on top of it and opened a window.' She was plainly transported with happiness.

Biddy cast an awkward glance at the note under the stone. 'Miss . . . Sybil . . .' she tried to say, 'I really can't . . . well . . .'

'Is that your little bag packed?' asked Sybil of the portmanteau by Biddy's side.

'Yes . . . yes it is,' said Biddy, 'and I must tell you why.'

'No need,' said Sybil, 'You've put it all in the note for me, haven't you?'

'Note?'

Sybil stooped and snatched the piece of paper.

'Wait, miss!'

But Sybil had it open and had practically finished reading it before she realised it wasn't meant for her. She looked back to Biddy with some puzzlement.

Biddy squirmed. 'It's intended for a friend – another friend.'

Sybil placed the note beneath the stone again.

'What I wrote about working as a cook, well, it's a little story, you see, but not a malicious one. I swear it. I only wrote that for good reasons.'

'Of course you did,' said Sybil, beaming. She clapped her hands excitedly. 'Oh, Biddy, you've had the very same thought as I have! Were you awake all night as well? I hardly slept at all, not that Pup much let me anyway. As soon as it was first light I came to my resolve. Yet now it seems I don't even have to ask you it.'

Biddy squinted with confusion. 'Ask me what?'

'Well, we're friends, aren't we? And this is what friendship must mean. We can read each other's minds.'

'Sybil,' Biddy began again, looking more determined now. 'I must tell you I am leaving here.'

'Well, of course you are, Biddy,' said Sybil. 'How else can I bring you back to Summersby?'

'Bring me back?' Biddy filled with dread. 'That's fair enough. What I did was wrong. If it's the policemen you mean me for, then I'll face them, I really will.'

Sybil gave her an incredulous stare. 'Biddy,' she said carefully, 'I mean to bring you back to Summersby so that you might commence your employment.'

Biddy stared back. 'You mean the Chinaman cook's job is mine after all?'

'The cook's position?' said Sybil in bewilderment. 'Good heavens no, are you mad? The position I've secured for you is as my companion.'

'Your what?'

'Dear Biddy,' said Sybil, affectionately, now stooping to pick up the portmanteau. 'You are to join the Summersby household in employment as my first official Sister.'

The astounded look upon Miss Garfield's face as she hurried down the stairs to where Biddy stood with Sybil in the Summersby entrance hall told Biddy that Sybil's definition of 'secured employment' probably differed from the dictionary's view. It was the first the governess had ever heard of Biddy's apparent position.

'This is impossible!' Miss Garfield responded, clinging to the balustrade.

'There's nothing impossible about it at all,' said Sybil, crossing her arms. 'I desired a sister and now I have found one.'

'But you don't understand, Sybil. This is *Biddy*.'

'Miss Biddy MacBryde, yes, a girl in need of companionship just as much as I am, Miss Garfield. You ought to be delighted that two such pressing needs have intersected.'

'But this is an untruthful, untrustworthy girl!'

'How can you condemn a person so cruelly upon appearances?' Sybil protested.

'*Appearances?*'

'Biddy's clothes are only ill-laundered for a lack of soap flakes, not intention,' said Sybil. 'She has scrubbed as best she could with nothing but her effort to attack the stains – and she has done so because she has standards to uphold; standards we applaud at Summersby.'

Miss Garfield's wits looked in danger of leaving her, forcing her to sink into a hall chair. Biddy stepped in, holding Pup in her arms. 'I understand why you might be feeling uneasy,' she began.

'I suppose for that alone you expect me to give gratitude?' said the governess, fanning her flushed cheeks with her hands.

'Never gratitude, only a chance,' said Biddy. 'A chance to make amends for my mistakes.'

This clearly struck Sybil as an unusual thing to say.

'You'll have as much success scrubbing away those stains as you had with scrubbing your wardrobe,' Miss Garfield snapped at her.

'You might at least show some gratitude for your own wardrobe then!' Biddy snapped back before she could stop herself.

Miss Garfield went white. 'Please lower your voice, I will not have Mrs Marshall dragged from her duties,' she said. Turning back to Sybil, she added, 'And do you imagine the Secret Heiress would dare to act in such a way?'

'Oh, the Secret Heiress!' cried Sybil, rising in volume to match Biddy's annoyance. 'I'm no longer eight years old, Miss Garfield. The Secret Heiress, the Tooth Fairy and Father Christmas no longer rule my behaviour. They are all figments of fiction once fed to a child.'

Miss Garfield fanned her face with vigour. 'You are quite determined to shock me.'

'What Secret Heiress?' Biddy asked, now looking confused.

Sybil didn't answer that, threatening tears. 'Can't you just see that I want a *friend?*' she demanded of Miss Garfield.

Biddy observed the governess attempt a careful extrication. 'But you always have me.'

'I do not in any way wish to hurt your feelings, Miss Garfield,' said Sybil, 'you who are so good and kind and loyal to me, you to whom I owe so very much, but you are not my friend. You are my governess.'

'Your relatives expressly forbid it,' said Miss Garfield. 'You know that full well, Sybil. You have always known it. So how can you imagine that things might suddenly be different?'

'We're not going to tell my relatives,' Sybil declared.

The governess was aghast. '*Sybil . . .* For this whim you would risk *everything?*'

Sybil wavered, before making a show of covering it. 'For the sake of a friend – a sister – I would.'

Biddy realised that there was much going on here to which she was not a part and could not understand. She cast a glance at Sybil and saw the determination behind her look to Miss Garfield, and saw her fear, too, her desperate uncertainty at all this.

'I will go,' said Biddy, abruptly. 'I'm sorry, Miss Garfield. You must think this some wicked plot of my making but it isn't, I swear. Miss Sybil found me and befriended me because she has a kind heart. I did not seek her out and did not give thought to all this.'

Sybil was thrown. 'Go where?'

'Go away. Go back to Melbourne. It's what I planned to do before you stopped me.'

Miss Garfield was silent.

'Biddy, you cannot!' insisted Sybil.

'Yes, I can,' said Biddy. 'You know nothing about me, so let me tell you I am not a good friend or sister or whatever you want to call me. Whatever story you think might see me safe in here will come at a cost, I can see it in your face. I can see it in your governess's face. I'd be an even worse friend if I let myself be the cause of that cost, so I won't allow it. I'm off.'

Relief washed over Miss Garfield.

'You agree, don't you, Miss Garfield?' Biddy asked her.

'Perhaps you could be a fine friend to Sybil *in time*,' Miss Garfield said, carefully, 'but you cannot remain, for reasons that are far too complex for me to begin explaining to you.'

Sybil was having none of it. 'Biddy, please,' she implored, 'I want you to stay – I need you to stay. You say I know nothing about you – well, you know nothing about me. But that will all change and very quickly, as soon as we start living like good sisters should. If you *are* my friend then you'll believe me. Nothing will be lost by having you here. I will not suffer because of it. My relatives don't even live at Summersby!'

'That's *enough*, Sybil,' Miss Garfield warned.

'You act as if they're hovering over me like some guardian angels, but they're my guardian devils!' Sybil cried, bitterly.

Biddy felt dreadful, not knowing what was going on or why it was so upsetting to Sybil and her governess. She placed an arm around Sybil's waist and put Pup between them. The little dog licked at Sybil's face. 'I don't know what all this is about, but it sounds very strange.'

Sybil fixed a hard look at her governess and Miss Garfield in turn looked beseechingly at Biddy.

'Miss Garfield doesn't want me here and I can see she's not intending to be cruel by saying it,' said Biddy, seeing the truth of this in the governess's eyes. 'It's because she too is a friend, despite what you think, and she only wants what's best for you. You must listen to her and let me leave.'

Sybil could only cry in response.

'Here,' said Biddy, placing the little dog fully in Sybil's arms, 'take little Pup. He's a friend you can keep. No one can possibly object to him, can they, Miss Garfield?' Biddy looked up at the governess again.

Miss Garfield was unhopeful. 'Summersby has very little history of pets.'

'They're not allowed either!' cried Sybil. 'You'll have to take him with you, too.'

Biddy's heart visibly sank. 'But I really don't think I can, you see—'

'My relatives disallow everything that might bring me joy!'

'What is all this high emotion?' a voice called beyond the great stairs.

Miss Garfield looked faint again and placed a hand at her throat. 'Now see what you've done.'

The harried housekeeper emerged from the door that led to the kitchen, wiping floury hands on her apron.

Miss Garfield stood up from her chair, her face full of dread. 'Mrs Marshall, you must believe me, I know nothing of how this untruthful girl keeps turning up like this.'

'Joey!' cried the housekeeper, stopping dead in her tracks.

The little pup whined and wiggled and then leapt from Sybil's arms, whereupon he shot across the floor to Mrs Marshall, who scooped him up and kissed him in joy. 'Oh you little mite,' cried Mrs Marshall, 'I thought you were gone from me, I thought I'd lost you for good . . .'

Miss Garfield gaped in amazement. 'Is that your dog?'

The housekeeper flushed with guilt. 'He's just a little thing. I had him sent to us,' she started to say, 'I know it's unorthodox, yet I couldn't see the harm. And then I lost him.' Her words trailed off as she realised who it was that stood between Miss Garfield and Sybil. 'You!'

Biddy squirmed.

'What are *you* doing here?'

Sybil had no idea how Biddy and the housekeeper might have ever been previously acquainted but she clearly knew a God-sent opportunity when she saw one. 'This is Miss MacBryde,' she said, her tears vanishing as she stepped forward and beamed at the housekeeper, 'and you should feel very grateful for her, Mrs Marshall. It was Biddy who found your dog!'

'You must despise me,' Mrs Marshall moaned into her floury hands. Joey, formerly known as Pup, whined and she reached for him and clutched him to her bosom. 'I am a hypocrite, I know, but I've always loved dogs and an opportunity came.'

'Mrs Marshall, you have always told us that dogs are forbidden here,' Miss Garfield replied, stiffly. 'What is Sybil to think with one rule for us and another rule for you?'

Biddy and Sybil stood awkwardly together watching on from the green baize door while the two older women sat in discussion at the kitchen table.

Never having married, despite the 'Mrs' in her title like all housekeepers, Mrs Marshall had been denied the opportunity to mother a child, Biddy suspected. She guessed then that the little pup had been given to her by someone she loved and Biddy wondered whom this might have been.

'I had a dog once before, you see' said Mrs Marshall, blowing her nose, 'many years ago – a dog I was forced to give up when I came here. I have never forgotten that little dog, never forgiven myself for doing it.' She hugged Joey again. 'I thought I was making amends somehow. He looks so very like my poor Yip . . .'

Miss Garfield was listening with impassion. 'Who gave you this dog?'

Mrs Marshall evaded answering. 'I was trying to hide him,' she said, 'he'd already escaped once. When he ran off the first time I only knew it when he was returned to the door by Lewis Fitzwater, who'd been out searching for lost bullocks and didn't know any better. Luck made him think to take Joey back here. But the little mite only escaped again, didn't you, Joey?' She kissed the little dog's head. 'And don't you need a good bath?'

The joining of dots revealed a picture that touched Biddy's heart. Clearly, when Joey had somehow escaped the second time he had again been found by Lewis, who'd intended to return the little dog to its mistress once more when he'd stumbled upon Biddy wielding the axe handle. Lewis had given Biddy the news of the cook's position and had also given her the little dog, so that Joey might win Biddy a favour. Although the path she had taken had proved somewhat winding, the destination had turned out to be the same, thanks to Lewis's kindness. Biddy had officially 'found' Joey and for this Mrs Marshall would surely have to tolerate her presence.

Miss Garfield seemed to be weighing up an ethical dilemma in her mind, before arriving at a decision. 'I will say nothing of the dog to our employers in my next correspondence,' she told the housekeeper. 'And I am sure you will continue to say nothing in yours.'

Mrs Marshall looked shamefaced but made no protest.

'Who doesn't have need of a friend?' Miss Garfield went on. Biddy realised with surprise that a point had been made and that Miss Garfield had an expectation in return. She glanced at Sybil whose look confirmed it.

'The girl Biddy is an outright liar,' Mrs Marshall countered.

Biddy slumped.

'The girl is likely a fantasist,' said Miss Garfield, glancing in Biddy's direction, 'and burdened with unrestrained imagination, certainly, but my heart tells me she is not dishonest.'

Biddy was dying to respond but knew it would be wise to keep quiet for the moment.

'She came here claiming to be a widow! We know nothing of her true situation.'

'No doubt it doesn't bear repeating,' the governess agreed. 'Sybil hasn't asked and the girl hasn't told her. Although I am sure we shall learn more in time.'

Sybil squeezed Biddy's hand for reassurance.

'When she's run out of lies to tell us?' Mrs Marshall suggested.

'Quite possibly,' was all Miss Garfield offered.

Mrs Marshall seemed at a loss. 'How will we ever live with the knowledge of doing this?'

'By thinking only of Sybil,' said Miss Garfield. 'Just as we only ever do. She has chosen Biddy. No doubt she could have chosen more wisely, but it is done.'

'But the risk that this brings?'

'A risk we can manage,' said the governess. 'Consider it, Mrs Marshall. If this experience is denied Sybil then she will only seek another experience in its place. It is to be expected in a young person.'

Finding the whole conversation excruciating, Biddy watched the housekeeper digest this.

'Threats of the Secret Heiress no longer hold weight,' Miss Garfield added, quieter. 'More's the pity of it, but there it is. It was always to be expected, I suppose, as she began to mature.'

Sybil frowned. They talked of her almost as if she wasn't even there.

'If Sybil is ever to succeed in the role that is rightfully hers,' Miss Garfield said, 'then it will be achieved by her choices; choices that neither you nor I can make. We can educate and nurture her, yes, but we cannot act in Sybil's stead when the time comes. Therefore, let her discover the consequences of *this* choice, the first real choice she has ever made, in such a way that we can cushion her from the fall, safe still in Summersby. After all, it is from mistakes that we learn to perfect ourselves, isn't that true, Mrs Marshall?'

Mrs Marshall looked at the governess a long time before she assented.

'Biddy will be your companion now,' Miss Garfield told Sybil a few minutes later as the two girls took their seats in the splendid Summersby drawing room. 'Do you comprehend what I am saying to you?'

Sybil's determination and optimism threatened to waver.

'Do you?' repeated the governess.

'I believe I do,' said Sybil, at last. But as Biddy looked at her it seemed that Sybil's pleasure at having won what she had strived for was somehow missing.

'Are you fearful of it?' Miss Garfield asked.

Sybil seemed about to nod, but stopped herself. 'No. I am not.'

'It is natural to feel fear at momentous occasions,' said Miss Garfield. 'And this is a momentous occasion for us all.'

Sybil stuck her chin out, resolute. 'Biddy is now my sister and I am glad of it.'

'Very well,' said Miss Garfield. She cast a look at Biddy, who had found this, along with every other exchange she had so far witnessed here, mystifying. Biddy saw little to illuminate her further in the governess's well-composed face.

'What does a companion actually *do* then?' Biddy asked Sybil, once Miss Garfield had left them alone in the drawing room to make arrangements.

Sybil was vague. 'Friendly things,' she said.

'Like what?'

Biddy had read novels where there had been graceful and charming companions in residence and the notion had seemed lovely then, but now that she thought about it, she could recall little of their actual tasks.

'Keeping me company,' Sybil suggested.

'All day long?'

'Oh no, I shouldn't think so, Miss Garfield wouldn't approve of anything distracting me from my lessons; no, only in my non-lesson hours, Biddy. You should keep me company before and during breakfast, I feel, also during luncheon, and then again at tea time and on until supper – unless I ask you not to, of course, which I will definitely do from time to time.' She looked away from Biddy as she said this.

Biddy realised that this left her with much of the day unaccounted for. 'Won't I be accused of skiving?' she asked.

Sybil had no idea what this was.

'What should I do when keeping you company, then?' Biddy asked.

'Do what you did when we met in the kitchen garden,' Sybil suggested. 'We had such a lovely time then, didn't we, Biddy?'

'Yes.'

'So, we'll do more of that.'

'You mean . . . make conversation?'

'Of course,' said Sybil, clapping her hands, 'I really like that very much!'

'You mean that's *all* I do, then?' said Biddy. She looked pitifully at sea.

'Well, yes, and amuse me,' Sybil went on, 'create little entertainments. Games and tricks; dancing and singing; reading aloud from books. You're so good at all that, Biddy, I just know.'

Biddy nodded and smiled with what she hoped was confidence that Sybil could not have found a more suitable companion had she searched the length and breadth of the continent. But inside she felt lost with the speed in which her situation had changed. She'd had no time to make plans for it; she hadn't thought the role through. The reversal of fortune had been thrust at her so abruptly that Biddy couldn't see where there was any map for it.

'Come, Biddy,' Sybil said, standing up and wrinkling her nose. 'Let me find you a bedroom to call your own. And perhaps a little bathroom, too.'

Upon being shown to the third floor servants' bathroom allotted to her, Biddy gave every appearance of being familiar with such an amenity, until the door was closed upon her and she was left alone. Biddy had never been inside a room dedicated solely to bodily cleansing in her life. The Manse had held no such room, washing being achieved via big porcelain bowls in the bedrooms for servant and master alike. Before she had lived with the Reverend, the sanitation Biddy had experienced at home in Carlton had been even more rudimentary. But Biddy wasn't one of those types who claimed that bathing more than once a week leached the body's natural oils. She liked to feel clean, and knew the difference to what it felt like being dirty. Biddy tried the taps above the bath and found the temperature and flow to be adjustable.

Soaking in the bath – a delicious experience – Biddy had time to think over several interesting notions that had occurred to her in the course of the day so far. This was something her mother Ida often did when faced with things that intrigued her and Biddy found herself following her example.

One. This house had a curious attitude towards truth: it was something to be hidden away – a folly Biddy recognised. The truth was turned into secrets at Summersby and experience had given Biddy a low tolerance for those.

Two. Mrs Marshall had been given a pup, Joey, but when asked who the giver was had pretended the question hadn't been asked. Why would something like that matter?

Three. A bogey haunted the household, called the Secret Heiress. This was a red rag to Biddy's bull. What was she to imagine this personage was? A ghost?

Four. Sybil seemed remarkably unconcerned by Biddy's plainly chequered past. Enough had emerged from Miss Garfield and Mrs Marshall's discussion to put off any prospective new friend, but not Sybil, who had not followed up with a single question about where Biddy had come from or why. She had not even asked about Alston & Brown. Clearly, her need for a companion outweighed all other concerns. The well-to-do girl must be very lonely, or failing that, she had some other reason for wanting Biddy near.

Once she was washed, Biddy was reluctant to put her Sunday best back on again, but it was either she wear those garments or put on her kitchen maid's uniform, which Biddy guessed would not befit a companion, so she stepped into her skirt and buttoned up her shirtwaist once more.

Sybil had asked her to wait in the hall outside once she was done and so Biddy did. There was no chair, so she stood, her portmanteau at her side. The great house was extremely quiet. From somewhere outside she could hear mocking laughs of kookaburras, but within the walls all was noiseless save the deep tick of a pendulum clock in the entrance hall two floors below. Biddy waited, the ticking clock growing louder in her ears as the clock chimed a half past and then, after an interval that felt far longer than thirty minutes, an o'clock. Biddy's nerves began to fray. 'Why do they have to know the blessed time anyway?' she exclaimed aloud. 'Can't they just look at the sun like any other normal person?'

Biddy turned with a start to find the housekeeper there with her keys.

'We have a clock because of the importance we place upon punctuality, girl,' said Mrs Marshall.

Biddy thought this was ripe given she'd been left waiting there for so long, but said nothing.

'Come this way, won't you,' Mrs Marshall said, and led Biddy down the hall. Walking ahead, the housekeeper kept her hand inside a skirt pocket.

'So then,' said Biddy, after a moment or two's progress. 'What happens now?'

'You are to fulfil the position of paid companion six days out of seven,' Mrs Marshall instructed, without turning around, 'although, if you show signs of diligence and application, you may be accorded the right to take Saturday afternoons off.'

Biddy thought she might have water in her ears. 'Did you say *paid* companion?'

'Well, of course it's paid. Do you think we practise slavery?'

Biddy flushed with pleasure. 'How much then?'

Mrs Marshall's look suggested that such a question was an insult to Summersby and those within it. 'Thirty pounds per annum, the standard rate.'

That really wasn't very much, Biddy thought, although she tried to hide the disappointment. The Reverend had paid her twenty-five to work in the kitchen. 'I'll take it.'

'You'd be a fool if you didn't,' said Mrs Marshall. 'You'll receive your meals and board in addition.'

The housekeeper stopped and jangled the keys she carried on a big brass ring. Biddy marvelled to herself at how many there were. How could anyone remember what opened what, she wondered? Only one key seemed marked to stand out in any way – a piece of string had been looped through its hole. Mrs Marshall selected a different key and slid it into the lock of a narrow door. It opened effortlessly. Inside was a plainly furnished room containing a little iron bed with a quilted coverlet; an old and faded armchair; a small valet's wardrobe; a pine tallboy and a little table, upon which stood a washbasin. It was filled with light streaming through the lace curtains. It was the loveliest room Biddy had ever called her own.

'I hope this will suit you,' said Mrs Marshall, making it plain that it would be unfortunate for Biddy if it didn't.

Biddy didn't have to make up stories. 'It will suit me very nicely, Mrs Marshall, thank you.' She laid her hand on the bed quilt. It was thick and soft.

'Further to your meals and board, you will also receive your clothes,' Mrs Marshall told her. She gave a meaningful glance at Biddy's Sunday best. 'The paid companion's position comes with certain . . . expectations regarding attire. And you do not meet those expectations.'

In any other circumstances Biddy would have been offended, but she could sense more good news coming.

'Please open the wardrobe,' Mrs Marshall directed.

Biddy did so. Inside were half a dozen ensembles; skirts, jackets, blouses and even a gown, in a lovely array of colours and shades, and made from fine fabrics that Biddy had never known near her skin. There were two hatboxes on top of the wardrobe containing, Biddy hoped, some equally delightful hats, and there were several pairs of shoes and slippers arranged on the wardrobe floor.

'In the tallboy drawers you will find stockings and gloves, and various undergarments,' Mrs Marshall said.

Biddy was overwhelmed. 'I . . . don't know what to say.'

The housekeeper held up a hand. 'They are a *loan*, not a gift. They belong to Miss Sybil; fashions from seasons past. It is fortunate you are of such a similar frame. Where items do not fit you it is your responsibility to make them fit. You will also find needles and thread in the drawers.'

Biddy nodded and waited for anything more. The housekeeper remained where she was, staring at Sybil's no longer wanted clothes with what seemed to Biddy almost a faraway look in her eye.

'Do you have other instructions for me?' Biddy asked.

Mrs Marshall started a little, her hand balled tight in her skirt pocket. It almost seemed as if she'd forgotten where she was, and Biddy saw an unexpected depth of feeling in her face. 'We have not had a companion at Summersby before,' Mrs Marshall said, 'it is something new for us – and new for Miss Sybil.'

'I understand,' said Biddy.

'I don't know that you do,' said the housekeeper, sharp. 'You will find Sybil to be . . . unlike other girls you may have known before.'

'She is very well-to-do,' Biddy agreed.

'That she is but it's not what makes her uncommon. Her life is . . .' Mrs Marshall took her hand from her pocket. 'Her life is *protected*,' she said. 'It has been so since she was a born. She is on a path that has been laid out to ensure her utmost welfare.'

Biddy nodded as if she comprehended what that meant, even though she didn't remotely. 'By Miss Sybil's relatives?'

Mrs Marshall didn't reply.

'Who are these people? An aunt?'

'That is not your concern.'

Biddy blinked. 'I'm not to know them?'

'You are not.'

Biddy tried her best not to look even more puzzled by this. The day so far had been one of continued confusion in Biddy's view, but she would not be caught complaining about it.

'Miss Sybil's relatives are her only family,' said Mrs Marshall. 'If you are to succeed as companion . . .' she said.

Biddy guessed there was something she needed to speak of, but was unable. 'You can trust me, Mrs Marshall; I want only to do well here.'

The housekeeper looked searchingly at her. 'If you hope to win that trust then you will do so by ensuring that Miss Sybil sticks to the path. You will not, in truth, be a companion at all, but a colleague to Miss Garfield and me in our own work. You will strive, Biddy, just as we do, towards one goal: Miss Sybil's success. Do you see?'

'I see completely,' said Biddy, even though she didn't. 'Everything you say makes perfect sense, don't you worry.'

Mrs Marshall became emotional. *'Scandal . . .'* she implored. *'It is scandal I fear, do you see that?'*

Biddy nodded, a little unnerved, thinking of Mr Hackett with his lovely fair hair, barging into her mother's Carlton kitchen and telling Biddy that nothing she had ever believed to be true was actually true at all; a disgusting scandal. 'I would not bring any shame,' she said with as much conviction as she could pray for.

Mrs Marshall gave the first smile Biddy had yet seen from her. 'I know none of it makes sense at all,' she said, 'but it does not matter. You will come to understand in time.'

'I know I will,' said Biddy, hoping this was what was needed from her. 'You can rely on me, Mrs Marshall. Just let me prove myself.'

Left alone, Biddy felt filled with happiness. She stood in the exact middle of the little room and turned around on the spot, letting her eyes fall on every single thing that the tidy space contained, committing it all to her memory, letting it swell in her heart.

'It's just so perfect,' she whispered to herself. She sat upon the bed and found to her delight that it bounced. 'A real spring mattress!' She jumped up and down, her dusty portmanteau bobbing along with her. One bounce too many saw the bag topple from the edge. 'Oh, blow.'

She got onto her hands and knees to retrieve her bits and pieces. Each little thing she owned seemed soiled and cheap in contrast to the items in the room.

Biddy realised she'd lost her old pencil stub in the spill and decided she didn't care – pencils were unlikely to be scarce at Summersby – but sentimentality took hold and she thought of how Lewis Fitzwater had held the bit of pencil when he'd written on the paper scrap. Biddy peered under the bed and saw that the stub had rolled right into the corner. She tried to reach for it but her arm wouldn't go that far. Taking care not scuff the floor, Biddy pulled the bed away, creating a gap, so she could reach down from above. She seized the pencil only to see that something had been scratched into the skirting board – two or three little words. Craning to see from above, she couldn't quite read what they said. She gave up, the contents of the wardrobe more interesting. Then the urge to read the words returned, unaccountably strong. She felt compelled to know what they said, as if someone else, someone who had been in this room long before her, needed her to read what was scratched there. The feeling was strange, uncanny, yet it would not be ignored.

Biddy pulled the bed further away from the wall, giving her enough space to squeeze in between, crouched on her knees. There were many years of dust on the particular spot on the skirting, it being too inaccessible for half-hearted maids to reach with their brooms. Biddy scraped at it with her fingers until the words revealed themselves.

Ida. Go away.

Shocked, she felt a chill run straight up her back. The skin on her forearms prickled. She shoved the bed into place again as fast as she could, covering the words. The coincidence of seeing her mother's name was shocking. And yet it could only be coincidence, Biddy knew, some other Ida had once been here, among so many thousands and thousands of Idas in the world.

The room seemed less appealing.

'Don't be so stupid, it's still a lovely room; it's just a coincidence, that's all.' She took deep breaths to steady herself. 'It's a coincidence. Don't be so stupid, Biddy.'

Two days later, attired in some of Sybil's unwanted clothes, which fit very well, Biddy came downstairs at four o'clock, marking the end of Sybil's lessons and the start of Biddy's companion duties for the afternoon. Biddy went to the drawing room, prepared for the task, having found a book that she hoped might be deemed suitable for reading aloud.

Sybil was already waiting and sprang from a chair, embracing her. 'Happy birthday!'

Biddy was taken aback. 'It's not my birthday, it was months ago.'

'Happy belated birthday, I meant to say,' said Sybil, no less excited.

'Well, that's nice,' said Biddy, mystified. 'Thank you.'

'Didn't you tell me that your sixteenth birthday was a very under-celebrated affair?' Sybil asked.

Biddy winced at the memory of herself, Queenie, and stern Mrs Rattray consuming a day-old sponge cake in five minutes of deathly silence before Mrs Rattray had pronounced the 'birthday party' over and made Biddy wash up the plates. 'It could have been worse,' she fibbed.

'I doubt it,' said Sybil, 'which is why we're putting it to rights. Come in, Mrs Marshall!' she called out.

Having evidently been waiting in the hall, the housekeeper entered carrying an iced fruitcake on a tray, followed by Miss Garfield cradling a bowl of fruit punch.

'Oh,' said Biddy, genuinely surprised.

As parties went, Biddy had known livelier and better-attended gatherings, if not at the Reverend's household, then certainly at home, but the thought behind it was touching. Biddy vowed to herself to accept whatever was given in the unique circumstances of her employment, and not to hanker after more. But it was the unique circumstances that had begun to intrigue Biddy. Sybil's absent relatives, the presumed owners of Summersby, had 'rules', it was clear.

'How am I to know when I'm going against something your relatives have wished for?' Biddy asked Sybil when the little party had been cleared away again. She thought this a very sensible question.

'You mustn't worry about any of that,' said Sybil.

'But how will I know so that I won't do it?'

'Shall we play pinochle now?' Sybil suggested. 'I do enjoy that game.'

'I've never played it.'

'I shall teach you then!'

Biddy retrieved the cards and table as directed and began to examine the deck, glancing at the other girl. Sybil's smile remained a lovely one but behind it Biddy could see the unease she'd first noticed when Miss Garfield had confirmed the companion's position. Biddy said no more while Sybil instructed her in the game, and they played a hand until Sybil declared herself fatigued.

'Will you answer my question?' Biddy asked, as Sybil was standing to leave the drawing room.

Sybil stopped and looked hard at her companion. 'You must not irritate me, Biddy, I am afraid I need to be insistent on that.'

'I'm sorry,' Biddy said. 'I didn't mean to do that.'

'Yet, I think that you might have,' said Sybil. 'Do you think the Secret Heiress would?' The question sounded like something parroted automatically, a phrase repeated by rote.

'Who?'

Sybil seemed to realise what she'd said and sidestepped it. 'I shall forgive you for it, for we must all err once. But to err again is less forgivable, don't you think?'

Biddy nodded, thrown. 'Yes, miss.'

'You must call me Sybil, remember,' said the well-to-do girl, assuming her smile.

Companionship, Biddy told herself as she put away the table and cards, was not the same thing as friendship despite any appearance that suggested it was. Friends considered themselves equals, because without equality friendship couldn't exist. Companions didn't consider themselves equals so much as they behaved as if they were.

Biddy had genuinely hoped for a friend. Yet somehow it still didn't feel beyond her achievement.

'When you have a moment to spare for me, Miss Garfield, perhaps you could dictate the Summersby rules I must follow?' Biddy stood before the governess with a pencil and notebook.

The governess gave her a level glance from the library sofa. 'Wash your hands thoroughly before meals. Refrain from running upon the stairs.'

Giving the impression of being pleased, Biddy noted these down and waited.

'Don't sniff,' Miss Garfield added. 'The sound of it carries in the halls and is most disquieting.'

Biddy wrote that down, too, and then looked back to the governess. 'Aren't these rules a bit, well, common sense?'

'Of course they are, Biddy, and it dismays me to think you need any instruction in them,' said Miss Garfield, sternly. 'Did you learn nothing in your previous service?'

'Of course I did, Miss Garfield, Mrs Rattray trained me very well.'

'Is this the same Mrs Rattray you once claimed to be?'

Biddy had the good grace to blush.

'Put your silly notebook away and prepare to amuse Sybil for the hour þefore supper,' said the governess. 'If you do then all will be well, you'll see.'

Biddy looked about her as if in fear of being overheard. 'I mean her relatives' rules,' she whispered. 'Can't you just tell me about those?'

Miss Garfield bristled. 'Such rules have absolutely nothing to do with you.'

'They do if I break them.'

'They are not yours to break. They are not your concern.'

'But they are my concern if I'm to be here,' Biddy pressed. 'I can't seem to find anything about them written down anywhere. There's no leatherbound book of them, and surely that's where such rules ought to be?'

'Biddy . . .'

'There's not even a framed needlepoint with them stitched on it either.' Biddy paused for breath for a moment. 'And who is the Secret Heiress?'

Miss Garfield rose from the sofa and stood half a head taller than Biddy, eyeing her off. 'How do you know of that?'

'Something I overheard,' said Biddy, losing confidence.

Miss Garfield's silence told her there would be no answer forthcoming.

'I'm only trying to be a good companion,' Biddy pleaded.

'You'll be a far more exemplary one if you desist from discussing these matters again,' said Miss Garfield.

Biddy narrowed her eyes as the governess removed herself from the room.

She heard her inquisitive mother's example again, compulsively listing in her head the things that niggled her.

One. Why would a person's relatives remain so unknown and mysterious? Why would they insist on it? Why would others enforce it? Why would a person accept it?

Biddy tapped at Sybil's door and waited in the hallway. When, after a moment, the door had not been answered, Biddy knocked again. When that brought no response, Biddy tried the handle. 'Sybil?' she called into the room. 'I'm here for our fun before supper.'

The room was unoccupied.

Biddy saw the folded note left upon the lace pillow of Sybil's bed.

Closing the door behind her she slipped inside and took the paper, perching on the edge of the bed as she read it.

I do not require amusement just now, Biddy. When you encounter Miss Garfield or Mrs Marshall later this is not something they need know. Rather, you must tell them the very opposite should they ask: much amusement was provided and you well fulfilled your duty as companion. In truth, you will well fulfil your duty by remaining in my room alone and doing all that might be required to make it seem that I am in here with you. Please do not fail in this. It is very important to our friendship that you succeed, and if you succeed (which I know you will) then I will have cause to ask it of you again. Your loving Sybil.

Biddy sat and thought about the letter for a long time, a smile on her face. She could not help letting her thoughts wander to Lewis Fitzwater, the handsome young man whom she had not seen since the morning at the hut when he had left little Joey in her care. She thought about Lewis's soft lips upon hers; a thought that could only *be* a thought because she had not actually experienced it.

When Sybil returned to the room an hour later, Biddy was playing her umpteenth game of solitaire. She looked up and grinned at the well-to-do girl, who grinned happily back, giving nothing away as to where she had been. Biddy did not ask and did not allude to the contents of the note at all. The two girls began a different game of cards, laughing in fun until the bell for supper rang.

Sybil seemed radiant as she descended the stairs, Biddy following one step behind, hands crossed at her waist. Taking their seats at the dining table together, Biddy looked at Sybil with new eyes as they ate their simple meal.

Sybil was involved in a clandestine romance. Biddy knew every one of the signs. This was the real reason why Sybil had wanted her here.

Biddy was the smokescreen.

*

Seeking ways to fill the hours when a companion was not required, Biddy invaded Mrs Marshall's domain. Oddly, it seemed to her, no replacement cook had been found and Mrs Marshall remained the source of Summersby's meals. Biddy came to know Mrs Marshall's narrow, albeit tasty, repertoire well. She observed Mrs Marshall's kitchen duties without comment from a chair at the scrubbed pine table; silence being a rare thing for her, but a more natural state for Mrs Marshall, who was used to working with very few staff around her at the best of times. After a while the housekeeper forgot that Biddy was even in the room. Then, without being asked, Biddy made brown soup from the meat bones leftover from Monday's roast beef. Mrs Marshall, thrown upon discovering what Biddy was doing, observed Biddy's work with high scepticism, but said nothing about it. Finally, when Biddy stood aside from the stove, Mrs Marshall deigned to sample the work. She still said nothing, but was apparently happy enough with the results, for the soup was served with supper.

Biddy repeated the process, again without Mrs Marshall saying a word about it, this time using bones from the boiled mutton. Then she prepared Scotch broth wholly on her own initiative from the neck of a mutton forequarter. Mrs Marshall again tasted both these soups, making her approval apparent only in her act of allowing them to be served.

'Summersby has no mincing machine,' Biddy remarked as the housekeeper prepared yet another roast beef dinner.

Mrs Marshall stopped. 'Summersby has no need of one.'

Biddy shrugged. 'Still, with the purchase of a mincer, I could use the leftovers to make rissoles for breakfast,' she said. 'The Reverend always liked it. I just add some onion with a little parsley and thyme.'

Mrs Marshall narrowed her eyes while Biddy smiled from the table.

'The brown soups were well received, if unexpected,' said the housekeeper, 'but they are not required of a lady's companion, and it must be said, do debase the position.'

'Tripe,' said Biddy.

Mrs Marshall flushed red and dropped her dishcloth. 'What did you just say to me . . .?'

'Tripe and offal,' said Biddy, winningly, 'I'm very handy with them, too. Tripe done with onions; it's always a tasty supper and very pleasing near the end of the week when the housekeeping budget's slim. You can go a long way with tripe.'

The housekeeper glared at her. 'Did you hear what I just said?'

'Did you give up the idea of finding another cook then? Is that because you actually rather like cooking? I like it, too,' said Biddy.

'That is none of your concern,' the housekeeper spluttered.

'Of course it's not, but the happy state of Summersby is, at least a bit, if I'm to be a part of things here. Miss Sybil might want a companion, but truth is she only wants one when she's not hard at work on her lessons, which is much of the time, or resting, which is quite often, too. I wasn't brought up to be idle, Mrs Marshall, and I don't care if it debases the position or not. Perhaps you could use another pair of hands in here? I know I could use the company – and the learning. There are many things you could teach me about running a great house like this, and I, for one, would like to know them.'

The housekeeper slowly smoothed her apron. 'As if I have the time or inclination to teach anyone anything, especially some slip of a girl who's landed her position with nothing more than lies and coincidence.'

The comment stung but Biddy's calm expression showed no trace of it. 'It's not as if I can't pull my weight. Why don't you ask me something?'

'I'm sorry?'

'Ask me something,' Biddy repeated, 'about household tasks; cooking, cleaning; things a useful girl ought to know. Ask me. Go on. I'm far more useful than I look.'

'This is a waste of my time,' Mrs Marshall muttered.

'Scared, are you? That's a shame.'

Mrs Marshall nearly fell backwards onto her stove at being spoken to with such impudence, but somehow she found the wit to right herself and, infuriated by Biddy, cast her eyes about the room until they landed on something to call her bluff. 'There. In the bowl,' she said, pointing to where a plain brown mixing bowl sat upon a dresser top. 'Think you know it all, do you? What's in the bowl?'

'Oats,' said Biddy.

'Wrong!' the housekeeper started to crow.

'*Scottish* oats,' Biddy clarified, without even needing to look at the contents. 'There's a difference, obviously, Scottish oats being far superior.'

The housekeeper didn't miss a beat. 'What makes them superior?'

'Well, the conditions in which they're grown, of course. That oats can grow at all in Scotland is a miracle, with such poor soil, so rocky and hard, and very cruel weather – there's hardly a growing season to speak of there, and nothing to harvest until well into autumn, I'm told. Each grain is a triumph, really, and that's what they bring with them: triumph. I wouldn't make porridge with anything but imported Scottish oats, and I'm relieved, Mrs Marshall, to see that you wouldn't either.'

The housekeeper's mouth hung open before she had the presence of mind to close it. Robbed of reply, given that Biddy was correct, she returned to preparing the roast. Biddy wasted no further time, getting up from the table and moving towards a tray of apricots that one of the gardener's boys had brought in and left near the door.

'Very fine fruit here,' said Biddy, hefting the tray towards the sink, 'they'll make a lovely jam, don't you think, Mrs Marshall? And don't you worry any; I'll break the stones with a hammer. The creamy white kernels are the very best bits in a good apricot jam. It amazes me how few people know this.'

Mrs Marshall looked up only once more. 'You'll find preserving jars in the stillroom,' was all she said.

Happy, Biddy headed into the room where Mrs Marshall aired her cakes and bread, and stored various sundries. She gave a little leap in the air once she was sure the other woman couldn't see her. Then, for the sheer joy at what had been achieved, she gave another little leap and another again. Biddy pulled herself together then, not wanting it to seem like she was rubbing some kind of victory into the other woman's face, and began gathering what she'd need for the jam. For the first time she felt able to assess the contents of Mrs Marshall's stillroom shelves properly. Two inviting cakes stood beneath glass lids, waiting to be iced. A crusty loaf of soft, white bread lay invitingly beneath a cloth.

There was a fine array of preserving jars in varying sizes and Biddy selected ten of the smaller sort, better suited for the breakfast table. She picked up and examined some of the other things stored along with the jars and noted bits of chipped or orphaned glassware that she guessed Mrs Marshall clung to for reasons of sentiment. A flash of sapphire blue caught her eye and, shifting some larger things aside, Biddy found an old perfume vial lost at the very back of the shelf. Biddy retrieved it and held it to the light from the upper windows. It glowed like a blue jewel in her hand. There was nothing inside. She put the thing back where she found it, until something made her turn to look at it again as she assembled the other jars. It *was* very pretty. Biddy wondered if it would be missed if it fell inside her apron pocket.

Deciding it wasn't worth the risk to her current good standing with the housekeeper, Biddy let the vial be but succumbed instead to the lure of the soft white bread. With memories of all the thick slices denied her while in the Reverend's employ, Biddy lifted the cloth from the loaf and carved herself a slice as thick as her wrist. As she did, a pleasing waft of herbs rose from the bread.

'Rosemary . . .?' Biddy wondered as she lifted the slice to her nose. She sniffed again. It was rosemary. 'That's unusual.' Yet it was by no means unpleasant. Biddy began to devour the scented slice unbuttered.

Her neck snapped back in a seizure before she'd swallowed half of it. Biddy felt as if her legs and spine were splintering. She hit the flagstone floor, the preserving jars taking the worst of her fall, her arms flinging and flailing as the fit consumed her and her consciousness slipped away.

In the final seconds before she knew no more, Biddy's thoughts flashed not to the pretty blue vial but the bottles next to it. They had all been dusty but the blue had not. It was clean.

Yet the blue vial was at the very back of the shelf with the appearance of having sat there for years.

IDA

DECEMBER 1886

3

Ida retired to bed early, almost as soon as she'd cleaned up from supper, denying herself even her treasured half hour of reading time before she blew out her bedside candle. She was expected to be up before dawn now that she had a new mistress, and she didn't want to do anything that risked putting herself in a bad light with Mr Hackett, or indeed with Miss Gregory, with whom Ida was very keen to make a continued good first impression. But without a book to send her nodding, Ida found it difficult to get to sleep. She was too excited about the day she'd had. At some point she must have drifted off, however, because the next she knew the hair on her arms was prickling and she was rubbing at them in her dream, telling herself not to wake up for it. But her skin went to goose pimples then and she felt a distinct shiver up her spine, before remembering the cold, dead hand that once had pressed at her there. The memory was more than enough to wake her and Ida lay blinking in her little bed, feeling oppressed by the dark.

She was rewarded for waking, if she could possibly call it that. She heard the faint tap-tap-tapping of dog's nails upon boards. Knowing that she *had* to be imagining the sound, given what Barker had told her, Ida tried to block it out with her pillow.

It was only because she was all alone, she told herself, pillow to her ears, that she was hearing such noises at all. It was only because there was no one else for company. The noises had Ida at their mercy, their audience of one.

Curled up in her sheets, trying to fool herself back to sleep, Ida didn't want to think upon what the noise might really be, but couldn't help herself. Was it the ghost of the poor little pup that had died with his mistress? Was the animal prowling the halls outside Ida's little third floor room? Sometimes the sound seemed loud, as if very near the door itself, other times faint, as if the dog was sniffing in the rooms below. Yet always the hard little nails kept clipping on polished wooden floors. The poor dead thing was only looking for his mistress. God was horrible, Ida thought, to curse a poor little dog to this fate, so blameless in its soul.

The taps grew louder and closer again. Ida held her breath and pulled the blanket up to her eyes. She begged herself to believe that it was all in her head, just like Barker had said it was. She kept holding her breath until she felt her face turning blue and couldn't control her lungs any longer.

The tapping stopped.

In the total silence that followed, it took something of Ida's willpower to force herself up from her bed and across to the door, where she pressed her ear against it to listen.

The sound of scratching broke out from the other side, a desperate attempt to get to her.

'I'm not your mistress!'

The scratching stopped.

Now stiff with fear, Ida told herself that she must open the door and prove to herself that the dog was *real*, and not a ghost at all, and not a figment of her imagination either, because this was the only possible explanation to convince herself she wasn't going mad as a hatter.

She curled her fingers around the handle, took a deep breath for courage and flung the door wide.

The hallway was empty. There was nothing out there but the

dark. She padded towards the great stairs and listened. There was nothing. She descended a flight until she reached the floor below. From somewhere above came a draught of late evening air, fresh and cool upon Ida's face.

She went to climb the stairs again to return to her bed, worried for what the whole silly experience might mean for her state of mind. Then she saw a figure looming towards her in the hallway and almost screamed the roof off.

'Mr Hackett?'

Wearing nothing but a nightshirt, he nearly cried out, too, upon seeing her appear at him from the dark. 'Ida? Ida, what are doing there?'

'I . . .' She was lost for words in the shock. 'I thought I heard something in the hall.'

'You, too?'

Her stomach tightened. 'What is it, Mr Hackett?'

'*Something is wrong*,' he whispered. 'I awoke feeling certain of it. I was soaked with sweat and panting, Ida, I felt need of a glass of water. My room was humid.' A shiver gripped him. 'I felt sure that something was waiting for me outside my door.'

Ida's heart beat faster. 'Oh, Mr Hackett.'

'I couldn't hear anything but I was so certain of it, I know I wasn't dreaming – something *was* there, waiting for me, just on the other side of the door.'

The hallway was empty.

His nightshirt glued to his chest, Samuel peered to his left, where the great stairs led to the ground floor below.

There was nothing to be seen in the dark. He glanced to his right.

'Are you ill, Samuel?' asked Matilda from the shadows.

The surprise was so great for both of them they sprang backwards, Ida striking her elbow against the wall with a flash of pain.

Matilda was barefoot in her own night attire, ghostlike and pale in the pre-dawn light. How long had she been with them?

'Did I frighten you?'

It was as if Ida wasn't there. Matilda could only see Samuel.

'Forgive me.' He found his wits again to recover himself. 'I did not expect you there.'

She was in no way ashamed of herself. 'I did frighten you. That was terrible of me. I was unable to sleep.'

Samuel gazed at her nightgown; soft and sheer, clinging to her lovely form. He glanced down at himself and was self-conscious. His nightshirt adhered to him like tar. Embarrassed at what she could see, Ida averted her eyes. He tried to cover himself. 'Is your bed uncomfortable?'

'Oh no,' Matilda said, 'that's not it. It's just, well . . . I am home again. I wanted to see everything – the things I forgot.' Her eyes lingered on his before flicking to his body beneath the sweat-soaked shirt. Her gaze aroused something within him. Her eyes returned to his again and he was made almost breathless by the look he saw there.

'Miss?' Ida said, from behind them in the gloom.

Samuel remembered her with a start.

'Miss, are you feeling ill?'

'Miss Gregory is having trouble getting to sleep,' Samuel said. He seemed to be hoping that Ida would read the look on his face and leave.

Ida didn't. 'I'll take you to the kitchen, miss,' she told Matilda, holding out her hand. 'I reckon there's some valerian tea in there, that'll help you sleep.'

Matilda pulled her eyes from Samuel's and directed them at Ida. 'No thank you,' was all she said. She turned in the direction of the stairs, leaving Samuel staring after her in the dark.

'Miss,' Ida whispered. 'Best take care in the shadows!' She wanted to run after Matilda but was frightened of somehow upsetting her if she did. In stark distinction to how she had been at the Hall, there was now nothing fragile about her, nothing vulnerable at all.

She turned to Samuel. 'Did she seem . . . strange to you, Mr Hackett?'

'I . . . I really don't know,' he said. He dabbed at his face with his sleeve. He collected himself. 'Go back to your bed now, Ida, and thank you. I shall see you again in the morning.'

Matilda awoke again at dawn when Ida followed Aggie into the Chinese Room where Matilda had slept. The young woman briefly believed herself back at Constantine Hall until Aggie threw the curtains aside and the room this action exposed bore no resemblance to the room Matilda had been kept in for so long.

She sat upright, staring about her. 'Where are we? What has happened?'

'It's all right, miss,' said Aggie.

Ida waited discreetly with a tray of breakfast things, having not yet mentioned what she had seen last night. Matilda took in the sight of her, moving about the room behind Aggie, and now bringing the tray to the bed.

'We're at Summersby,' Aggie reminded. 'Your home.'

Ida gave Matilda a sideways, searching look as she settled the tray. Something of the previous day's events seem to come back to Matilda. 'The long carriage journey from the railway station . . .' she said.

'That's right, miss,' said Aggie.

'We arrived at night . . . the great house emerged from the trees, only half seen until the trees cleared.'

Aggie smiled. 'You remember it now. You are not at the Hall and never will be again.'

Matilda patted the pillows and Aggie rearranged them at her back. 'This is a comfortable bed.'

'I'm pleased to hear it,' said Aggie. She winked at her. 'Mine was acceptable, too.'

Observing all this avidly, Ida took it as reason to join in. 'Pleased to hear it likewise!' she said, revealing her brightest smile. 'All my handiwork, you know. Nothing in your rooms I haven't touched.'

Matilda cast a look of some surprise at her, and then to Aggie, who was looking rather more aghast.

'Mr Hackett would wish you to address your mistress as "Miss Gregory", I think,' Aggie said to Ida.

'Oh, sure,' said Ida. She stood there a moment before she remembered. *'Miss Gregory.'*

Matilda smiled shyly and fell to eating her boiled egg.

'Thank you, Ida,' said Aggie, attempting to usher her from the room.

Ida missed the hint and took this attention as praise for her actions. 'My pleasure, miss, I'm at your beck and call. Don't think to stop yourself from shouting for me.'

Matilda was looking about her as she ate. The large Chinoiserie screen was the room's most attractive feature and Matilda's eyes remained upon it as she ate. 'Do you think my sister slept here?' she asked.

Ida didn't have an answer.

'I wouldn't have thought so,' said Aggie, beginning to take out clothing from an opened trunk. 'She would have slept in the master bedroom, I imagine.'

Matilda nodded. 'So many nice things.'

Ida was quietly ecstatic.

With her back to her mistress Aggie opened the doors of a wardrobe, placing items upon the hangers she had been too tired to put away the night before. Matilda's eye settled on the flat, round box decorated in a Moorish style that Ida had placed atop a little pile of books at the bedside.

Ida watched on, pleased, as Matilda opened the box, but was surprised when Matilda withdrew a photographic image pasted on a card. Sure that the box had been empty when she herself had placed it there, Ida squinted to see what the photograph was from where she stood, but could only half make out a portrait of a young woman, beautifully dressed, with rich, dark hair cascading like a fall of coal down her back. Matilda stared at the portrait a moment and then turned the photograph over. A name and a date had been inked onto the back in smooth, flowing copperplate. Ida couldn't quite read it from where she stood.

Samuel stood smiling from the open door. Ida gave a start as she realised it and Matilda slipped the box and its contents beneath the bed cover. 'I trust you slept better?' he enquired.

Matilda blushed and clearly didn't know how to respond. She looked to Aggie and saw that she was blushing, too. Aggie curtsied to Samuel as an afterthought.

'Better than?' Aggie began.

Samuel seemed to hesitate, searching Matilda's face for something, but unable to find it. He caught eyes with Ida. 'Last night.' he prompted, addressing himself to Matilda. 'You said you couldn't sleep at all. When I found you.'

It was Aggie's turn to look bewildered. 'But Miss Gregory slept very soundly indeed, Mr Hackett.'

Ida shook her head to tell her otherwise but Aggie missed it.

Samuel realised then that he had erred in some way. 'I am sorry,' he said, 'we have not had ladies at Summersby for quite a time. I am used to having the roam of this house. Forgive me for disturbing you.' He gave a little bow and left.

'Brother Samuel?' Matilda called out after him.

Aggie turned to look at her, but could say nothing before Samuel reappeared at the door, his smile wider still.

Matilda seemed to find her words at risk of failing her once more. 'This . . . this is a lovely room,' she managed.

'I'm pleased you like it,' said Samuel. He seemed to be hoping for very much more.

'Was it my sister's?' she wondered.

A cloud passed across his face. 'Why would you think that?'

It looked to Ida as if Matilda was now about to show the photograph but then stopped. 'So many nice things . . .' she replied instead.

Samuel's cloud seemed to pass. 'All of Summersby's rooms have nice things in them,' he said, smiling again, 'as you will soon remember. Come down to me when you have dressed and eaten and I will show you them all.'

He departed once more and Ida saw Matilda's finger trace

the photograph's smooth, shiny surface beneath the sheet. 'I do believe this *was* my sister's room,' Matilda said to Aggie, after a moment. 'But I do not mind. Perhaps he fears I will find the fact unpleasant, but I really do not. She is my twin after all. I know that we are united again.' She returned to her breakfast, taking a spoonful of egg. 'Even if she is dead . . .'

Ida badly wanted to tell Aggie that Matilda had not slept soundly at all. But the other servant was too preoccupied with tasks to be bothered now, and Ida was hesitant to raise it in front of Matilda herself. It seemed like Matilda had forgotten it.

By mid-morning Ida found herself at a loss for things to do. Not daring to be idle, she revisited rooms she'd cleaned in recent days to see if they needed another going over. She returned to the dining room again, and found herself staring at a spot on the carpet where she imagined the late Miss Gregory had breathed her last. She tried to blink all thoughts of this away and bent to check the room's dust traps. She lifted the heavy curtains from where they gathered at the floor to make sure were hiding nothing. The left-side drape revealed mice droppings. Curling her lip, Ida took her dustpan and broom to the pile, unsurprised that rodents had made their way inside the house, given how few people there were to scare them off. On her hands and knees to sweep up the last of it, Ida was surprised to see the glint of something she recognised beneath the settee against the far wall. Puzzled, Ida made her way across the room and reached underneath.

Her hand emerged clutching the same blue perfume vial she'd previously placed in the Chinese room. It took Ida a moment to understand how this could possibly be. She tried to remember if she'd seen it earlier on Matilda's dressing table, but couldn't recall.

'But why would someone move it?' she wondered aloud.

She held it to the window light to see the level of perfume inside. It seemed much the same.

Sometimes this house was strange, Ida thought. Tucking the vial away inside her apron pocket, she thanked her stars that at least Barker hadn't found the vial before she did. He'd think she never cleaned behind curtains. She turned to see the valet himself slouched at the door, smirking at her.

Ida jumped in surprise.

'She led us on a merry dance last night,' he said.

Ida blinked. 'Who did?'

'The mistress did, who else, you cretin?'

Ida blinked again, lost. 'But I know she did. I saw her.'

Barker looked at her like she was truly deficient. 'She was there outside His Lordship's rooms. God almighty knows what she was doing.'

'I was *there*, Mr Barker. I don't remember seeing you.'

Barker's smile was lewd. 'And him wearing nothing but his nightshirt.'

Ida felt herself growing hot. 'I don't know why you're telling me this. If you were there, too, why didn't you say something?'

'Who gives a Buckley's what you think?' he said, dismissing this. 'You're needed elsewhere this morning, cretin. His Lordship wants to take her to the graveyard.'

The blue glass vial felt heavy in Ida's apron pocket. 'What am I supposed to do there?'

Barker shrugged and sniffed. 'Keep an eye on 'em. He's your fancy man, ain't he?'

Ida went red to the rim of her housemaid's cap.

Barker smirked at having scored himself a bullseye. 'Thought as much.'

The granite memorial stone was extremely new, erected only a day or so before Matilda's return, and so stood out among the other memorials atop the older graves for looking crisp, sharp and spotless. Matilda ran her gloved hand across the chiselled, gilded lettering as Ida watched on in attendance at the graveyard periphery – the very spot she had stood at the funeral.

Margaret Louisa Gregory

1867 – 1886

At Peace with the Lamb of the Lord

'I should have liked it to have said "Beloved sister",' Matilda remarked, looking up at Samuel from the inscription.

His hand clasped his walking stick. 'There is space upon the stone. I can ask the mason to letter it,' he suggested. It seemed to Ida from where she observed Samuel that he searched Matilda's eyes for any hint of something that he could not or would not put into words. Whatever this was, Matilda gave no recognition of it.

'There could never have been a more beloved sister,' said Matilda, '*anywhere* . . . And there was nothing she would not do to express her deep and abiding love for me. She so often said it. Her every action reflected it.'

Samuel met eyes with Ida and looked awkward. 'A beautiful resting place . . .'

Matilda nodded and then smiled, her face veiled against the buzzing insects. Ida had no veil and had to shoo them with her hands. Ancient eucalypts towered above, sparse branches swaying in the breeze. The grassy hills surrounding were a golden yellow, baked dry by the sun. Matilda nodded again and echoed Samuel's words. 'A truly beautiful resting place, indeed, brother,' she agreed.

He seemed to search her face again but still found nothing of what he sought there.

Two young boys came through the cemetery gate with a man whose face was shielded by the broad brim of his hat.

'Would you like to visit the other graves?' Samuel asked Matilda, with one eye upon the new arrivals.

Matilda knelt again to brush her fingers against the petals of the flowers she had left at Margaret's stone. 'How did she die, brother?'

There was a sense that Samuel had given this answer already. 'It was a sudden turn,' he told her – or reminded her, Ida suspected.

'Her constitution had been very weak.' He cleared his throat, as if preparing to say something that was difficult for him. 'It is my belief, however, that it was the weight of conscience that led her to succumb.' Flies crusted about his eyes and he shooed them as Ida did.

Matilda stood once more, looking up at him. 'What things?'

He was gentle with her. 'Matilda, your sister was a very untruthful person. She told some quite shameful lies.'

'Such things are enough to take a person?'

Samuel nodded. The flies were determined to harass him.

Matilda looked shamefaced. 'I am sure I have asked you the question already, and that you have answered it too, brother. You must forgive me.' Her hands fluttered at her side. 'My memory is . . . never as it might be.'

Ida squinted a little, wondering at this. Had she also forgotten what she did last night or was she merely pretending so?

'You must apologise for nothing,' Samuel told her. He held his arm out for her and she took it, as naturally and unquestioningly as she had taken it when he had led her from Constantine Hall. 'Shall we see your father's grave?' he suggested.

Matilda nodded.

A child's cry from somewhere behind made them turn. One of the small boys who had entered through the gate now stood a little way off, staring at Matilda with his mouth open; sticking his hand out in a point. 'She's a ghost!'

Matilda flushed beneath her veil netting.

'She's a ghost!' the boy yelled, alerting the other boy as well as the man he had come with. Ida thought she recognised the man from town.

Startled, Matilda clutched at Samuel's arm.

Samuel raised his walking cane, as if to strike at the child. 'You ill-mannered brat – is this how you behave before a lady?'

The boy spluttered, his eyes wide with shock. 'But she was *dead*,' he insisted, 'and now she's here at the graveyard – she's a ghost!'

The man now came up behind the boy, the other child with him, and Ida confirmed to herself that this was Mr Skews, a somewhat skittish man of Samuel's age, if not quite his blond good looks. Ida knew of him as the young apothecary from doddery Dr Foal's surgery in Castlemaine. She glanced at Samuel and thought that he looked discomforted at seeing him.

'I'm very sorry, Mr Hackett,' said Skews. 'My word, Jim, where's your manners?' He seemed to rake Matilda's features beneath her veil, just as the boy had done. He scratched at his arms.

'This is Miss Gregory,' said Samuel, very aware of Skews studying her. 'She has returned to Summersby with the passing of her sister.'

Skews lifted his hat, embarrassed, drawing closer the child that had been shocked. 'Please forgive me, miss. My son, Jim, he knew your poor sister by sight – we all did, my word, yes.' He scratched at himself again and gave a brief, fearful look to Samuel, before whatever meaning was behind it vanished.

It was as if the boy still couldn't believe what he was seeing. 'You're not the same Miss Gregory?'

'I am Miss Gregory . . .' Matilda started to say.

'She is the poor lady's sister, son, see?' said Skews. 'She is her twin.'

Matilda nodded and on an impulse lifted her veil, letting them see her fully. The boy's eyes popped anew. Hiding behind Skews, the second boy, unidentified, stared too, but with a clear note of scepticism in his face, as if he believed what he saw but somehow doubted whatever it was that had brought it to pass.

'We're visiting the boy's late mother, God rest her soul,' said Skews, indicating another, less decorated grave nearer the enclosure's far side.

The reminder of this seemed to sober the first boy. 'Mum died of the diffthery,' he offered, 'just like Lew's ma.'

The other boy screwed up his mouth. Nervous Skews tipped his hat again, making to leave with the boys.

'My mother died, too,' said Matilda. This made them stop

short. It seemed she would say no more, however, and Skews was about to pull the boys away again when Matilda found further words. 'It was typhus,' she added, 'when Summersby was newly built. I was very small, I think.' She paused again, and they waited. 'My memory plays tricks,' she said apologetically, 'but I remember this, her death, I remember it. I do . . .'

Skews spoke first. 'I'm sorry to hear it, miss, my word, yes.'

Matilda acknowledged this, perhaps seeing sympathy in his watery eyes. He rubbed at his nostrils as Ida watched him, enthralled.

Matilda then looked to the two boys, and kneeled down again to be level with their faces. 'To lose a loved one is a very cruel thing,' she told them, 'yet I believe we never really lose them. They remain with us, you see, and not just in our hearts, but right there beside us.' Her eyes were shining. 'We simply need to look – or learn *how* to look – and then we will see those who have gone.' As if to illustrate what she meant, she looked to her other side, the side opposite to where Samuel stood, and there she seemed to focus on something that perhaps was clear to her but invisible to everyone else. She looked back to the boys again. 'Do you see?'

Their expressions were awed.

Ida couldn't pull her eyes from Matilda either. 'What is it you see there, miss?' she asked.

Samuel looked acutely uncomfortable. 'Shall we return to the house now, Matilda?' He made to help her rise and lead her away.

The boy Jim spoke. 'You were right, miss.'

Matilda turned. 'Yes?'

'You're not the same Miss Gregory.'

'My word, Jim . . .' Skews started to say, a warning in his voice, but the little boy was sincere.

'Well, she's not,' he said. He looked to Matilda again. 'You're different from the other one.' He turned back to his father. 'You see it, Pa? She's a very nice lady, not just pretty, but *nice*.' He gave a final smile to Matilda before his father managed to get him moving. 'The other Miss Gregory wasn't nice at all, remember?'

he said, with his awkward father leading him away. 'Hardly no one liked her.'

On the walk across the paddocks to the great house, following respectfully behind Matilda and Samuel, Ida found herself asking questions in her head. She couldn't stop herself. Seeing the late Miss Gregory's grave had done it; the last resting place of the woman who had liked Ida for her inquisitiveness.

One. Apart from herself and the never-there Mrs Jack, Summersby had lost the rest of its servants. Why was it that Barker was untroubled by the lack of fellow staff?

Two. Why did Samuel and Barker accept the inadequate explanation that Margaret had died of a 'turn'?

Three. Less pressing, but interesting all the same. How did the nervous Mr Skews know Margaret Gregory intimately enough for his own son to have formed an opinion of her character?

'I must ask you to turn your apron pocket out,' said Aggie in exasperation, when she found Ida in an upstairs hall after luncheon.

Ida felt neither astonishment nor resentment at the request, and produced from her apron a tortoiseshell hairbrush – and the blue glass vial. 'Oh, I almost forgot I had this,' she declared.

Aggie took the hairbrush from her, thin lipped. 'I must ask you not to touch Miss Gregory's things again.'

'Oh, I didn't mean *that*,' said Ida, dismissing the brush, 'I was only taking it to dip in the vinegar for nits. No, I meant *this*.' She waved the vial.

Aggie seemed offended by the suggestion that Matilda's hairbrush held vermin and turned on her heel for the stairs.

'What should I do with it?' Ida called after her.

'Do with what?' replied Aggie, not bothering to stop.

'The pretty blue glass.'

Aggie gave the vial another glance over her shoulder. 'It doesn't belong to my mistress.'

'I know that. I think it belonged to her dead sister.'

Aggie stopped, her foot on the first descending stair. Ida trotted up to her, still waving the vial. Aggie seemed to be doing her best to stay patient. 'I'm not sure what the problem is, Ida.'

'Well, I found it again, you see? Just like the first time,' Ida tried to make clear.

'Yes?'

'In the death room.'

Aggie looked pained at the choice of words. 'Then you should put it back there.'

'I don't think it belongs. Not from the two spots I found it in, anyway – first under the curtains and then under the settee. Seemed very odd.'

Aggie waited.

Ida waited, too. 'So, what do you think?' she asked, finally.

'I find you confusing today, Ida,' said Aggie.

'Oh.' Ida gawped at her, a little dismayed. She popped the vial into her apron pocket again and chose to beam her brightest smile instead. Aggie just shook her head and began her descent to the floor below.

Ida kept close by her heels. 'I supposed you've noticed I do bloomin' everything around here?' she remarked, by way of a fresh conversation starter. She could tell that Aggie had most definitely noticed this, although she was disappointed that Aggie didn't now say that she did everything *well*.

'Summersby is extremely understaffed,' Aggie replied instead.

'Is it what,' said Ida.

Aggie stopped on the stair. 'When I asked Mr Barker the reason for this he was most short with me about it,' she said. 'Quite rude, in fact.'

'Oh, *him*,' said Ida, dismissively. 'Did you ask him why he keeps a poker up his bum?'

Aggie frowned. 'Ida, really.' She continued the descent again.

'Servants hand in notices here like they're scared they'll catch something off the doorknobs,' Ida remarked, keeping pace.

'Your common mouth does not become you,' said Aggie.

'Sorry,' said Ida, remembering herself. 'I've not met many *polite* people before, miss. Sometimes I'm a bit at sea.'

Aggie turned and saw that Ida was genuine.

'I just don't think many things through before I say them,' said Ida, 'I never have much. I forget I'm not at home.' The sudden thought of this made Ida's face crease up as she was struck by the obvious truth that she was homesick.

'You must be lonely,' said Aggie, gentler now.

Ida scrubbed a tear from her eye, before pulling herself together again. 'That's why it's just so nice having the company,' she said. She beamed her smile again and realised then that Aggie's heart had gone out to her.

'Who is giving you training?' Aggie asked. They began descending the stairs again, slower now.

'No one,' said Ida. 'Well, that's not true. Mum taught me chores. I'm used to doing them.'

'But no one's training you properly here?' Aggie wondered.

Ida shook her head. 'I make it up as I go along.'

She wasn't surprised that this struck Aggie as peculiar. 'But Mr Hackett is a very refined gentleman,' said Aggie. 'I know he doesn't own Summersby, but he was engaged to the late Miss Gregory and, for the moment at least, he continues to live here. He has his standards, doesn't he?'

Ida didn't have an answer for that.

Aggie stopped on the stairs again. 'Why did the other servants hand in their notices?'

Ida had come up with a theory, but as a girl who little thought before she spoke, she felt it best to think carefully now.

'What is it?' Aggie asked.

Ida felt very conflicted.

Aggie let the matter go. 'Don't worry,' she said. 'It's none of my business, anyway.'

'If I tell you what I think it might wreck it all for Evie,' Ida said, worried.

'Who's Evie?'

'My sister, Evangeline, the only one of us born with any brains. She's thirteen and being kept at school. Mum and all my aunties have high hopes. My wages pay for her books.'

'I see,' said Aggie, even though she didn't seem to see really.

'Those who talked got the flick,' whispered Ida, pained. 'I didn't guess it to begin with, but that's what it was, they *talked*, you see, and when poker-bum Barker heard he told 'em they were through.' She paused to let the significance of this be felt. '"Handing in their notice" was all bunkum!' she declared. 'They were sacked! Course it only made things worse. Soon as they were out they talked to anyone who'd listen. Now the whole world must know. If I speak another word then it's Evie who'll suffer the most.'

Digesting this information, Aggie proceeded with care. 'Then you shouldn't tell me anything of it at all, Ida. I mean it,' she said. 'If that's the way things are here then I must respect that, just as you do.'

Ida struggled another moment, before succumbing to acceptance. She nodded her profound gratitude to Aggie, tears once more in her eyes.

'There now,' said Aggie, maternally, patting Ida's hand.

'I think Miss Gregory killed herself!' Ida blurted out.

'What?'

'I think she did it from shame for what she'd done to her sister! I've been thinking and thinking about it and it all makes sense. It's why no one speaks of it. It's why everyone says she had a "turn". She couldn't live with herself for what she'd done. She killed herself.'

Aggie was horribly shocked.

'People have said she was ill before she died,' Ida went on, *'ill in her mind* . . . It was the guilt making her ill. I think she couldn't bear it.'

'Oh, Ida,' Aggie said, putting her hands to mouth. 'You mustn't say another word about this.'

'I won't.'

'I mean it. If what you say is true, well . . .' Aggie was pale.

'It's a terrible sin, I know.'

'It's far worse than that,' said Aggie. '*It's a terrible scandal.*'

Later, when the hushed conversation was done, Ida felt so vastly better about getting it all off her chest that she attacked her endless cleaning round with real energy. She had a friend in Aggie, she knew, a genuine friend, and if she was lucky she'd gain another one in Aggie's strange yet lovely mistress, who was also her mistress now, too, Ida had to remind herself. It was to Matilda's room – the Chinese room – that Ida applied herself, cleaning not "tidying", with a fervour and commitment she'd little felt at Summersby before.

It was only when she came to dust the surfaces that she remembered the blue perfume vial. With no better idea coming to mind, she put it back where she had originally placed it upon the dressing table, mystified that it had ever found its way back to the dining room at all. Who on earth had moved it and why?

When the room was looking as fine as Ida felt she could make it, she took herself to the room allotted to Aggie on the floor above, not far from the little nook that was her own bedroom. Ida attacked her new friend's room with a vengeance, keen for it to mirror the Chinese Room in cleanliness as much as was possible. Once she felt it truly sparkled, a bolt of inspiration hit. Skipping down the servants' stairs to the kitchen, Ida went through to the walled garden beyond where the household's herbs and vegetables grew. Ida knew little about flowers, only that they were pretty. She looked for what might be in bloom, scared to go beyond the garden walls into the grounds proper where anything she snipped would surely be missed. Confining herself only to what grew among the kitchen produce, Ida took out her scissors and snipped some yellow marigolds, a few sprigs of salvia in lilac and blue, and some pretty, white, daisy-like blooms of feverfew.

On her way inside again Ida remembered a lovely lead crystal vase that belonged in the library. It was criminally wasted where it was, in Ida's view, such a pretty thing should live in the rooms that ladies more often frequented, not gentlemen. She decided to borrow it. Carefully resting the snipped flowers upon a hall table, Ida twisted the handle of the library door and ducked inside, making straight for the cabinet that contained the vase. It was only when she'd retrieved it that she realised the room was occupied.

'Miss Gregory!' she gasped, and nearly dropped the thing.

Matilda was hunched over a writing desk, pen and paper before her. She looked up in surprise at Ida, blinking like a startled mouse.

'I'm so sorry, miss, I didn't realise you were in here,' said Ida, curtseying with rare presence of mind.

Matilda regarded Ida as if she had never met her before.

'It's Ida,' said Ida, feeling the need to remind her, and curtseying again.

Matilda seemed to look her up and down highly critically and Ida felt very conscious of the vase in her hands. She returned it to the cabinet without another word, as if her purpose in coming to the room had merely been to look at the thing.

'Did you have a nice time at the graveyard, miss?' she asked when she was done, in an effort to fill the silence.

'I am at my work,' said Matilda, taking her eyes off Ida at last and returning to her pen.

'My mistake,' said Ida, cheerily, making for the door. She glanced at the writing desk as she passed. The paper Matilda worked upon was covered in thick, uneven handwriting, functional just, where it wasn't marred by ink spots. It was very unattractive on the whole; the sort of penmanship that would have earned Ida a sharp rap over the knuckles from the schoolmistress once upon a time, had she ever dared let it be seen. 'Penning a letter?' she asked.

Matilda stopped very still and said nothing.

Ida closed the door behind her again as quietly as she could. She was starting to realise that Matilda was somewhat changeable. She'd seemed warmer at the graveyard, nicer, but now she was cold and reserved. Ida knew she would simply have to get as used to this unpredictability in her.

Cradling the flowers in her apron, Ida returned upstairs to Matilda's room first, where she arranged the blooms into two small bouquets. Choosing two other vases from among the several the room contained, Ida upended water from the washbasin jug into them before adding the flowers. The effect in each was very pretty.

She heard the low rumble of Barker's voice from somewhere in the hallway outside. 'You ought to get her out there, give her a bit of an airing,' he was saying.

'Miss Gregory is not some open wound to be exposed to the elements,' Samuel replied.

The relationship between the two men was very strange to Ida's mind. The violence with which she'd seen Samuel treat Barker on the carriage, and the insolence with which Barker had driven him to it, spoke of things unsaid between them. And yet they were speaking now. Ida crept to the door and peeked out. At the other end of the hallway the valet was slouched at the open door to Samuel's rooms. Ida couldn't see Samuel within, but his voice carried, polished and higher class.

'Isn't she?' The valet asked. 'Some in town might differ there, Mr Hackett, especially now that gossip's done its work.'

'I abhor gossip,' Samuel responded.

'Not this gossip you don't, and you've got me to thank for it.' Barker tapped his long, straight nose. 'Thank me and the tongues of all the disgruntled.'

'That's enough!' Samuel shouted. He came red-faced to his door and Barker backed away a little.

'You're missing my point,' Barker said.

'I get your point perfectly well,' Samuel told him.

'Do you?' said Barker. 'Let's see then. What do you reckon will come when you listen to some common sense and start squiring that wax-headed noodle on your arm for a bit?'

Samuel seemed to bite back a flush of anger and Ida made sure no part of her was protruding past the door of the Chinese room where either man might spot her. She couldn't quite see them now, but their voices stayed clear. 'You call your mistress "wax-headed", do you?' Samuel objected.

The valet was very dry. 'Sorry. I forget you're slow on the uptake, yourself, Hackett.' He altered his tone to one more appropriate for a child. 'You might not have noticed it, but the other Miss Gregory, the one that's not dead, she has a memory like a billy can that upset a shotgun – full of holes.'

'I suppose you think that my conducting Miss Gregory in public will illicit some manner of sympathy?' said Samuel, clearly weary of Barker. 'The fiancée and the sister taking comfort in each other's grief?'

'You surprise me,' said Barker. 'It's sympathy that won't go astray, neither, not for her and not for you, which might very well be a good thing.'

Ida dared peek again and saw that Samuel had reached for his door handle. 'Thank you very much, Barker, that will be all.' He shut the door.

Ida thought she knew what at least part of the conversation meant, and it was gratifying to learn she'd been right in her suspicions. The gossip mentioned was surely that concerning Margaret Gregory's suicide. From the way that Barker had spoken it seemed like he felt that Samuel should be grateful he had had a hand in spreading it. Who would be grateful for scandal? Yet, the scandal was still acknowledged by Barker as real. Sympathy that might be elicited from taking Miss Matilda out in public was seen as an antidote for it.

Ida hated that Samuel was somehow beholden to his awful servant and that Barker presumed to advise him. Samuel was in every way Barker's better; a beautiful man, gentry born. Why wouldn't he rid himself of such a bad valet?

She took the larger of the two floral arrangements to the dressing table – which was when she got a further shock.

The blue glass vial was gone again.

Ida glanced all around for it but the piece had vanished once more.

Ida thought of Matilda downstairs in the library writing in her ink-spotted hand. She adjusted the vase of flowers. 'Someone's playing silly buggers with me,' she muttered.

When Samuel proposed the notion of Matilda accompanying him to the Castlemaine District Ball, Matilda said yes. But only once Samuel had left the breakfast table and Aggie had come into the dining room did Matilda express the fear that she would not last from dusk to dawn, the necessary number of hours required to grace a country ball. Ida listened to this with interest, placing the used breakfast things on a tray.

'I will fall asleep,' Matilda worried. 'I will be found beneath a table somewhere, or outside in the grass. I will be unable to stop myself from sleeping.'

Ida saw Aggie's eyes wander to the same spot on the floor where she herself had imagined Matilda's dead sister might have been found.

'I will bring disgrace upon dear brother Samuel for it,' Matilda feared.

Aggie pulled her eyes away and made assurances that nothing so dire would occur.

'But how would you know, Marshall?' Matilda asked of her. 'You have never been to a ball, either.'

Aggie glanced then at her own reflection in the mirror above the fireplace. 'Nor do I expect to, miss,' she said, looking away from the glass. 'But I shall enjoy your enjoyment of one. You must go if Mr Samuel has asked you.'

'I'm dreading it now,' said Matilda.

'But you told him yes.'

'I couldn't refuse him. He's so kind to me . . .' She trailed off, plainly beset with insecurity.

'Sympathy,' said Ida. 'It'll help bring some sympathy.'

Matilda and Aggie looked at her.

'Why is that needed?' Aggie asked. She looked annoyed

with Ida for sticking her nose in. In truth, Ida didn't know why sympathy might be a good thing and it bothered her. The overheard chat between Samuel and Barker had not made it clear. Yet it had still seemed like something useful to contribute.

Aggie made Matilda examine herself in the mantle mirror in her place – a distraction. 'Now listen to me,' Aggie told her, 'is it not true that when you were a little girl and your father was still with you, you and your sister dreamed and dreamed of being invited to balls, and were enchanted with the notion of dancing until dawn?'

Matilda's suspicious look came over her. 'How could you know such a thing about me, Marshall?'

Ida saw Aggie's attention drifting to the spot on the floor again. 'Is it true?'

'Well . . .' Matilda seemed to fight inside herself. 'Perhaps it is. I do not know. My memory.'

Aggie nodded, understanding.

'But I don't see how *you* could know of it, if I don't,' Matilda said.

'I know it because every girl dreams it, miss,' Aggie smiled. 'Isn't that true, Ida?'

Ida jumped at being included in the conversation again, and nearly dropped a saucer. 'Oh yes,' she said. 'I'd love to go to a ball.'

Aggie nodded at her. She took a brush from her dress pocket and began stroking Matilda's long, unpinned hair, not yet put up for the day.

'Oh,' said Matilda. The beauty of her reflection and the motion of the hairbrush had their effect; she began to seem calmer.

'That's better, isn't it?' Aggie asked.

Matilda nodded, eyelids closed. 'Matilda went to a ball once . . .'

Aggie paused with the brush. 'You're Matilda,' she reminded.

Matilda's eyelids opened. 'No, I'm not.' She looked searchingly at Aggie's reflection in the mirror, and in that same mirror saw puzzled Ida.

Not knowing what else to do, Ida nodded politely at Matilda's reflected face.

'Am I really, though?' Matilda wondered, vulnerable.

Aggie was patient. 'Mr Clarkenwell told you a dreadful lie, remember? And so did a lot of other people. You were never Margaret at all – *she* was. She was the one who was ill, too. You're Matilda and you're not ill.' She waited as the beautiful young woman once again digested this. 'So, it must have been Margaret that went to a ball,' she added, as gently as she could.

Matilda's look was bitter. 'Sometimes I quite resent my sister.'

'Well, no one would blame you for that,' said Aggie, resuming with the brush. 'She caused the wrong in the first place.'

'I resent her for ruining my certainty.'

Aggie didn't understand. Matilda turned to her. 'I was sure. I had become so *sure*, Marshall.'

She'd lost Aggie. 'Sure of what, miss?'

'Sure of whom I was, at last, after so very long of not being sure . . .' There were tears beginning to well in Matilda's huge brown eyes. 'I really thought I knew for certain.'

'That was the viciousness of the lie confusing you, confusing everybody. You're Miss Matilda. You always were.'

Matilda seemed to give in. 'You're quite right.' She let her eyelids close again with Aggie's brush strokes.

'You'll not have the chance to fall asleep, Matilda.'

Matilda's eyes sprang open and she, Aggie and Ida turned to the dining room door. Samuel was there, dressed ready to go into town.

'Well, you won't,' he said, smiling, stepping into the room, 'so you mustn't worry. Only the tipsy old men nod off at the balls. Everyone else has too fine a time in the hullabaloo to even think about sleep.'

Ida glanced at Matilda and saw that she was blushing, robbed of reply.

'Miss Matilda has never attended such an affair, Mr Hackett,' Aggie answered, curtseying.

Samuel's kind blue eyes met Ida's and she saw that he wanted her to leave him and Matilda alone.

Smiling shyly back at him, she took the tray of used breakfast things to the hall, fully intending to park there and listen while Samuel sat down with Matilda – but Aggie followed her.

'Why are you standing there, Ida, aren't those things meant for the kitchen?'

'Sssh,' Ida hissed.

'People only dance until dawn because it is preferable to travelling home along bad country roads in darkness,' said Samuel from inside the room, 'but I'm informed that the District Ball is only held following consultation with the almanac.'

Aggie looked shocked anew by Ida. 'It is shameful to eavesdrop upon your betters' she admonished. 'Go to the kitchen at once.'

Ida was pained. 'The mistress didn't sleep well at all the first night. She was wandering around the house.' She spoke in a barely audible whisper. *'Wandering near Mr Samuel's rooms.'*

'That's not true!'

Ida shook her head, apologetic. 'I saw them. Nothing happened that shouldn't have, but what did happen was enough.'

Aggie needed to lean against a wall to steady herself, she was so mortified.

'Now we've got to eavesdrop, don't we?' Ida insisted.

'We will know what our mistress permits us to know,' said Aggie, appalled by everything. 'Now go.' She pushed Ida in the direction of the green baize door.

'The almanac tells us when the moon is at its brightest,' Samuel continued from the dining room. 'So I promise you, Matilda, on the night of our ball, the moon will be full in the sky. The almanac will have ensured it. There'll be plenty of light to make the drive home long before dawn.'

Ida didn't move far. 'Mr Barker eavesdrops all the time,' she hissed at Aggie. 'I never know when he's going to appear.'

'Don't be ridiculous. What interest does that man have in the business of women?'

Inside the room Matilda asked, 'But what if there are clouds, brother?'

Samuel just laughed.

Matilda was quiet for a moment before laughing, too. 'What if there are clouds?' she repeated, as if this was now a joke. 'What happens then?'

Suddenly there was a cry and the sound of someone knocking into the table. Aggie and Ida heard the noise and rushed to the open door to find Samuel and Matilda awkwardly looking away from each other.

'I . . . I thought he meant to bite me,' Matilda blurted.

Aggie reeled.

The smooth, fair skin at Samuel's throat went red. 'Miss Gregory . . .'

'I'm so silly, aren't I?' said Matilda. 'It's not what he meant to do at all.'

Samuel somehow left the room with all the dignity he could gather.

Aggie said nothing for a moment, before her eyes fell reflexively to the spot on the floor. She pulled them away.

'Did he try to kiss you, miss?' Ida asked, gently. She could only dream of receiving such a wonderful thing from Samuel.

Matilda looked at her with surprise for a moment. Ida felt as if she were being weighed for her qualification in something, but what that might be Ida couldn't suppose. After another moment of this Matilda nodded. 'He did, Ida. I . . . I misunderstood it.'

Ida's heart went out to her. Matilda seemed as fragile as glass again, like she'd been at the graveyard, or the day she'd been collected from the Hall. Her changeability was extraordinary.

'Well, if it happens again, you'll know what to do, won't you, miss?' Aggie said, softly, taking charge once more. 'You'll be more prepared for it.'

Ida wished she herself had been the subject of that kiss.

It was only afterwards, when Matilda had gone out to stroll in the grounds, that Ida found herself unsettled by what she'd witnessed.

She tried to concentrate on her tasks but was unable to keep her head from the increasing strangeness of it all. Samuel had tried to kiss Matilda, which meant he was rapidly acquiring feelings for her, very rapidly indeed. Was this respectable, Ida wondered? She didn't know. A proposal could be forthcoming, in itself a happy prospect for any girl, but given the events that had seen Matilda return to Summersby in the first place.

Ida knew herself to be young and inexperienced in life, despite her efforts to be otherwise, yet Samuel had been engaged to Matilda's dead sister. What would people make of things if he got himself betrothed to Matilda? This, she realised, could be a very good reason to illicit sympathy from people beforehand. If people felt sympathetic they might also feel better disposed towards such an unexpected announcement.

Ida stepped out from the shadow of the entrance porch as Samuel stepped down from the carriage and strode towards Summersby's great door. She knew Barker waited somewhere within the house and she wished to speak with Samuel without the risk of the black-clad valet overhearing.

'You've come back from town then, Mr Hackett?' she said, by way of alerting her presence to him.

Samuel was taken off guard at seeing her, but at once recovered and actually looked pleased to see her. 'Ida,' he said, acknowledging her with a smile.

'Can I speak to you a minute?' she asked, with what she hoped was suitable appeal.

Samuel's brow creased a little and Ida realised with alarm that he thought she meant to bring up the kiss. She was quick to disavow it. 'Something very distressing has come to my ears, Mr Hackett,' she said, 'something I overheard when I went into town yesterday on my afternoon free.'

Samuel's brow creased deeper, but his smile remained.

Ida kept to the story she'd rehearsed. 'It upset me that such wicked things could be said, Mr Hackett, and I . . . well, I thought you should know about it . . .' she trailed away as Samuel's expression remained unaltered.

'What did you hear?' he asked, kindly.

Ida steeled herself, studying him without, she hoped, looking as if she was doing so. 'I heard that the late Miss Gregory died by her own hand.'

Samuel's expression revealed absolutely nothing.

Ida's nerve failed her. 'It's terrible what people will say,' she blurted, 'people with nothing better to do than sow misery over other people's sorrow – if I'd known the gossipers I would have given them a piece of my mind, but being just a maid and only sixteen . . .'

Tears pricked Samuel's eyes and this silenced her. 'It's true,' he said.

Ida went very still.

'My fiancée took her own life.'

Ida was left with nothing in reply.

'I have so badly wanted to tell you of it,' he said. 'Your kindness of heart was obvious from the very first day we met each other, as was your honesty and loyalty, Ida, but all the same, it is so very difficult to speak of such a thing.'

Ida felt ashamed of herself.

'We found her on the floor that morning,' said Samuel, 'still warm as if her heart was beating, but she was gone, Ida.'

'Who's we?' she asked without thinking.

He pulled up slightly at this. 'Barker and I.'

'Him?'

He smiled sadly at her. 'You find our arrangement perplexing, Ida, he can be very uncouth at times, I know, but you must believe me when I tell you he is indispensible to me. I would have fallen to pieces that day without Barker; I was distraught at the loss. He took care of everything, you understand, all the sad arrangements afterwards. There was no one else to do it, you see.'

Ida nodded.

'But I am afraid we have lost the battle to still the tongues of the town,' Samuel said, softly. 'People know what she did.'

'It would seem so – I'm sorry, Mr Hackett,' Ida said. She hated herself for having raised the matter with him so dishonestly.

Samuel nodded once and smiled at her again, with genuine warmth and gratitude. 'I was right to call you a friend.' He reached for her hand, grasping the tips of her fingers in his before letting them go again.

He continued past her to the great front door, where he stopped and turned to look at her once more. The door began to swing open behind him. 'My fiancée was unbalanced, do you understand?' he asked her.

Ida did.

'I don't know that you do understand it, Ida.' Samuel said, not unkindly. 'She hid it very well to begin with, you see, but by the end she could hide nothing from me. She was determined to destroy herself and that is what she did. I now know it was guilt at what she'd done to her sister that drove her to it.'

Ida opened her mouth to ask a question that burned inside her, but shut it again.

'You understand why I should have wanted such a shameful thing kept secret?' he asked her. 'Even if it was impossible to do so.'

Ida nodded. She did understand. 'The scandal.'

'Not for my sake, but for hers,' he pressed, 'for her memory. She was not a bad person, really. I have to believe that.'

The door was open behind him and Barker revealed himself, gloved fingers curling and flexing.

'She was like her sister once, like her sister is now,' Samuel said, and at once Ida saw everything. 'She had her sister's same innocence, her sister's same lightness,' said Samuel. 'Your new mistress is just how my fiancée was when we were betrothed; before the change came over her.'

'I understand, Mr Hackett,' said Ida, meaning it. He had loved Margaret and she had betrayed him with lies. Now Matilda had come into his life and perhaps he was hoping – however unattainable it might be – to love her in her dead sister's place. Was that a crime, Ida wondered? Of course it wasn't. No one would be hurt. 'I understand how it is,' she told him.

Samuel looked at her with deep affection in his eyes, before he turned to go inside. But as he crossed the threshold, Barker standing aside for him, he said over his shoulder, 'You will never tell your mistress how it happened, Ida. Promise me that?'

Ida shook her head. She would never tell.

'Matilda is everything her sister was,' said Samuel, 'and perhaps, if God allows, she will be everything her sister might have been.'

'Yes, Mr Hackett,' Ida said, moved for him.

Samuel entered the house and was gone.

Ida looked at her feet for some seconds, humbled, processing what she had learned. Then she remembered the question she had burned to ask but in the end hadn't dared. 'But how did she do it?' she whispered, giving voice to the thought. 'How did she kill herself?'

She looked up with a shock to see that Barker hadn't followed Samuel into the house. The dark servant stepped onto the porch, the whites of his eyes glowing beneath his hair in the glare of sunlight. 'That's a thing to ask,' he said. 'What would you use, cretin?'

She bristled. 'I beg your pardon?'

'To top yourself,' said Barker, 'I asked what you would use?'

'Mr Barker, I didn't mean anything by it—' Ida started to say.

'But you *did* mean,' he said. 'So what method would you fancy?' He grew impatient when she gave him nothing. 'Come on. Are you really so much of an idiot? How would you meet your Maker before your due time?'

Ida felt the muscles in her arms tighten. She felt like hitting him for his continued unpleasantness. It was a mystery to her why any of the girls in town had talked of him as if he was somehow special. He was repellent. The valet smiled without smiling, his mouth in a rictus of hard, white teeth, and his black eyes hard.

'Maybe I would use a noose,' Ida offered him.

'In the dining room?' Barker scoffed. 'You'd need a ladder for that to reach the chandelier, and still I'd not wager the thing would hold your great weight.' He looked her up and down, as if condemning her for girth she didn't even possess.

Ida set her jaw at him.

'Come on, then,' said Barker, 'is that the best you can do?'

'A pistol,' Ida suggested. 'I'd use a pistol.'

'With all that mess?' he said, laughing at her. 'Blood and brains all over the walls? You'd never get stains like that hidden without fresh wallpapering. Does the dining room look like it's fresh papered to you?'

'No,' Ida agreed, 'it doesn't.'

'What was that?'

'You heard me.'

Barker snatched her wrist in his grip, twisting it.

'Ow!' Ida gasped.

'So, what else is it, then?' he prodded her. 'You're hell bent on doing yourself a nasty, but you're yet to find the means. I said you were an idiot but maybe you're worse? Maybe you're a Mongoloid – thicker than dung?'

A tear of anger rolled down Ida's cheek. 'You're hurting me.'

'No more than the mistress hurt,' he chuckled, 'hurt so much she killed herself.'

'Poison,' Ida spat at him. 'I'd use poison.'

'Ah, now that'd take some brains.' He stroked his chin, pretending to contemplate the idea.

She pulled her wrist free of him. 'I might ask you a question, Mr Barker,' she said, eyes blazing. 'How do you seem to know so much about the Gregory sisters' silly childhood games? "So they say" was your explanation for knowing of it, but who is "they" and when did they tell you?'

He was brought up short.

'Here's another one,' Ida went on. 'Miss Matilda seemed to recognise you that day we took her away from the Hall, but not as a valet, she said. She seemed to think she knew you when you'd held some other position once.'

He scoffed. 'She's a nutter. She's lucky to remember how to use a bloody chamber pot.'

Ida was pleased to see he was defensive. 'Did you work here once before, many years ago perhaps . . . before you met Mr Samuel?'

His dark eyes flashed. 'You want a slap for an answer?'

'Are you all right there, Mr Barker?' said a voice behind them.

The valet spun around to find Aggie there. She wasn't looking at Barker but at Ida, her face fearful. 'Get back to your work,' he shot at her.

Relief made Ida feel giddy. 'Done it all,' she said, keeping her eyes fixed on Aggie, her saviour and friend. 'Got nothing left. Maybe I'll have the afternoon off?'

'No fear you will!'

'But I feel tired. Can I have a little lie down?' she asked, contemptuously.

Barker went to raise his hand.

'Mr Barker!' Aggie cried out.

The valet froze.

Aggie stepped past him through the door, taking Ida by the arm. 'Let me give you some jobs to do, you lazy girl,' she admonished her. 'Poor Mr Barker must be feeling very provoked.' They moved with speed together back into the entrance hall and toward the marble stairs. Not once did either of them turn to glance at Barker on their way to the floor above. Only when they had reached the safety of the Chinese Room, closing and securing the door behind them, did they catch their breaths and stare at each other.

'She poisoned herself,' Ida said finally, pale.

Aggie nodded, frightened by what had occurred.

'Mr Samuel said she was ill.'

'She pretended to be her own sister.'

'She must have been ill then.' Ida tried to convince herself that deception was evidence. 'She must have been very ill with all the guilt of lying about it. Miss Matilda locked up by the lie. Terrible guilt it must have been.'

'Yes. Yes, that was it . . .' Aggie trailed away.

'Poor Mr Samuel,' Ida remarked. 'Such a young and handsome man to suffer such a trick.'

'Yes,' Aggie echoed.

They fell quiet.

'Still, you've got to marvel . . .' offered Ida, thinking things through.

'At what?'

'Miss Margaret's cunning. She fooled poor Mr Samuel most of all.'

Aggie looked at her. 'What do you mean?'

'Well, Mr Samuel would have met Miss Margaret when she was living in the care of her old dad and Mr Hackett was working as his secretary.'

She watched Aggie try to order the facts in her head. 'Did you say Mr Hackett first worked for the late Mr Gregory?'

Ida nodded. 'That's what Mr Samuel said that day we took our mistress away from the Hall. He's a gentleman after all, he would have asked Mr Gregory for Miss Margaret's hand in marriage.'

'A woman may accept a man's proposal without her father's permission, Ida,' Aggie said, 'especially if her father's deceased.'

Ida scoffed. 'As if she'd have got herself engaged without observing the due proprieties,' she said. 'Of course her old dad was asked, you mark my words, even if the poor bugger was on his death bed when it happened. She might have been ill but she was still brought up proper. Both girls were.'

Aggie shook her head at Ida's logic.

'Well, I *know*,' said Ida, 'I've read lots of very interesting novels and I know how ladies are, and if our poor little mistress only got locked up under a falsehood once her dear old dad was gathered, then that means she was also around when Mr Hackett showed up in the first place and fell in love with her sister. I mean, where else would Miss Matilda have been but here?'

The real truth of this suddenly seemed to strike Aggie, even if Ida somehow missed the significance of what she had said. 'Ida, have you been eavesdropping with complete abandon?'

'Not really,' Ida lied.

'How else could you know such things?'

Ida waved this away. 'I just think about it,' she said, 'a lot. Therefore,' she added, looking quite triumphant, 'you have to marvel at just how cunning that Miss Margaret really was. Mr Samuel didn't know that the sister he was engaged to was really Miss Margaret and that the one who got locked away was really Miss Matilda. It's especially cunning when you consider that their dad must have told him who was actually who when he first turned up at Summersby. Yet still Miss Margaret managed to switch places and fool him later on.'

Aggie just stared at her.

'What is it?' said Ida, seeing her friend's expression change.

'My God, Ida, he *knew*,' said Aggie, aghast.

'We just said that, didn't we?'

'No, no, he *knew* who he was courting, he *knew* who he was proposing to,' Aggie whispered, 'it was Margaret – and he knew her by that name, of course he did. He knew everything.'

Ida squinted, not quite following the logic now, even though she'd been responsible for it.

'When Mr Gregory died and our mistress was collected to be taken away to the Hall,' Aggie elaborated, 'she would have protested who she really was, surely? She would have said she was Matilda, the wrong girl, but her lying sister would have claimed she was Margaret.'

'One sister's word against the other,' lamented Ida. 'Makes you wonder how anyone believed anything at all.'

'Exactly,' said Aggie, gripping Ida by the arm, 'so why *did* anyone else believe it? Because someone supported the lie, someone whose word held weight.'

Ida's puzzlement remained for another moment until she saw what Aggie meant. 'You don't mean Mr Samuel?'

Aggie nodded. 'He *lied* for Margaret . . . He knew everything.'

This shocked Ida greatly. 'He would never do that!'

'Well, he loved her, I suppose,' Aggie ventured, 'and perhaps, as Mr Gregory's secretary, he may have learned what was intended in the will.'

'That Margaret was to be sent to the Hall?'

'Yes,' Aggie went on, 'and perhaps it was all too much for him to allow because of his love for Miss Margaret . . .' She paused, considering another possibility. 'Or perhaps he just saw a golden opportunity.'

'What opportunity?' said Ida, feeling very upset on Samuel's behalf and regretting the conversation now.

'To make a dishonest profit,' Aggie suggested. 'And Margaret was very happy to oblige because she needed him so as not to get locked away. They hatched a plan together to lie to the whole world.'

Ida thought of the second will and the revelation it contained that dead Matilda was not Matilda, but dead Margaret. If what Aggie believed was true, then Samuel had known of this already and the will was not a revelation to him at all. If this was so then he would have been pretending throughout the entire meeting with Hargreaves Cooper, and then ever since. But how could he have carried this off?

Ida wrapped her arms about herself, shivering. 'I won't believe it of Mr Samuel, Aggie. I won't! Miss Margaret was the rotter, not him; he was tricked along with everyone else. And anyway, Margaret took poison in guilt, didn't she? That's what Barker wanted me to guess. So, why isn't Mr Samuel feeling guilty, then?' she asked. 'There's proof right there that he's blameless.'

Aggie gave her a wry look. 'What's going all the way to Melbourne to let poor Miss Matilda out of the Hall if it's not guilt then?'

Ida just screwed up her mouth, hurt on Samuel's behalf.

'I don't know about you,' said Aggie, 'but I don't like the sound of this one little bit and I intend looking out for my mistress – *our* mistress – where I can.' She folded her arms across her chest, determined. 'Are you planning on helping me, Ida?'

Ida tried to maintain a glare at her friend but failed. She nodded, looking away. 'Of course I will. What do you take me for?'

But to her mind 'helping the mistress' did not mean doing the opposite thing to Samuel. She knew he was blameless. Yet Ida's inquisitive mind would not be silenced, no matter how kind her heart.

One. Samuel and Barker were bound together by something unknown. Could it have been the shared secret of the mistress of Summersby's real identity?

Two. When eavesdropping Ida told Barker of what she had heard about the shocking deception and the second will he had taken it in his stride. Was this because there was no reason to be shocked if he already knew?

Three. Could both these things combined explain why Barker treated Samuel so contemptuously? Was the supposedly loyal valet using the secret to his own advantage?

'Has your memory always been so rotten?' Ida tactlessly asked, smoothing the silken fabric of the ball gown once Matilda had stepped inside and Ida had helped pull it up to her shoulders.

Aggie cringed, but said nothing to censure her. Four days had passed and Ida and Aggie were helping Matilda get dressed for the District Ball.

Matilda caught Ida's eye reflected in her looking glass. 'I can't remember.'

A smile appeared at Ida's mouth before she collected herself. 'Must be awful,' she said, 'not to recall the things that have happened to you.'

With Aggie holding pins ready to arrange Matilda's hair, Ida watched Matilda process this remark. More often than not, the lack of recollection meant nothing to Matilda at all, it seemed. Matilda plainly didn't know what it was to have her past at reaching distance. In Matilda's mind, Ida guessed, nothing was easily reached at all.

'Do you remember when you first went to the Hall?' Ida wondered.

'No,' said Matilda, shaking her head. 'I can't remember that.'

'What about your sister and Mr Samuel?' Ida pressed, with an eyebrow raised for Aggie's benefit. 'What do you remember of them being together?'

Aggie frowned at Ida, but still didn't say anything. She wanted to hear Matilda's answer, if she had one. She began to work on pinning Matilda's beautiful hair as the young woman thought upon this.

Ida recognised the startled look her mistress took on when something dislodged itself inside her mind.

'Matilda went to a ball once,' Matilda said.

Aggie and Ida looked at each other, pained. 'You are Matilda,' Aggie reminded her once again, gently.

'I remember what she wore!' Matilda exclaimed.

'What your *sister* wore, miss,' Aggie interjected, but Matilda leapt up from the dressing stool and made for the table at the side of her bed. 'Your hair, miss, careful . . .' Aggie called after her.

Matilda took the Moorish patterned box from where it sat on the bedside pile of books. She prized open the lid and seized the photograph that Ida had been surprised to learn was inside.

Ida only realised then that other items had since been placed beneath it. She saw what looked like letter paper and below that, the hint of some other object.

'See – see here,' Matilda said, dropping the box onto the bed. She held the photograph in her hand. 'This is what she wore – isn't it lovely?'

Ida and Aggie regarded the portrait with some interest. 'Beautiful,' Aggie murmured. She turned the photograph over and they both saw what was written there in smooth, flowing copperplate.

Matilda, 1884.

Matilda turned the photograph over again in Aggie's hands. 'That is what she wore to the ball.'

But Aggie studied the back of the photograph. 'Do you recognise the handwriting, miss?'

Matilda stared at it. 'It is my own,' she said at last.

Aggie nodded. 'You wrote your own name and the date on the back – over two years ago, not long before your father died and you went to the Hall – perhaps to help you remember?' She turned the photograph back to the portrait side. 'Because that's you there, isn't it?'

Matilda looked at the beautiful face in uncertainty. 'Is it?' She glanced up to see Aggie and Ida nodding.

'That's you, miss,' said Ida. 'You must have gone to a ball.'

Matilda resumed her seat, a little deflated.

'And I owe you an apology, miss,' said Aggie, pinning Matilda's hair. 'You told me before that Matilda went to a ball, and I said you were confused and that really you must have meant that Miss Margaret had been to one, but I see now that you really meant yourself. What else can you recall of it?'

Ida watched as Matilda tried to focus her mind. She wondered what images, if any, might be fighting to emerge: feet in dancing slippers, perhaps, laced with ribbons that wound tight around ankles; fingers at piano keys; a man with a violin; an airy hall on a balmy summer's eve.

'The Messieurs and Miss Roberts,' Matilda suddenly said, 'they gave us dancing lessons, Matilda and—' she stopped herself. 'My sister and I.'

Ida was delighted. 'You learnt as an accomplishment?'

Matilda nodded, delighted too. 'We went to Castlemaine,' she said, 'where the Messieurs and Miss Roberts had come from Melbourne to give lessons in a church. They taught us the quadrille, the waltz, the Balmoral, and the minuet.' She marvelled at the pictures that were plainly filling her head. 'My father had been urged to have us taught. He was informed that the skill of dancing was just as important as polite address, elegant manners and a kindness of disposition to equip young ladies for everyday life.'

Ida could tell that Matilda's mind was back in the past, hearing the piano, basking in effusive praise.

'I don't think I was very good at it,' Matilda said. 'I enjoyed it but I do believe my sister was much more naturally talented. She received compliments for it.' She looked back to Ida and Aggie to see the mild surprise upon their faces. 'What is it?' she wondered.

'It is pleasing to see you remember something like that,' said Aggie. 'Perhaps being back in your own home again is helping?'

Matilda looked at her reflection in the glass and seemed to like what she saw there. 'Oh, it is, Marshall,' she replied. 'It is helping me very much. My heart feels uplifted every day.'

Aggie smiled. 'That is because you are your own person again, miss,' she said, in a manner that she plainly hoped would ring true with the young woman. 'Your life is your own to live as you wish here. There is no one to decide things on your behalf anymore, no one to control you. You understand that, don't you, miss?'

Ida could tell that Matilda saw only love and hopefulness in Aggie's face. 'I do,' Matilda said. 'I will make all my own decisions here, you mustn't fear for me.'

Aggie now seized opportunity, and Ida realised that she had been steering the conversation to this very point the whole time. 'And perhaps you will decide on Mr Samuel's position soon?' Aggie wondered.

Matilda stopped. 'Brother Samuel?'

Ida's heart began to beat faster.

'As secretary, miss,' said Aggie, 'a position of service to a gentleman, certainly, but perhaps a less needed position in service to a lady . . .?'

There was silence. Desperate, Ida shot a pleading look to Aggie to desist, but she ignored her.

'Should Samuel leave Summersby's employ?' Matilda asked at last.

'Not in any disgrace,' Aggie said quickly, 'just as a means of maintaining propriety, that's all. So that people don't gossip.'

Matilda mused on the notion. 'Ask Samuel to leave . . .'

'Miss!' Ida went to pipe up in Samuel's defence, but Aggie spoke over her.

'*Tell* him to leave,' said Aggie, pushing it now. 'You're the mistress here, you pay his wages, and he's not your brother really, you know. The look Ida gave Aggie was furious, but she was unabashed. 'After the ball's over, I mean,' Aggie added, 'there's no need to spoil your fun.'

Ida waited, speechless with anxiety, as the idea of prising Samuel loose from Summersby sat with Matilda for the very first time. 'I had never thought of brother Samuel in that way . . .' Matilda whispered, 'as someone to *tell*.'

Ida's heart sank.

'No one's saying Mr Samuel is not a nice man,' said Aggie, plainly as much for Ida's benefit as Matilda's, 'but the need to keep him as your secretary is yours to decide, no one else's. We just want to help you see it, that's all.'

Matilda stood abruptly from the stool, causing Aggie to stumble back. 'You're wrong.'

Aggie was thrown. 'Miss?'

'Completely wrong,' Matilda said, frowning at her. 'The decision is not mine in this regard, far from it. Whether brother Samuel stays or leaves is nothing to do with me at all and I'm very cross with you for even thinking it,' she said. Matilda took to her dressing table, picking up items and dropping them again.

Aggie was mortified. 'But . . . but whose decision is it, then, miss, if it's not your own?'

Matilda rested the photograph of herself against her dressing table mirror. Then she turned to depart the room without answering.

'Miss?' Aggie shot after her. 'Whose decision is it?'

Matilda stopped in the doorway and turned to glare at Aggie. 'It is *my sister's* decision. She was engaged to brother Samuel.

All decisions about him must therefore be hers to make and hers alone – just as decisions have always been. Her love for me is unwavering, I will not betray her now.'

Ida's mouth fell open at the startling statement, but Aggie stayed composed.

Matilda looked fixedly at each of them from the door, letting the weight of her words sink in. 'It upsets me that you should even need to ask.'

Aggie saw her mistress's little purse sitting on the bed where she had forgotten it.

Ida was still reeling. 'She actually thinks her sister's *not dead . . .?*'

'No time for that, look what she's forgotten.'

'Sometimes she gives me shivers,' said Ida.

'Put your shawl on then,' said Aggie. 'I'm taking this down before I miss her.'

'No, you're not. I'll take it,' said Ida, snatching the thing from Aggie's hands.

She walked quickly into the hallway before Aggie could object, harbouring intentions of somehow putting in a good word for Samuel, to show that Aggie alone thought ill of the handsome secretary and that Ida held a different view.

She reached the stairs and looked down to the entrance hall below. She could see no sign of Matilda. 'Miss . . .?' she called hopefully. 'Are you still down there?'

No reply came, so Ida began to descend. 'You've forgotten your purse, miss!'

As she reached the first landing Ida felt the tiny hairs along the back of her wrists and forearms stand on end. It came upon her in an instant, the flesh beneath her sleeve prickling, and when she went to rub it with her hand she felt it ripple into gooseflesh. She shuddered; a familiar chill shot along her spine like a hard, iron hand was pressing at her, pushing her forward, willing her to trip and fall, to break her neck. She gripped the banister, looking slowly about her. She was alone.

Then and there she heard the sound of a dog's nails tapping somewhere upon floorboards high above. A cool draught stirred and she felt the now familiar motion of fresh air upon her skin. The gooseflesh prickled her shoulders, reaching her throat.

She heard the dog's nails louder, closer.

Ida stopped and turned again, truly frightened. 'Miss Margaret?'

There was nothing.

Filled with a dread of remaining where she stood, while still telling herself she was being a fool for getting the spooks in the first place, Ida held the marble balustrade tightly as she continued to the ground floor.

The reception rooms were deserted. Ida wondered whether Samuel could really have collected Matilda so quickly and driven away. There was light from the dusk outside, so Ida went to pull open the great door to look for Matilda. As she reached for the handle the door was pushed inwards from the other side.

It was Barker. 'Watch it,' he grunted, displeased to see her.

'Where's my mistress?' Ida demanded, refusing to be cowed by him. 'She needs her purse.' She looked past and saw Matilda in the distance, standing alone in the shadows on the long gravel drive.

'Leave off,' said Barker. 'She's with your fancy bloke.'

Ida shot him a disgusted look. 'Don't you think you should speak with more respect about the lady who pays you, Mr Barker?'

'I'll do as I please,' said Barker, picking at his hard, white teeth. 'Give it here.' He held out his hand for the purse.

Ida clutched it to her chest and barrelled past him. Smirking at her defiance, Barker stayed, watching her from the door.

'Miss!' Ida called out. 'Your nice purse, miss!'

Matilda turned. In the soft, pink light of sunset the expression upon her face was unearthly, as if she was standing in the garden enjoying the warmth of the summer's evening, yet not quite standing in the garden at all, but somewhere else, miles away. Ida ran towards her, boots crunching on the gravel, and in a moment arrived, panting, to slip the purse into Matilda's hand. She was struck by the strange expression on her mistress's face.

Ida launched into what she wanted to say. 'What Aggie said, miss, back in your room, it's not what I think, and I want you to know.'

Matilda looked at her uncomprehendingly.

'Aggie means well and she loves you, miss, everyone does, but she just worries for you, that's all, and the worry makes her say things that she knows she shouldn't.'

It now struck Ida that Matilda had not the faintest notion of what she was saying to her. 'Are you all right, miss?'

Matilda considered. 'I am well,' she said.

Ida placed her hand against her mistress's forehead to see if she was fevered, but Matilda pulled back in alarm. The look Ida returned was equally as startled. 'I didn't mean . . . You look a bit feverish. I wanted to see if you have a temperature.'

Matilda was looking at Ida in the very same way she'd looked at her the day in the library.

'What is it, miss?' asked Ida, feeling uncomfortable. 'Are you sure you still want to go?'

Matilda recomposed her features, making an effort to become more pleasing. 'Of course I wish to go, Ida, I couldn't possibly miss it,' she said. 'Yet, if only I could take a long walk around the grounds first, they are absolutely splendid in this sunset.' She pointed to a beautiful tree with glowing, golden leaves. 'Look at how the last of the rays light up the robinia's leaves . . .' Matilda closed her eyes, breathing in the garden's scents.

Ida looked to where her mistress had meant and then looked back at her. 'Oh, your hair,' she exclaimed. 'Whatever's happened to it? That's not how Aggie arranged it at all.'

Matilda shook Ida's fingers away. 'I don't care if it's loose. I prefer it.'

'Well, that's what you get for running down the stairs. The pins must have dropped out along the way.'

The sound of footsteps on the gravel made them turn. Samuel had come from the side of the great house. Ida gave an involuntary gasp at how handsome he looked in his evening clothes. She had seen little of him in the last few days, and looking at him now, as striking a man as she was ever likely to see, she couldn't stop questioning his actions in her mind. Had it all been pretend that day at the Hall when it had truly seemed as if each was meeting the other for the first time? She could believe it of Matilda; her damaged memory made so much seem like new to her, even when it wasn't. But what of Samuel?

Matilda didn't care that her own reaction to his appearance was noticed. 'You are resplendent,' she purred at him.

Samuel looked taken aback by this familiarity for a moment. Then Matilda's own appearance struck him in turn. 'And you are simply beautiful,' he told her.

She held his gaze, appraising him, a cat-like smile starting to curl about her lips. Ida was shocked anew to see such a wanton look clear in her mistress's face. It was the look she had had the night they found her in the hallway. 'Where is the carriage?' Matilda asked.

Samuel was lost in her eyes, lost in the heat of her look to him. But something seemed wrong to Ida, something she couldn't quite see. This was Matilda, who had been so alarmed when Samuel had tried to kiss her.

'Samuel?' Matilda prompted.

'No carriage this evening, I have a surprise,' he told her, remembering himself. 'Come with me to the stables.'

Matilda glanced at Ida. 'What could it be, I wonder?'

Ida felt awkward, in the way. 'Shall I go now, miss?'

'Whatever for?' laughed Matilda. 'You're coming with us tonight, remember?'

Ida did a double take.

Samuel held out his arm and Matilda slipped her own through his, her fingers brushing against the tight ball of muscles she found beneath his sleeve. She smiled appreciatively.

'Miss?' Ida piped.

'You're coming with us,' Matilda said, harder now. 'How can you have forgotten? I need you with me.' She turned to Samuel. 'Isn't that right?'

'Ida is very welcome to join us,' said Samuel. He seemed barely aware of Ida at all.

Ida was stunned. Matilda had never said anything about accompanying her. 'But . . . but what will I wear?'

Matilda waved her away, heading towards the rear of the house with Samuel.

Ida looked at her dowdy black housemaid's dress with despair. There was no time to change into anything more suitable – not that she had anything suitable anyway. 'I'll fetch my shawl!' she shouted to her mistress's back.

Ida returned to the grand front door to find Barker still slouched there, his smirk unchanged. He revealed a lit cigar, the tip glowing red as he sucked upon it. When he gave no sign of standing aside so that she might squeeze past, Ida made to barrel through him again. He stepped out fully, blocking the way altogether. 'Where d'you reckon you're going?'

'Let me in, please, Mr Barker,' said Ida, in no mood for him, 'I'm to go with the mistress.'

'Are you now? There's a treat. Mind you keep your eyes peeled.'

'Why?'

Barker tapped the side of his nose as if somehow she already knew the reason. He released a cloud of acrid smoke. Fed up, Ida made to force her way in – just as Barker kicked the door shut in her face.

'You'll be wanting the servants' entrance,' he shot at her from the other side.

The rough and raucous dancing so enjoyed in Castlemaine a generation earlier, when Matilda's father had made a fortune on the goldfields and Ida's grandfather had gone to a pauper's grave instead was looked upon now, with the town having outgrown its uncivilised start, as unsuitable, somewhat to Ida's disappointment. The boisterous hugging and swinging of partners, which the elders had once so enjoyed when young, was now viewed as offensive and objectionable behaviour by newer District folk seeking to create 'Society'. Ida just wished she'd been alive to witness it all before the wowsers spoiled the fun. With the New Year of 1887 marking the start of Queen Victoria's Golden Jubilee, the upper tier of Castlemaine was united in opposition to anything that risked the new and improved etiquette of modern dancing. For this class's younger people, and for those still facing a climb up the social ladder, ballroom dancing was the essential accomplishment. It was very plain to Ida, watching on as she was from the sidelines, that Matilda and her late sister were by no means the only ones to have benefited from the instruction of the Messieurs and Miss Roberts.

Samuel beamed broadly, welcoming the admiring stares of others as he and Matilda stepped onto the Town Hall's polished floor for the waltz. Her ears trained to the sound of their voices, Ida found she could largely follow what the two of them said to each other as they danced. 'Do you know,' Samuel to Matilda, his voiced raised above the music, 'the gaiety of Australian social life would be the envy of civilised nations if only the word would get out about it.'

Matilda seemed to Ida to be just as aware as Samuel was of all the pairs of eyes that found them fascinating. Matilda's head and feet were already lost in the music of the orchestra. She smiled back at Samuel, wonderfully happy, letting him lead her.

'And the ladies of the colony of Victoria, it has been my very good fortune to discover,' Samuel went on, 'are by far the most accomplished dancers in the Empire.'

Matilda's smile remained, her feet moving effortlessly, perfectly in time with the music's sweeping chords.

'The gift of dancing comes as naturally to you colonial girls as walking,' Samuel declared, his rhythm and poise matching her own. 'It is as rare to find a woman who dances badly here as it to find a woman in England who dances well.'

Matilda allowed her eyes to meet his in her obvious pleasure at the compliment. Ida glimpsed the desire there again and forced herself to glance away. Matilda's provocative look tantalised Samuel, teasing him on to do what? Ida didn't know. It was the most intoxicating look she had ever seen a woman give a man.

'*That's Matilda Gregory for certain, I'd recognise her anywhere.*'

Ida's head turned to see a tiny woman in green, dancing alongside them with a pencil-thin rake of a man.

'Miss Roberts!' Matilda exclaimed from the floor, clearly remembering the woman at once.

The lady nodded her head; her partner gave a courtly wave and bow, all without losing a step. 'Well, of course you're Matilda, who else would you be?' said Miss Roberts, gaily.

Samuel seemed to be looking for a gap in the throng that he might lead Matilda away from these two.

'It astonishes me so many people here could be confused by it, much less waste the whole evening talking about it,' the dance instructress trilled. 'All they ever need do is look at your feet, Matilda, your graceful feet!'

Matilda playfully pointed a toe.

Miss Roberts was appreciative. 'You were simply the finer dancer, *mon chéri*; your sister never attained the required elegance. I'm telling everyone who'll listen.'

Matilda beamed. '*Merci, mademoiselle,*' she said, in rather smoother French than Miss Roberts. '*Mon nom est Matilda.*'

Miss Roberts turned to her partner. 'You recollect it, too, *mon cher frère*?'

But the too-thin man looked pained and hissed something in French that was as badly accented as his sister's. Miss Roberts flushed to her hair. '*Mon dieu . . .*' she said, horrified, 'but why didn't you stop me?' She looked back to Matilda, mortified, and then to Samuel. 'I didn't know of the tragedy . . . We've been elsewhere for some time. Please forgive me my *faux pas*.'

Her brother spied a widening gap among the dancers before Samuel did and propelled the blushing Miss Roberts away.

Still watching intently from the side, Ida was left in some surprise by the strange exchange, and yet Matilda seemed untroubled by it. She and Samuel moved beyond Ida's earshot. The music transported Matilda, consuming her as she dipped and swayed in Samuel's strong, young arms. To Ida it seemed that the breath near left Samuel at the look she continued to return; a look that said without words that all other men were eclipsed by his presence. Desire must surely roar inside him to receive such a look, Ida supposed, even though she only half understood what desire was at all. To Ida it was an emotion closer to envy, for she felt very envious as she watched them, fantasising herself to be where Matilda was. Her own hair, her own eyes, her own smile would be just as enthralling to Samuel as the dead sister's identical looks had ever been – just like Matilda's features so clearly were to him. Ida wondered what it would be like to feel his soft lips press against her most sensitive skin.

Samuel and Matilda made a rotation of the Hall and Ida found that she could follow their conversation again.

'Why didn't you say that you had called upon me before?' Matilda was asking him.

Ida strained to catch the words, unsure she'd heard properly.

Samuel cocked his head, spinning Matilda around. 'What was that?' he asked, smiling.

'At Constantine Hall,' Matilda said, glowing from the exertion, 'that day you came for me – why didn't you say that you had already called upon me there once before?'

It seemed to Ida that Samuel experienced a sudden stab of dread.

'I am right, aren't I, Samuel?' Matilda beamed at him. 'You *did* come to visit me before, and when you did you charged me with a task.' The face she presented him was radiant with the triumph.

Samuel frowned as if puzzled, while seemingly still delighted by her amusing turns of talk. 'I'm afraid you have lost me.'

Matilda stopped still. The whirling dancers around them lurched off their feet trying not to collide with her.

'Then I must help you find yourself again,' Matilda told him, loud and clear, and no longer smiling.

Annoyed with having been sent off to find refreshments at the very moment when her inquisitive mind most wanted to be at the heart of the startling conversation, Ida returned to find Matilda seated with Samuel on bales of hay against a long wall at almost exactly the point where the Town Hall ballroom was dissected by a thick chalk line. On one half danced the 'scrub aristocracy': the bank clerks, the solicitors and their lads, the doctors and their families, along with their various employees, and with them the post office clerks and the storekeepers. On the other side of the chalk energetically danced the servants of all these folk, along with other people of ample aspiration for someday crossing the line, but with little means, at present, to succeed. There was small discernible difference between the two groups to Ida's mind; both were well turned out in their finery and greatly enjoying the dance.

Ida had procured refreshments; for Samuel a tankard of brandy and ice, known to all as 'smash'; for Matilda a cup of fruit punch.

'Do you know Mr Skews, Ida?'

Ida was startled to find herself the centre of introductions. Dr Foal's nervous young apothecary sat on the hay bale next to Matilda, at the very edge of the chalk line. 'Yes, miss, I have met Mr Skews.' She carefully handed out the drinks.

Skews nodded to Ida, scratching at his nostrils, before returning his attention to Samuel as the conversation was resumed. 'I was offering Miss Gregory here my deepest condolences again at the passing of her sister,' Skews said to him.

Ida realised that like her, Samuel had been apart from Matilda for some minutes, during which time Mr Skews had somehow appeared on the scene. The apothecary looked as if he would rather be elsewhere, and not conversing with the people from Summersby. He nervously rubbed at his nostrils again and sniffed.

'Your condolences were more than adequate at the graveyard,' Samuel told him.

'What graveyard?' wondered Matilda.

'We encountered Mr Skews there,' said Samuel. 'At the headstone. Do you remember?'

'It's of no matter if you don't, Miss Gregory, my word,' said Skews, sniffing again. His eyes were very watery and red, Ida noted. She put it down to the dust from the bales.

Samuel was patently little enamoured of the skittish apothecary.

'Oh yes, of course!' said Matilda, nodding at Skews. 'So kind of you come out all that way just to pay your respects to my father's stone.'

'Weren't they visiting Mr Skews' late wife?' Ida asked aloud.

Matilda blinked at her and turned to Samuel again. 'The apothecary has been telling me that it was he who found my sister's body. It must have been so distressing.'

Ida almost gasped, thrown to hear this extraordinary new information. Yet the look on Skews' face made her wonder whether he'd been saying anything of the kind at all. The man looked horrified. 'It was a very distressing thing to happen,' he managed to say, 'for everyone there.'

Samuel said absolutely nothing.

'How did she die again, Mr Skews?' Matilda asked.

Ida tried to look as if she wasn't listening as avidly as she was.

'Matilda, is this really a conversation to be had at the ball?' Samuel objected.

Skews' nervous red eyes met Samuel's again, but he answered Matilda's question. 'It was a bad turn, I believe, Miss Gregory, hard to comprehend, my word.'

'I wonder that I never thought to ask about it before,' Matilda pondered.

Ida saw Samuel glance sideways to see whether Matilda's eyes were upon his. They were. 'Or have I already asked it?' Matilda said. She went on before Samuel might answer. 'What does it *mean*,' she turned back to Skews, 'to have a "bad turn"?'

Skews seemed to struggle with finding the right words. 'Well, a person's body just gives out sometimes, Miss Gregory, suffice to say,' he replied. 'I've seen it happen many a time working with old Dr Foal, my word, yes. So hard for those left behind to try to understand it.'

Matilda nodded.

'The human constitution is the greatest mystery,' Skews went on. He pulled a handkerchief from his waistcoat and dragged it across his forehead before applying it to his nose. He was perspiring greatly in the heat of the ballroom. He scratched under his nostrils with a fingernail. It was raw from his doing it so much. His nervous eyes darted about the room, as if looking for the means of escape.

Matilda nodded again, seemingly lapsing into thought. Samuel took her hand, making to lift her to her feet. 'Shall we sample the air outside?' he wondered.

'Do you think she killed herself?'

Samuel stiffened.

'Do you?' she asked.

'Matilda, please . . .' he began, looking about him. Ida realised with alarm that she wasn't the only one whose attention was glued upon them. The residents of Summersby were of high interest to plenty of other ball goers.

Matilda turned to the apothecary. 'Was that really what happened, Mr Skews?' she wondered, remaining exactly where she was on the hay. 'From your experience of such sad things, do you think my sister took her own life and somehow it only *looked* like a turn?'

Skews was ashen. He shifted on his bale. 'Well, now, my word, Miss Gregory, I couldn't possibly say a thing about that sort of business.'

'Well, I don't think it,' said Matilda.

Ida was holding her breath.

'*I don't think it at all,*' she went on, 'not one bit. My sister would never have killed herself, and I should know. She was simply too fond of living, you see. She was simply too fond of *me.*'

The tankard slipped from Samuel's hand, spilling brandy to the floor.

Matilda only then seemed aware of herself. She placed a hand to her lips. 'Oh, please forgive me,' she stammered. She looked to the faces of those nearby. 'Please forgive me. I barely know what I say sometimes . . .'

Some of the eavesdroppers, but not all, looked away in embarrassment. Others kept their eyes fixed hard upon squirming Samuel.

'The apology is mine to make, Miss Gregory, my word it is.' Skews rose now and bowed, relieved the conversation was over. 'Tragedy leaves many questions in its wake, my word.'

Matilda rose and walked away, smiling in acknowledgment of the many pairs of eyes. 'How kind everyone is,' she whispered.

In the tiny window of time before Ida snapped to her senses and ran after her mistress, she witnessed Samuel grip Skews by his jacket sleeve and hiss something in his ear that Ida didn't catch.

'Mr Hackett . . . she came to me, I didn't start it,' said Skews, trying to explain.

'Remember you have two motherless boys . . .' Samuel pressed, pulling away from him now.

Skews paled and glanced away in fear, only to meet Ida's shocked stare.

Samuel caught up with Matilda just after Ida did. Ida dropped respectfully behind them as Matilda left on his arm, neither of them turning to look again at Skews. When they reached the coolness of the courtyard beyond the Town Hall doors, Samuel took a long, grateful gulp of summer night's air, looking around him only to see that Matilda had become an object of attention for yet more people outside. It was clearly too much for him.

'Let us stroll together,' he suggested. 'Ida can remain behind. You don't mind, do you? Perhaps you might secure me a second tankard of smash?'

His smile was as lovely as ever, as if nothing had occurred that was in any way strange. Ida bobbed, finding herself lost in him once more. Yet her mind was still racing. 'Of course, Mr Hackett.' She made to return inside to the refreshment trestle.

'Do you remember the task you gave me now?' Matilda asked him, sipping from her fruit punch.

Ida stopped, half turned to leave, her eyes already upon the doors but her ears on edge for whatever Samuel might say in reply.

'I'm not sure,' said Samuel, carefully. 'Do you remember it?'

Ida glanced to see that Matilda seemed about to answer and was creasing her brow as if trying to grasp at something, until whatever it was or might have been slipped away. 'No . . .' Matilda's face fell with the disappointment of it. 'No, I cannot now. I thought there was something, but now it's quite gone. Oh, what a shame, Samuel.'

'It is nothing I recall either, I'm afraid,' Samuel said, echoing her disappointment. 'Perhaps you were mistaken?'

He walked her from the chattering crowd and Ida's eyes, which followed them all the way to the shadows.

The pleasing tenor of Samuel's voice, the musical quality it possessed to Ida's ear, kept the orchestra's sounds alive during the long, moonlit journey home. Matilda and Samuel sat high upon a dray together, up front upon a candle box where Samuel steered the Clydesdale horses, this mode of transport being as unlikely for people of their class as it was also charming. Matilda had expressed delight at Samuel's sense of fun when he'd revealed this humbler choice of transport to her at the Summersby farmyard. He had wanted the evening to be memorable, he had said. Ida sat in the tray at their rear, cushioned by a spread of sacking cloth. To her mind the night was proving more than memorable, but not in any way that made sense. She had passed the ball in confusion, as if witness to a play performed in some unknown language. She knew there had been meaning behind all she had been privy to, but as to what it was she was in bewilderment. Everyone had been engaged in conversations in which the words were irrelevant; whatever it was that had really been discussed had been conveyed by some other means.

One. Why did Matilda believe that her sister had not taken her own life at all? If she didn't think Margaret had killed herself in guilt, then how did she think she had died?

Two. Did something bind Samuel and Mr Skews? Was it the same secret thing that bound Samuel and Barker? Had all three of them known of Margaret Gregory's deception?

Samuel was holding forth on a subject that seemed straightforward enough, but in light of the night's events Ida couldn't be sure. She strained to listen between the lines.

'It is my belief that we have entered upon an era of science discoveries without precedence,' he was saying to Matilda from the front of the dray. 'The wildest predictions of the most imaginative writers in the world will fall far short of what will actually be realised in the next fifty years,' he effused, 'just think of it.'

Matilda was giving the appearance of trying to do so, and Ida saw her hand slip inside his as his other hand held the reins.

'Read any journal of science,' Samuel went on, plainly enjoying her audience, 'and you will see it said that steam will be superseded. Scientists say we will experience the journey from London to Sydney made in no more than a fortnight. Imagine such speed! The efforts of science will then be directed, the journals say, towards extending the spans of our lifetimes – people may live well into the hundreds, thanks to the removal of disease.' He cast a beaming look to Matilda that she returned. 'There is so much to be hopeful for in the future,' he said as the dray made its way along the unlit track. 'Our lives will become that much more beautiful and that much happier.'

'Stop,' Matilda said.

'What's that?'

'Stop, if you please.' Matilda pulled free her hand.

Ida sat up straight in the back. 'What is it, miss?'

Matilda pointed into the dark. 'See there. Do you see?' She pulled at Samuel's jacket sleeve. You must stop and let me visit it once more.'

Ida strained to see what it was that Matilda meant. Vast eucalypts soared above, the moonlight dappled and diffused by branches. There was little to be seen but gloom.

'See it? Do stop, Samuel!' Matilda insisted.

He reined the great horses. Matilda leapt from the candle box to the ground in her beautiful ball gown before the dray had slowed.

'Miss!' Ida cried out in alarm.

'Matilda, do take care!' Samuel called after her.

Ida saw what was there deep in shadow from the trees, hidden from the glow of the moon. It was a bark and box hut, abandoned many years, but still upright, evidently well erected. Samuel gave the horses their heads and leapt to the ground after Matilda. She had vanished into the dark.

'Mr Hackett!' Ida cried after him, scared of being left alone. As quickly as she dared without risk of injuring herself, Ida shinned down the side of the dray and followed in Samuel's wake. She could just make him out ahead in the shadow.

He came to the hut's battered tin door, which was hanging ajar. 'Are you in here?'

Ida saw him vanish inside. 'Wait, Mr Hackett!' she called after him. Cobwebs fell in her eyes as she reached the door.

Matilda stood some way inside the hut, surveying the cramped and dirty room in the darkness. She turned to Samuel. 'It was my father's,' she marvelled. 'This is where he dwelled when prospecting for gold. It's where he found it, what's more. Long before he built Summersby, of course.'

Ida looked around at the rudimentary furnishings, the stark lack of modern comforts.

'It's barely fit for a native,' said Samuel.

'It suited him well,' smiled Matilda. 'He made his fortune in it. Married our mother, too.' She looked back to the dusty odds and ends scattered throughout the room. 'My sister and I were conceived in here.'

Ida's uncomfortable look was lost in the dark.

'I suspect only tiger snakes are conceived in here now,' Samuel suggested. 'Do let's go.' He held out his hand.

Matilda suddenly seemed to glimpse something within her own mind. 'I remember it now! Oh, Samuel, I remember it!'

'Remember?'

'My task,' she said, 'my task was writing messages – tiny little messages on scraps, never anything longer than a sentence, but so many of them.' She beamed with delight. 'Do you remember it now, too?'

The gloom hid whatever reaction Samuel had from Ida.

'Such a lot of little messages, such a lot of little scraps,' said Matilda. 'You said you admired my lovely hand. Surely you must remember it now, Samuel? You dictated every one of them I should write.' She strained to remember. *'Matilda says . . . Matilda says . . .'* She shook her head, as if the rest of the words wouldn't come. 'Just little things, fragments. *Matilda says . . .* I was so happy doing it.' She smiled warmly at him. 'Happy because I was pleasing you.'

Samuel said nothing. Ida felt her throat tighten, she was getting the shivers. 'Do let's go home now, miss,' she pleaded.

'I really am becoming whole again,' Matilda said, emotionally. 'It is your goodwill towards me that does it, Samuel, your attentiveness and care.'

'I am very glad of it.'

Eucalypt branches swayed in the breeze and the moon's glow brightened outside the hut's window. Ida saw the light strike a folded piece of paper wedged in a gap in the pane.

'Look,' said Matilda, seeing it, too. She made no move to take it.

Ida plucked the paper without thinking, just as Samuel's hand shot out to do the same. She opened it. It was a long letter, covering one side of a full foolscap page, and written in a stolid, unattractive hand, its writer having taken no pleasure in the appearance of the thing. She saw the words *Dear Margaret* before her eyes fell somewhere on the second paragraph.

. . . We played this little game in an unusual way. Rather than each of us swapping identities, only one of us would make the change. I, the sister whose mind was whole, would tell the Summersby household that I was really you. You, the twin whose mind was so cruelly damaged, never swapped at all . . .

Matilda abruptly slapped the note from Ida's fingers as if it was burning her. Shocked, Ida looked up as Matilda moved to the open tin door, rubbing her hand against the silk of her gown. 'Let's go,' she said, 'I have kept us too long.'

She ran outside towards the waiting dray.

Alarmed, Samuel looked after her and then to the dusty hut floor.

Ida was the most bewildered she had been all night.

'What did it say, Ida?' Samuel's composure had left him.

Ida tried to tell him. 'It was some kind of letter, Mr Hackett, about the twin Gregory girls, I think.'

He was very shocked. 'The handwriting – what did it look like?'

Ida tried to describe. 'Not very nice, there were ink stains all over it.'

'Are you sure?'

'Yes, Mr Hackett, it was very messy.'

He seemed incredibly relieved. 'Help me find it, Ida, whatever it is. It may be important.'

She joined him in the dirt, trying to find it again. 'But what was she talking about – writing little messages on scraps?'

Samuel paused. 'Ida, are you truly my friend?'

'Of course I am, Mr Hackett—'

He shook his head, stopping her. 'Friendship is so easily professed, anyone can claim it; it falls from the lips without thinking.'

'I'm your friend,' Ida implored him, 'you know that I am.

I'm your loyalest friend if you'll put me to the test, but tell me what is happening here?'

Emotion caught in his throat. 'Ida . . .' he began, 'Margaret was very unwell, you realise that now.'

'Yes, sir.'

'And Matilda is her sister, her twin sister . . . her *identical* twin.'

'Of course, but what is it, Mr Hackett, what is this all about?'

'Her mind, Ida, her memory – have you noticed how she changes, how her very manner of being can seem so different, so completely different, from one occasion to the next? Tell me I'm not the only one who has seen this in her, Ida?'

Ida swallowed. 'I have seen it, too, Mr Hackett.'

He was helpless. 'Thank God I'm not alone in this. So help me, Ida, I am starting to fear that perhaps she is identical to her late sister in more than just her appearance. I am starting to fear that Matilda, like her sister, is *ill.*'

They did not find the letter that had been placed in the window-pane. Whatever it had been, it remained lost to them in the dark.

In the Chinese Room, well past midnight, Ida and Aggie picked and carried items, rehanging clothes, putting away hats and shoes, and rearranging things that did not need rearranging as a means to pass the time while they talked. Having returned from the ball, and with Matilda and Samuel taking refreshments downstairs in the drawing room, Ida gave Aggie her impressions of the night's events. Aggie was trying her best to make any sense of it.

'You say this Mr Skews found Miss Margaret's body?'

'That's what was said,' Ida told her, 'although he seemed very nervous that it had been said at all. He was very nervous all round, scratching at himself and sniffing. And Mr Samuel didn't like him talking to the mistress about it one little bit, but I think Miss Matilda was the one who started the conversation with Mr Skews in the first place. It was very strange.'

Aggie clearly didn't know what to think of this.

In her mind Ida saw an image of Margaret dead on the floor, poisoned by her own hand. 'Mr Samuel was very upset by it.'

She thought of what had happened in the hut. 'And then there was the letter, just popped inside a crack in the windowpane for someone to find it – and we did find it – right after the mistress remembered that she had once written some 'message scraps' she called them, when at the Hall. I hardly got to read it before she slapped my hands and I dropped it. We couldn't find it again in the dark. It was something about twins changing places to trick people.' The next part was very troubling to Ida because she knew it would feed Aggie's growing unease about Samuel. 'She said she had written the message scraps for Mr Hackett . . .'

Aggie stopped folding clothes. 'Written messages *for* him?'

'She said he had once come to the Hall and *asked* her to write them.'

'What for?'

'Well, that's just it – Mr Samuel didn't know what she was talking about. He really didn't.' She hesitated, thinking on what Samuel *had* said. 'Aggie, what if she's ill, really ill, just like Miss Margaret was ill – ill inside her mind?'

Aggie studied her, frowning. 'He did know her already, just like I thought, he knew who she really was. She just couldn't remember it before.'

'That's not what's important here – you're not listening.'

Aggie was disgusted. 'Why wouldn't he have mentioned any of that himself then, Ida? Why would he have pretended they were strangers that day?'

Ida felt anxious. 'Because they were strangers, don't you see? He didn't know what she meant by any of it!'

'The mistress's sister took her own life, don't forget!'

Ida remembered then what Matilda had said. 'But that's another thing, the mistress doesn't think she did at all.'

'She said something?'

'She asked what Mr Skews thought about it, whether he thought her sister had killed herself – he didn't know what to say in reply when she asked. Then she said that she didn't think her sister killed herself anyway.'

Aggie blinked at her.

'It's what she said,' Ida was emphatic. 'I heard her. She said she didn't think that's what happened.'

'Then what did happen?'

Ida just looked helplessly at her. 'I think she might be ill . . . think about it, Aggie.'

Aggie's face set in determination. '*No.* Something's going on with that Mr Hackett and it's going on right under our very noses.'

But Ida couldn't agree. 'It's the mistress who is acting so strange,' she insisted, 'stranger than she normally is – ten times stranger. You weren't there to see it. It's the things she's been coming out with all night that put him so on edge. I've never seen her like that before, Aggie. I know she's always a bit odd, but tonight she was *really* odd.'

'She's just confused,' defended Aggie, 'she doesn't see him as she should because he's so nice to her. She can't conceive of someone nice meaning her harm.' She gave Ida a pointed look. 'And she's not the only one.'

'But he is nice!' Ida insisted. 'If there is something going on he's not part of it, I swear to you. More likely it's disgusting Mr Barker! Or that sniffing Mr Skews! I think they've both got something over him—' Ida's attention was suddenly distracted by something. 'Well, knock me down,' She pointed to the Moorish box at the end of the bed where Matilda had opened and forgotten it. 'That blessed thing's got a mind of its own.'

'What's wrong with it?' said Aggie, reaching for the box. But Ida got there first. Pulling aside some folded writing paper on top, she uncovered the sapphire vial.

'The pretty blue perfume bottle. It must have been the mistress who took it!'

'Didn't you say you found that in the dining room?'

'Oh, I did,' said Ida, cradling the glass, 'I found it twice. I put it on the dressing table after the first time but then it went and disappeared. When it turned up in the dining room again I put it back on the dressing table. Then it took off a second time,' Ida marvelled, 'but I suppose I shouldn't think anything odd when it comes to our mistress – if only you'd start believing me.' She shook the contents of the vial. 'She hasn't felt a burning need for the stuff.'

A sickening look came over Aggie. 'Drop it . . .'

'What's that?'

'Drop it . . . drop it, Ida!'

'But it's so nice?'

Aggie struck at the vial and it fell from Ida's hand, landing upon the bed.

'What the matter with you, for Gawd's sake?'

Aggie clutched at her. '*It's the poison.*'

'No, it's not, it's just scent. I opened it.'

Aggie's eye went to the folded letter Ida had scooped aside. On impulse, she picked it up, unfolding it. Her eyes widened.

'What's wrong now?' said Ida, rubbing at her hands.

Aggie showed her.

Dear Margaret,

This is for your Remember Box.

At about the time of our father's long illness he hired a private secretary. This young man was Samuel Hackett. Well turned out and extremely handsome, Mr Hackett was an arrival from England, where he had been born and raised in the very best of circles. He was also of reduced prospects. As the third son of gentry Mr Hackett could inherit nothing of his family's fortune.

Samuel Hackett was a profoundly indolent gentleman who attempted to better himself only by use of his looks and charm. Honest work and industry were unknown to him. Our father hired Mr Hackett because of his charm. It is also possible that he saw in his secretary a son-in-law. The Englishman was tall and well formed; ladies liked him. He was not especially bright. In the likelihood of love arising, perhaps our father guessed that I, his heiress, would be less likely to have my fortune wrested away in wedlock if my groom was beneath my intelligence. But if so, then our father underestimated both his secretary and his daughter. Samuel Hackett possessed a fine talent for low scheming – along with the patience to carry such things out – that was little hinted at by his good looks. I, on the other hand, possessed such utter unscrupulousness that our father, should he ever have guessed at the true extent, would only have been hastened to his end.

Samuel may have believed he was first to uncover the clause pertaining to me inheriting the estate and you becoming confined, but I knew of it before he did, before Samuel was even hired by our father. Samuel's arrival at Summersby was a pleasant happenstance for me, manna from the heavens. Samuel's arrival gave me the very best means to carry out a plan that could only have been conceived by someone who is an identical twin.

Some people fail to understand what it really means to be a twin. Our father, despite having sired twin girls, was one such person. In willing you, following his death, to be confined for your own protection to Constantine Hall he failed to grasp what separation feels like when born as one of two. The very notion of being kept apart from one's 'other self' is too horrific to contemplate. It is like death.

When I learned of what our father intended, despite being named as his heiress, I vowed one thing: you would not remain apart from me. But to achieve this required much cunning. The will's clauses were cast iron. Any departure from our father's instructions would have seen either of us cut off with nothing. I dearly loved you, but I loved the money, too. So, I intended to have both.

Your sister who loves you,
Matilda

It was the same unattractive lettering, marred by spots of ink. Ida blinked in the lamplight. 'It's just like the one in the hut.'

Aggie took the letter back from her. 'But she didn't write this.'

'Yes, she did – there's her name.' Ida squinted at the displeasing lettering. 'She put the first letter in the windowpane just before Mr Samuel and I followed her in there. She put this one inside the box.'

Aggie went to the dressing table and took up the mounted photograph Matilda had placed against the looking glass. 'I don't dispute that it looks very much like she put the letters there, Ida,' she told her, 'but she certainly didn't write them.' She turned the photograph over, showing Ida the writing on the reverse. 'Our mistress wrote her own name here, see, along with the date.' She held this next to the wording on the letter. 'The handwriting is very different.' Indeed it was: the photograph back showed a smooth copperplate; a lady's lovely hand.

'That's not her handwriting,' said Ida.

'Of course it is,' said Aggie, 'I'd know it anywhere.'

Ida tried to recall the day she went into the library and found Matilda at the writing desk. Hadn't she seen thick, uneven words like those on the letter, worthy of a knuckle rap? Or had she seen the same smooth, finely worked penmanship on the back of the photograph?

Aggie was adamant. 'That letter is not in her hand. It's far too ugly. She's very proud of her handwriting.'

Ida thought of what shocked Samuel had asked her in the hut when they'd found the first letter – *what had the handwriting looked like?*

Ida felt she had to accept what Aggie said. She still knew their mistress better, after all, ill or otherwise. 'Yet she put it inside the thing that's called the Remember Box,' said Ida, 'along with the blue glass and the photograph.' She re-read the lines.

Aggie seemed to guess where Ida's mind was wandering. 'Ida, Margaret Gregory is stone cold dead in her grave,' she reminded her.

'You don't have to bloody tell me about it!' Ida protested. 'Our mistress is the one thinking there's spooks in the night!'

An awkward pause fell between them.

'I hear that poor little dog sometimes . . .' Ida confessed. 'I heard it on the stairs.'

Aggie blanched, as if stung by a memory of Yip left behind at the Hall.

Ida's eyes brimmed with tears. 'Miss Margaret's poor dog, it died when she died, in the dining room. I heard it in the night.'

This was the first Aggie had learned of any dogs at Summersby, ghosts or otherwise. 'Ida Garfield, you did not hear anything of the kind.'

Ida bit at her bottom lip. 'I know what I heard.'

Aggie scoffed at her. 'Now we're just being silly and spooking ourselves.'

'The ghosts of suicides wander the earth,' Ida whispered. 'That's what they say.'

'Didn't you say you heard a *dog*? Pets don't suicide.'

'Well, I don't know what to think,' Ida wailed. 'I'm just trying to get to the bottom of things.'

They each sat on the bed.

Ida poked at the vial with a finger. 'Rosemary oil, that's all it is, harmless. Nothing like a poison at all. I'll show you.' She picked up the glass again and twisted at the stopper.

'Ida, for goodness sake!'

'Keep your hair on, I won't bloomin' drink it, will I?' Ida struggled with the thing. The stopper was tight. 'Cripes, it's like it's been glued shut.'

'Please take a bit of care!'

The stopper came loose with a pop.

The unmistakable smell of rosemary reached their nostrils.

Ida sniffed deeply. 'See, it's nice.'

Aggie thought she heard a floorboard creak from the hallway. 'It's Barker,' she hissed. She slid off the bed and crept to the door, listening.

Ida placed her nose closer to the vial, inhaling the scent. 'Odd . . .'

Aggie pressed her ear to the door panel. 'He's not coming inside here,' she vowed, 'he'll get the fight of his life if he tries, the disgusting man.'

A louder creak from behind made Aggie turn around again with a start.

Ida slumped senseless to the floor, the vial and its contents spilling from her fingers.

BIDDY

DECEMBER 1903

4

*B*iddy sensed she was sprawled upon the flagstone floor, her head cradled in Miss Garfield's lap, a wet towel applied to her forehead. She was awake, yet somehow not. She felt her chest struggle to rise with each breath. She heard Sybil cry out in shock.

'What is it? What has happened to Biddy?'

Biddy sensed Mrs Marshall there, trying to speak but somehow not making herself lucid.

'Biddy has had a turn,' said Miss Garfield, sounding very strained. 'I found her fallen in the stillroom. I managed to pull her out here but she is still unconscious.'

Biddy sensed Sybil fly to her side and take her unresponsive hand. 'Biddy, Biddy . . .' Sybil rubbed her fingers and palms. 'You must wake up, Biddy; you're giving us a nasty fright.'

But Biddy stayed still.

'We must send for the doctor, Mrs Marshall,' Sybil implored.

Biddy sensed Mrs Marshall was shaking, still unable to speak, rooted to the floor.

'I have sent a farmhand to town in the trap to fetch him,' said Miss Garfield.

Sybil started to cry. 'Oh, please wake up . . . This isn't very fun of you at all.'

Biddy's eyes flickered.

'Biddy!' cried Mrs Marshall, finding her own tongue again. She took the towel from Miss Garfield's hands and dabbed at Biddy's cheeks with it. 'There you are, come back to us now, that's the way.'

Biddy murmured and groaned. 'My head . . .' She opened her eyes and shut them again, the glare from the windows painful.

'There, there,' said Mrs Marshall, 'you lie still.'

'Rosemary . . . It was only rosemary . . .'

The housekeeper's voice caught in her throat. 'What did you say?'

'That's all it was, just rosemary.'

Biddy opened her eyes again to see the housekeeper looking as if she was experiencing a sickening deja vu.

'Mrs Marshall, not you, too!'

Biddy saw the housekeeper catch at Sybil's arm and succumb to a faint of her own.

When the commotion was all over and the patients, both, examined by a doctor from town, Mrs Marshall nodded in assent that bed rest was essential for herself and Biddy, and of several days duration, if not a full week. Mrs Marshall had been meek in the face of medicine, blaming the cessation of her monthly bleeds for her fainting spell. The doctor was sympathetic and easily swayed, turning his attention back to Biddy, whose own collapse was viewed by him with rather more mystery and significantly less conclusion. 'The onset of womanly maturity' was the best he could do, which was likely a tactful avoidance of the most likely culprit, Mrs Marshall's bread. Biddy knew it was by no means unknown for rye to go rotten before it was baked. People who ate it could end up with hallucinations, or worse. Mrs Marshall was far too respected for anyone to cast aspersions at her baking, but the unsaid was clear. She said she would take it upon herself to dispose of all the baking ingredients as a caution.

Once the doctor had gone and Summersby returned to quietude, Mrs Marshall removed herself from her bedroom and descended the stairs. Reaching the deserted kitchen, she slipped out the rear door and entered the kitchen garden. She moved swiftly along the path that led to the far wall gate, which, when pushed aside, revealed a stretch of the Summersby grounds with the little stone cottage for the outdoors staff in the distance. Shielding her eyes in the late afternoon sun, the housekeeper began the short walk to get there, the hem of her dress snagging and catching at grass seeds.

'Where are you going, Mrs Marshall?'

The housekeeper turned with a start to find Biddy watching her from the garden gate. She had followed the housekeeper when she'd seen her making her way down the stairs. Just like Mrs Marshall, Biddy had no intention of remaining in bed if she was feeling better.

'To the groundsmen's cottage,' said Mrs Marshall. 'There is a fellow in there I haven't seen in some time. I like to check on him when I can.'

'Do you mind if I join you for the stroll?' Biddy wondered. 'I'm feeling that much better for having a little rest.'

Mrs Marshall looked as if she would have liked to say no, so Biddy started walking through the grass anyway before she could get the chance. Mrs Marshall frowned but didn't object. Biddy's near miss with the rotten rye seemed to have tempered the housekeeper's sternness towards her to a degree.

They reached the cottage, seeing ample evidence of those who lived inside from the kicked-off boots and spat-out cigarette ends. It was an inescapably male domain.

'Who lives here then?' Biddy wondered. She'd never gone to this part of the grounds before.

'Lewis and his cousin,' said Mrs Marshall. 'And their uncle.'

Biddy caught at the name. 'Lewis?'

'He works in the grounds.'

Biddy tried not to look as keenly interested as she was. 'I don't think I've met him before. He's the one who found Joey the first time, isn't he? Is he an old bloke then?'

'No,' said Mrs Marshall. 'He's the same age as his cousin – twenty-one, I believe.' She seemed to brace herself, composing her face as she took her bare knuckles to the cottage door.

Biddy braced herself, too. Would handsome Lewis Fitzwater come to the door and see her standing there on the doorstep and get the surprise of his life? She hoped in her heart that he would, and that it would be a surprise, too – a nice one.

The knock went unanswered. They waited, Mrs Marshall thinking in silence for a moment, not bothering to knock a second time. Without saying a word to Biddy, she walked around to the side of the cottage, her eyes fixed hard on one of the high windows.

Biddy followed her. 'I don't think anyone's home, Mrs Marshall.'

Halting beneath the window, the housekeeper stood on her toes to peer through the glass, but wasn't tall enough. An old candle box caught her attention. 'Help me, will you, Biddy?'

Dragging it from where it had been left, Biddy helped Mrs Marshall place it where she could climb on top and achieve her desired view. Face pressed to the grimy glass, Mrs Marshall cupped her hands to her eyes, the better to see in with.

'What's inside?' Biddy asked.

Mrs Marshall stepped down from the box, satisfied.

'What did you see?'

Mrs Marshall started striding in the direction of the great house again. 'I saw that deja vu is only that and nothing more, Biddy,' she replied over her shoulder, 'and I was a silly woman for ever fearing otherwise.'

Biddy was set to follow when an impulse seized her. With one eye on the retreating housekeeper, she jumped onto the box and peered where Mrs Marshall had peered.

Little was clear in the gloom at first, until the shocking form of a grey, cadaverous man rose and gaped at her from a narrow iron bed. What struck Biddy most were his eyes: as cold and black as jet; piercing out from beneath a net of greying hair. They were eyes that could see right through her; hateful eyes; windows to an ugly, misshapen soul. A pair of battered crutches leant against the wall. This was the 'fellow', as Mrs Marshall had called him. He was plainly crippled and sick. Shuddering, Biddy leapt down from the box, and ran after Mrs Marshall, ashamed for acting like some Peeping Tom.

When Mrs Marshall returned to her kitchen, she went to a large dresser drawer labelled 'castor oil' and opened it. No castor oil was inside; rather, she kept in the drawer a number of homely items she had made with her own hands: a display of pressed violas arranged in a pretty frame; a little Australian coat of arms done in needlepoint; a pair of knitted mittens; a collage of pretty girls clipped from ladies' journals; a doll made from the Japanese silk of a torn cushion cover. The drawer was deliberately, misleadingly labelled so that no one would ever wish to open it but her.

Mrs Marshall selected the pressed violas in the frame just as Biddy came inside. Mrs Marshall looked up at her once and then returned to her task.

'Was that the uncle?' Biddy asked. 'Alone in the bed? He didn't look very well, did he?'

Mrs Marshall didn't admonish her for looking in the window. Biddy didn't think she would anyway, given she'd done the same thing. 'Mr Barker has reaped what he has sown,' she told her by way of reply. Nothing else was forthcoming.

Mrs Marshall wrapped the frame in a length of linen, and then added a layer of plain brown paper. Before tying the paper with string, she slipped inside a little card, on which she wrote in ink some brief words.

Mrs Marshall tied the package tight and then turned her pen to inking an address she clearly knew by heart. When that was done she placed the package in her wicker shopping basket. The entire process, taking no more than five minutes, had plainly made Mrs Marshall feel somewhat better in her heart and mind, Biddy thought, because she became more cheerful.

'Why don't we make one of your delicious brown soups, Biddy?' she suggested.

The importance and significance of telegraph messages at Summersby did not occur to Biddy at first. The warm summer days stretched into mid January, which was when she casually noted the wire that stretched from a connecting box. The box was perched high on the house's outer eastern wall; the wire that ran from it was supported by poles that stretched across a section of the grounds and disappeared into the distant paddocks. Biddy didn't consider the wire again for several days, presuming it to be the bearer of electricity, just like the wires she knew in Melbourne. But it was only after she had experienced playing cards by the light of kerosene lamps that it struck her that electricity wasn't present in the great house. Then she looked at the wire anew and wondered if it was the means of sending telegraph messages. This intrigued Biddy. She pondered on what a place Summersby was to possess a private means of communication enjoyed by no other house she had known. She studied the direction the wire came from and guessed it began at Castlemaine.

Biddy decided then to determine which room it was that housed the telegraph machine. By gauging the exact position of the connecting box outside, Biddy surmised that the corresponding room lay somewhere in the Summersby attics. These were servants' rooms, but with Summersby's indoor staff being countable on one hand, there were far more rooms than staff to sleep in them. It made sense to put the telegraph machine somewhere up there, too.

Biddy ascended the servants' stairs to reach the third storey. On her mission to find the room that met the connecting box, Biddy located the most likely by deductive reasoning. There was a door she had noted in passing for its unusual appearance; a door half disguised to look more like the wall that supported it. This door was locked, which was also unusual. Biddy could think of no other door in the house to which entry was barred. Peering through the keyhole gave Biddy nothing.

The importance and significance of Jim Skews' role at Summersby did not occur to Biddy to begin with, either. She noticed the tall, lean and quite attractive young man appear very early one morning in Mrs Marshall's kitchen before the house-keeper ushered him through the baize door to another part of the house. With the glare of the morning sun in her eyes as he'd come inside, Biddy's heart had almost leapt to her mouth when he'd greeted Mrs Marshall. The young man bore a resemblance to Lewis Fitzwater, being very similar in voice and frame. He was certainly handsome, but in a sign that good looks are never quite all, there was something about his manner that Biddy was unsure about. Somehow more guarded than Lewis, Jim tipped his bowler hat at Biddy as he passed without a word. She didn't see him leave.

Biddy didn't think of Jim Skews again until his second appear-ance, one week later, when she was sitting in the kitchen garden with Joey by her side for company. She was blacking Sybil's boots for want of something better to do, all while keeping an eye out for Mrs Marshall in the process. Jim appeared loping along the path from the direction of the stables.

'Hello again,' he called to her, tipping his bowler. He carried nothing else with him and stooped to give Joey a pat.

'Hello,' said Biddy, having no idea who he was or what he did for the household.

Later, when Biddy was returning Sybil's shining boots to her room she encountered Jim on the servants' stairs descending from the third floor.

'You again,' he said. The hat stayed on his head, but he flashed his toothy smile at her. Joey was close by her heels and Jim stooped to pat him again.

'Me again,' said Biddy, smiling back for politeness's sake.

'Just off for my dinner,' said Jim. 'Mrs Marshall's pasties make it worthwhile.' He winked at her as he passed and continued heading down.

'They are nice, aren't they?' said Biddy after him.

It was only once she had returned the boots to Sybil's bedroom that it occurred to her that she could think of no other purpose for Jim being on the third floor except one. Darting up the stairs again to the landing, Biddy made sure that all was quiet before she ducked along the hallway to the room she imagined the telegraph machine resided in.

She tried the unusual, half-disguised door. 'Still locked, Joey,' she said to the little dog.

'Mrs Marshall's not ready for me yet,' said a voice behind her.

Biddy leapt out of her skin.

'It's only me,' said Jim. 'Did I give you a scare?'

Glad now that he'd already seen her when she was blacking Sybil's shoes, Biddy felt a story forming. 'Should this door be locked?' she asked, recovering.

He frowned. 'Shouldn't it?'

'Not if I'm supposed to clean inside it,' said Biddy.

Jim's smile flashed again, in what was clearly an automatic response to things that required his consideration. 'I didn't notice it was dirty.'

'Well, Mrs Marshall did . . .'

The smile flashed again. 'We've met but we haven't met, Miss—'

'Biddy,' said Biddy. 'I work here, you know.'

'As do I,' said Jim.

'Not often,' said Biddy. 'I've only seen you here twice.'

'I'm in here as needed,' said Jim. 'Once or twice a week, sometimes more.'

Biddy just waited. The door stayed locked. Joey the pup looked up at her expectantly.

'Fair enough then,' said Biddy. 'We might as well go downstairs together for a pasty. I'll tell Mrs Marshall you didn't think the room needed cleaning then, shall I?'

He fumbled in his waistcoat pocket. 'Don't go getting her all upset. She might think she can find another lightning squirter in this district but I can tell you now there isn't another one for fifty miles.'

'A what?'

He produced a key that Biddy recognised, if not for the key itself, but for the little bit of string used to mark it. She realised that it normally lived on Mrs Marshall's big brass key ring.

'Lightning squirter,' said Jim. 'Just put a cork in it and let me enjoy my pasty, eh?' He said with a wink. He unlocked the door and opened it. Biddy felt a draught of air upon her face, unexpectedly cool. 'Where's your cleaning things?' Jim asked her.

Biddy thought on her feet. 'In the cupboard, where they're supposed to be.'

He nodded and left her to it. 'I'll go back down. Maybe there'll be a copy of the *Mail* I can read while my dinner does its last in the oven.'

Biddy nodded at him and ducked inside the door, Joey following her. She stood a moment listening to Jim's footsteps recede down the hall. When she was certain he was gone, she turned and was surprised to discover what was inside.

It wasn't a room so much as a staircase. Narrow and wooden, it wound in a spiral to an unseen floor above. It was gloomy and close, but the room above was light-filled, spilling sunshine on to the uppermost stairs.

'It's the tower,' Biddy realised. 'What a twit I am for not guessing it. Stay here, Joey,' she whispered.

The dog ignored the command and followed, sniffing every stair he mounted with particularly keen interest. The sound of his claws on the boards seemed to become magnified by the unusual dimensions of the room. The effect of it was very strange.

When Biddy reached the space above she was pleased to find confirmation of her powers of deduction. The light and airy upper room was filled with sunshine from four round windows that afforded a lovely view of the grounds. It would have made a very charming bedroom, Biddy thought, and she wondered if anyone had ever lived up here in the past. The room itself contained a banker's swivelling chair fronting a sturdy oak table, upon which rested a telegraphic machine. A relatively compact device, similar in size to a lady's largest hatbox, it was handsomely made and looked well cared for. A second machine, less impressive and lacking the tortoiseshell keys and glass valves of the first, sat alongside. Biddy guessed this was the means of empowerment; some kind of chemical battery. A ladder and trap door in the corner of the room led to the tower roof.

Pleased with herself for having solved a puzzle, Biddy would have left the room following a cursory wipe of the dust had it not been for the papers laid in a wire desk basket labelled 'Out'.

Biddy recognised Miss Garfield's penmanship on the uppermost sheet, and before she knew quite what she was doing, she read what it said.

. . . progress with the translations of Tacitus has afforded me the greatest pride of all in Sybil's achievements this week, a pride I have little doubt you will echo tenfold when you learn of it . . .

Biddy felt her heart race. It was a letter penned to one or more of Sybil's relatives. It was clearly not to be entrusted to His Majesty's Mail, but rather was to be laboriously keyed and transmitted using Morse code. Biddy boggled at the effort and likely cost. As far as she knew, telegrams cost six pence to send six words within Victoria. She had never known of a single person to send a message any longer than that.

Biddy glanced at the sheets underneath. Miss Garfield's neat penmanship continued before it gave way to another hand, less expertly wrought, on a fresh letter.

Sybil has continued to partake of well-prepared meals this week, made by my own hands and using the finest ingredients Summersby provides. We are still to find a new cook to relieve me of the burden, but it is not really a burden when my reward is Sybil's good health and robust constitution. On Monday luncheon Sybil enjoyed a spiced kedgeree made with egg and ham, and a strawberry fool for her sweet. On Monday tea-time she partook of some apricot jam and cream-filled crepes . . .

It was a letter from Mrs Marshall. Biddy read it to the end. She then returned to Miss Garfield's letter and read that in its entirety, too. Half of it lay outside the basket, writing side down on the desk. This suggested to Biddy that much of it had already been sent in code. What remained in the basket would follow once Jim Skews had eaten his dinner.

Neither letter made any mention of Biddy.

She was seized by an impulse to tell a story so provocative it almost made her laugh. Biddy peered at the two letters. Miss Garfield's script was a lady's hand. Mrs Marshall's writing was almost entirely made up of capitals, full of crossings out and underlining, one page done in pencil and the other done in ink.

Biddy opened the desk drawers to see what they contained and was pleased to find a pencil there. Of the two letters, Biddy hoped that Mrs Marshall's hand presented the lesser challenge. There was just enough space between the housekeeper's final sentence and *"Your Faithful Servant"* to insert, if lucky, two additional lines.

Biddy took several seconds to compose her words before she carefully wrote them on the sheet, using capitals and being sure to cross out and underline. She squinted at her handiwork when done.

The girl Biddy has joined us. She is honest, hardworking and of good character; a companion to Sybil, a sister. What should I tell her of your rules?

It looked like an afterthought. If there was a difference in style, perhaps it might be explained by Mrs Marshall being overworked.

The dusting Biddy gave to the room was thorough. She wanted Jim Skews to notice it. If she was lucky, Biddy told herself, he wouldn't notice anything else.

*

Jim did not reappear at Summersby until seven days had passed, and then, when he did, Biddy only saw him arrive from a distance while she was walking with Sybil in the grounds. Intrigued to know what, if anything, Sybil knew of Jim's strange role at Summersby, Biddy tested the waters. 'There's that funny man again,' she said, pointing in the lightning squirter's direction.

Sybil turned to see him in the act of doffing his hat to Mrs Marshall at the kitchen door, before the housekeeper admitted him inside. Sybil's face held no expression at all.

'I saw him here a week ago,' said Biddy, 'and a week before that. He's got teeth on him like a hare.'

'That's not true at all. He has quite a handsome face.'

This surprised Biddy. 'If you like that sort of thing,' she said, airily. 'What sort of tradesman is he, then? He comes here without any tools.'

But it was already apparent that Sybil intended dismissing all lines of enquiry. 'It is much cooler today,' she said, pulling a light shawl across her shoulders. 'I should think that autumn is getting nearer, Biddy.'

Biddy looked at Sybil carefully, but didn't ask another thing about Jim. Sybil's evasion was all the answer she'd sought anyway. The well-to-do girl knew exactly what task the young man did at Summersby. 'Shall we go in?' Biddy said.

'Not yet,' said Sybil, 'I'm enjoying our nice walk. And Miss Garfield will only propose something dull for me to do.'

Biddy nodded and linked her arm through Sybil's. Both girls glanced at the wire that stretched from the eastern wall, across the grounds, and all the way to Castlemaine.

Biddy and Sybil returned to the house via the kitchen door. The big room was hot and deserted. Something delicious baked in the oven and preparations had been made for luncheon, but Mrs Marshall was not in evidence.

'I'm hungry,' said Biddy.

'So am I,' said Sybil.

'You had an upset tummy at breakfast and don't pretend.'

Sybil looked profoundly shocked that Biddy had guessed this without being told.

'Well, you did,' said Biddy, 'you were looking very green around the gills. Do you feel better now?'

'A little,' said Sybil, self-consciously. 'Enough to feel hungry.'

'Shall we rob the pantry?'

'Biddy, you're so sinful.'

'We'll only be *borrowing*,' said Biddy. 'I'll just add it to my long list.'

'Biddy, you're very naughty, and if I didn't know you better I'd almost think you were making fun of me.'

'Never, my beloved dear friend,' said Biddy, striking an angelic pose. 'Now what do you feel like eating? If I were still with the Reverend, I'd be going straight for the tins of condensed milk.'

'Is that something nice?'

'Heaven!' said Biddy, in raptures. 'But Mrs Marshall won't get it in, so it's no surprise you've never tried it.'

Sybil tentatively poked around. 'Mrs Marshall's made some fresh butter.'

Biddy was dismissive of this. 'Very inferior, I'm used to factory-made butter,' she said. 'Mrs Marshall's butter comes straight from the cow.'

Sybil laughed. 'Well, where else would it come from?'

'It's no laughing matter, Sybil, Summersby's backward when it comes to Pasteurisation. Don't you know milk's got germs in it?'

'There's nothing wrong with Summersby's cows.'

'That we *know* of,' said Biddy. 'What if they've been eating cape weed? That'll knock the flavour halfway to Easter. And if it's been churned too much? There'll be lumps in it the size of your ear. And what if it tastes like soap? Someone forgot to wash the butter pail properly, that's what. And if it tastes a bit flat? The dairy's got riddled with damp. And God help us if it tastes like carrots. That means the butter turned out far too pale so someone went and made it yellow by fakery.'

Sybil often seemed to marvel at the things Biddy knew – or gave the appearance of knowing. 'How do you even have room for things like that inside your head?'

Biddy considered. 'I suppose I want them there. There's nothing I don't know that isn't useful. How do you have the room for all that French and Latin inside your head?'

'I have room because my relatives have instructed me to,' said Sybil, matter-of-fact.

Biddy let that sit uncommented upon. 'My relatives wish it' had come to be the explanation for far too many dull and dispiriting things at Summersby, which was especially rich, in Biddy's view, given these mysterious personages didn't even live here.

'Something sweet,' Sybil pleaded. 'I'm starving.'

'Who'll keep lookout then?'

'I will,' said Sybil, 'I couldn't hold my nerve to do any of the stealing.'

'Borrowing.'

'I still couldn't do it. I'd go to pieces.'

'And you won't go to pieces if Mrs Marshall comes back and you have to distract her at the door?'

Sybil looked comically stricken. 'Gaining a sister has proved to be educating in ways I could never have imagined before I found you, Biddy.'

'Quick! The clock is ticking.'

'Just find some food!' said Sybil, laughing.

She went and stood at the baize door as Biddy popped into Mrs Marshall's stillroom to see what she might uncover. Biddy was rewarded by the sight of several dozen freshly baked biscuits. Pinching four of them, she was about to conceal the booty in a fold of her skirt when she heard a cry from somewhere in the rooms outside. It was Mrs Marshall. Immediately there was a second noise, like a wail about to break out only to be cut off before barely a sound had emerged.

'Sybil . . .?' Biddy hissed. She could half hear voices from a hushed conversation being held beyond the baize door. Mrs Marshall had evidently returned, found Sybil's 'guarding' to be rightly suspicious, and the nervous girl was now spilling everything. Biddy felt a rush of indignation. 'Whose house is it, anyway?' she said to herself. 'Why can't she have a bit of food? She's not bloody Oliver Twist!'

But Biddy looked at the biscuits in her skirt fold and immediately shoved them back where she had found them, guilty. She crept to the stillroom door and stood, not daring to peak out. She heard the low tones of Mrs Marshall's voice distinctly now, and some kind of halting reply from Sybil, before the fluty tones of Miss Garfield came in on top of both of them. Biddy felt ill. 'They've both got into it . . .' she said. 'That's it then.'

Smoothing down her skirt and trying to hide her escaped fronds of hair, Biddy took a deep breath. She couldn't let Sybil make a mess of things all alone.

'Who's there?' called Biddy, brightly, and stepping out from the stillroom as if being discovered in there was the most natural thing in the world. She was at once brought up short by Sybil, the housekeeper and the governess all staring at her from the baize door, their expressions as one in shock.

Biddy decided it was pointless attempting to make up stories when indignation might prove the stronger weapon. 'Why shouldn't she have a snack between her meal times?' she demanded. 'It's not going to kill anybody and there's plenty to spare!'

'Biddy . . .' a pale Miss Garfield started to say.

'She's got growing pains!' Biddy overrode her. 'If you two crows knew how bad she had them you'd be ashamed of yourselves for denying her the sustenance.'

Miss Garfield flushed. 'Biddy!'

'Well, it's true. You're both so stiff and sour you've forgotten what growing pains feel like.'

Mrs Marshall stepped forward, angry. 'That's quite enough, my girl.'

Biddy flinched, her gall failing. 'I'm only trying to be a good companion.'

This unexpectedly silenced both women.

'Well, I am,' said Biddy.

Sybil stepped forward and Biddy only saw now that she had taken on an air of calm, at odds with the two women who corralled her. 'It doesn't matter about the food.'

Biddy blinked. Sybil was transformed, empowered somehow, yet dignified with it and suddenly looking older. The girl clearly believed she possessed some kind of upper hand, but Biddy knew she was deluded. 'It *does* matter,' she said, ashamed. 'I'm a dreadful companion making you do wicked things, Sybil. If Mrs Marshall doesn't want you to eat between your mealtimes then I'm terrible for making you go against it. She wants what's best for you and I've got no right to tell you otherwise.'

'Enough!' barked Mrs Marshall.

Biddy blanched.

'Biddy,' said Sybil, 'you mustn't worry about any of that now.'

'All right . . .' Biddy realised then that something of considerable importance was about to be made known to her, and a sudden, fleeting image of Jim Skews huddled over the telegraph machine entered her head before it snapped from her sight like a lightning bolt.

'My relatives have sent a telegraph message,' said Sybil. 'That is what the young man you saw earlier does for us—'

'Sybil . . .' Miss Garfield warned.

The girl ignored her governess. 'He sends and receives such things for us.'

Biddy tried to look as if this was news. 'Why not just send letters?'

'The message that came this morning concerns *you.*'

Biddy's heart stopped. The housekeeper and governess, standing on either side of Sybil, looked stunned, Biddy realised; both were at sea with whatever it was that had happened.

'Our dear Mrs Marshall and Miss Garfield are mystified,' said

Sybil. 'They did not know my relatives knew I had taken a companion at all. They had not told my relatives themselves, you see.'

Biddy did see, but gave no indication of it.

'Nobody told them and yet somehow they knew.'

Biddy ventured to say something but stopped. She realised that she wasn't about to be accused of anything.

'My relatives are very resourceful and this is a reminder to me and to all of us that we are wise not to underestimate what this resourcefulness might achieve.'

'What do your relatives say about me?' Biddy whispered.

Mrs Marshall cleared her throat, about to object, but Miss Garfield held up a silencing hand. 'It is nothing unpleasant, Biddy,' she assured.

Sybil lifted a sheet of paper she had been holding in her gloved hand. It was Jim's transcription of Sybil's relatives' telegraphed words. 'This is what they sent,' said Sybil, turning the paper so that Biddy could read it.

Biddy has been wronged. You must tell her what she needs to know.

Biddy felt as if the floor had dropped from under her. Wronged?

'Is that all?' she asked in a small voice.

'Yes. That is all,' Sybil said, 'but Mrs Marshall and Miss Garfield both agree it is more than enough.'

'So how can it be that you know *nothing* of the parents who brought you into the world?' Biddy demanded of Sybil, when they sat alone together in Sybil's room. Some information had now been explained to her by Miss Garfield and Mrs Marshall in chorus, but to Biddy's mind all their words were worthless until elaborated upon in private by Sybil herself.

Sybil rubbed at her tummy, feeling decidedly unwell again. She had taken off her corset in the privacy of her room. 'It's because I have no memory of them.'

'But how can it be that no one has ever told you anything about them at all?'

Sybil was seeking a way to answer this question. 'Miss Garfield and Mrs Marshall have been given no facts regarding my birth,' she told her, 'aside from the knowledge that I have relatives, who are also their employers, and who also own Summersby. What Miss Garfield and Mrs Marshall *have* been given are my relatives' expressed wishes that I be discouraged from acquiring the facts myself.'

Biddy couldn't help but think of how her once-mother Ida might have responded if told such information. 'Well, that's all very convenient, isn't it?' she sniffed.

Sybil looked startled.

'Well, isn't it? Miss Garfield and Mrs Marshall don't know anything and they're under orders to stop *you* from knowing anything, too. Therefore, nobody knows a sausage! Your relatives might as well have made this rule just to cause curiosity, not to end it.'

She watched the other girl processing these words.

Sybil went to her mahogany dressing table and slipped open a drawer. Beneath a layer of silks was a small photograph mounted on card. She returned with it to Biddy by the bed. 'I have this,' she said. It was a portrait of a young woman, perhaps a little older than Biddy and Sybil were now, but with clothes arranged in the style of the 1880s. The woman was beautifully dressed, her dark hair falling down her back, her body angled away from the lens, her face turned over her shoulder to greet the viewer's gaze.

Biddy was almost struck dumb by the young woman's dark beauty. 'Is she an actress? She looks like she should be on stage at the Princess Theatre.'

The woman in the photograph seemed to smile with her eyes only; eyes that knew secrets. Biddy turned the photo over. On the reverse, someone had written a name and date in fine, smooth copperplate.

Matilda. 1884.

'I believe she could be my mother,' said Sybil.

The name struck a chord for Biddy. Hadn't the letter she had found and accidently burned at the hut been written by a Matilda? Biddy stared at the fine features of the young woman and could see a resemblance to Sybil that was undeniable. They shared each other's large, smooth brow, and the gentle curve of their upper lips. They could be mother and daughter easily. And yet Biddy had thought the letter-writing Matilda sounded like rather a sinister person with her story of changing places to fool people, and the servant who had not been fooled.

'I have had this photograph for as long as I can remember,' said Sybil, rubbing her tummy again where it ached. 'I found it when I was very small. I have never told anyone else of it, or shown anyone. Miss Garfield and Mrs Marshall have no idea I have it.' She looked sadly at the photograph again, at the other young woman, so attractive in her 1880s finery. 'I know nothing more than her name. The truth of her is, I suspect, that's she's long dead.'

Biddy suspected this was right, given her letter had been lost in the hut. She felt sad for her. 'Sit down and rest, you still look very peaky today,' she said.

Sybil shook her head and returned the photograph to the dressing-table drawer. 'Perhaps my relatives *do* want me to be curious,' she said, turning to Biddy, 'and that, of course, is the test.'

Biddy raised her eyebrows.

'My life is full of tests and this is just another one,' said Sybil. 'I have every faith that one day I will be permitted to know my mother's name, and know my father's name, too, and indeed the names of all my relatives. But if I go and try to find things out for myself, whatever I find will only get back to them and bring displeasure.'

'But these people don't even live here,' said Biddy in dismay.

'They found out about you, didn't they?'

Biddy let the circumstances of that discovery remain obscure. 'Why should it be forbidden to know the truth about your own beginnings?' she asked. 'It seems very cruel.'

Sybil looked uncomfortable. 'I believe that the circumstances of my birth must be a source of great shame, Biddy.'

Biddy opened her mouth and closed it again without saying anything. She remembered Mrs Marshall's dread of scandal.

'The circumstances have never been called as such and I have never heard them uttered so by anyone, but shameful they can only be, for what other reason could there be for hiding them?'

'But these people are your blood, aren't they?' Biddy asked, hurt for her. 'Don't they have love for you at all?'

'My relatives love me with all their hearts,' Sybil said, quickly, 'I have never doubted that for a moment. It's because I'm loved so much that everything, well . . .' she gestured around her at the room and the house and the grounds beyond the windows, 'everything *is* . . .'

'Everything is strange and mysterious you mean?'

'That's not true . . .' said Sybil, offended.

Biddy dropped onto Sybil's big, lace-covered bed, and looked up at the ornate ceiling as she sought a way to begin afresh. 'Listen, Sybil,' she started, 'I'm your companion, aren't I? Companions tell you their honest thoughts about things and I'm telling you that everything here is like nothing out *there*.'

Sybil sat down next to her with a degree more delicacy, taking care not to crease her skirt. 'I've seen so little of the world to compare it to.'

'That's something that you and I are going to put to rights.'

'What do you mean?' said Sybil, alarmed.

Biddy waved the question away for the moment. 'Why do these people keep you here when they don't live here themselves? Tell me about that again.'

'You'll be tiring of me talking about it soon,' said Sybil.

'No, I won't,' said Biddy, 'I'll never tire of it. It's like something out of a book. *You're* like something out of a book. It's the most fascinating topic in the universe to me. No one could make up this sort of thing.'

Sybil smiled at that. 'All right then. They keep me here in readiness.'

'For what? Kingdom come?'

'Don't blaspheme, Biddy. My readiness requires much preparation by way of education and refinement under Miss Garfield's direction, and now that you're here, preparation through companionship, too. When my relatives declare the preparation complete, why, then I'll be *ready*.'

Biddy waited.

'For my inheritance.'

'Which is?'

Sybil got to her feet again and spread her arms wide. 'All *this*. I am the Summersby heiress,' she said.

Biddy was looking at her cock-eyed.

'Well, I am,' said Sybil with a toss of her head. 'My relatives own it.'

Biddy studied the girl. 'So, you're the Summersby heiress, who has lived at Summersby your whole life.'

'I am.'

'Who has never known anything else but this grand house and its beautiful grounds . . .'

'And the little village of Summersby, I know that, too.'

'And Castlemaine when allowed chaperoned visits.'

'That's correct.'

'But anywhere beyond that?'

Sybil shook her head. 'My relatives' wishes are clear. I am not to journey any further until such time as it is permitted. That is, if I wish to *remain* the heiress. But I have every faith that one day the reasons for my restriction will be revealed to me.'

Biddy narrowed her eyes. 'So, you're the Summersby heiress who has never known anything *except* Summersby and your whole life has been lived in preparation to inherit it . . . but you still might not?'

Sybil set her mouth in a firm line.

'Did I get that wrong?'

'No,' said Sybil, finally. 'You understood what Miss Garfield told you quite correctly, Biddy. I am the Summersby heiress, but I will not inherit my relatives' wealth and property if I'm found . . . to be wanting in some way, when the call comes to meet my relatives in person . . .'

Biddy sat up in the bed. 'And what if that happens?'

'It won't, Biddy,' Sybil said, determined.

'But if it does?'

'It never will. It can't. I am the Summersby heiress. I will inherit it all, Biddy. I must.' But somehow Sybil lacked conviction.

'But if your relatives decide that you *are* found wanting?'

There was a silence.

'I want to hear you tell me,' Biddy pressed. 'Not Miss Garfield or Mrs Marshall, I want to hear it from you – it's your life and your inheritance, after all, not theirs, and I'm *your* companion.'

Sybil gathered herself. 'There is a person we call the Secret Heiress,' she said, finally, 'the second heiress, there are two of us. I've always known of it and she is the greatest mystery of my life, greater than all the others combined. I don't know who she is or what she looks like or even where she lives. So I can only call her the Secret Heiress. I have always believed, because I have always been told, that she will have everything if I am found to be wanting – *everything*. Despite the years and years of training and lessons and refinement to get there, I will be left with nothing at all. Just like that – nothing, Biddy. I will be cast out from Summersby, poor and alone.'

Sybil's circumstances were sounding more like the Brothers Grimm with every word, Biddy thought. And while she didn't doubt that Sybil believed it all, to Biddy's ear it sounded more like a story that only someone kept shut away from the rest of the world *would* believe. 'I'm sorry,' she said, as Sybil waited for her to reply, 'it's just, well . . . it's just so unlike anything I've ever known before.'

'It's all I've ever known,' said Sybil. 'Mrs Marshall, and Miss Garfield have held the existence of the Secret Heiress over me throughout my childhood. They turned her into some kind of bad fairy – or rather, a fairy so impossibly *good* that I could only be seen as bad in comparison to her.'

'And you're sure she's even real?' asked Biddy, sceptical.

It was revealing, Biddy thought, that Sybil didn't answer at once.

'I believe that she must be,' she said at last, 'if only because Mrs Marshall and Miss Garfield persist with using her against me. If she'd been a fabrication, like Father Christmas was or the Bunyip, then they would have abandoned her as soon I began to question. But whenever I've doubted the existence of the Secret Heiress Mrs Marshall in particular has redoubled the efforts to control me with the threat of her. It's never gone away. Yes, I'm quite sure she exists.'

Biddy took Sybil's hands in her own. 'But you will not fail. You said so yourself.' Yet she couldn't help thinking of the unspoken thing that existed between them: Sybil's clandestine romance. Biddy had never once raised the matter, never once hinted that she had guessed that a love affair was going on, and she intended remaining mum until Sybil herself raised it. Yet as to whom Sybil's secret beau actually was, Biddy couldn't imagine. But what might happen if the relatives learned of it, she wondered?

Sybil trembled, perhaps thinking of the very same thing. 'You do not know that, Biddy. I could fail easily.' She rubbed at her tummy again. 'There are so many things I must still perfect, so many accomplishments I'm yet to attain. I'm barely refined at all and I must be, and must be soon. I could be summoned by my relatives at any time, there will be no warning, and when it happens . . .'

'You will *not* fail,' Biddy repeated, 'I mean it.'

'You cannot be sure.'

'But I am. Do you know why?'

Sybil looked at her hands curled inside Biddy's own.

'Because I am here,' said Biddy.

Sybil slipped her hands free. 'That is very sweet of you to say, but it is naïve. You cannot gain my inheritance for me,' she said. 'No one can. It is solely my task to achieve.'

Biddy was insistent. 'Of course I can't,' she said. 'Only you can do that – I wouldn't know where to start. But one thing I can do is even up the odds a bit.' She gave her most cunning smile. 'Honestly, I don't know what you people did before I came along. No imagination and hardly any gumption. You needed a dose of me.'

'Biddy . . .'

'I'll make you a wager,' said Biddy. 'Your very last Summersby shilling says I can dig up this Secret Heiress for you and discover if she's even real or just some storybook witch made up to keep your nose clean. Seems to me you could do a lot better if you had few more of the facts up your sleeve.'

Sybil paled. 'Biddy, that's . . .' The words failed her.

'Good, because if there's one thing I just can't stand it's other people presuming to hide the truth. I'm going to find the truth out for you, and when I do, well, who knows what we'll then uncover! Secrets by the score, I'll bet – useful secrets, just you see. Nothing's going to get in the way of Miss Sybil Gregory and her rightful inheritance – not if her faithful companion Biddy MacBryde has anything to do with it.'

Sybil leapt up from the bed. 'Biddy, you've gone mad!'

'Well, what's the matter? Aren't you pleased?'

'This is not even a thing that should concern you . . .' Sybil started.

'For heaven's sake, I keep telling you I'm your companion, don't I?'

'This is not something a companion does.'

'What else have I got to worry about but your health and happiness?' Biddy asked, smiling with all the confidence she could muster to hide the uncomfortable truth of the words.

Sybil opened and closed her mouth like a goldfish. 'But my relatives have forbidden me knowing anything of the other heiress at all.'

'Again, very convenient,' said Biddy, dismissive. 'Have your relatives forbidden *me* knowing anything?'

'Well, I . . .'

'Of course they haven't. There's the loophole.'

Sybil stood there, floundering. 'But if my relatives should learn of it . . .' She started to wring her hands.

Knowing she was the vessel by which the relatives had discovered her own existence, Biddy was unconcerned. 'These people's so-called power to see from the other side of the world, or wherever they happen to be, seems all pretty convenient, too,' she declared.

'What will you do exactly . . . to find things out?'

Biddy waved her hands, airily. 'The less you're told, the safer your inheritance. Keep your own hands clean.'

'Biddy, what will you *do*?' Sybil insisted.

'Use your noggin,' said Biddy, 'you're always going on about how much you like Sherlock Holmes stories.'

'This is real, not a detective fiction!'

Biddy just shrugged, before tapping the side of her nose, enigmatically.

'Will this involve dishonesty?'

'Goodness no!' Biddy exclaimed. 'I never lie.'

Sybil weighed up Biddy's answer and then plainly decided to be relieved. 'And neither do I,' she said, quietly. 'So long as lies are avoided then perhaps it could be useful to know who my rival is,' said Sybil.

'I'll flush her out of the woodwork,' declared Biddy.

Sybil seemed to dislike this coarse choice of words.

'I'll *investigate* her,' Biddy rephrased.

'If you really think you could ever find out such a thing for me discreetly?'

Biddy smiled. 'So many people underestimate me, you know,' she said. 'They're the easiest ones to pull the wool over.'

'You said no dishonesty.'

'And I meant it,' said Biddy, crossing her heart with the fingers of her right hand. The fingers of her left hand crossed themselves and crept behind her back where Sybil couldn't see them.

Sybil looked long at Biddy's beaming face before succumbing to hope. 'Oh, Biddy, if you find out if the Secret Heiress really exists at all I will never forget you, no matter what might happen. I will always look out for you and I will always be your friend.'

Biddy felt a rush of emotion. She hugged Sybil. 'That's all the encouragement I need. Just what you said, nothing more than that.'

But as they held each other, Biddy's feelings churned inside her. She was frightened. Her promise was ill thought out and reckless. She didn't have the first idea how to find this strange person. But this was what friendship required, she knew, when one side was so unequal to the other.

The lesser friend must prove herself worthy of having a friend at all.

IDA

JANUARY 1887

5

*I*da felt detached from herself, as if a hundred miles away and on the train again to Melbourne, cushioned and snug in the comfort of a first class carriage.

'Ida! Ida, wake up, please . . .'

She was vaguely aware of Aggie slapping at her cheeks to no response.

'Ida!'

They were her cheeks and yet they were not her cheeks. She was not at Summersby anymore, but safe on the train. Samuel sat across the compartment from her, his smile tender and warm.

'Ida, please don't die.'

She heard Aggie sobbing and felt her take her wrist; the wrist that was not her wrist. She felt fingers jab between her tendons, trying to detect signs of life perhaps. Ida sensed Aggie press her head against her chest, listening for a heartbeat. Across the compartment, Samuel beckoned Ida to sit with him. She did so, bashfully.

'God, help me!' Aggie cried from somewhere even further away now. 'Don't let her be dead.'

Ida heard a door flung open, footsteps running into the hall. 'Mr Barker! Mr Barker!' she heard Aggie call out. 'Are you up here?'

Ida looked to Samuel sitting next to her on the soft, warm compartment seat and realised with a shock that Barker was now slouched there, his long legs stretched out insolently before him. Samuel was gone.

'What's got into you, woman?' Barker answered Aggie, yet he looked Ida hard in the eye.

'Mr Barker, please help, it's Ida,' Aggie's voice said, so many miles away.

The valet picked his hard, white teeth with a nail. 'What's wrong with her?'

'She's . . . she's fallen,' Aggie told him.

He dug out some forgotten morsel and regarded it on the end of his finger for a moment before popping it back in his mouth. 'From the roof? Good riddance.'

Ida felt her stomach turn.

'In our mistress's room,' said Aggie's voice. 'She's in there on the floor. Please help me.'

Ida heard Aggie's running steps, followed by another set of feet, not running at all.

'What's the hurry?' said Barker

'She's fallen!' Aggie yelled at him. 'She's on the floor!'

Both voices seemed nearer, yet Barker hadn't moved and Ida couldn't see Aggie anywhere. It was confusing, and with Samuel gone and only Barker to share the compartment with, unpleasant.

'Felt for a pulse?' Barker wondered.

'Yes!' cried Aggie's voice. 'I can't feel one.'

Barker seemed to consider this prospect. 'Don't waste your breath then,' he told her. 'There's a rubbish pile up the back paddock. I'll toss her on top in the morning.'

Ida distinctly heard Aggie cry out at this remark and she decided there and then that she'd had enough. 'Go on and try it, you lanky bastard,' she yelled at him, 'I'll snap your pretty nose like a pencil!'

'Ida!'

The train compartment was gone and Ida found herself lying on the carpet in the Chinese room with Aggie crouching over her.

'Spoke too soon,' muttered Barker from where he leant against the doorframe. He sloped off into the hallway.

Aggie hugged Ida. 'I thought you were gone.'

Ida was shaking, weak in her limbs. She clutched her friend. 'I've got such a shocking headache, like you wouldn't believe . . . worst one I've ever had . . .'

'For God's sake, you were knocked out cold!' Aggie admonished her, helping her stand.

'I'm fine now,' Ida insisted. But her legs gave out beneath her and she looked like slipping to the floor again.

Aggie steadied her with difficulty. 'Have you lost your senses, Ida? Something very bad is going on and you were almost made the worse for it!'

Ida's bottom lip began to tremble, more shocked by what had occurred than she was letting on. She looked at the blue glass vial on the floor. Aggie had had the presence of mind to put the stopper back in, preventing whatever was inside from leaking out entirely.

'What would have happened if you'd done more than smell the stuff?' Aggie wanted to know.

Ida didn't have a reply.

Aggie pleaded with her. 'We've got to forget about this business, Ida, whatever it all is. It's getting too dangerous. Whatever's going on, it's nothing to do with us. All we do is work here. We'll look out for our mistress, but that's the limit of it. Promise me you'll keep your nose out of it.'

Ida said nothing. She was beginning to feel angry now, angry that someone was treating her like a fool.

'Promise me,' said Aggie.

Ida looked at the sapphire perfume vial, the thing that was making her angriest of all. It was as if it was taunting her. Why did it keep moving around seemingly of its own accord, but never quite hiding itself properly? Why did it always manage to get *found* again?

'Promise me, Ida!'

She refused to promise anything of the kind.

Evie was horrified by what she'd just been told. *'Poisoned?'*

Ida took a sip of her bottled lemon barley water, as if scrapes with death were par for the course for girls with inquisitive minds. 'Thing is, though, it's a funny kind of poison – it makes me wonder now if it's even a poison at all.'

Evie nearly choked on her pie. They were seated on a long bench together, outside the bakery in Mostyn Street, Castlemaine. The schoolhouse across the road thronged with children on their dinnertime break. Ida had come to see her sister on her one afternoon off for the month. 'You smelled it and you fell into a stupor!' Evie reminded her. 'If that's not a nasty poison, what is?'

Ida had to agree it was mystifying. 'I've got so many questions, Evie, and answers are thin on the ground.'

'I don't see why you're making this your affair at all – especially since being poisoned!'

'For instance,' said Ida, ignoring this concern, 'Miss Matilda wrote the letter to Miss Margaret, but when did she write it and why? To put in her Remember Box the letter said, but Miss Matilda's the one who can't remember anything.' She thought of the few words she'd managed to read of the hut letter before it had been slapped it from her hand. 'Yet Matilda wrote that it was *Margaret* whose mind was damaged.'

'Well, obviously it was, you already said that everyone thought she was ill – ill enough to top herself in the first place,' said Evie, returning to her pie.

'True,' said Ida, 'but is it the same as being damaged? My mistress's mind is as damaged a mind as I've ever seen in a person – her memory's all in little bits and pieces.'

'But she's *Matilda*, not Margaret,' Evie reminded her. 'You and I both saw Margaret get put in a hole in the ground.'

'Then there's the handwriting,' said Ida, 'Aggie swears it's not our mistress's and I believe her, but handwriting was what Mr Samuel wanted to know about when we found the first letter and lost it – he wanted to know what it looked like and I told him: it looked awful.'

'What did he say to that then?' asked Evie, intrigued despite everything.

'He didn't say anything at all,' said Ida, thinking on it now. 'But he did seem relieved. I only wish that we'd found it again in the dark, I should liked to have read all of it.'

They heard the Post Office clock chime the half hour.

'I've got fifteen minutes left,' said Evie.

'Let's take a walk. I want to stretch my legs.'

'A *quick* one,' warned Evie.

The two girls walked west along Mostyn Street, Evie peering in all the shop windows as they went, while Ida's inquisitive head stayed with her questions, ordering them and reordering them as she strolled. They reached the corner where the street of shops met the road that went north to Bendigo. Evie wanted to turn around again. 'One more block,' said Ida. 'You've still got ten minutes.'

'I don't want to have to *run* back,' said Evie, 'it's undignified.'

But they crossed the road and made their way up the Mostyn Street hill towards the Castlemaine Railway Station. They neared a double-fronted villa, painted white, with a steep flight of steps leading to the red front door. Pink and red pelargoniums made a cheery little front garden. Ida studied at the polished brass plaque that was screwed to the wall.

Dr A. L. Foal, Physician

'I feel a bit unwell,' said Ida.

Evie looked at her worriedly. 'Well, of course you do, you went and smelled that horrible poison.'

'I think I should see the doctor about it.'

'What? But that's ruinous expense, Mum'll tell you.'

Ida opened the little wrought-iron gate. 'I'll say goodbye to you here, Evie, and come and see you again next month.'

'Wait . . . what?' She realised what her older sister was doing. 'You can't go in there, that's for toffy people!'

'I'm sick,' said Ida. 'I need a doctor's care.'

Evie was on to her. 'You're inquisitive to a fault, Ida Garfield, and one day soon it's going to bite you on the unmentionable!'

'I earn a wage. I've got every right to come here.'

Evie screwed up her face. 'If you don't stop doing whatever it is you think you're going to do, I'll be telling Mum!'

The school bell began to peal from the other end of Mostyn Street.

Ida kissed her on the cheek. 'Sorry, Evie, looks like you'll have to run.'

The woman who answered the door was pleasant enough, but reserved. Standing on the doorstep, Ida felt as if her character was being assessed. 'Dr Foal,' she repeated, 'would it be possible for me to see him, miss?'

The woman looked to be about forty and had pince-nez, which she adjusted upon her small, button nose. Ida thought they ill-fitted her. 'But are you a patient, Miss –?' The woman looked past Ida and seemed to address herself to busy Mostyn Street.

'Garfield,' Ida told her.

The woman nodded. 'Not a patient then.' A dose of failure was implied by the words. 'Perhaps I might direct you to the Benevolent Asylum, Miss Garfield?'

'I have money,' she told the woman. She could feel her umbrage threatening to show itself. 'I'm not a charity case.'

'No one said that you were.'

'I work at Summersby,' said Ida.

The woman was pulled up short.

'The big house,' said Ida. 'Do you know it?'

The woman's expression told her that she did. Ida hoped that the doctor's doorkeeper was suitably impressed, or failing that, put back inside her box, being little more than a servant herself. The woman did seem at a loss for words.

'The doctor?' Ida reminded her.

The woman pulled the front door open. 'Please come in,' she told her. 'You may wait in the parlour.' She indicated a dark front room off the hall.

'I didn't get your name?' said Ida, hopefully.

The woman looked at her worriedly for a second or two, before retreating to the rooms beyond a curtained hallway. She parted the drapes and closed them behind her again, avoiding Ida's eye. Suspicious of this without quite knowing why, Ida took a position on the parlour's horsehair sofa and prepared for the real reason for her visit, which had nothing to do with Dr Foal. A woman was dead, she reminded herself; a woman who valued Ida's inquisitive mind.

After a short time, Ida became aware that her presence had been noted by a skittish man of passable looks, who walked by the door to the room twice, seemingly on an errand and looking in at her each time. He now repeated the performance again. Ida knew exactly who it was: Mr Skews. She looked up from her lap for the first two inspections, smiling politely, and was doing the same again when Skews broke his pattern and addressed her.

'Can I help you there, miss?'

'I don't think so,' said Ida, 'unless you're Dr Foal?'

'I'm afraid not,' said Mr Skews, 'I am his apothecary. But aren't you Ida from Summersby House?'

Ida beamed and stood up. 'I was hoping to speak to the doctor when he can see me. I was told by a lady to wait.'

Skews nodded. 'Miss Haines, yes, you're a patient?'

Ida shook her head.

'Well, Dr Foal is very busy with those who are, I'm afraid, and won't be able to see you.'

Ida pinched at her hand behind her back until her eyes glistened. She looked up at him, cow-eyed. 'If there's no one here who can help me, I do understand. Maybe if I rest a bit I'll soon come good.'

She dropped onto the settee in an approximation of a swoon.

'Ida?' Mr Skews was at her side. 'Are you all right? My word . . .'

'Don't worry about me,' she said, sounding far away.

He brought her a glass of water from a jug on the side table.

She sipped at it. 'It comes and goes,' she explained, taking a moment to recover. 'It's been happening for days now. Aggie begged me to get some medicine for it. She's my only friend, you know.'

'You're dizzy, you say?'

'In spells. Ever since I opened that pretty blue perfume glass.'

He gave a perceptible flinch.

'Such a pretty thing. I found it when doing my cleaning,' she went on. 'When I opened it, it smelled of rosemary. Then I woke up and I was on the floor.'

'That must have been very distressing, my word, yes,' said Mr Skews. He began to scratch at his inflamed nostrils.

'More so for Aggie than me,' Ida insisted. 'She was very upset. I'm *her* only friend, too, you see. I brought it in with me.'

'Brought what?'

She retrieved the blue glass vial from the little bag she carried with her.

He stared at it blankly for a moment. 'But that is only Hungary water – rosemary oil,' he told her, 'prescribed by Dr Foal as a stimulant applied externally. The vial is from my apothecary's rooms. It's quite harmless, I promise you. It would never make you ill.'

'Oh,' said Ida, blinking at it in her hand. 'I am sure you're right.' She looked at him beseechingly. 'Something else must have given me the dizzy spells. What do you think it could be?'

'Vertigo,' said Mr Skews, without hesitation. 'Why don't you let me give you some pills for it? There's no need to see Dr Foal, the pills will put you right, my word, they will.'

'Oh, that would be very nice.' Ida beamed at him again.

The parlour door was flung open. The face of a small boy peered around from the hall. 'What time's dinner, Pa?'

'Jim! Outside at once,' Skews ordered.

Ida recognised the boy as the one who had spoken to Matilda at the graveyard.

'But I'm starving,' he complained.

'Can't you see I'm talking to the nice young lady?'

The face of another boy joined the first and Ida recognised him as the second boy from the graveyard – the one who'd stayed quiet. She smiled at the sight of them both; peas in a pod, barefoot and baked brown by the sun, each as grubby as the other. She guessed that neither was old enough for school. Jim, the first boy, stuck a finger in his nose.

'Out!' said Skews. 'We'll find you some dinner when it's the proper time to eat.'

Skews ushered the boys outside and returned, a minute or so later, with a small bottle of tablets. 'I'm sorry,' he began, 'that was my son Jim and his cousin. I'm a widower, you see. My wife's sister passed, too, and left me with her own boy as well. I'm bringing up both.'

Ida was touched. 'Two nice-looking boys, Mr Skews.'

'Jim has a bright future. The money I earn will go to sending him to a good school in Melbourne one day, when he's ready, my word, yes.'

Ida nodded approvingly.

'My sister's boy, Lewis . . .' He looked awkward. 'Well, it's not possible to send two boys to Melbourne on an apothecary's wage, you understand.'

Ida wanted him to know that she did understand. 'I'm sure he'll get good schooling here in Castlemaine. Why, my own sister Evie—'

He interrupted her. 'I am . . . *familiar* with Summersby,' he said.

There was a moment's pause as they assessed each other.

'Oh yes?' said Ida.

Skews edged towards her, nodding and scratching at himself. 'It was a great tragedy what happened, my word it was, a terrible thing . . .'

Ida nodded back. 'I only met the late Miss Gregory once. I serve her sister, you see.'

'Ah,' Skews said. 'I filled prescriptions for the late Miss Gregory, you see, and her late father before that.'

Ida saw that he was perspiring; his forehead damp. He rubbed under his nose again and sniffed. Something badly bothered him there. 'Mr Skews—'

He cut her off. 'Is there something *wrong* at Summersby?'

It felt to Ida that she was standing on the edge of a precipice. If she stepped into the void would she plummet to her death? She did not know – and could not know. She took the leap of faith. 'No, I don't think so.' She cleared her throat in an effort to contain herself. 'Should there be?'

He looked quietly relieved. 'No, no, my word, no, not at all . . . I was just wondering.'

'Miss Matilda says you were at Summersby when her sister died,' Ida revealed, as if it was of little importance.

He shifted. It looked to Ida that he was thinking very carefully on what he would now say. 'Not at the moment of her death,' he began, 'but I'm afraid I was there when her poor body was found, yes . . .'

Ida said nothing, waiting.

'I'd been asked to deliver medicines that day,' he said, 'that was nothing unusual. I come to Summersby from time to time with prescriptions from Dr Foal. But that morning when I arrived at the house, Mr Hackett was very concerned. He told me that Miss Gregory had been talking of harming herself, and indeed, it was an order of sedative powders that I had brought upon his request. He directed me towards the dining room – it was not long after Miss Gregory had eaten breakfast, you see – and Mr Hackett told me she was waiting for me there. I had the sedatives and was ready to prepare a draught, but when I went into the room, well, I couldn't see Miss Gregory in there and presumed she had gone . . .' He wiped his brow again. 'I was about to leave and look elsewhere, when I saw the hem of Miss Gregory's dress on the floor behind the table.'

'Oh, Mr Skews,' said Ida, bringing a hand to her mouth.

He shook his head, plainly distressed at the memory. 'She'd collapsed, you see. Oh, my word, I felt for her heartbeat. There was none.'

'How terrible for you.'

He looked at her with red and watery eyes. 'She was quite dead. I called for Hackett. He was devastated, utterly distraught. I ministered the sedatives for him in the end. His man Barker took charge. I returned to town and sent the undertaker for him.'

Ida trod with care. 'Mr Skews, forgive me for asking such a thing, but it sounds as if you knew the late Miss Margaret better than I did.'

Skews nodded. 'A fine lady, very elegant, my word, yes.'

'Was she . . . ill in her mind?'

Skews looked thrown that she should ask such a thing. Then his expression became bitter. 'I told Mr Hackett that it was my professional belief that his fiancée was not ill in any way,' he said. 'I told him this on the very day she died.' He scratched at his nostrils again. Ida glanced at the nasty inflammation on the skin.

'I was very wrong,' said Skews. He looked imploringly at her. 'Margaret Gregory was deeply disturbed, Ida. I know she *was* ill, very ill indeed.'

As Mr Skews escorted Ida down the steep flight of steps from Dr Foal's front door to the hilly end of Mostyn Street, she made a mental note of the three interesting things that had struck her in the course of their conversation.

One. Mr Skews had been adamant that the vial contained Hungary water, as he called it, and yet he didn't open the thing to make sure. How could he be certain without checking?

'You have done the right thing, Ida,' he told her. They shook hands in farewell, standing on either side of the doctor's wrought iron gate. 'Dizzy spells can be worrying, but if you take one of those pills each time you feel faint you'll be put good again, just you see.'

'Thank you, Mr Skews,' said Ida, smiling. 'I am so grateful for your time.'

Two. When she told him that Matilda said he had been present at Margaret's death he had been freely forthcoming with information. Yet he had not asked how or why Matilda should think such a thing. He accepted it at once.

'Farewell, Ida,' Mr Skews said, turning to go back up the steps.

'Good day, sir.'

Three. Mr Skews was utterly certain that Margaret Gregory had been ill in her mind, and Ida had no doubt he was telling the truth. He was adamant that Margaret had been extremely unwell.

Thinking on the importance of all this, Ida slowly walked up and then down the rest of the hill to where the coach to Summersby waited for her at the railway station. The slate tiles on the station roof looked almost purple in the glow of the afternoon sun. As she was about to cross the street she recognised a woman coming out of one of the little houses to shake out a tablecloth.

'Mrs Jack!'

The sometimes cook looked up at her in surprise. 'Hello there, Ida. Chucked it in at last, have we?' she wondered, folding up the cloth.

'Chucked what in?'

'The big house. Summersby.'

'Oh no,' said Ida, 'I wouldn't dream of doing that.'

Mrs Jack wrinkled her powdered nose. 'Just a matter of time, mark my words. You're too good for 'em, my love. Come and look me up, when you do it,' she winked. 'This is where I live. I'll help you find another position. Something suitable.'

Ida suspected that something suitable was more likely something unrespectable. 'Oh no, Mrs Jack, I'm very happy there,' she said quickly, ready to depart.

'Are you now? With all those goings on?'

Ida stopped. 'Goings on?'

Mrs Jack just raised an eyebrow, knowing.

On an impulse Ida took a gamble. 'Do you mean Mr Barker?'

'Ha!' the older woman scoffed.

Ida stepped closer to Mrs Jack's front gate. 'He's a strange man, not often very nice.'

'Oh, he's nice enough when he wants to be.'

'When? I've never seen it.'

'He's nice to those he wants to be nice to,' Mrs Jack said, enigmatically.

'Who? Not to Mr Samuel he's not.'

Mrs Jack dismissed that.

'Who?'

The sometime cook looked sceptically at her. 'Well, I suppose it's a bit before your time.'

'What is?'

A man's voice called out from inside Mrs Jack's cottage, incoherent. 'Pour your own bloody glass!' she yelled back over her shoulder. 'I best be going, love,' she said to Ida with another wink.

'What's before my time?' Ida pressed. 'Who is it Mr Barker was nice to?'

'*Miss Gregory, of course,*' the older woman whispered. 'There was nothing he wouldn't do for her, besotted you might call it. In lust is what I'd call it.'

Ida was startled. 'Not Miss Matilda?'

Mrs Jack tapped the side of her nose as if hinting at something saucy. Then she winked again and was gone inside her front door.

Ida crossed the street, her head full of this conversation. She began traversing the little path that took her down an embankment to where the coaches waited in the forecourt when she saw who watched her from the tall tree shadows.

Barker.

She almost yelped. She stopped still. Barker stared back without shifting his pose, his black eyes glinting.

'Keep going,' Ida told herself. 'It's your afternoon off; you can be where you please. For all he knows you've been shopping . . .'

She went on towards the coaches. Barker continued to watch as she waved to one of the drivers and conducted a brief discourse before being helped inside the coach. She saw him watching still as the horses were flicked with the driver's whip and the transport began to clatter away.

Only when the coach was pulling out from the forecourt did Ida see Barker move away from the shadows, pulling out his tobacco makings from a pouch as he went. He stood in sunlight, apparently considering things for a moment, while he rolled a cigarette. Gripping it in his lips, he struck a match against a fence post and only then, just as the scene vanished from Ida's view, did she see the pair of boys playing marbles on the gravelled street: little Jim Skews and his orphaned cousin, Lewis.

The last Ida saw was the shock-haired valet heading towards them in the dust.

When Ida returned to Summersby in the late afternoon, she found Matilda in the Chinese room seated at her dressing table and engaged in the act of copying poetry from a book. Ida peeped at the work over her shoulder. Matilda's handwriting was beautiful, a fine, smooth copperplate, free of spots and smudges, and nothing like the ugly mess Ida had seen her produce before. 'What a lovely hand you have, miss,' said Ida. She watched her carefully, thinking on this, thinking on everything. 'Do you always write so prettily?'

'Oh yes,' said Matilda, pleased for the compliment. 'Always. I take pride in my penmanship.'

Matilda tapped the Moorish-patterned box. It had been moved from her bedside to the dressing table. 'Do you know what's written inside the lid?'

Ida did know, but pretended she didn't.

Matilda opened the box and showed her. 'It says Remember Box.'

Ida felt acutely conscious of the blue vial, taken from the box and still hidden inside her own little bag from when she had gone into Castlemaine. She had hoped to return it without Matilda guessing it had been taken. Yet, Matilda seemed none the wiser that it had ever been inside the box at all.

'It gave me an idea,' Matilda said. 'Perhaps I should write things down to help me remember them – important things – and put them in this box?' She showed the poem she was copying. 'I am practising my hand. It has been some time. I would hate to make a mess of anything I meant to keep.'

'Well, that is a very good idea, miss,' said Ida. 'We all forget things sometimes.'

Matilda nodded, satisfied. 'It's what my sister does, write things down. It's very useful indeed.'

Ida shifted, uneasy. 'Oh yes?'

'Summersby is full of such clever hiding places for letters,' Matilda mused, continuing to pen in her elegant hand, 'this I already knew, of course, but now that I know my sister's intentions regarding those hiding places, well, many of them can be dismissed, I think.'

Ida had no idea what she referred to, but she stayed attentive. 'If you say so, miss.'

'Their purpose is not to hide what might be placed inside them,' Matilda told her, continuing to write, 'but to expose. They are not true hiding places at all.' She paused and looked up at Ida. 'That lovely robinia tree, for instance, outside in the grounds. My sister has picked it as just such a place for reasons I do not exactly know but can guess at, I believe. Was it the same place Samuel asked her to wed him?' She waited to hear what Ida thought of this idea.

But Ida was staring at what she had failed to see when she had first come into the room. Matilda was wearing a jewelled ring, something that Ida had never seen on her hand before. 'It that something new?' she asked, pointing.

'Oh, yes,' said Matilda, remembering it.

'It is a very pretty ring,' Ida said.

'The largest stone is a diamond,' Matilda told her, showing it. 'The stones that surround it are sapphires.'

'Very pretty,' Ida said. 'They catch at the light.'

'Samuel means for me to wear it.'

Ida's heart skipped. It was a betrothal ring. Samuel had given it to her. Samuel had proposed. She steeled herself. 'Was it your sister's?'

Matilda looked knowing. 'I asked brother Samuel that, too. Do you know what he said? He said, "How could you think so, Matilda?" It was the wrong thing to ask him but I have no idea why it was wrong. I said, didn't you give her pretty things, too, brother?'

'What did he say?'

'He said, "I should like you to cease calling me brother."'

Ida watched her closely.

'Then he said, "Of course I loved your sister. I loved her very much. But now I love you."' She indicated the poem she had copied. 'I have practised enough. I think I might write it all down, everything that was said. What do you think?'

Matilda looked to her with a beaming smile so bright that Ida's eyes welled up. She had never seen such a look upon her mistress's face before. Ida imagined how she herself might have felt had Samuel just asked for her hand. She knew she would have smiled just like Matilda did. 'Do you love Mr Samuel, then?'

Matilda didn't answer. She returned to her painstaking copperplate for a moment, before adding, 'When he gave me the ring I closed my eyes expecting a kiss from him, but do you know, nothing came? I opened them again. He had left me alone beneath the robinia tree. That's when my attention was caught by something wedged into a gap in the tree's trunk.'

Ida felt a chill. 'You didn't find another letter, miss?'

'Yes,' said Matilda, surprised that Ida could have guessed it. 'I found another letter entirely – from my sister, of course – which is what I mean by hiding places that are not for that purpose at all. I tried to pry it out with my fingers at first, but the thing was wedged in. I found a stick and succeeded in dislodging it.'

She withdrew a piece of paper from beneath the sheet she had been writing on. The other paper was identical, apart from being soiled and creased from where it had been placed in the tree trunk. The handwriting was not the beautiful copperplate, however, but the ugly, stolid hand that Ida was already familiar with.

'What does it say?' Ida asked in a trembling voice.

Matilda was about to show her when Aggie spoke up from the door. 'You have accepted him, then?' She had seen the ring on Matilda's hand and was struggling to hide her own shock. Ida couldn't guess how long Aggie had been standing there listening. She tried to tell from the look on her face.

'I believe so,' Matilda said, not sounding particularly sure. The jewels on the ring flashed blue in the glow of the lamplight.

'You believe so?' said Aggie, stressed. 'Did you tell him yes or no, miss?'

'I didn't say either,' said Matilda.

Aggie was made speechless.

Ida stepped in. 'Miss, shouldn't you give Mr Samuel a clear answer on such an important thing?'

'But Samuel is in no doubt about it,' Matilda responded. 'He knows I mean yes, even if I didn't quite say it that way. He actually knows me very well, I think. Almost as well as you both do.'

They watched her stand up and start to wander about the room picking up small items and releasing them – a glove, a shoe, a stocking – all while studying how the stones of the ring captured and reflected the light. 'And besides, Matilda knows, too,' she went to add, before stopping herself. 'I mean, *I* am Matilda,' she said, quickly.

'*Are* you Matilda?' Ida asked, watching her.

Aggie gave her a questioning look. Ida shook her head.

'Aren't I?' Matilda wondered.

'Who do you believe yourself to be?' Ida asked.

Matilda pondered this.

Aggie stepped closer, reaching with the hairbrush to begin stroking Matilda's long, dark hair. Matilda met eyes with Aggie in the looking glass. She gave no reply to Ida's question, and now Ida wondered if she was unwilling to let her know any more of the true state of her mind.

Aggie changed the subject. 'One day soon you and Mr Hackett will move into the master bedroom,' she said. 'Just think.'

Matilda looked about her. 'I will begin a married life with him,' she said. 'I will be Mrs Hackett.' She took on a dreamy look. 'I am so fond of his hair,' she said. 'It is very . . . yellow.'

Ida thought to herself that Samuel's hair was indeed very appealing.

'I wonder if your sister liked his hair, too?' Aggie said, apparently without thinking. When she dared to raise her eyes, she found Matilda eye's looking hard upon her. There was jealousy in her face.

'Perhaps we might pack away some of your less-needed things for the move,' Ida said, breaking the tension.

Ida felt a draught of cool air, over almost as soon as it began, by no means the first time she had felt it. She wondered vaguely at what continued to cause it.

Matilda drifted to the hall outside, happy with her thoughts, leaving Ida and Aggie shocked and alone with their own.

'She knows that I fear for her,' Aggie whispered to Ida, looking at the door though which Matilda had gone.

Ida tried to match Aggie's unease but found she could not get Samuel from her mind. All she could think of was how nice it would be to have him as her betrothed. Had he asked Ida she would have said yes to him on the spot, even if she was an unlucky quadruplet and he had been engaged to her identical dead sisters. A man with Samuel Hackett's looks could make any past misfortune go away. She clung to this conviction like glue. 'Perhaps we should just be happy for her?' she offered.

Aggie's look was withering.

The day's events pressed at Ida's conscience. 'Aggie, I did something today which might make you cross, but I couldn't *not* do it, you see. I had to find something out.'

Aggie wasn't listening, looking out into the hall again. 'I have to speak with her about it. I can't let this continue.'

'Wait, before you do—'

But Aggie had left the room.

Ida looked at the Moorish box and thought of the blue vial and the visit to Mr Skews. She thought of Matilda at the ball and her comment that she didn't think her sister had killed herself – a comment that no one else echoed at all. If Matilda didn't think her sister had taken her own life, then how did she think she had died?

Ida took the vial from her little bag to put it back in the box. Just as she curled her fingernails under the lid to open it, Matilda appeared in the room from nowhere.

'Stop it!' She flew at Ida and snatched the box from her hand. 'That is not yours to see!'

Ida blushed at being caught, the blue vial still in her hand. 'I'm . . . I'm sorry, miss, I didn't mean . . .' She let the vial slip to the floor.

Startled, Aggie reappeared at the door. 'I didn't see you come back in here, miss!'

Matilda hugged the box to her chest. 'We'll say no more of it,' she muttered, turning to walk past her and leave.

'Actually, I think we will say more of it, miss,' said Aggie.

Matilda stopped dead.

'If not about the box exactly, then about some other things,' Aggie said, treading with the greatest of care. 'And when I've said what I have to say, *then* we will say no more about it, if that is your wish. But until I've said it I will not rest.'

Ida held her breath as she waited for their mistress's response to this shocking speech.

The look upon Matilda's face was one of cold incredulity. 'Speak then,' she said.

Aggie cleared her throat. 'It is my belief that Mr Samuel had . . . an *understanding* with your late sister.'

Ida waited for another show of jealousy from Matilda but there was none.

'It was more than simply being betrothed,' Aggie said, 'he had an arrangement with her, a deal.'

Ida couldn't believe that Aggie was daring to talk of this, but Aggie kept her quiet with a look.

'It was an arrangement that saw you wrongly confined at Constantine Hall, miss.' Aggie's voice caught in her throat and Ida saw how much she truly loved Matilda. Nothing she said was from malice.

'It was a deal that required Mr Samuel to lie about who you really were, and maintain that lie all through your false confinement and up to and beyond your sister's passing.' Aggie braced herself to deliver the worst of it. 'It's a lie that he continues with even now . . .' She paused, eyes shining with feeling. 'It has become a lie of omission, a disgusting lie, a lie that did you great wrong and will continue to do so, I fear it, miss,' she implored. 'Mr Samuel is a *liar*,' she said, placing all the terrible emphasis she could upon the word.

Ida's heart stopped as she waited for Matilda's reaction. Yet Matilda said nothing, holding the box tightly before her as she stared in wide-eyed silence at her maids.

Aggie took another deep breath. 'That you are now engaged to be married to him is of great concern.' She softened her tone, taking a step towards Matilda. 'Surely you see that he is untrustworthy and undeserving of your heart?'

Matilda flinched and took a step away.

Aggie hardened herself. 'He stood by while you suffered the loss of your liberty; he enabled it. He remains silent on it now, exploiting your natural confusion, imagining that the truth of what he did will never be known.'

'My "natural confusion"?' Matilda said at last. Her look was suddenly dangerous.

Ida felt Aggie falter. 'Your memory, miss,' Aggie said, 'it is not as it might be, you're the first to admit.'

'My memory is excellent,' said Matilda.

Aggie stood blinking at her in surprise for a second, and then seemed to spot an advantage that might be pressed home. 'Perhaps you remember when Mr Samuel first came to Summersby then, when your father was still alive?'

Matilda's eyes had a burning new intensity to them that alarmed Ida. She could easily have believed then that her mistress *did* remember the event and was replaying it in her mind. Yet the answer, when it came, was the expected one. 'I have forgotten,' Matilda said.

Aggie was gentle. 'It is because of your confusion that Mr Samuel exploits you. If you did remember it, miss, you would remember meeting him as who you really are – as Matilda, not Margaret, whom he so wrongly told people you were much later. Do you see, miss?'

Matilda pulled herself up to her full height. 'I see perfectly, Aggie.'

Aggie smiled in relief. 'I'm so pleased, miss.'

But Matilda was icy. 'And if this matter is ever, in even the tiniest way, mentioned by you again, you will be the worse for it, do you hear me?'

Aggie took a shocked step backwards. 'Worse, miss?'

'You will be dismissed from here.' Matilda advanced upon her. 'Expelled from this house. You will receive no references from me or from anyone else. Your prospects will be nothing if this happens, do you understand? You will be made futureless by your own actions.'

Ida felt a sob breaking in her throat and tried to say something to help her friend. 'Aggie doesn't mean to upset you.'

Matilda turned on her. 'But she upsets me greatly. She outrages me.'

'Please . . .' Aggie tried to counter.

Matilda shook her head, turning to Aggie again. 'That you dare to hold opinions on my life at all is a dismissible action. That you dare to impose those opinions to my very face in an effort to somehow control me is a criminal act. What business there might have been between Mr Samuel and my sister has so little to do with you as to be laughable.'

Aggie began to tremble.

'You are just a servant here, nothing more,' Matilda spat at her, 'and as of today, substantially less.'

Aggie began to cry. 'But how can you ever trust him? How can you ever marry him?'

With one swift action, Matilda stepped forward and struck Aggie hard in the face with the box she held. Aggie cried out and fell to the floor.

'Miss!' Ida screamed.

Matilda turned to Ida, knuckles white as she clutched at the box. *'Because I love my sister,'* she said. 'Ida understands that, don't you, Ida?'

Ida was frozen.

'Don't you, Ida?' Matilda repeated.

'Yes, miss,' she answered in a tiny voice.

Matilda smiled. 'Of course you do. And I will continue to love her, what's more, on terms that are wholly my own and no one else's.' She regarded Aggie sobbing at her feet. 'Most especially yours.'

Matilda left the room.

Shattered, Aggie retired to her bed at Ida's insistence. Ida succumbed to tears of her own for some time until her inquisitive mind told her she must pull herself together again.

On Matilda's dressing table sat the letter found in the trunk of the robinia tree, the handwriting ugly and ink smeared.

Ida couldn't stop herself.

Dear Margaret,

This is for your Remember Box.

At the heart of my plan was the age-old game so loved by all identical twins: swapping places. But here I did something new. I took my time in befriending Samuel Hackett when he came to Summersby, remaining elusive to begin with, perhaps, but never anything less than seductive. I allowed time for old stories of our little games to reach Samuel's ears from the servant gossip, so that he would become accustomed to the notion of identity being a somewhat changeable thing. Then, when I was quite sure that two things had occurred – first, that Samuel had uncovered for himself the terms of our father's last will and testament; and second, that Samuel was highly aroused by me – I claimed that I was you, Margaret, and that hitherto I had only been pretending to be me, Matilda.

Samuel Hackett believed it. In not having lived through our childhood history of trickery, and only hearing second-hand about the chaos it wrought, Samuel overlooked what it was that had made all our earlier deceits effective: your damaged mind. And so, in claiming to Samuel that I was you, and that you were actually me, I relied on this being Samuel's first experience of our game playing. He presumed that our identical appearance alone was enough for the ruse, and I didn't tell him otherwise. What convinced him that I was really you was this: in claiming myself to be Margaret I was risking confinement at Constantine Hall. Who would ever put up their hand for such a thing? And here I hooked amoral Samuel with what I had planned.

That I was confident that Samuel would agree to my plan – which of course he did – reveals so much about my true abilities. Where my father saw a handsome, charming young man in Samuel with potential to bend to my whims, I saw all that and much more. I saw what our father did not see – that Samuel was a dishonest, opportunistic man who would agree to any secret arrangement that might benefit him, but always in the assumption that a better secret arrangement might yet be found. A dishonest man will treat all arrangements dishonestly: this was the important life lesson that I already well knew and wisely heeded.

Your sister who loves you,
Matilda

Ida finished the letter and folded it, breathing fast. Snatched words stayed in her mind among so much that was shocking.

... What convinced him that I was really you was this: in claiming myself to be Margaret, I was risking confinement at Constantine Hall...

The writer of the letter had falsely claimed to Samuel that she was Margaret. That meant she was actually Matilda. Matilda had written the letter *to* Margaret. Yet the letter was not in Matilda's beautiful copperplate hand. Regardless of who had written anything, Margaret was dead and Matilda had been released from the Hall.

She felt sure that someone was intended to be deceived in all this, but the question was who?

Her head spinning with trying to fathom it, Ida opened the letter again and re-read the first line.

At the heart of my plan was the age-old game so loved by all identical twins: swapping places...

That was the key to it, Ida realised with a jolt.

Ida's mistress reappeared at the door: the young woman that she and everyone else had been calling Matilda when perhaps she was not Matilda at all, but Margaret, as she had repeatedly told them herself.

Her hands were empty. She no longer had the Moorish box.

Ida wondered what she had done with it but did not intend to ask. She deliberately turned her back on Matilda and began to place things in a drawer, trying to think of what she might say to her mistress now that she was starting to *see*. Another cool draught stirred the hair escaping from her housemaid's cap, and once again, the gust was over almost as soon as it had begun.

Something flashed near the bed in the lamplight from the corner of Ida's eye. She turned to see but there was nothing. Matilda remained where she was at the door.

The Moorish box now sat on its little pile of books upon the bedside table. Ida blinked in surprise. 'How did it?'

Matilda crossed the room to the bed. 'Why has she moved my Remember Box?' she asked. She picked up the box, moving to the chest of drawers. Unable to conceive how it could have returned to the room unseen and of its own accord, Ida felt her flesh begin to creep. She stood aside as Matilda pulled open the desired drawer and stashed the box deep inside.

It was too much to deal with. Ida ran from the room.

BIDDY

JANUARY 1904

6

When the long discussion between Biddy and Sybil was over it was past the time for luncheon. Sybil withdrew to the library to eat with Miss Garfield. Biddy was not required and was not offended at being excluded. Mrs Marshall closed the baize door, her signal that she wished an hour or two of soul-searching. Biddy was given her own meal on her tray, plus a meal for Jim Skews, and asked to take the latter upstairs to him. Biddy kept her composure while the house-keeper explained how she might locate the telegraph room. Mrs Marshall made no suggestion as to where Biddy might eat her own meal and so Biddy took the two plates all the way to where Jim was working and tapped upon the door. She hadn't intended returning to the telegraph room again if she could help it, but now the possibility of further information it might contain began to suggest itself.

'Who is it?' Jim called down from inside the tower.

'It's Biddy. I've brought you your pasty, Mr Skews.'

After a moment she heard Jim's feet coming down the spiral stairs and the door opened. The smiling lightning squirter greeted her like an old friend. If the significance of Sybil's relatives' words from the morning had caused a seismic upheaval downstairs, Jim gave no indication of it bringing anything amiss above.

Her mind filled with the task ahead of her, Biddy came up the staircase with him to eat, seating herself on the room's stuffed leather armchair, the tray on her knee. Jim gave no sign of this being amiss, either, dining at his desk.

'You don't wear a maid's uniform, Biddy. Don't they mind?' he wondered.

'They probably would if I was a maid,' said Biddy.

Jim seemed to mull on this. 'Not a maid at all then? Well, that's a bit rum.'

'Not for me,' said Biddy with a smile. 'And I *do* work here, you know. It's not as if I'd make up stories about such a thing.'

'You don't strike me as the fibbing sort,' said Jim.

Biddy was disconcerted by this and looked to see if he was having a joke. 'I'm sorry, I thought you knew,' she said, when it seemed apparent that he wasn't. 'I'm Miss Sybil's companion.'

'Ah . . .'

Biddy still thought she saw a glimmer of a tease in his eyes. 'Sybil's relatives have mentioned me in their telegraph message,' she said, after a time, deciding to proceed with care.

Jim chewed upon his pastry. 'They don't miss much,' he said.

Biddy nodded, as if this was something of which she was all too aware.

'But sometimes I wonder if I do,' said Jim. His eyes twinkled.

The pasty went leaden in Biddy's mouth.

Jim kept on smiling while he ate.

The rest of her meal was hastily consumed. Biddy rose to take up the plates and cutlery, and as Jim passed his plate to her he held his grip upon it when she took the other edge. 'I'm just going along to the convenience now,' he said. 'Keep an eye on the room while I'm gone, will you, Biddy? I don't like to think of anyone trying to get in.'

A sweat bead broke and ran down Biddy's back. 'Yes, Mr Skews.'

'Why don't you call me Jim?' He released the willow pattern plate and went down the spiral staircase.

Biddy leapt at the wire desk tray labelled 'Out' and rifled through the papers. The new week's letters yet to be sent were there and, miraculously, beneath them were the letters from the previous week, face down to show they were done. They hadn't been returned to their senders and they hadn't been thrown away. Biddy flipped the sheets aside, discarding Miss Garfield's penmanship first, before she reached Mrs Marshall's block capitals. She flicked over the first, then the second page of the correspondence, seeking the third and final sheet; the sheet to which Biddy had added the postscript.

It wasn't there.

Biddy looked under the wire basket, and then in the drawers, but the doctored sheet of Mrs Marshall's letter wasn't to be found. With sickening certainty beginning to form in her stomach that Jim was one step ahead of her, Biddy looked in the rubbish bin. It was empty of anything except peach stones.

When Jim returned, Biddy was standing at the base of the staircase, waiting for him with the tray of luncheon things in her hands.

'Best get back to it, then,' said Jim. Biddy was more than ready to leave. 'Oh, and Biddy?'

She turned and found he was right at her shoulder.

'Some people find independence wrong in a girl,' he said, 'do you think that's fair?'

The tray grew heavy in Biddy's hands. 'What some people find is of no interest to me,' said Biddy, carefully.

'I don't think it's fair at all,' said Jim. 'Why shouldn't a girl want what she wants? Some people think they can dictate a girl's heart.'

Biddy span around to glare at him, the tray things before her like a shield. 'Are you trying to intimidate me, Mr Skews?' she asked. 'Because I wouldn't if I were you.'

Thrown, he stepped back a pace. 'What are you talking about?'

'What are *you* talking about?' she said. 'Is it the threat of something improper? Sounds like it might be, and if so, think again. You might think you're safe in Summersby, but I'll tell you something for nothing: I'm safer. I've got a protector. Want to put him to the test?'

He stared at Biddy for a shocked moment. 'What are you getting worked up for? You misunderstand my meaning.'

But Biddy walked outside to the corridor, the tray still in her hand, before he could say any more. If he'd been trying to convey something important to her, Biddy's nerves and guilty conscience had stopped her from hearing it.

All the long way down the servants' stairs, the tray things rattled like an earth tremor was under them. Biddy's nerves had been stretched as if she'd just run half a mile. For the first time in her life she feared where her stories might take her. The promise made to Sybil had been rash and ill conceived, and she couldn't perceive how she would fulfil it. Beyond subterfuge in the telegraph room, she had no further source of illicit information, and now that source was to be avoided, too. Worse, the story told to Jim about having a 'protector' was made in the spur of duress. Biddy had no protector; a fact easily exposed should Jim set his mind to doing so. Biddy feared the next encounter with him. What would he do? What would he say? Who else would he say it to?

Biddy's mind was in a tumult as she reached the kitchen. She resolved to throw herself before Sybil and tell her the truth behind the relatives' words. This seemed the only way to disarm Jim. But as she placed the luncheon knives and forks in the sink and automatically began to wash them, she saw the hopelessness of this plan. Her friendship with Sybil was unequal. The well-to-do girl was skittish. Why would she forgive an untrustworthy friend when certainty could come with that friend's banishment?

As Biddy began to wash the plates she saw the consequences of confession stretching before her. Her companion's position would end forthwith and Miss Garfield and Mrs Marshall would revert to their true selves, sheltering Sybil from all further pain while she, Biddy, was driven back to the abandoned hut. But then the hut would be denied her, too, given that it stood on Summersby land, so Biddy would be forced to return to Castlemaine, to stand at the lonely railway platform. And if Mrs Marshall and Miss Garfield were of a greater vindictive mind – and who could blame them if they were? – then Castlemaine Gaol would be her destination. Biddy would be locked up in prison for all of her stories, and the terrible truths that she'd shunned and ignored and tried to outrun would meet her in a rush, and everyone would know what she really was and why she had nothing and no one at all.

This picture of what her existence would be was so stark that Biddy burst into tears over the dishwater. She tried to wipe the tears from her face, but they couldn't be stopped, so she gave into them and allowed herself the comfort of crying, grateful for being alone where no one would see it.

'G'day, Biddy!' called a surprised voice behind her, 'don't tell me you've come back home to us again?'

She turned around in shock and saw the tall, broad-shouldered form of Lewis Fitzwater at the door, caught in the act of wiping his boots and removing his hat.

'Hey, hey now, what's happened to you? You're all cut up and crying, Biddy, don't do that,' he said, coming towards her at the sink.

Biddy tried to reply but couldn't make the words, and she continued to cry until she was led to a chair by a strong, brown arm about her shoulder, and encouraged to sit down.

'This is your heart breaking for your friend, the Reverend, isn't it?' Lewis asked her. 'I suppose he's been gathered by now, has he? Well, that's very sad, and you're right to grieve for him as a good friend should. But this was his time, Biddy, and there is nothing to be done.'

Her tears ceased and she looked at him in confusion.

'Your mate, the Reverend,' said Lewis. 'I'm sorry he's died.'

Biddy suddenly remembered the story she had written in the letter she'd left him at the hut, claiming she had returned to Melbourne. 'Yes . . . yes . . . there was nothing to be done to save him.'

'If I was a God-bothering bloke I'd say a prayer for him,' said Lewis, sympathetic, 'but I'm supposing he did enough God-bothering of his own while still breathing, and the Almighty's probably heard enough prayers to have made his mind up about him long ago.'

Biddy almost smiled, maintaining the fiction. 'He was a very good man,' she agreed. 'Straight to heaven. No stops along the way.' She found her handkerchief and dabbed at her eyes.

'Doesn't mean you won't miss him before you get up there yourself though, does it?' he ventured. 'I've had a blub for everyone I've lost in my time. And there's been a few.'

Biddy looked at him anew.

'So you're back here at Summersby then?'

Biddy nodded, searching for something to say to support the story that she'd worked as the Summersby cook. 'Everyone's been very kind.'

'It's a good house, this.'

'I owe you my thanks, Mr Fitzwater,' she told him, in a rush of feeling. 'It's all worked out for me.'

'You're calling me "Mr" now? Didn't I tell you my name was Lewis?'

Biddy beamed back at him until she remembered Jim and the promise made to Sybil, and her smile fell away.

'Getting yourself some tucker, mate?' called another male voice behind them.

Biddy lurched in her chair. Jim stood, giving an identical grin from the bottom of the servants' stairs. But behind the cheer he was wary. There was unease in his eyes.

Lewis at once stood up, looking caught out. 'This is Biddy,' he said, 'she cooks here.'

Biddy looked from one to the other.

'This is Jim,' Lewis said to her. 'He's me cousin, works as a lightning squirter.'

Biddy's mouth went dry.

'Biddy, is it?' said Jim to her with a wink, 'Well, you're a looker, ain't she, Lew?'

'Keep a smart tongue in your head,' said Lewis, 'she's suffered bereavement.'

Jim looked genuinely abashed to hear this. 'I meant nothing by it. Sorry for your loss.'

'No offence taken,' said Biddy, narrowing her eyes at him. Jim's own eyes reflected sympathy, yet the wariness remained. He almost seemed keen for his cousin to remain under the impression that he and Biddy hadn't met.

Lewis turned to Biddy again. 'Jim's practically all I've got in the world and I'm all he's got, like it or lump it.'

'Nice to meet you, Jim,' said Biddy, carefully.

Jim held out his hand and Biddy felt she had no option but to shake it. His grip was warm.

Mrs Marshall entered the room through the baize door and all three of them sprang from each other as if guilty of something. 'Is it a holiday?' asked the housekeeper.

'No, Mrs Marshall,' said Biddy, speaking first. 'Lewis is here to have his dinner, I think.'

'Wait outside, please, Lewis,' said the housekeeper. 'I'll not have your dusty clothes in the kitchen.'

Lewis made haste for the door. 'See you later then, Biddy,' he said with a wink.

'Unless I see her first,' Jim added lightly from the stairs.

Biddy willed herself not to look at Jim as he made his way back up to the telegraph room.

'Biddy,' called Mrs Marshall on a late January morning when the day ahead looked to be milder. 'I am going into town, will you accompany me?'

'To Castlemaine, Mrs Marshall?'

'To Summersby village,' the housekeeper said. 'Everything I require will be found there. No need to go any further afield today.' She had a brown paper parcel before her on the table, in the process of securing it with string.

'Yes, Mrs Marshall. I'll fetch my hat and gloves.' Biddy was excited. She had skirted the little local village when she'd been forced to live in the hut, but she hadn't dared walk along the main street, fearful she'd be seen and talked about, and ultimately found. But the village of Summersby had seemed attractive from a distance, with its several little shops and even a restaurant of sorts. She wanted to see it. And it was also possible, Biddy thought, that the visit might unearth a clue that would help her in her quest.

When Biddy returned to the kitchen attired for the excursion, she found Mrs Marshall at the door to the yard. 'She is coming now,' the housekeeper called out to someone when she saw Biddy, 'we are ready to leave.'

Biddy came to where Mrs Marshall was waiting and saw Lewis outside with a horse and surrey. He gave Biddy a wink and doffed his hat at her. 'Morning, Biddy,' he grinned.

'This is *Miss MacBryde*,' Mrs Marshall informed him as she took Lewis's arm to mount the transport, 'she is a companion here, not a servant, and should be addressed as such, Lewis.'

Biddy went pink.

'My mistake, miss,' Lewis said. It was Biddy's turn to be helped aboard and Lewis kept his grin in place, but raised an eyebrow at her. 'Companion now, is it?'

'To Miss Sybil,' said Mrs Marshall.

Lewis narrowed his eyes at Biddy, assessing her anew, as she steadied her gloved hand on his arm, making to climb the step. He didn't seem perturbed by the discovery, but Biddy was embarrassed that she hadn't been able to explain her altered circumstances to him in her own terms. 'It doesn't mean I'm up myself,' she whispered to him.

'Biddy,' said the housekeeper, warningly, and Biddy went quiet. Lewis flicked the horse's reins and the surrey set forth down the long Summersby drive.

Mrs Marshall settled the brown paper parcel in her basket and began her favoured conversation, that of household tips and domestic matters. These chats were an education of sorts, an ongoing test of their respective domestic knowledge. Biddy was rarely found wanting.

'What is a method to rid a home of mosquitoes?' asked Mrs Marshall, launching in over the rhythm of the horse's hooves.

'There are several methods that I know of, Mrs Marshall,' Biddy replied. Her eyes were on the back of Lewis's hat, where he sat in front of them, pretending he wasn't listening to her words. Biddy had a mind to show off a little. 'The one I favour is to place a piece of cow pat on the fire embers before I go to bed. Not a fresh one, mind, because that won't do anything. You need to make sure it's dried. I'd keep a store of them for the purpose if I had my own household. They throw out a scented smoke, a bit peculiar but not nasty, and the mozzies don't like it at all.' She turned her smile to Mrs Marshall and found the housekeeper looking askance.

'That sounds like a very *old* method,' said Mrs Marshall, and Biddy perceived how unladylike the mention of cow pats had been. She thought she heard Lewis stifling a laugh in front.

'But no doubt it's effective,' the housekeeper added. 'I will list it in my book of household remedies for ever such time as I find myself living in a shearing shed.'

Lewis stifled his laugh again and this time Biddy heard it distinctly.

'And what of fleas?' Mrs Marshall went on. 'What is your remedy for those?'

Biddy didn't hesitate. 'Half a teaspoon of black pepper, a teaspoon of sugar and a teaspoon of cream.'

'And how do you apply it?'

'Well, you don't rub it in your hair,' Biddy clarified for listening Lewis's benefit. 'You mix it all on a saucer and leave it in a room where the fleas are. They hate it as much as the mozzies hate the cow pat.'

'Clever girl,' said Mrs Marshall, approvingly. 'Someone taught you well.'

Biddy kept her eyes on the back of Lewis's hat. 'Someone did,' was all she said. As to who that someone was Biddy didn't explain, and Mrs Marshall, who had already sensed that there were things from Biddy's past about which she would not be pressed, did not enquire further.

'I'll remember that one when I put my head down tonight,' Lewis offered from the front, without turning around. 'That many fleas in our cottage, I could spread 'em on toast for me breakfast.'

It was Biddy's turn to stifle a laugh.

'Are you saying Summersby has provided you with an inadequate cottage, Lewis?' the housekeeper shot at him.

'No, Mrs Marshall,' said Lewis, still not turning around, 'real comfortable it is. Apart from the fleas.'

There was an affronted pause from Mrs Marshall, where only the clip-clop of the hooves was heard. 'Remind me to prepare a saucer of the remedy for Lewis when we return, Biddy,' she said at last.

The surrey hit a hole in the gravelled road and all three of them lurched forward with a jolt. The parcel flipped from the shopping basket on Mrs Marshall's knee and landed on the seat in front.

'All right, ladies?' Lewis asked.

'Will you please drive with more care?' complained the housekeeper.

Lewis fished the parcel from where it had fallen next to him and returned it to Mrs Marshall.

The three of them remained silent for the rest of the ride.

As Lewis steered the horse and surrey along Mitchell Street, named for the explorer who had first sighted the region, they neared some ladies selling delicacies from a cake stall, arranged on trestles outside the Presbyterian Church. 'Halt here please, Lewis,' instructed Mrs Marshall. Lewis reined the horse and assisted the housekeeper and then Biddy to the ground. 'We shall not require you for an hour,' Mrs Marshall told him. 'Collect us from the front of the Railway Stores. Your time is your own until then.'

'Thank you, Mrs Marshall,' Lewis tipped his hat at her.

Biddy flicked her eyes in his direction and was pleased to see he was smiling at her as Mrs Marshall went ahead to the ladies' stall.

'You *sure* you're not up yourself?' he wondered.

Biddy harrumphed and followed Mrs Marshall, but when she snuck a look over her shoulder again, Lewis hadn't moved and was only grinning more. 'Thought so,' he mouthed at her.

Although she made plenty of cakes and biscuits of her own at the great house, Mrs Marshall bought several on offer from the Presbyterian Ladies Committee, given that they were raising funds for the parish poor. Biddy suspected that the best of the cakes may have been purchased already and that these were the also-rans, but Mrs Marshall reacted to them as if they were worthy of a Buckingham Palace high tea. The three ladies in attendance were vocal in their gratitude.

'And look at Miss Sybil?' cried one, smiling at Biddy. 'My, how lovely she's becoming.'

'This is Miss MacBryde,' said the housekeeper, 'Miss Sybil's *companion*.'

The woman was evidently thrown, as were her colleagues. 'But you look so like her,' said the lady, 'especially your beautiful hair. Please forgive me, dear.' Biddy saw the ladies adjust their attitude towards her. Their respectfulness went down a notch, but by no means disappeared altogether.

'You should eat more, child,' said one of the other women to Biddy. 'You mind you get some of that sponge into you before Mrs Marshall lets the farm boys have it.'

The other ladies laughed and Mrs Marshall led Biddy along the street towards the butcher's shop.

*

'Mr Taylor is always to be treated with politeness,' said Mrs Marshall, once she and Biddy had exited the butcher's shop, 'but his gossip is really not to be encouraged, Biddy.'

'Even when it's interesting?' Biddy asked, in apparent innocence.

Mrs Marshall pursed her lips by way of an answer and then looked towards the Railway Stores. Lewis had tethered the horse and surrey out front and was waiting in the shade of the veranda. 'I need to use the postal service,' said the housekeeper as they strolled towards him. 'Wait with Lewis while I go inside, Biddy.'

Biddy did so, Lewis barely acknowledging her presence until Mrs Marshall had gone. 'Got you a present,' he grinned at her.

'You what?' said Biddy, taken aback.

'A present,' said Lewis. 'I bought you something.'

For the second time that morning Biddy blushed at him. 'You really shouldn't have,' she stammered, 'you hardly know me.'

Lewis dismissed this. 'It's not an engagement ring,' he retorted and Biddy rode the wave of a third blush.

A rolled-up journal was placed in her hand. 'What's this?'

'You already told me you can read.'

Biddy unrolled it to reveal the cover of the *Bulletin*.

'You ever read it?' Lewis asked her. 'Comes all the way from Sydney.'

Biddy shook her head.

Lewis tapped his temple. 'Good stuff in there. *Ideas*. It'll make you think about the times we live in.'

Biddy looked up at him in some amazement. 'Think? Do I need a printed journal to let me do that?'

'You might,' said Lewis, 'to think about certain things, anyway.' He tapped his temple again. 'I did.'

Biddy wasn't sure what to make of it, but thanked him for it anyway. 'I hope it wasn't dear.'

'Good ideas are worth paying something for.'

Biddy tucked the journal under the things in her basket just as Mrs Marshall emerged from the store, now minus her parcel and carrying a folded newspaper under her arm. She looked at Biddy warmly before placing the newspaper in her hands. 'Just because you have no governess to tutor you, does not mean you must remain ignorant of the world about you, Biddy,' she said. 'I have bought you *The Australasian*, a respectable publication that I shall continue to purchase for you once a week. It is from Melbourne and therefore sound. New South Wales publications have found their way to our climes, and rabble rousing along with them.'

Biddy felt the *Bulletin* grow heavy in her basket.

'Flamboyant publications,' said Mrs Marshall, 'and unsuitable for any young woman. *The Australasian* has never been anything less than trustworthy in my view and I look forward to discussing its issues with you.'

When the three of them returned to Summersby, Mrs Marshall alighted from the surrey before Lewis could even assist her. She hurried to the kitchens, claiming they'd taken too long at shopping and that the midday dinner would be delayed. Biddy offered assistance but the housekeeper was through the door and Biddy didn't hear her reply.

Lewis helped her down from the surrey and neither rushed the process. She liked placing her hand on his arm for balance. 'Thank you for your present,' she told him. 'I'll read it cover to cover.'

'Make sure you do,' said Lewis. 'You won't regret an education.'

Biddy turned to go inside and then stopped, looking back at him, thoughtfully. She considered herself to be a resourceful girl, but a girl who knew when to seek assistance from those who were well disposed towards her was the most resourceful of all.

'Something wrong?' Lewis asked as she looked at him.

She wondered how she might phrase her words without risking the things Sybil most feared. 'There's a mystery . . .' she started to say.

'What's that?'

Biddy cleared her throat. 'A mystery,' she began again. 'There's a puzzle I'd like to solve. Well, need to solve really.'

Lewis cocked his head at her, plainly not sure if she was pulling his leg. 'Like the mystery of the Flannan Isle lighthouse keepers? I've got a theory on what happened to them.'

Biddy chose her words with care. 'It's a bit like that. I want to find something that's gone missing, too. Something important.'

Lewis tipped his hat from his brow and scratched at his hairline. 'Tell me.'

Biddy steeled herself. 'It's not even a some*thing*, it's a someone.'

'A person's gone missing?'

Biddy nodded.

'Got lost in the bush?'

'Not like that. At least, I don't think so. They're missing in another way – a way that doesn't make people worried.'

'You look worried,' said Lewis, giving his grin again.

She cleared her throat once more; aware she wasn't doing this very well.

'I'm sorry,' said Lewis, 'you're fair dinkum, aren't you?'

'Yes,' said Biddy.

'You're looking for someone and you'd like me to help you?'

Biddy sighed in gratitude. 'I like to think I'm canny about things,' she told him, 'but being canny means you can tell when someone else is canny, too. Two canny heads on a puzzle solves it in half the time.'

The horse was growing impatient, wanting its bag of oats. Lewis stroked its mane. 'Come with me to the stables where we can talk properly, Biddy.'

She cast a glance towards the door to the kitchen and Mrs Marshall no doubt expecting her inside. 'All right then . . .'

Glad to be detached from the surrey, the horse chewed its oats as Biddy and Lewis leant on the corral to talk.

'So who is it that's missing then?' he asked.

'I don't know their name.'

'Rightio. What do they do? Where are they from?'

'I don't know that either.'

Lewis creased his brow. 'So, as mysteries go, I'm gunna have better luck with the lighthouse keepers? What *do* you know?'

'It's a girl,' said Biddy.

That refreshed Lewis's interest. 'What's happened to her?'

Biddy felt her anxiety rise as she wondered whether she'd bitten off more than she could chew. Sybil's fear of her relatives was very real, and while Biddy had her doubts, they clearly posed something of a threat. 'It's not that anything's happened,' she explained, 'but rather, all the evidence of who she is and where she lives and what she does with herself is being kept from view – if she's even real at all. There's something very strange about it.'

'Is any of this supposed to make sense?' Lewis wondered.

Biddy deflated. 'Maybe that's part of what's so strange about it . . .'

'Well, this ain't much to go on, Biddy.'

'I know,' she conceded.

'Cooooo-ee!' A piercing yell startled them. Jim appeared at the stable door. Biddy kept her face composed at the sight of him.

Lewis turned in his cousin's direction. 'What's your damn racket about?'

'You're wanted at the cottage,' Jim told him. 'The old bastard's awake.'

He disappeared and Biddy was relieved he hadn't decided to join them.

Lewis turned back to Biddy, apologetic. 'Can you tell me the rest of it quick? The old bugger's sobered himself up and he'll be waiting for me to bow to him.'

'Is that your uncle?'

'That's him,' Lewis rolled his eyes. 'A misery.'

Biddy felt as if her plan had failed her. 'I don't think I should have said anything about it. Will you forget I did?'

He was plainly puzzled by her. 'If you say so.'

Biddy made to take off. 'Thanks for the present again.'

Lewis nodded and smiled.

A sudden thought hit her. 'I've just thought of how to explain it!'

'Cripes! You coming or going?'

Biddy returned to the corral. 'This girl who's missing, this girl I need to find,' she whispered, 'the only thing I know for certain is a *big* thing: she's important. She has to be – she means too much to Summersby for her to be nobody. She's *somebody*. She's as important as Summersby itself in her own way. People know of her and they talk about her, too. Whoever she is.'

Lewis squinted at her. 'Sounds like we've got more to go on than we thought we did.'

Biddy was pleased he'd said 'we'. 'She's very important to *me*, Lewis. I know we don't have much to go on to actually find this girl, but maybe we've got just enough to find a *way* to find her, if that makes any sense.'

Lewis nodded. 'I suppose it does. Sort of.' He mused for a moment.

Biddy was heading in the direction of the stable door again when he added, 'Margaret Gregory.'

Biddy stopped. 'Who?'

He shrugged. 'I don't know. You tell me. Margaret Gregory.'

Biddy returned to his side. 'Who are you talking about?'

'This missing girl, who's so important – missing yet not missing, as you put it; missing in view – her name might be Margaret Gregory.'

Biddy stared at him. She remembered the name as the recipient of the letter from the hut, yet that had been written many years ago. 'But who is she? How do you know this name?'

'Mrs Marshall. Every week she sends a parcel, wrapped in brown paper – sometimes a small one, sometimes a bit bigger. They mean a lot to Mrs Marshall those parcels because she never lets 'em out of her sight until they're safely posted at the Railway Stores. I know this because I'm the one who drives her into town.' He watched Biddy digest this. 'She's very regular in her habits.'

With a start Biddy realised this was true. She had seen Mrs Marshall carefully cradling parcels on a number of occasions, but had never given further thought to it. 'But who is Margaret Gregory?'

'No idea,' said Lewis, 'but you might say she's hidden in view. When today's parcel jumped from Mrs Marshall's basket and landed in my lap, I saw the name on it: Miss Margaret Gregory, care of Number One Hundred and Eight, Auburn Grove, Hawthorn. I reckon that's in Melbourne.'

Biddy just stared at him. 'Auburn Grove . . .' she repeated, 'Auburn Grove . . .'

'Know of it?' Lewis asked.

A tiny part of Biddy actually thought that she did know of it in some little way, but how?

'Never heard of it,' she said.

Jim reappeared at the door, rolling a cigarette. He took in Biddy and Lewis still talking together and apparently decided to make it a party. 'Thought I told you the bastard's awake?' he offered. 'He spent his morning kip dreaming up jobs for you to do.'

Biddy felt herself growing tense.

Lewis gave no regard to this, and when his cousin came into the corral he plucked the rolled cigarette from Jim's hand and claimed it as his five-minute smoko. Jim blithely started on rolling another one.

'Margaret Gregory,' said Lewis, exhaling a cloud of blue-grey smoke once he'd lit it. 'That name ever come up in your lightning squirts, Jim?'

Biddy stopped breathing.

Jim tapped his nose. 'I owe my security of position to a healthy respect for discretion,' he said, a twinkle in his eye.

'A yes or a no,' said Lewis. 'Does that name sound familiar?'

'Let me repeat myself on account of your small brain, Lew: I owe my security of position—'

Lewis cut him off. 'We all know you've got tickets on yourself – no lead to labour it. Just tell me if you've seen the bloody name.'

Jim licked the edge of the rice paper into a tight, white tube. 'What does it matter if I have?'

'Matters to me,' Lewis told him.

Jim grinned; an expression that would have perfectly matched his cousin had the latter been in a more jovial frame of mind. Lewis's look stayed serious. 'This about your little sweetheart?' Jim teased.

Biddy wanted the ground to swallow her up with the embarrassment. Lewis looked like he might hit him.

'Ah ha,' said Jim, 'that's taken off a bit fast, hasn't it?'

Lewis's hands clenched into fists but the grin on Jim's face only widened, good-natured laughter in his eyes. 'All right, keep your hat on. Just having a lark.'

'Biddy's flesh and blood,' said Lewis. 'You like girls made out of ectoplasm, I reckon.'

Jim looked less amused. 'My sweetheart's *real*. You can take my word for it.'

'So real I've never seen her yet,' said Lewis, 'despite you singing her praises for months. Not allowed to see her, not allowed to know one provable fact about her. Yeah, she's a phantom sweetheart, I'd say. She's set up shop inside your imagination.'

'Margaret Gregory,' said Jim.

Lewis stopped short, the half-smoked cigarette between his lips. 'She's not your bloody sweetheart?'

Jim savoured a lungful of smoke, releasing it slowly through his nostrils. 'Nup,' he said at last. Then he laughed at Lewis's angry look. 'Never heard of a Margaret, you dozy bugger, on the lightning squirts or otherwise. Who is she, anyway?'

Lewis looked to Biddy, apologetic. 'None of your business,' he said.

Lewis took off to find the bedridden uncle and the list of chores, leaving Jim to his own devices. Biddy left the stables to make her way back to the house, knowing Jim was watching her from the door. She didn't rush. She knew that *he* knew something about Margaret Gregory. It was obvious. But Biddy knew something now, too, something she had not known before the conversation in the stable, but had certainly wondered at. It was about Jim's sweetheart.

She was not surprised when Jim appeared by her side as she strolled towards the kitchen door. He had rolled himself another cigarette.

Biddy got a word in first. 'Must be annoying,' she told him.

'What must?' said Jim.

'Having so little control of your own private life.' She looked sympathetically at him. 'What with Sybil dictating the times and places of all your secret trysting, you must wonder what the benefits are of having such a pretty girl at all?'

There was a long moment while he assessed her anew. Eventually he said, 'I knew you'd work it out.'

'Did you now?'

'Told Sybil you would, too. You're no drip, Biddy. You've got a good head on your shoulders.'

She took that as a compliment. 'And yet I'm still just the smoke-screen, aren't I? I'm only here to make sure everyone else looks in the wrong direction?'

For the first time since meeting him, Jim suddenly seemed contrite to Biddy. His face softened and she saw that there was real feeling behind all his apparent mirth. He seemed like a worried little boy. 'It's not like that,' he began.

'Isn't it?'

'Maybe to begin with . . .' He stepped closer, appealing to her. 'Sybil really loves you, Bid. Don't think it's otherwise. She hates having to lie and keep secrets, but that's how things have to be, at least for the time being.'

'How things have to be because she loves *you*?'

Tears pricked in his eyes. He was at her mercy, she realised. 'Gunna tell anyone?'

Biddy made a show of considering. 'When we're on the same side? Why would I?' she said. 'Last thing I'd want to do is stand in the way of true love.' She stopped to study him. The breeze rippled the long, dry grass at their feet as she thought of the words she had written at the end of Mrs Marshall's letter, the words Jim had telegraphed that had told Sybil's relatives of Biddy's existence. 'If you ask me, everyone has a few things they'd like left quiet,' she mused.

His demeanour changed. The smile he now gave her was suddenly pally. He trusted her. 'Syb's got such fine prospects, too – and I can't even brag in the open about her or squire her on me arm.'

'Very unfair,' said Biddy.

'This whole business is unfair. Secret Heiress rubbish, relatives she's not allowed to know.'

'Do you really love her?'

Jim actually looked hurt. 'Of course I do. She's everything to me.'

Biddy took a long moment to regard him closely. She wanted to doubt him, wanted to call him a liar for such easily spoken sentiments, given how little he'd seemingly offered her before this moment to make her think of him as someone who might be capable of sincerity, let alone love. And yet as she looked into his eyes she saw with surprise that he was sincere and always had been, if only she'd realised it. The man she glimpsed was vulnerable, scared of the situation in which he had unwittingly found himself, scared of his complete lack of say in any of it, and scared of being forced to keep such an enormous thing to himself. He was scared because he was so in love with Sybil, deliriously and hopelessly. To Biddy's final surprise she found that she pitied him for it. He mightn't have been the most trustworthy of young men in her view, or for that matter the nicest, but even someone of Jim's character could find themselves at the mercy of their hearts.

'Truth is though,' he went on in a quiet voice, 'sometimes love feels like resentment; resentment that she gets to be more of a man than I do.'

He tossed his cigarette into the garden before he'd finished smoking it.

'Who's Margaret Gregory?' Biddy asked. 'And don't fib to me, Jim.'

'I don't know,' he told her.

She crinkled her eyes at him.

'I don't,' he repeated.

'Could she be this Secret Heiress?'

'Could be,' said Jim, sucking his teeth. 'Could be someone else again.'

'Why is everything made so bloomin' mysterious around here?' Biddy asked him, exasperated.

'Because Mrs Marshall's got something she wants hidden away, something scandalous, that's why,' he told her. 'It's why everything's sent in telegraph messages – she's scared of sending letters the normal way in case someone reads 'em by mistake. Don't ask me what the scandalous thing is, though, because I swear I don't know – all I do know is Sybil's part of it, but she's not allowed to know either. Mrs Marshall won't *let* her know.'

In light of Biddy's own experience of an unwitting life of lies, she knew she couldn't live with herself if she let Sybil remain at the mercy of others who claimed to know better. Nothing was ever better than the truth. *Nothing*.

'Do you know, Jim,' she mused, 'if I were a man feeling restless and frustrated in a situation like yours, I reckon I'd be looking for ways I could take some action that might make certain things change.'

He tilted the hat from his brow. 'Such as?'

Biddy glanced at the Summersby tower where the telegraph machine lived.

'Such as the lightning squirts, for a start.'

Biddy pressed the door to the drawing room shut before taking to the sofa, training her ears for the telltale signs of footsteps in the hall while she and Sybil kept their voices low. 'You've never heard that name Margaret Gregory before?' Biddy clarified.

She was holding her tongue for now on what she had learned from Jim Skews.

'Never,' said Sybil, already seated.

'Not once? Never in your entire life?'

'I'd remember it if I had,' said Sybil, 'it's the same as my own!'

'*Gregory*. It can't be a coincidence, can it?'

Sybil agreed it was unlikely.

'Identical twins changing places, a servant who was never once fooled – does any of that mean anything to you?' Biddy went on.

'No,' said Sybil.

'None of it?'

'No. Should it?'

Biddy frowned. 'I sort of feel like it should, yes,' she said, 'but I'm blessed if I know why yet. Twins might have something to do with all this – one called Margaret, and the other, Matilda.'

'Oh, Biddy,' Sybil began again, trying to keep the excitement from her voice, 'you're very clever to work it out.'

Biddy held up her hand. 'Nothing is clear yet, Sybil, and I've hardly done anything. So tell me, how much of Mrs Marshall's life do you know about?'

Biddy suspected this was the first time the idea of the house-keeper even having a life outside Summersby had occurred to Sybil. 'Well, I know she originally comes from Beechworth,' she said, after a moment. 'Wait, I think it was Myrtleford.'

Biddy smiled, her suspicion confirmed. 'Who might she know called Margaret Gregory that she'd have reason to send parcels to?'

Sybil looked shamefaced. 'She's been the Summersby house-keeper all my life, but I know nothing of her family.'

Biddy would have laughed at this, thinking it typical of those who employed servants, until she saw a parallel with her own situation. This made her see the housekeeper in an alternative light. 'It may be then that Mrs Marshall has no family – or friends,' said Biddy, speaking from experience, 'meaning she never talks of those that don't exist. It's not a slight on you for knowing so little about her, Sybil; it's just that what friends and family she has are all here at Summersby.'

Sybil nodded. 'Now that I think of it, she has never gone on a holiday,' she said, 'in all these years. She has never gone to visit someone. If she had people of her own outside Summersby, surely she would see them?'

'And yet she sends a weekly parcel to someone,' said Biddy, 'and this week the parcel went to a Miss Margaret Gregory. You do realise this makes her a liar then?'

Sybil looked alarmed. 'Who's lying?'

'Mrs Marshall, of course; she who would have you believe she knows as much about everything as you do – that is to say "nothing". But if she knows the name and address of this person, and knows enough to send parcels, then she's a liar, isn't she? Mrs Marshall knows far more about secret Summersby things than she's ever been prepared to let on. She's been lying to your face for years!'

'But . . . but Mrs Marshall was the one who told me there was another heiress in the first place – she first told me when I was a little girl, years and years ago.'

'Well, yes,' said Biddy, 'but it's not like Mrs Marshall told you any actual facts about her, did she?'

'That's what I like to see,' said Mrs Marshall's voice at the drawing room door, 'broadening your mind already.'

Biddy and Sybil nearly leapt from their seats as the house-keeper entered.

Biddy looked up and smiled pleasantly, casting a sideways glance at Sybil, who was doing the same with impressive ease.

'Enjoying some instructive reading already?' Mrs Marshall wondered.

Biddy glanced at her own lap and thanked her guardian angels that she'd placed the 'sound' *Australasian* over the 'flamboyant' *Bulletin* when she'd sat down, ostensibly to read.

Joey trotted in behind and took a place he felt was rightly his on an armchair before Mrs Marshall shooed him off and took the seat herself. He curled up at Biddy's feet on the carpet.

'So then . . .' said Mrs Marshall, with a motherly smile.

Biddy and Sybil maintained their own smiles, not daring to throw each other another glance. Biddy tormented herself in imagining how much Mrs Marshall might have overheard.

'I see you've caught Lewis Fitzwater's eye,' the housekeeper said to Biddy.

Biddy went pink.

'There's no crime in it,' Mrs Marshall said, 'it's natural that you would. You're a very pretty girl, Biddy, and boys like Lewis always have an eye for pretty girls.'

Biddy sought the safety of denial. 'I . . . I don't know what you mean by that, Mrs Marshall. I haven't led him to expect things that he shouldn't, if that's what you think.'

'Of course you haven't, you're a good girl,' the housekeeper reassured her. 'I didn't mean to chastise you for anything. What catches a boy's eye is hardly the fault of a girl, unless she's a girl of poor virtue, and you'll not be accused of that by me.'

Sybil stood up. 'Is this is a conversation that best be had with Biddy alone, Mrs Marshall? I'm sure you'll not mind if I leave . . .'

The housekeeper encouraged Sybil to resume her seat. 'Companionship is a two-way street, Sybil,' she said, 'and what I must say to Biddy will do your ears no harm.'

Sybil sat again. Biddy resumed tormenting herself, convinced the housekeeper had heard everything and was taking a very drawn-out path towards revealing it.

Mrs Marshall shifted in her seat, her corset making it hard to get comfortable. She pulled a cushion to the small of her back, before something about Sybil's own posture seemed to strike her as odd. 'Sybil!' she exclaimed, shocked. 'Have you taken your corset off?'

Sybil blushed, straightening herself at once. 'No, Mrs Marshall.'

The housekeeper stared at the girl's torso. 'You most certainly have. I can see every curve of your abdomen. Oh, Sybil,' she said, dismayed.

It was only now that Biddy realised it, too. Sybil *was* free of her corset. It wasn't as if either of them needed such constrictive things anyway, although as she glanced at Sybil again, she wondered if perhaps her friend did require a little more support.

Sybil was plainly mortified. 'It is too tight. It cuts into me.'

'Then you could only have gained weight from all my good food,' pronounced Mrs Marshall, 'because your undergarments were measured to fit you perfectly.'

'I'm sorry, Mrs Marshall,' Sybil muttered, embarrassed.

The housekeeper changed the subject. 'You have no mother to guide you, do you, Biddy?' she enquired after a pause. 'No mother alive, I mean?'

Biddy sensed Sybil listening keenly. 'No,' she fibbed.

The housekeeper nodded. 'The circumstances are no one's business, although I presume they are sad?'

Biddy said nothing, but gave a single nod. She'd been made sad by them, it wasn't a total untruth.

'What *is* our business is your welfare, however,' said Mrs Marshall, continuing. 'At least while you're under this roof, and likely when you're no longer under it, too.'

Biddy dared risk a glance to Sybil, unsure of what to say. But Sybil's own look gave her no clue.

Mrs Marshall took Biddy's hand. Biddy used her other hand to keep the *Bulletin* securely in place under the *Australasian*. 'You're a good girl,' Mrs Marshall repeated, 'but I won't have you fail to stay that way for want of a mother's advice.'

'But my mother is gone,' said Biddy, continuing the story.

'And I'm sorry for you that she is,' said Mrs Marshall. 'I myself am not a mother, although once I wished that I might have been, but it wasn't to be. I know when mothering is needed, however.'

Biddy was confused.

'What is it Biddy needs mothering for, Mrs Marshall?' asked Sybil.

The housekeeper withdrew her hand. 'I should tell you that Lewis Fitzwater is somewhat *boisterous*. He's known throughout the district for it – and all because he never had the benefit of a father's strap on his rear when he might have benefited from it. His cousin Jim, at least, has acquired a respectable skill.'

Biddy absorbed this in confusion 'What do you mean, Mrs Marshall?'

'Sybil knows, don't you, child?' said the housekeeper, turning to her.

Sybil's look to Mrs Marshall was stern. 'I fear that is somewhat unfair of you to taint Mr Fitzwater's character, Mrs Marshall,' Sybil said, 'given I have seen nothing to suggest insolence in his manner.'

Mrs Marshall was quick to disavow. 'He has never been insolent, of course he hasn't, merely *high-spirited*.' She cleared her throat and attempted to begin again. 'When Lewis Fitzwater was sixteen he was given sole charge of a herd of cattle to drive to Newmarket,' she said. 'In disregard for laws, he took the herd through the streets of *Melbourne*, if you please, spinning shameless stories to the constables who tried to stop him.'

Mrs Marshall waited for Biddy to react to this apparently scandalous anecdote, but Biddy's opinion of Lewis shot up higher at an event she only wished she'd seen for herself.

The housekeeper went on. 'When a gentleman proved immune to Mr Fitzwater's comedy and set loose his dogs on the cattle, Lewis slashed the man's shirt with a stockwhip and would have flogged him insensible had not the dogs then been controlled. Needless to say, word of these antics reached Summersby.'

'Did he still get the cattle safely to market, then?' Biddy asked.

'That is not the point,' said Mrs Marshall.

Biddy guessed that the answer was yes.

'His moleskin trousers are far too tight and his spurs are unnecessarily large,' Mrs Marshall condemned. 'Too often have I heard that he frequents the Bush Inn, meaning his interests lie only in drinking, swearing and brawling, for that is all that any man does in there.'

Biddy was flabbergasted. 'But I've never once smelled drink on his breath.'

'Neither have I,' said Sybil.

Mrs Marshall was clearly struggling. 'Remember what I've told you when you look at him,' she said to Biddy. 'I know he's very handsome – very handsome indeed – but a boy who starts his adult life with such outlandish behaviour goes to his early grave with it, too.'

Biddy felt an injustice was being done, but the sincerity in the housekeeper's face made it hard to see any malice behind.

'His cousin Jim, on the other hand,' Mrs Marshall went on, 'seems to have avoided the family curse. He did very well in his schooling and gained himself a valuable skill.' Mrs Marshall leaned close to her. 'Should you ever find yourself catching Jim Skews' eye, Biddy, well, you could do a lot worse.'

Biddy made a quick intake of breath and glanced at Sybil, who looked mortified. Mrs Marshall was trying to play matchmaker.

'Mrs Marshall,' said Sybil, severely, 'I'm sure Biddy has no interest whatsoever in catching the eye of Mr Skews, now or in the future.'

'Well, that strikes me as a great pity,' said Mrs Marshall, 'a fine young man like Jim Skews could suit someone like Biddy very nicely.'

'Someone like Biddy?' said Sybil, her voice rising.

Biddy said nothing.

'Well, he'd suit any nice young woman, I'm sure,' Mrs Marshall attempted to explain herself. 'I'm just suggesting that Biddy would be foolish to limit her choices. After all, Jim has all his cousin's looks and none of his impediments.'

'What's a pong that would strip the slates from a roof if it's not an impediment?' Biddy cracked.

'Biddy!' cried Sybil. She looked far more shocked at this remark than Mrs Marshall did.

'Very nasty pong on him,' Biddy said, po-faced. 'It's a mystery to me if he takes the time to wash.'

'Biddy, that is most uncharitable and I am quite sure, untrue,' said Sybil.

Biddy had to stop herself smiling. If only Sybil knew what she had learned from her clandestine sweetheart, she thought!

There was sharp tap at the drawing room door and Miss Garfield admitted herself before anyone responded. She was flushed in the face.

'What is it, Miss Garfield?' asked Sybil, making the most of the interruption.

'Some extraordinary news, completely unexpected.' The governess held a piece of paper in her hand.

Mrs Marshall looked wary. 'Is that a telegraph transcription?'

'It is indeed,' said Miss Garfield. The two women held each other's weighted looks for a moment. 'Mr Skews was retrieving something from the telegraph room when the machine came to life,' said Miss Garfield, 'and it is very fortunate that he was.'

Biddy kept a poker face.

'It is something for all of us to hear . . .?' Mrs Marshall asked. There was an unmistakable note of warning in her voice.

Miss Garfield nodded, visibly steeled herself, and then turned to Sybil. 'Your relatives have issued an instruction that I'm sure you will find both surprising and delightful.'

Sybil sat up straight, held by the expression on her governess's face. 'This isn't my *summons* . . .?'

The governess glanced nervously at Mrs Marshall. 'I'm not quite sure.'

'You're not sure? Is it or isn't it, Evie?' Mrs Marshall spluttered.

'Perhaps it is, I can't be certain.'

Mrs Marshall sprang from her seat. 'The day Sybil receives her summons from her relatives is one we have keenly anticipated. We have never been told when it will come, only that it *will* come, so surely there can be little confusion if it has arrived?'

Agitated, the governess handed the transcription to the house-keeper. Mrs Marshall read what was there for a moment.

'You see my confusion,' said Miss Garfield.

Sybil stood up, glaring at them both. 'Please tell me what my relatives have instructed right now.'

The two women just looked each other.

Miss Garfield cleared her throat. 'You are to be taken on a visit.'

'A what?'

'You are to come away.'

Sybil stared in amazement. 'I'm to leave Summersby?'

'For a *visit*,' said Miss Garfield.

Sybil grew visibly faint and Biddy stood to assist her, guiding Sybil to a seat again. 'Oh, Biddy,' she muttered, 'this *is* my summons, it's come at last.'

Knowing more than anyone, Biddy said nothing.

The governess struck an unmistakable note of doubt. 'I'm afraid this is why we are uncertain as to whether this is your summons at all,' she said. She caught Mrs Marshall's look. 'At least, *I* am uncertain . . .' she trailed off.

'But . . . but where is it that I am going?' Sybil asked.

'Melbourne,' Mrs Marshall said, speaking up at last. Miss Garfield continued to look at her questioningly. The housekeeper braced herself. 'It is not an address your governess recognised because she has no reason to. But I recognise it.' She seemed to be wrestling with what would come next. 'It is the home of your relatives. Auburn Grove, Hawthorn.'

Biddy almost gave a little cry, risking giving herself away. Sybil kept calm. Miss Garfield looked greatly shocked, however. It became apparent at once to Biddy that Mrs Marshall had long been privy to information that Miss Garfield never had. The governess had *not* known the address.

'Your relatives have decided it is time for you to enlarge your experience of society – and of them,' said Mrs Marshall. 'The message is emphatic. This address is where you shall visit, accompanied by Miss Garfield, of course, and . . . well.'

'And Biddy?'

'Yes, Biddy,' said Miss Garfield. 'She, too, has been mentioned.'

Biddy smiled in apparent surprise.

'Your relatives feel that a pair of reliable men are needed to provide assistance on the journey,' said Miss Garfield, chiming in again and trying to mask her earlier shock, 'and rather than having Mrs Marshall go to the trouble of hiring two who are wholly unproven, they have requested we utilise two young men already known to us here at Summersby.'

Biddy saw what was coming and could have laughed at Jim's playfulness.

'They have asked we use Jim Skews and his cousin, Lewis Fitzwater.'

If Biddy expected surprise from Sybil at this development, she didn't get it. Instead Sybil fell into silence.

Miss Garfield felt obliged to fill the hush. 'A wise choice from your relatives, I am sure, Sybil,' she said, hopefully. 'Both Lewis and Jim are very fine young men, well regarded in the district.'

Biddy gave a deliberately droll look in Mrs Marshall's direction.

The housekeeper was a picture of acute discomfort. 'This aspect of the direction is very unorthodox.'

Sybil stood up again, looking the housekeeper firmly in the eye. 'We are in agreement that my relatives' knowledge of Summersby is unsurpassed, are we not?'

'Well, of course we are,' said Mrs Marshall, taken aback.

'And we also agree that their means of acquiring that knowledge do occasionally surprise us?'

The housekeeper frowned. 'I will remind you of the respect due to me as a faithful servant of this household, Sybil.'

'And I will remind you that my relatives' wishes are all,' said Sybil. She held her hand out for the transcribed telegraph, and after a brief hesitation Mrs Marshall gave it to her. Sybil scanned what it said, before folding it neatly in two, satisfied with its contents. She turned to Biddy. 'We are to journey to Melbourne then?'

Biddy smiled, a picture of joyful innocence. 'And what do you suppose we shall find there?'

IDA

FEBRUARY 1887

7

*I*da squeezed herself tighter under the bed, fists at her ears to block out the sound. 'Go away!' Even with the late summer thunderstorm howling in the night outside, the noise of the ghost dog in her head was relentless, clawing at her door like a demon, hell-bent on getting to her, hell-bent on tearing her to shreds.

'What do you want from me?' she cried out, angry more than she was frightened. 'Why don't you just leave me alone?'

The ghost dog began to whine.

'Aggie!' Ida called out. 'Can't you hear it, too, Aggie?'

But Aggie, fast asleep in her own room further down the hallway, made no reply. No one would come to her aid. 'It's all a dream,' she told herself. 'It's all a dream. This isn't real . . .'

Trying to squeeze herself tighter and smaller, she felt the prick of something sharp. Daring to look, she found a lost hatpin, forgotten under the bed. 'This isn't real, it's only a bad dream.'

As if to prove it to herself she scraped the hatpin along the skirting board. A short, shallow mark scored the paint. She took to the board with a fury, gouging with the pin.

Ida, she scratched, then, *Go away.*

Something crashed hard against the windowpane in the gale outside, and then crashed again. Ida shrieked and shot out from under the bed, clutching the hatpin. She hurled herself at her bedroom door, flinging it open. Whatever it was she imagined to be outside flew back in shock as Ida ran into the hallway, slashing and jabbing at the air. She ran headlong through the dark, making for the servants' stairs, the ghost dog's nails hard on the floorboards behind her.

'You stay away!' she screamed, too frightened to look and see what it really was. She hit the stairs and took them two at a time.

By the final landing the ghost dog no longer followed her.

Ida stopped and listened. She could hear nothing but the gale outside and her own breathing. Pressing her hand against her chest, she felt her heart. 'It's gone . . .' she told herself. 'It *was* all a dream, of course it was, and now you've woken up from it . . .'

She looked back up the two flights of stairs to where her little room was and didn't much feel like repeating the whole experience. From the kitchen beneath her a light glowed. 'That's where Aggie's gone,' she whispered to herself. 'No wonder she didn't come.'

Ida descended the final flight. It was only when she peeped around the door, hoping to find her friend in the act of brewing a comforting pot of tea, that she realised Aggie was still asleep upstairs and someone else was in the kitchen.

Samuel was barefoot, clad in his nightshirt with a waistcoat thrown over the top. He was hunched at the wood stove, engaged in something that wasn't clear. Ida's surprise was replaced by curiosity. She had so few opportunities to watch him unobserved; it was strange to see him as others rarely did. His appearance, while not exactly less impressive without his fine clothes, was at least *different*. Parts of him normally hidden from view, like his ankles and feet, were there to be gazed at. These parts seemed ordinary. Had she expected something more? Samuel seemed almost vulnerable now as she watched him, a lost little boy.

The smell of charred paper reached her nostrils.

Samuel sensed her and turned, just as she withdrew to the shadows. Ida froze, one foot upon the servants' stair, one foot upon the floor, just outside his line of sight and scared to retreat further in case she gave herself away with creaks. She couldn't see Samuel from this position, and he couldn't see her, but she knew she wouldn't hear him either if he crept up upon her in his bare feet upon the flagstones.

She willed him to stay at the stove, and keep on doing whatever it was that he was doing, and not poke his head around the door and find her.

'What are you doing there, Ida?'

Samuel spotted her. She found her presence of mind. 'What are *you* doing there, Mr Samuel?'

'I beg your pardon?' He came closer. 'It's unlike you to forget your manners, Ida.'

She bobbed a curtsey. 'I'm sorry, that was very rude.'

He was not offended. 'No harm done.'

She waited for an explanation but nothing came. 'You'll be lucky to burn anything in that fire,' she said at last, cheerily, 'it hasn't been lit since supper time and the flu's choked up as it is.' She realised now that she had exposed him in doing something he'd meant to keep secret.

'I am to be married tomorrow,' he said, as if this somehow explained himself.

'Yes,' said Ida. She put both feet upon the stair, and then stepped up another one, making herself almost level with his height. 'You'll make a lovely couple, too; everyone says so, especially me.'

'Do you, really?'

'Oh yes, of course I do.' She found herself once again losing herself in his eyes.

Samuel stared at her for what seemed like forever, before breaking into his lovely smile. 'That's a very nice thing to say.'

'But I mean it,' she said, even though she didn't. More than anything in the world she wished it was her marrying Samuel in the morning.

He held her look as if he knew what she was thinking. There was longing in his eyes, a need to speak of something vital. 'Go back to your room now, Ida. I'm sorry if I woke you.'

Nothing would make her leave. 'I might as well stay up. It's practically light anyway.'

'Don't be silly, off you go.' He was sweetly insistent, yet the longing remained. He wanted her to stay.

'Yes, Mr Hackett.' She turned and slowly took the stairs, knowing he was watching her. She reached the first landing and stopped. She dared to look back. Samuel hadn't shifted.

She went to say something else but Samuel spoke first. 'You imagine I don't love her then, I suppose?'

This disarmed her. She began to make an automatic reply, and then thought again. 'I'm never going to let myself think that you don't,' she told him, sincerely, 'even though others might think it.' Her mind went to Aggie and what such opinions had cost her with their mistress.

'I can understand that some might think such a thing,' Samuel said. 'I would think it, too, perhaps, if I was her maid and serving her as loyally as you do.' His eyes met hers and held them again.

'What is it, Mr Samuel? Is something wrong?'

'Ida . . .'

'Are you ill? Has something happened?'

He bit at his lip, and then seemed to arise at some decision. 'Can I tell you something, something important? Tell you as my friend?'

Her heart was in her throat. 'You know you can.'

'I do not love her at all.'

Shocked, she put a hand to her lips.

'I have tried and tried with everything I have – I have tried to force my heart, but it has done no good. I loved her sister, or I thought I did, but I was wrong there, too, I'm certain of it now. Whatever I knew back then was a copy of love, not real. Whatever I know now – with Matilda, at least – is just a copy again, not love.'

The words echoed in her heart. *". . . with Matilda, at least . . ."*

There was no untruth in his eyes. She let this sit between them, saying absolutely nothing, and knew that she was poised upon the precipice again. Did she have the courage to take another leap of faith?

She went down the stairs until she was almost level with his face once more. 'Perhaps you should not be getting married, Mr Samuel?'

He shook his head. 'I must.'

'But why? If you are not in love, how can you?'

'Love is not needed in a marriage, not for people like us.'

'But surely it is?' Ida insisted. 'How can it not?'

'What matters is position, standing.'

'But you are not in England now – you yourself said so. Australia is a different place. A person has opportunities here that would not found in the old country.' She felt herself swimming in him, drowning, swept away by his beautiful eyes. 'Here you can follow your heart.'

On impulse she half held out her hand, her fingers.

He took them in his without hesitating. *'Oh, Ida . . .'*

She gasped at the longed-for touch of his skin.

'What if she is not the one you think she is?' she said, breathless.

He blinked. 'What's that?'

'What if she is not Miss Matilda but Miss Margaret, and she has been all along?'

He stared at her, trying to fathom her words. 'What are you telling me?'

'The second will,' Ida said, 'what if it was all just some deception? What if it was still the sister who died that wrote it, but she was *not* Miss Margaret as she had you believe in that will, but was actually Miss Matilda, and that's why she wanted to use solicitors from Kyneton?'

'Kyneton?'

'Where the Gregorys are less known – where the truth wouldn't be guessed. What if she was always Miss Matilda? What if it's actually Miss Matilda who's in the ground dead?'

Samuel's eyes flashed confusion. 'You don't know what you're saying, Ida.'

She came down the two stairs, her fingers still in his, looking up at him now. 'I know I'm not all that bright, but I'm inquisitive, you see, and I've been starting to work it all out.'

'Work what out?'

'What I couldn't understand was who Miss Matilda meant to deceive by it. Then I worked that out, too. What if it was you?'

His eyes widened. 'Deceive *me*?'

She looked imploringly at him. 'Please don't be angry with me, Mr Samuel, I'm on your side, you know that I am. It's dead Miss Matilda who's the rotter here, I've said so all along. No one could blame you for what you did – you were in love, or you thought you were in love – everyone does things they really shouldn't do when they're led by their hearts—'

He stopped her with a kiss.

His soft lips against hers, Ida thought of what she was doing right now and knew she was no different. She was as in love with Samuel as it was possible to be in love with any person. Her heart was bursting with love for him.

She never wanted the kiss to end, but it did. He released her gently. Samuel's smile reappeared, bright and wide. 'What is it you think I've done, Ida?'

'You came to an agreement with her. You knew about Mr Gregory's will and the clause that said Miss Margaret was to go to the Hall for her own protection when he died. Then Miss Matilda told you that *she* was Miss Margaret and you believed her and agreed to help her and let her sister go into the Hall in her place.'

Samuel still smiled but his eyes took on a new emotion.

'But what if she lied to you?' Ida went on. 'What if she was always Miss Matilda? And what if it was Miss Margaret who went to the Hall just like she was always meant to do?'

Samuel let her fingers drop. 'This is . . . dismaying.'

'Don't worry,' she assured him, 'I won't tell anyone, you know

I won't, and really, when you think about it, what is there to tell? You haven't done anything bad now, have you?'

He blanched. 'Bad?'

'No one was put away who shouldn't have been, and poor Miss Margaret's been freed. What sort of dad wants his daughter locked up like that? You're her saviour, Mr Samuel, and I'm your friend. I intend to keep on calling her Miss Matilda out loud just like I always have and no one need ever know.' She made a button sign at her mouth. 'My lips are sealed.'

Samuel took a long minute to process all this. 'I have just kissed those lips.'

It was almost as if another girl had been kissed, Ida realised; a girl who was not inquisitive at all, a girl who simply longed to be held and loved. 'I know you have,' she whispered.

'I have longed for it.'

'So have I. It was lovely.'

He leant forward to kiss her again.

'And something else,' she whispered, before he was able to, 'why don't you get rid of Barker now?'

'What's that?' he said, startled.

'Get rid of him. Mr Barker. He's an awful man and he's got something over you, I know he has. If it was this, and I bet that it was, then why not be rid of him? No hurt's been done. He can't touch you, Mr Hackett.' She looked at him with loving, devoted eyes. '*Sack him.*'

He claimed the second kiss from her.

She gasped once more and put her hand to where his soft lips had touched her again.

'I'm very lucky to have such a good friend,' he whispered.

'I'll be there for you,' she told him. 'I'll never doubt you. Just you see.'

'And I'll be there for *you*. Trust me, Ida. It will all come well. Just trust me.'

Samuel made to return to the kitchen.

'But what *were* you doing before?' she asked him as an afterthought.

Samuel stopped. 'What's that?'

'When I came in, what were you burning at the stove?'

His face was unchanged. 'I was just getting rid of something.'

Ida returned to her room and shut the door, all thoughts of the ghostly dog forgotten. When she felt that enough time had passed, she opened her door again and retraced her steps down the stairs and into the kitchen.

Samuel was gone.

There was hardly any light to see by but Ida didn't want to risk sparking a candle.

She opened the door to the wood stove and peered inside. Smoke billowed out, the choked-up flu preventing it from blowing through the chimney. Ida found the poker and stuck it inside. Whatever Samuel had placed on the embers was reduced to ashes. Disappointed without quite knowing why, Ida went to close the stove again when something white emerged from the blackness. Her hand reached into the stove and withdrew the one scrap of unburnt paper that was left. It had the remains of something written on it.

Matilda says drink it

The hand was a fine, smooth copperplate, just like the hand that had written on the photograph. Margaret's hand.

Ida was proud of herself and her inquisitive mind for working out all that she had so far. Yet she had to agree that still there were several worrying loose ends. Was this why Samuel had seemed somewhat unconvinced by her theory?

One. What was it that Samuel went to the Hall to get Margaret to write for him?

Two. Why did Matilda kill herself, if the previously supposed reason, guilt at her sister's false confinement, wasn't actually false and therefore not cause for guilt at all?

Three. How was it possible to be so hopelessly in love with a person who lied?

'Oh, it was a lovely occasion, it really was,' said Ida the following afternoon, smoothing the covers on Aggie's bed, 'considering February's such an unlucky month to get wed.'

'That's another old wife's tale,' Aggie sniffled. She was bed-ridden with a dose of summer flu.

'Is it now?' Ida wondered. 'You mean you don't believe in that rubbish? Could have fooled me.'

Aggie tried to sit up higher against the pillows but the ache in her chest plainly got worse with the movement and she gave up the effort.

'What are you squirming for, can't you just lie still?' Ida complained.

Aggie did so, sinking back. 'Tell me more,' she said, pained. Ida knew that Aggie's throat hurt to talk much above a whisper. 'What happened in the church?'

Ida considered. 'Someone in the congregation fell down dead as a stone when Mr Samuel gave his "I do". Straight after that our mistress's bridal veil caught fire. No sooner had we got the flames out when Mr Barker became so sulky he said he was heading off early to hang himself.' She looked at Aggie, po-faced, waiting for her reaction.

'That all sounds very nice, then,' Aggie said, frowning at her.

'Our mistress looked very happy to be wed,' said Ida, telling the truth now. Her heart felt the pangs of it.

'Are you sure?' Aggie pressed.

'Of course I am. Shouldn't I be?'

'I didn't say that,' Aggie said.

'No, what you did say,' Ida said, crossing her arms, 'if not today then yesterday and also the day before that, was that you had been very wrong in interfering and worrying about our mistress, when she is perfectly able to look after herself and is not confused and possibly ill at all.' Ida was a picture of condemnation. A difficult silence fell between them, by no means the first in recent weeks. 'Well, you did say that, didn't you?' she harped.

'Was Mr Skews there?' Aggie asked from her bed, changing the subject.

'I see. Conversation's closed again, is it?' Ida wondered.

'Was he there?' Aggie fumbled for the glass of water at her bedside, but lost her grip and sent the glass spilling to the floor.

'He was not,' said Ida. Ignoring the puddle, she picked up the glass, which had landed without breaking. She poured more water into it from the jug and handed it back to Aggie.

Her older friend sipped with difficulty, sickness clear in her face.

'What's wrong?' said Ida, watching her. 'Changed your mind again now, have we? I know she shouldn't have hit you, but you've got to get it in your head that they're married now, and that's the end of it.' Ida bit back her own despair at the thought. She knew she would do just about anything to be kissed by Samuel again. 'Just as well they've got me looking out for *both* of them, isn't it, seeing as you've given up?'

'Leave me, Ida. I'm too unwell for this,' said Aggie. She placed the glass upon the table again with difficulty, the strength sapped from her hands.

'I only hope your brains return as soon as this flu passes,' Ida declared, going to the door.

'Ida . . .' Aggie started to say.

But she shut the door on Aggie, leaving her alone in her sick bed.

Ida made her way with a pile of folded linen in her arms, up the great stairs towards the western wing's second floor. She stopped still upon the last step, hearing the voice of her mistress she now privately thought of as Margaret, no longer Matilda.

'*He has married me . . . You cannot marry him, too, dearest. You are dead.*'

Leaving the stairs she neared the door to the master suite of rooms. Margaret was inside, Ida having already moved all her things from the Chinese room.

'These rooms are riddled with hiding spots,' Margaret was saying, 'places for letters you never actually intended for *me* to uncover at all but someone else. Is it Samuel you want to find them? Is that why you persist with this?'

Looking up and then down the deserted hallway, listening for tell-tale sounds of anyone else, Ida tested the handle of the door. It turned. In a single motion she was inside the room leaving the door ajar behind her.

'Excuse me, miss?'

Margaret was waiting alone in the master bedroom inside the great, canopied bed that had once been her father's and now belonged to her – and her husband.

'Just thought I'd look in,' said Ida, tormented by thoughts of the wedding night. 'Are you comfy there, miss?'

Margaret ran her arm between the sheets of the opposite side and felt the coolness there, the smoothness of the unrumpled linen. 'Soon my husband will come,' she whispered. 'I will triumph over my sister.'

'Yes, miss,' said Ida.

'What is keeping him, do you think? Has he tired of me so soon?'

'No, miss!' said Ida. She wondered, too, what was delaying Samuel from the room. Was he so exhausted that he had fallen asleep inside his old room out of habit, forgetting all about his bride? Or was he thinking of the night-time kiss upon the stairs, just like Ida was thinking of it, unable to stop, reliving it again and again in her heart? 'Why don't you have something to eat while you're waiting?' she suggested.

Margaret slipped out of the great bed and examined, one by one, the things Ida had already placed in the room with the hope of pleasing Samuel. Candles cast a soft light upon the walls, throwing shadows and mystery into the corners. Bowls of dried and perfumed rose petals gave off sweet scents. Champagne waited to be popped and drunk. A tray of tiny titbits invited consumption. Everything had been placed there with love.

Ida watched her and took a moment to stand still, breathing in the exotic scents of the male environ. She could smell traces of Samuel's pomade, and behind it the cologne he favoured, too.

Still holding the linens, she moved towards his dressing room and lingered at that door. An open wardrobe displayed Samuel's suits and coats, at its base his pairs of boots. Ida stepped inside the little room for a moment to put the linen down. She touched the fabrics of his clothes, the fine-spun wools and the rougher tweeds. She slipped her hands inside the pockets, pulling out and examining each small item that she found. She felt inside the boots.

Ida took another moment to stand very still, the pine-scented pomade sharp in her nostrils. A flicker of movement from the bedroom outside revealed Margaret standing now behind the same door that Ida had opened to enter from the hallway. When had she moved there?

'I'll go now, miss . . .' Ida started to say, caught out.

The dressing room door slammed shut in her face.

'Miss!' She rattled the door. It was locked.

'Why did I write those scraps?' Margaret asked from outside.

'Write what scraps, miss? Let me out,' Ida implored her.

'For him,' Margaret answered herself, 'You wrote them to make him happy, why else?' There was a brief second's pause before she posed another question. 'Did it work?' There was another pause, less than a second long, before she answered in a voice that at first seemed the same as the one she had used to pose the question, but in fact held the very subtlest of differences. 'Oh yes, he was very pleased. You gave him what he needed. Or rather, what he thought he needed, which was much the same thing in his view.'

Ida rapped at the door. 'Miss, I don't understand what you're saying! Please let me out at once.'

'But what did he need them for?' Margaret asked. She immediately laughed in response and there was the difference to her
voice again. 'Are you really such a fool?' The laugh stopped just as
quickly and with it the change in Margaret's voice. 'I may not be
as wise as you but people say I am kinder.'

'Miss, *please*,' Ida insisted, 'I've still got work to do and Mr
Samuel will be coming along any minute. I don't want him to find
me in here.'

'He needed them for *me*,' said Margaret.

'I don't understand,' said Margaret, 'I didn't write them for you.'

'No,' Margaret agreed, 'but that was their purpose. He gave
each and every one of them to me. Not all at once, of course, but
over time, a scrap here and there, sometimes weeks apart, at other
times barely hours. The process was quite relentless really, insidi-
ous, too. Some of his hiding spots actually shocked me.'

Ida listened, suddenly mesmerised by what was being said in
the bedroom outside. Was she talking about the so-called scraps
she had written for Samuel when still at the Hall? Whether she
was or not, another truth was inescapable: Margaret was holding
a conversation with both her *dead sister* and *herself*. . .

Ida's mind whirled and ticked. Her mistress had once said
that her sister had been the more graceful dancer when taught
by the Messieurs and Miss Roberts. When she encountered
Miss Roberts again at the ball the instructress had praised her
dancing, and exclaimed that she'd recognise her anywhere *as*
Matilda *because* of her elegant steps. The mistress was changeable, swinging to extremes. So much of the time she was gentle,
kind, if scattered and confused, but there were other occasions,
fewer, when she was none of those things. At those times she was
cold, harsh and cunning. She was also wanton; her eyes ablaze
with desire. Why were there two poles of behaviour in Margaret?
Had she and Matilda created confusion too many times as girls?
Did it now seem to Margaret that sometimes she really *was* her
own sister? Is this why she still thought of her as alive? Had she
had *become* her sister while somehow remaining herself?

Samuel had been right, she was ill. She was more than ill, she was insane.

'But what did I imagine you felt guilty about?' Margaret asked.

Margaret laughed again. 'Me? Nothing!' This was the sister's personality, the sister's reply. The delicate change to her voice was the voice of *Matilda*, the twin who was cold in the ground.

'And yet I wrote the scraps?' Margaret pressed.

'At Samuel's behest, he gave you the words. You merely transcribed, dearest.'

'Then what did *he* imagine you felt guilty about?'

'Ah, well,' said Margaret, now sounding thoughtful in her sister's voice, 'rather a lot I'm afraid.' There was cruelty in her inflection, in her sigh; the sister's cruelty, not Margaret herself. 'He thought me wracked with guilt, poor Samuel and I know I allowed him to think it, but truly, he was all too easily fooled. Like a tiny little boy. I wasn't guilty of anything. He only thought I was. Just like he thought I was really you.'

'You've been unkind to him then, sister?' said Margaret, bristling. 'Lying to him?'

'He's been unkind to me. Do you realise what his purpose was with all those little scraps? They were meant to drive me mad with the guilt he imagined I had – drive me so mad I would kill myself!'

'But I love him,' Margaret answered in a hurt little voice.

'Dearest,' said Margaret, patiently, her voice unmistakably her twin's again, 'he has thought to *fool* me, and this dismaying pride is simply bestial in a gentleman. So he will be punished for it in order that he might change his ways.'

'I will not let you hurt him,' Margaret vowed.

'We shall see . . .'

Margaret lapsed into a final silence. The conversation had ended. Ida waited to hear any more but there was nothing. As she reached out to rattle the handle again, the door sprang open. Margaret had unlocked it. She looked at Ida, deeply ashamed. 'I am so sorry. It was all my sister. She locked the door.'

She held a crumpled letter in her hand – written in the same ugly hand.

Ida indicated it, no longer surprised by anything now. 'She left something new for you to find?'

'Not for *me* to find,' Margaret whispered. Her nerves were in shreds. 'It's meant for someone else, I realise it now; they all are. They are not meant for me at all.'

Who then, Ida wondered? What was really going on inside her mistress's shattered mind? 'May I see it?' She gently held out her hand.

They heard the creak of a footfall in the hallway.

'Samuel?' Margaret called. The shivers of the house replied.

Clutching the letter still Margaret took a lighted candle and went to the bedroom door. She peered into the hall outside. 'Samu—'

'What is it, madam?' Barker asked her from the shadows.

Margaret leapt back, causing the candle to fall, splashing wax upon the carpet. Ida sprang forward to pick up the candle before it took flame. She thrust the glow before the valet's surly face. 'What are you doing lurking out there, Mr Barker?'

He ignored her. 'You wanted help with something, madam?' he said to Margaret. Wedding alcohol was sour upon his breath.

Margaret struggled to make words. 'Why are you waiting there?'

'In case madam needed me.'

Ida took a step away from his fumes. 'Where is Mr Samuel?'

'Coming along,' said Barker. 'All in due course.' He lapsed into a moment's silence before seemingly remembering himself again. He gave them a laboured wink, showing his too white, too wide grin.

Ida shuddered. 'Why is he delayed?'

'Who says he is?' Barker tapped his long nose. 'Probably just scrubbing himself nice and sparkling clean.' He found this funny and began chuckling in his drunkenness.

Margaret's face filled with anger. A forgotten raindrop of memory suddenly fell from the branches of her mind. 'You were a stable boy here in my father's time,' she said accusingly, 'a foul, disgusting boy. We laughed at you!'

Barker stopped chuckling.

Ida was transfixed. She had been right. Margaret *had* recognised him that day in the Hall and had not been mistaken at all. Barker had worked at Summersby before. And what was it Mrs Jack had said about him? He had been 'nice' to Miss Gregory.

'When did you become a valet?' Margaret demanded. '*How* did you?'

'Now, now,' said Barker, 'we all have hope for advancement. Some of us have means for making hope real.' He watched her with glinting black eyes.

'What means? What could you have had that ever would have seen you let past the kitchen door?'

Barker's eyes flashed in the glow of the candle. 'Not all were so uncharitable, madam. Some saw my potential.'

'Who? Who did?' she wanted to know.

'Your sister for one.'

Ida's inquisitive mind was racing.

Margaret scoffed. 'But she laughed at you, I tell you. She laughed louder than I did.'

Ida imagined the memory: now dead Matilda laughing, pointing at the strange shock-haired youth hefting manure on a fork; spitting words of scorn at him, calling him 'devil' and 'beast'. He had loved her for it, worshipped her.

'Until the day she stopped,' said Barker, meaningfully.

Margaret gripped the bedroom door, frightened by him now. 'Leave me. Go to your bed and sober yourself.'

'I'm in no hurry,' said Barker. He blew out the candle.

'Mr Barker, what are you doing—' Ida cried out.

'Leave me, I said. Get out!' Margaret screamed.

They could no longer see where he stood in the gloom. 'Toey little filly, aren't you, eh?' came his voice from the dark. 'Soon your stallion will put all that to rights.'

Margaret made to slam the door on him. 'Leave!'

But Barker had his boot in the doorjamb. 'There, there,' he said. 'Just you put yourself to bed instead, eh?'

Ida rushed forward and kicked at his foot, stamping on it. 'Aggie! Aggie, we need you!' she screamed into the hallway.

Barker lashed out with a single slap and Ida fell to the floor.

'That fat lump's come down with a dose,' he said, chuckling again. 'Won't be rousing her in a hurry.'

Margaret picked up the fallen brass candlestick and smashed it onto his boot. Barker withdrew with a yell. Margaret kicked the door closed and then locked it from inside with the key. She stood there a moment, panting in shock and dismay. 'Ida, are you hurt?'

Ida felt her cheek where he'd struck her. It was very sore. 'I might have a bruise in the morning.'

Barker remained on the other side of the door.

'I shall tell my husband of your outrage,' Margaret spat at him through the keyhole.

'Shame you've got a memory like a hessian sack,' he countered from the other side. 'Reckon you'll still remember it in five minutes?'

'*I'll* remember it!' Ida hissed at him. 'I'll tell him everything!'

Margaret's hands clenched at her sides. 'Where is Samuel? Bring him to me!'

'All in good time,' said Barker. They heard him fumbling with the big brass ring of keys he carried at his waist.

Margaret flew to the bed, pulling the covers up to her chin.

'What are you doing?' Ida trembled with dread.

'Never you mind,' said Barker.

'Don't worry, miss, he can't come in again,' Ida reassured her mistress.

'Don't you dare come back inside!' Margaret ordered him, wide-eyed in fear.

'Now, why would I want to do that?' the valet asked. They heard the noise of a key being inserted into the lock. The key with which Margaret had locked the door from inside fell dislodged to the floor.

Margaret gripped the bed covers 'Don't come inside . . . Please don't come in here . . .'

The door opened.

'Mr Barker, no!' Ida cried out.

The grinning valet advanced on her first, the glint of sapphire blue glass in his hand.

Ida opened her eyes at the sound of the door handle turning. She was on the dressing room floor. She saw Samuel's boots and clothes. She tried to move but couldn't. Her head felt as if it weighed more than her body.

'Samuel . . .' she murmured.

'Samuel, is that you?' It was Margaret's voice.

The dressing room door was partly ajar. Ida could half make out her mistress in the gloom. Margaret was still in the bed.

'Of course it is, my love,' Samuel held a candle in his hand and the soft light made his hair and skin glow like honey.

Margaret stretched between the sheets. 'Oh, husband,' she purred. 'I must have fallen asleep.' The change in her voice was there once more—Matilda's voice.

'Then I am sorry to have woken you,' he said. He placed the candle at the table by her bedside and kneeled on the floor before her. He was oblivious of Ida slumped on the dressing room floor. She could see him, she could see everything. Ida tried to move again, tried to call out for help. She was paralysed.

Samuel took Margaret's hand between his fingers, kissing the softness at her wrist.

'But I wanted to be awoken,' she told him. The catlike smile was there, curling at her lips, the desire. 'I was waiting for you.'

'Have I kept you very long?'

Margaret laughed; a rich peal of mirth as she threw her head back. 'Only many years,' she said.

He seemed to register the oddness of the answer for only a moment before her soft moans of pleasure told him to take her in his arms.

'So long I have waited,' said Margaret. 'So long I have dreamt of this.'

As he stepped from his robe, Margaret threw the bed covers wide, letting him see her fully. She was naked; her rich chestnut hair spread out on the pillows like a halo. 'Take me, husband,' she begged him. 'Take me and give me a child in our joy.'

This was the girl that Samuel once thought he loved, Ida knew; the girl that was dead Matilda, made alive once again in her sister.

Ida came to again, aware that more time had passed. It was still night, she was still on the dressing room floor. She still couldn't move or cry out. Her head was throbbing horribly. Through the crack in the door she could still see the bedroom outside. Her mistress's eyes were open, the surroundings plainly unfamiliar to her. Did she recognise her new bed, Ida wondered? Did she recognise her new room? Margaret propped herself up on her elbows and only then saw she was not alone. Samuel slept next to her. Startled, Margaret slipped from the sheets, snatching a robe from the floor to cover herself; Samuel's robe. She looked at the form of the man sharing the bed and only then seemed to recognise he was her husband.

'Samuel,' she whispered, her alarm subsiding. 'You came to me at last.' Her voice had returned to what it should be.

Ida watched her, mesmerised. Her mistress was two sisters in one. She had given herself to Samuel as dead Matilda. Now she was living Margaret again.

He stirred and shifted beneath the cover, not quite awake.

Margaret went to him, kneeling upon the floor, and her face near his. 'Why didn't you wake me? I thought you had forgotten.'

Unable to move, Ida tried to think of what else had happened while she and her mistress had waited for him. She half-recalled an exchange that had been unpleasant. But who it was with and what it had been about were now lost to her in the haze. She dismissed this shadow of a memory as irrelevant. The exchange had not been with Samuel, she knew.

Hesitant, Margaret reached out to stroke Samuel's hair, smoothing it away from his eyes. He awoke. 'Matilda?'

Margaret smiled at him. 'I thought you had forgotten me,' she said again.

He smiled back, a knowing smile. 'So soon?'

She giggled. 'I'm silly, aren't I?'

He slid through the sheets to the side where she had slept, and before she quite knew herself she was in the bed again, beside him. 'Samuel,' she breathed. 'Husband.'

'Shhh.' He pressed a finger to her lips, his other hand slipping the silken robe from her shoulders.

'I love you, Samuel,' she whispered. 'We will be happy together, yes?'

'Yes,' Samuel murmured, his lips against hers. Ida watched as Margaret gave herself to him for the first time then, a gift he received as naturally and thoughtlessly as any man might who guessed nothing of the moment's significance.

Ida found herself in the dining room in the middle of a yawn, paused in tidying away the last of the wedding supper. She realised with a jolt that she had no idea how or when she had entered this room, and yet here she was in the middle of tidying it up. How long had she been here? What had she been doing before? She was still in her uniform, at least. It was now very late at night. Nothing was amiss and yet it felt as if so much should be. Her head felt like it was filled up with fur.

She continued piling plates and glasses onto a wheeled trolley and regarded the mess of leftovers for a moment, before helping herself to the tastiest, scooping up bits and pieces with her hands. She was ravenous. Ida remembered then that the unreliable

Mrs Jack had proven reliable for once, turning out an impressive meal for two. But that was all she remembered. Somewhere there a gap in the evening's events. Yet it didn't seem to matter much. The leftovers would stretch to filling her up nicely and there'd be some tasty morsels for Aggie, too, if she ever shook off her flu. But not a morsel would she save for Barker. Let him have dirt, she thought. And then she wondered why Samuel still hadn't sacked him.

Something rustled in the pocket of her apron: paper. She slipped her hand inside and retrieved a letter. She knew the handwriting at once: ugly, ink stained. She half-remembered something more, very recent; something she had seen and heard. Had she been inside the master suite? Thick, warm fur was stuffed inside her head, making a fug of her mind. The smell of rosemary lingered at the back of her nose. She read the letter.

Dear Margaret,

This is for your Remember Box.

Our father duly died. His will was opened and read. You were sent to Constantine Hall. It was just as I expected, then, when Samuel finally showed me his true colours.

As part of our arrangement, Samuel and I announced our betrothal. Samuel had insisted I become his bride in exchange for his aiding me. I had agreed, although I told myself that I had no intention of going through it. But in order for you to be freed from confinement without any loss of the inheritance, my engagement to Samuel was necessary. To further maintain my ruse I took Samuel to a Kyneton solicitor – I didn't want to risk using a local man who might have known of me – and there we each signed a will. In the likelihood of death, all my property would go to my husband-to-be. This I signed as myself of course: Matilda.

Then, I did a very cunning thing. I visited another solicitor alone, also in Kyneton. There I created a second will, one that cancelled the first, because here I confessed to being you.

I willed that should I meet an untimely death the Summersby fortune must go to the 'real Matilda wrongly confined at the Hall'. I well suspected that Samuel would guess that I might do such a thing. Indeed, I didn't much hide my tracks so that he would guess. I banked that dishonest Samuel's inclination to double-cross would lead him to fear just such a double-cross from me. He was right to fear it. I did double-cross him. Just not in the way he supposed.

I had led Samuel to believe a number of lies, the utmost being: under the terms of my second will he would not inherit Summersby. In order to get his hands on the fortune, he would need to marry the sister he thought of as the real heiress – you. Everything was in place for you to be freed. All I had to do was wait, somewhat on guard, to see what Samuel would do. I did not have to wait very long.

The first scrap of paper I encountered bearing your unmistakable copperplate was not intended to torment me, at least at first, merely unsettle me. In contained some seemingly harmless words: 'Matilda says drink it'. It was not the words themselves that Samuel hoped would throw me, at least not at first, it was the fact that you had somehow written them and conveyed them all the way to Summersby without me knowing, and once here, hidden them in an unusual place, namely inside a glove in my dressing table drawer. He had planted it, of course. A second scrap followed not long after, found in a tree in the garden. Then a third; then many more.

'Matilda says you suffer the torture of guilt.'

'Matilda says love's happiness is a lie. You must choose death's release from your guilt.'

'Matilda says believe nothing of your joy. Your conscience torments you.'

'Matilda says only the grave brings redemption for all you have done.'

'Matilda says the weight of your guilt is a torture.'

'Matilda says drink it and we will know peace.'

I never mentioned finding these scraps to Samuel. He never revealed that he knew of their existence. He didn't need to. I guessed that he had paid a secret visit to you at the Hall, and there had arranged for you to write them all. He would not have encountered much resistance from you, for you were, I knew, attracted to Samuel, beguiled by his good looks and charm. For this I could hardly blame you, for I, too, was attracted to the man, despite everything. My physical desire for Samuel was a complication to my plans, but not an impossible one.

In order for my plans to continue, I had to allow Samuel to believe that the scraps were having an impact upon me. The words dwelt heavily upon guilt, implying that I should feel tortured by it for what I had done to you. I duly played at suffering. Then the mysterious message gave way to a mysterious object: a blue glass vial. Curious, I opened it to find only Hungary water. Then the vial inexplicably disappeared from my possession only to reappear a little time later. I opened it again, and again it was rosemary. Rightly, I suspected that the vial would play a crucial part in what might be ahead for me. Samuel's moves were approaching endgame – and so were my own.

Samuel was acting under the mistaken belief that I was ill, of course, and could be made yet worse with games such as these. Believing I was you, whom our late father willed be confined for illness, Samuel was employing the scraps – and the vial – to drive me towards a state of complete unhinging. His goal was clear, and for my purposes, quite perfect: I would be driven to suicide. When I was dead my secret will would surface, the deception, as Samuel believed it to be, would be exposed, and you would be returned to Summersby as the real Matilda and Summersby's true heiress. The path would then be open for Samuel to marry you in my wake.

Your sister who loves you,
Matilda

The letter held echoes from a conversation that Ida was sure she had held very recently, but she couldn't quite recall just when. It all seemed very fresh, and yet not, as if she'd actually held it years ago. Yet she knew that she hadn't. It was because of the fur in her head.

Ida folded the letter up again and returned it to her apron pocket. She intended to re-read it later when her head felt clearer and things might make more sense.

Loading as much of the crockery and leftovers as she dared onto the trolley, mindful of spills, Ida propelled her cargo through the dining room doors, glad she knew the route to the kitchen well enough to travel it in the dark. The gas lamps had been extinguished by Barker hours before; she remembered that, too. It had been an act of stinginess for which Ida had cursed him, given that responsibility for the clean-up was hers. It was no easy feat judging 'clean' in the dark. She trundled down the hall and negotiated the green baize door without mishap, backing into the kitchen. It was candlelit. Aggie must have come downstairs for a natter, Ida assumed. 'Feeling better now?' she called over her shoulder, as she pulled the trolley inside.

'Like a fine young buck on his wedding night,' Barker smirked at her.

Ida span around. 'Thought you were in bed?'

'Why should I be?' There was an open bottle of claret on the table. He poured himself another liberal glass, scraping a hand through his thick shock of hair.

Ida shot a glance at the leftovers exposed on the trolley and cursed her bad luck again. Her head still felt so heavy. 'Why shouldn't you be, more like it,' she said. 'You're as soused as a sauce bottle.'

'A man feels like celebrating,' he said, fixing his lips to the full glass. He misjudged the amount and spluttered it.

'Watch it,' Ida scolded. 'I only just scrubbed that table.' Barker slurped on the wine and Ida felt her gorge rise at the sight of him. 'Go to bed for Gawd's sake, look at the state of you.'

'The state of me?' Barker looked up with red ringed eyes. 'What's wrong with me then, you little sow?'

Ida laughed, banging dirty plates in the washing-up tub. 'Where do I start?' she exclaimed. She bent to the trolley's lower shelf to retrieve the soup terrine and nearly let it slip from her hands when she righted herself to find Barker out of his chair and right behind her. 'How'd you move so fast?'

'People make a habit of underestimating me,' he told her. A long hand reached out for her bottom.

Ida slapped him away and felt a bead of sweat run from her brow. 'Get out of my way, will you, I've got to wash these.'

Barker didn't move, his breath foul in her nostrils. His hand pinched at her apron bow. 'You look a bit peaky. Fancy a lie down?'

Ida ducked to the side, terrine before her, and scooted around so that the trolley stood between them.

'Hey, where you going now?' said Barker, disconcerted.

Ida clutched the terrine. 'I'm going to bed, if you're not. You're drunk, you dirty bugger.' She rubbed at her temple. 'And I don't feel well . . .'

Barker kicked the trolley aside with a shocking crash. Cups and saucers smashed to pieces. Ida stared at the wreckage in horror. 'Some blokes get their second wind with a skinful,' he told her. 'Sheilas, too.'

The look Ida saw in his eyes was one that her mother had warned her about. She'd never understood what intentions might lay behind such a look, but now she understood them exactly. The valet advanced upon her, leering. 'Mr Barker,' Ida warned, 'you keep away from me now.'

'Cheeky little piece,' he smirked, 'giving a respectable man the come on, eh?'

Ida started shaking, backing towards the servants' stairs. 'I never did that, I never would, Mr Barker . . . I'm a good girl.'

'A good little tart,' he mumbled. 'I know your sort. Why d'you think I put up with you?'

'Because I'm a good girl!' She reached behind with her free hand, feeling for the banister. 'I'm from a good Methodist family, now let me go up to my bed.'

'You're not going anywhere,' he told her.

Ida brought the terrine down on his head with a dull thud. The dish stayed in one piece. Barker stood blinking at her for a second, stunned. Ida raised it to hit him again. Barker's eyes flashed with rage and he caught her wrist before she could strike him. 'You'll break it!' Ida cried. Barker shook the terrine loose and it clattered to the floor, the handle snapping off. Ida spun on her heel and dashed for the first stair but Barker's lust empowered him and he caught her by the skirt hem. 'Stop it, let me go!'

Barker yanked her off balance, causing her to sprawl. He continued pulling at her skirt, tearing at it, pulling it up to her waist. 'No!' A hard hand smacked her in the mouth and then clawed at her hair, pulling it until the tears came.

'You little harlot, laugh at me, will you?' His black-clad form was on top of her now, thrusting himself into her belly, crushing her back against the sharp edges of the stairs.

'I've never laughed! I'm a good girl . . .'

'Let's see how bloody good,' the valet said.

IDA

APRIL 1887

8

*I*da couldn't remember the person she had been before it had happened, before he had forced himself onto her and made her what she was now. She could barely remember what her life had been like before he'd shattered her spirit on the stairs. The life he had left her with was one she lived now as a shadow life, a replica of how her life had once been; a fake. Ida went through the motions of living; nothing touched her now, nothing intrigued her, nothing got through.

Especially Samuel.

Ida's inquisitiveness, her questioning of things, belonged to the other Ida, the girl from before. She couldn't be that girl again, Barker had seen to that. She could no longer play the Ida who had cared.

Ida watched in silence as Margaret pressed her fingers to her belly, turning to see herself reflected in profile in the looking glass. Margaret turned to stand at another angle; pressing again, clearly fascinated by the changes to her naked self. The bump had formed and grown without her scarcely made aware of it at first, until, quite suddenly it seemed, she became very aware, the change to her figure small but undeniable. Her bleeding had already ceased. She had told Ida that she expected the bump as a consequence, hoped for it, but until she had been able to actually feel it beneath her fingertips, just as she did now, she could not be sure. There was no longer any doubt. She was with child. Samuel would be thrilled when she told him the news, Margaret said. Ida wondered if he'd already guessed. If he had, Ida would not let herself know of it.

Ida went to every length she could to avoid him now. She hid in doorways when she heard him approach. She kept her eyes to the floor if he was unavoidable and then would not answer if he spoke. It was all she could do, trapped as she was in the same house as the man who had let Barker hurt her. She lived as if Samuel wasn't there. The memory of his soft lips upon hers she erased.

Ida didn't know why Samuel hadn't sacked Barker, and likely would never sack him, but she thought she could guess. Barker did the things that Samuel had no stomach for.

For all his lovely words, Samuel had stomach for Ida least of all. This was why she would never tell him what Barker had done to her. If he knew the truth he still wouldn't do anything. Samuel needed Barker more than he needed her.

Ida selected underthings but Margaret rejected them. They would no longer do. Some women adhered to their corsets until well into pregnancy, she said, but she did not intend being one of them. She would eschew such restrictive things for her growing child's sake. She tossed the expensive underwear aside, stepping into her slip and petticoats only.

Margaret preferred to get dressed in this, her old room, the one with the Chinoiserie screen; it was comforting, she told Ida. She slipped inside her dress unaided, but struggled with the buttons at the back until Ida fastened them for her. This done, Margaret gathered the things she would need for the morning: the Remember Box with the collection of her sister's letters in their ugly hand; her pen and ink with paper to write on; the snatches of overheard talk she had recorded on paper already, even though she little knew to what they referred to. The act of recording things had become instinctual to her, she told Ida.

Ida no longer cared what some piece of paper might have written on it. She would never read such things again.

Ida hunched over the sink, weeping again like she found herself weeping so often now. She could no longer control it. Her own morning illness had persisted for weeks, and then had come the swelling. Her own bleeding had stopped, just like her mistress's had stopped. She knew what it all meant. Her mother had told her that much, at least. She was carrying Barker's bastard, conceived in violence, and no doubt malformed in her belly, twisted and foul in its soul. And yet it was nothing like him, Ida knew in her heart, it was a blameless child, an innocent thing, knowing nothing of how it was made. She would never tell it. She would love it with all the love she could give and would keep it safe from him. It was possible her baby would be born with something of its father's vileness and if so she would love it all the more, love it fiercely; love it in the face of all those who would despise it for its nature. But just perhaps, Ida hoped deep inside, the baby would be born pure of heart, with not a skerrick of the father to be seen. It was wrong to wish for that, Ida knew, a sin to wish for it, really, but she found it hard not to. It would be a blessing to give birth to a beautiful, healthy child. In Ida's heart she longed for a girl.

She sensed someone behind her and span around in fear. But it was only her mistress, clutching at the Remember Box.

'Miss?' Ida knew her face must look raw with the tears.

Margaret was plainly shocked to see her, given there'd been no sign of such grief when Ida had helped her dress earlier. 'I'm sorry, Ida, has something upset you?'

She made an effort to pull herself together. How could she tell her mistress what was wrong? How could she ever tell anyone? 'Don't mind me.' She looked around for something to explain herself. 'Bee sting,' she said. 'Why do they have to hurt so much?'

She gave no indication as to when or where a bee might have stung her.

The Remember Box seemed to grow heavy in Margaret's hands.

'Did you want something?' Ida asked.

'No, it is nothing . . .'

Barker entered the room behind her. 'Madam,' he said, by way of a greeting, before loping past. He moved to where Ida had laid out a meal on a tray. He picked up the plate and sniffed at it, disparagingly. 'Call that your best do you?'

Ida said nothing, eyes fixed to the flagstone floor. She wouldn't let him see the shame in her face; the shame that never left her, that wouldn't scrub clean.

Barker dropped the meal onto the table, causing her to start at the sound. Gravy slopped over the sides of the plate. 'That's for Aggie,' Ida somehow managed to say. 'She'll be getting hungry upstairs . . .'

The valet glowered. 'I said, is that your best?'

Ida shrank in on herself. 'Roast mutton. I only know a few dinners. I'm no trained cook.'

He raised his hand as if to slap her for it.

'Mr Barker!' Margaret cried out.

Barker only laughed. 'Don't worry yourself, madam, you'll forget all you've seen in a minute, won't she, Ida?'

She cast a look at her mistress. Margaret was scared, bewildered by the scene, but Ida knew he was right. It would soon be rendered meaningless, as was everything else. It didn't matter what she witnessed.

He cocked his chin at Ida. 'Lost all your cheek now, haven't you, idiot?'

She felt herself starting to cry again. 'Yes, Mr Barker.'

'Who would have known that's all it'd take, eh? Getting noticed by a man?'

She knew the disgrace and fear must be stark in her eyes. She could never hide it from him, he would always know.

'All the same, you ugly ones,' he told her. 'Curse and sass like sailors until someone shows you what your parts are for. Then you're as meek as little lambs.' He lurched forward and she cringed from him, but he merely picked up the plate. 'Nice to see a bit of feminine gratitude,' he smirked.

Ida somehow found a skerrick of courage. 'I want to see Aggie,' she told him. 'I'll take the meal up to her today.'

Barker froze. 'This again.'

'She'll be missing me,' Ida pressed, 'she'll be worried, and she's not getting any better with her flu.'

Barker's look was enough to see Ida's courage retreat, but inside her, buried somewhere deep within, she felt a stirring of rage. Had he done something terrible to Aggie, just like he had done to her? Had he hurt Aggie?

'And have you telling her your little lies about me?' Barker asked. 'You must think me as stupid as your mistress.'

Margaret stood rooted to the spot.

With a wink to her, he took the servants' stairs and was gone from the room, the plate of roast mutton gripped tight in his long, hard hands.

It was still an hour before dawn when Aggie felt her way down the servants' stairs, one step at a time, stopping still at every creak, pausing to pull air into her lungs.

'Aggie?' The sight of her friend slumped at the landing brought a cry of shock from Ida, coming down the stairs behind her. She was already dressed for the day ahead, unable to sleep. 'Oh, heavens.' She clamped a hand to her mouth and stood there staring, eyes filling with tears. 'You look so ill.'

'I am ill,' Aggie managed. Every joint in her body seemed to be grinding in pain; her skull was throbbing. Her vision was falling in and out of focus, her hearing with it. She could barely hold her balance against the rail. Sounds from the night beyond the windows seemed to be lurching and magnifying around her.

Aggie kept one hand pressed to her stomach; a sodden laundry bag swung from her waist where she'd tied it.

Ida helped her reach the bottom of the stairs and Aggie fell panting against the banister. The rasp of her lungs seemed to echo against the walls. She tried to still the noise, struggling to compose herself, but feared falling to the floor and being unable to rise again if she didn't give herself these minutes to rest and breathe.

After a time she felt recovered enough to go on. Making her way into the kitchen proper, Aggie took the bag from her waist to the scraps bin near the sink. Opening the bag, the swollen joints in her hands struggled with the effort of emptying what was in there: a day's worth of meals apparently consumed but in reality tipped inside the bag.

Ida was white with horror.

'I hoped you would look inside the bin in the morning and think it strange the uneaten food was in there,' Aggie whispered. 'Perhaps you would put two and two together . . .'

'To make what? Why haven't you been eating your food?'

'Shhh,' said Aggie, 'I don't want him to know.'

She ran the canvas bag beneath the tap, and Ida prayed that the sound of the pipe knocking and banging inside the wall would not alert Barker to there being someone downstairs. When done, Aggie gestured for Ida to help her towards the door that led to the garden.

'Tell me what's going on,' Ida pleaded. But Aggie put a hand to her lips.

Once outside, shivering in the damp, Aggie took another long moment to breathe in the cool night air. Then moving silently, carefully, she began tearing off edible items – a leaf of silver beet here, a tuft of kale there. She fed on all that the garden could offer, silently rejoicing in food that was clean and fresh and untouched by anyone's hand.

*

'I'm so sorry, Aggie,' Ida whispered later, when they had come back inside. 'I didn't know how bad it was.'

'Why didn't you know?' her friend looked at her carefully. 'Why haven't you come to see me?'

Ida's face creased in humiliation.

'What has been happening down here?' Aggie demanded. 'Has he been frightening you?'

Ida shook her head, unwilling to answer.

'You must tell me.'

'No, I can't.'

'Tell me!'

But Ida wouldn't say what had happened, what he'd done to her. She had told herself she'd never say it to anyone; she would never form the words. Yet the rage was there again, telling her to stop being so stupid.

Aggie hugged her close. 'It doesn't matter,' she said, 'let's not worry on it now.' But Ida knew that it mattered to Aggie very much and her heart ached to think of it. Her friend would get the truth out of her and wouldn't stop until she did. 'You must help me, Ida. I need to see Dr Foal,' Aggie whispered. 'Help me get the trap from the stables.'

'But Dr Foal has been to see you here each week?' said Ida.

'No, Ida, he hasn't.'

She stared at her friend in surprise for a moment, and then saw what the appalling reality was. Apart from the initial visit in the first days of Aggie's illness just before the wedding, the doctor had not attended again, despite Barker telling Ida he had. The valet had been stopping Aggie from getting well.

'I'm very ill, Ida.'

She started shaking. The certainty in her friend's face was terrible. 'Barker will know if I leave ... he'll punish me,' Ida started saying.

Aggie looked imploringly at her. 'Aren't you doing all the cooking now? Aren't you doing everything?'

Ida nodded that she was.

'How do you get the ingredients you need?'

'Deliveries,' said Ida, 'the store boys bring things from the village.'

Aggie nodded to a wooden produce box on the dresser, where a boy had left it yesterday. 'That food's spoiled then. I can tell it from here.'

Ida looked to the box, startled. 'No, it isn't.'

'It's all off,' said Aggie. 'Can't you smell it? It all needs to go back to the store for exchange. Mr Barker would be the first to say so.'

Ida's face creased again. 'No—'

Aggie lost her temper. *'I'm being poisoned!'*

Ida processed this in terrified silence.

It was Barker. It was Samuel. It was either of them, it was both of them, the difference didn't matter. All that did matter was that they were poisoning Aggie's food. She felt the rage surge.

The colour in Ida's face changed. She bolted for the porcelain sink, where she proceeded to be violently, noisily sick. Aggie stood watching her in alarm. When Ida stood upright again, dabbing at her mouth with water cupped in her hands, Aggie was behind her, rubbing her back. 'You're ill, too,' she said.

'I'm not,' said Ida, avoiding Aggie's eye.

'What do you call that, then? You're green in the face.'

'It's nothing,' Ida insisted. 'I'm all right.'

Aggie's lips compressed themselves into a thin, grim line. 'Ida, what is wrong with you?'

She knew that abject shame was etched into her eyes. She wanted so badly to tell. 'It's nothing, I said. I'm just a bit off colour, that's all.'

Aggie gripped her by the wrist and started pulling her towards the door to the kitchen garden.

'Stop it!' Ida pleaded.

'You'll have to hit me to stop,' said Aggie, 'hit a woman who's been dying in bed for weeks without a single friend to care about her. You'll have to do that if you want me to let go of you, Ida

Garfield.' She pulled her through the doorway and back into the garden. 'You're coming with me to Dr Foal. You need to see him as much as I do.'

Ida bit at her lips, her face looking greener still in the glow of the early sun. She remembered the girl she had been before, the girl who did anything to look out for a friend. She felt what that inquisitive girl had felt; her conviction, her certainty that truth only led to good. She started to softly cry.

Aggie tried to smooth the stained and crumpled dress she'd pulled on when she'd crept from her bed. She clutched her shawl tighter around her shoulders. 'Let's get to the stables quickly.'

With Aggie leaning on her for support as they stumbled into the grounds, Ida's other hand strayed to her abdomen, rubbing herself there. Aggie had lost a lot of weight in her own illness, her face and neck had been made gaunt by it. But Ida had experienced the opposite reaction. Her figure was fuller, more womanly, the fabric at her belly and breasts stretched tight at the seams.

An inexpert driver, Ida tethered the horse in hilly Mostyn Street as best she could, pleased to be near a water trough at least, and hoping the beast would still be found waiting for her when she returned, and not wandered off with the trap. She helped Aggie get down, and Aggie said she felt at least slightly improved, even if she little looked it. The fresh food had done what it could for her. She was fit enough to put up a fight at least, if not yet her best one, she said. Dr Foal would help her.

Ida supported Aggie as they headed up the hill against a chilly wind, Aggie's shawl pulled around them both, their uncovered hair whipping at their faces. Dr Foal's surgery and dispensing rooms sat at the summit in the little garden of pink pelargonium. Pushing open the low gate Ida ascended the five stone steps and pulled the cord of the bell. She stood there self-consciously a moment, very aware of her appearance. At least there was a real patient, this time, she told herself.

Doctor Foal's housekeeper opened the door. Ida couldn't remember her name. 'Please, we need to see Dr Foal,' she told her.

The woman gawped at Aggie at the foot of the steps and backed away, closing the door to a crack. 'She's too sick, go to the Benevolent Asylum.'

'Please miss . . .' said Aggie from below.

The woman held the door fast.

'Isn't this a place where people get made well?' Ida demanded, her rage surging hot inside her. 'Let us in to see Dr Foal at once.'

The woman was taken aback by Ida's tone. 'You're far too early. He's not even attending yet.'

'I don't believe you,' said Ida.

'How dare you!' the woman started to say, but Ida threw her weight against the door, barrelling in.

'You don't understand, she's been poisoned!'

'If you don't get out I shall run for the sergeant,' said the shocked housekeeper, rubbing her arm where the door had hit her.

'Do it, then,' said Ida, desperation making her dangerous now, 'and in the meantime we'll speak with Dr Foal.'

The other woman suddenly reacted with physical force of her own. Ida found herself picked up under the arms and about to be pushed out the door.

'Please, we need help – have compassion!'

'The Benevolent Asylum,' the housekeeper spat, 'we're not a charity!'

'Don't you even remember me?' Aggie begged.

The woman stopped.

'I'm Marshall, the lady's maid to Miss Gregory.'

The woman's jaw dropped.

'I'm very ill,' Aggie said.

Ida was confused. How did Aggie know this woman?

'Please,' the housekeeper told them, 'I don't want trouble. I left all that behind me.'

'Let me see Dr Foal,' Aggie pleaded, 'We don't want any trouble either.'

The housekeeper froze with indecision. Aggie mounted the steps with difficulty and stood facing her on the doorstep. 'You do remember me, don't you, Miss Haines?'

The housekeeper flushed with guilt. 'I'll take you in,' she whispered. She pulled Aggie down the hallway towards the hallway curtain. Her face was full of fear. 'Just be quick as you can.'

They disappeared, leaving Ida all alone.

Her eyes fell on a polished pine door on which was a sign: *Apothecary.*

The rage Ida felt remained, aimed at nothing specific now that Aggie was with Dr Foal, but still there all the same, aimed at everything. She felt fury at Mr Skews. She had once assembled questions about the apothecary.

One. Why had her mistress wanted Ida to accompany them to the ball that evening so many weeks ago? Her mistress had never mentioned it previously, even though she had claimed that she had. Why had she wanted her there at all?

Two. Why had Barker told her to keep her eyes peeled when she went? He had told her to do the same thing when she accompanied Samuel and her mistress to the graveyard. Barker said she should keep an eye out, but for what? Had she seen whatever it was that she was supposed to see? And why was she meant to see it at all?

Ida tapped at the apothecary's door. 'Mr Skews?' she called.

She waited.

'Are you there, Mr Skews?'

She heard a voice from somewhere within, distorted by the door. 'It's Ida, the maid from Summersby,' she spoke into the doorjamb. 'Do you have time for a word?'

She turned the handle.

She couldn't see the apothecary anywhere in the dispensary. A smell like a sick room hit her. She held a hand to her nose. 'Mr Skews . . .?'

A weak moan came from the other side of the dispensing counter. Ida went towards it and found the apothecary slumped on the floor behind. He had collapsed and vomited, ruining his clothes; his hair was sodden, his skin like chalk. His eyes had rolled in their sockets. 'Mr Skews!' She tried to lift his head from the floor. 'What has happened, Mr Skews!'

There was a glass hypodermic syringe near his side. Ida realised he had injected himself with something.

His eyes found focus. 'Two . . .' he rasped.

'You need help, let me find you Dr Foal.'

He clutched at her hands. 'Still two.' There was a bleak warning in his face.

Ida looked about her wildly. 'Help!' She called for the house-keeper, Miss Haines. 'Come in here please! It's an emergency!'

Skews' fingers clawed at her, twisting at her own. 'Stay with me,' she begged him. 'Please stay with me, Mr Skews.'

The life was dimming in his eyes.

'No!' she pleaded.

'Miss Garfield?' The frightened housekeeper stood at the door. Ida arose from behind the counter, the look on her face enough to bring Miss Haines inside. She came around the counter and saw what was there.

'He's gone,' said Ida, helplessly. 'Dying when I found him, now he's just gone.'

The housekeeper was staggered.

Ida shook her head. Her rage was all gone. 'He was trying to tell me something, something important, I think. *Still two*,' she said. 'It's all he could speak. *Still two.*' Her face fell into her hands.

Miss Haines went very still.

When Ida lifted her eyes again a change had overcome the housekeeper; her stern exterior had slipped away, along with her fear. A resolution had been reached and with it had come empathy for Ida. Miss Haines gently led her from the room, shutting the door behind them. 'Dr Foal,' Ida started to say, but Miss Haines hushed her, leading her into the front parlour, where she made her sit down.

'The doctor is seeing your friend now.'

A glass of water was found and handed to her. Ida gulped it, grateful, and put the glass down.

'The devil,' said Miss Haines, now that Ida was calmer, 'he drove him to this.'

'I beg your pardon?'

'The devil,' she repeated, 'from Summersby – that foul man.'

Ida caught her breath. 'You mean Barker?'

Miss Haines nodded, vehement at the memory. 'He still makes us suffer him here – letting himself inside whenever he pleases as if he belongs in here.'

'Barker knows Dr Foal?'

Miss Haines shook her head, growing angrier. 'Mr Skews. They're brothers-in-law. Barker had a hold over him. Mr Skews was made desperate. And now he's lying there dead.'

Ida struggled to grasp what she was saying.

'There are *things* in that dispensary, Miss Garfield,' the housekeeper whispered, 'things that entrap a person, make them vulnerable.'

Then Ida suddenly did understand. 'Mr Skews was a drug addict?'

Miss Haines nodded, ashamed for him. 'Barker was capable of exploiting him for it, using it against him, I know it.'

Ida felt as if the pieces of the puzzle, the mysterious game far larger and complicated than any she'd known, were finally falling into order. 'But *how* do you know?'

Trembling, the woman reached for Ida's water glass and poured herself a little more from the jug. She drank it down, steeling herself to reply. 'I once worked at Summersby, you see,' she said, at last, 'and after that I worked at an establishment in Melbourne called Constantine Hall.'

Ida fell back in her seat. 'What did you do there?'

'I was Margaret Gregory's lady's maid . . . Before your friend Aggie took the job.'

Ida stared, open-mouthed. 'You know of the tragedy, then? You know of what happened to Matilda?'

Miss Haines just looked back at her, sadly. 'That tragedy was not what it seemed, Miss Garfield.'

Once-dark clouds began to part in Ida's understanding.

Ida ran down Mostyn Street hill where she found the Summersby horse had indeed slipped its tether and was pulling the trap on its own towards Lyttleton Street. Miss Haines ran ahead and secured the horse, which seemed glad for the firm attention, while Ida ignored the negative remarks of onlookers. She needed Miss Haines' help to climb inside the trap and then found that her nerve was failing badly in the accumulated shock.

'You're not at all well, either,' Miss Haines told her.

'I'll be all right,' said Ida, determined. 'I've got to go back there. Stay with Aggie please, she needs someone like you near her. And there's also Mr Skews.'

'His life's been lost, but others can be helped yet,' Miss Haines insisted. 'Think of your Mr Samuel – he's just a puppet in all this.'

Ida did think of Samuel then and felt sick to her heart. She had thought she understood everything about him now, but she had been wrong. Yet still she knew he was little better than Aggie had always said he was, just not as bad as others.

Samuel had not understood Barker. Samuel had not understood Matilda.

Those two and what it was that they wanted Ida to do, she now understood fully.

She shook the reins and the horse fell into step in her hands.

The hour for midday dinner was approaching and the scene Ida foresaw of Barker taking Aggie her plate and discovering her gone was a torment. Ida knew he'd be made violent by it and the thought of what he might do made her sick with dread – sicker than she was already feeling. She remembered her rage, remembered how it had driven her. She looked for it again and found it, the faintest of echoes.

Her head started to throb. All she wanted was relief, just the chance to go on and face what she need to do and with her wits about her, if nothing else. Ida knew her mistress had a small supply of sedative powders in her old room. As she went about the kitchen peeling vegetables and adding more wood to keep the oven at an even temperature for the lamb, the lure of those powders grew strong. Ida had never stolen anything from her betters, and had never even thought about it, what's more, unlike so many other girls in service. But now she thought about those powders and the relief they might bring. She dropped the peeler and potato in the sink.

Ida crept up the servants' stairs to the second storey, emerging to find the hallway deserted. She stole along the passage towards the Chinese Room, just as she heard footsteps from the opposite wing. Panicking that it was Barker, Ida looked for somewhere to hide. An alcove was the best she could manage and she squeezed into the gap, feeling exposed, ready to deny everything until he resorted to slapping her.

It was Samuel who walked past, not seeing her at all, focused upon his destination.

Her chest pounding as hard as her head, Ida stepped from the alcove, peering after him. He entered the Chinese Room.

Ida made her way unhurriedly towards the room, hands clasped before her at her waist. Samuel emerged before she got there, and when he did, Ida merely curtsied. 'Be serving luncheon soon, Mr Hackett,' she told him, with her eyes to the floor, 'nice lamb shoulder today.' It was the most she had said to him in weeks.

If he was pleased at being spoken to by her, she did not care. And why should he be pleased, Ida thought to herself, he had everything he wanted now, thanks to his marriage. Well, almost everything. He did not have her.

'Ida, I see so little of you nowadays. Won't you talk to me awhile?'

There was hurt in his voice, but she refused to look up. 'I have my chores.'

She saw his fingers dart for hers. She pressed her hands in her dress pockets, where he could not get to them.

'What is it, Ida? Something's wrong, I know it is.'

'Nothing's wrong.'

'Then why won't you talk to me? I thought we were friends.'

Rage bit at her, growing stronger once more. She looked at him now. 'You're not my *friend*, you're my master.'

He was thrown. 'But nothing changes between us.'

'Everything has changed.'

He tried to appeal to her. 'I told you to trust me, to wait. Everything will come well.'

'How will it? You are married to my mistress. What do you propose? That "mistress" becomes a word I apply to myself?'

His face flushed.

'I believe everything *will* come well,' she told him, meaningfully, 'just not in the way you might have hoped.'

Ida continued down the hall, as if on a visit to another of the rooms, but when she heard his footsteps descending the great stairs, she turned around and went into the Chinese Room.

The blue vial stood on the dressing table.

Ida felt the sickness drain away without a grain of powder needed. Rage remained. Miss Haines had told everything she knew and Ida had worked the rest of it out, worked out why she had been so manipulated and lied to. The vial was at the heart of it, and of course she was meant to find the foul thing once again. For as long as Ida had served at Summersby the sapphire blue vial had taunted her, appearing and disappearing. It was intended that Ida know it intimately, and know exactly what it could do.

She picked the thing up. There was plenty of liquid in it, more than when she last had seen it. It had been topped up. But was it the same liquid, Ida wondered? She rather thought she knew: this time something different would be inside it.

Ida placed the vial inside her apron pocket, and then placed her mistress's powders there, too.

All the way down the servants' stairs the rage boiled inside her. When she reached the kitchen Barker was there.

'I'll be taking Aggie her dinner today,' she announced before he could say a word to her. The look on her face must have given him rare pause. Barker just nodded, seemingly dismissing her and little caring for once, but when she turned to go back to the spuds she saw him glance at her waist. Let him guess, she told herself, he'll never get his stinking claws on it. Barker left the room.

She peeled a potato, thinking of the blue vial. Her rage wouldn't lessen now. Bitterness for Samuel filled her. For all his good looks he was utterly characterless. Ida put down her peeler and withdrew the blue vial from her apron pocket. She tried the stopper. It easily came free in her fingers. She sniffed at the contents.

It still smelled of rosemary.

'Of course it does . . .' she said to herself. Whatever it was this time, it would do more than knock a person out.

She thought of Samuel anticipating his lamb.

Later, when the midday meal had been cooked and served, it hit Ida just what she had done. She felt a need for her chair. Calmer again, common sense returned. The blue vial must be hidden away where no one would think of it, she told herself, but not so hidden that she couldn't lay hands on it again, should she ever have another need.

Ida hid it at the very back of a shelf in the stillroom, behind the preserving jars.

Alone in the library, Samuel finished the last of his luncheon, using a bread slice to mop up the mint sauce. Observing him through the crack in the door, the long, long chain of fascinating questions and captivating things that Ida had assembled in her head from the very first day she had come to Summersby began to reform in her head. She thought about the day in the carriage, when it was made plain to her that Samuel and Barker were bound together by something secret, and that something, she had later worked out, was really *someone* secret: her mistress, and all of the secret wrongs that Samuel wrongly believed had been done. Ida now knew that Samuel and Barker were not bound together in quite the same way by those secrets – or by quite the same mistress.

As Ida watched Samuel eat the last of his meal, she wondered whether his thoughts were not on the food but on who his wife might actually *be*. Had Samuel seen his wife for who she really was yet, Ida wondered? Had the telling error to his wife's performance been no one particular thing he could have named, but rather, an accumulation of tells, tiny things seen over months, that together opened his eyes, just as Ida's had at last been opened? Or had Samuel failed to notice anything at all? Ida wondered whether it was truly possible that she, a sixteen-year-old nobody, fresh off the farm, with no breeding or prospects, and nothing but inquisitiveness to aid her, could have arrived at a conclusion before Samuel Hackett had, the fine English gentleman, and her superior in every way.

Samuel's wife was ill, but not in the way that he had tried to make her ill. His wife's instability of mind was at once far deeper, and in the same breath simpler than anything he had tried to drive her to becoming. Hers was a performer's illness, the madness of the actress leaping crazed upon the stage; for a stage was what Summersby had become to its mistress, Ida now understood, and she, along with Samuel, was the audience of two.

Ida opened the door to enter and clear the things away. She made herself attentive. 'Did you enjoy it, Mr Hackett?' she asked him, eyes bright. She looked fully at him.

He smiled and nodded in response, plainly delighted by her. But as he stood from the table he seemed light-headed.

'Are you all right?' His eyes seemed to be having trouble focusing upon her.

'Of course I'm all right, thank you, Ida, an excellent lamb.' He finished his glass of claret, and Ida watched him swallow it, gulp by gulp.

'It's just that you look very strange.'

He smiled at her again, his eyes struggling. Ida placed the luncheon things on her tea trolley.

A thought seemed to occur to him. 'Have you seen Mrs Hackett?'

'Not in a little while. She likes to take her dinner a bit later now.'

'You've not seen her at all?'

Ida pointed a finger to her chin, as if illustrating 'thinking' in pantomime. 'Well, I do know she's not in the Chinese Room, Mr Samuel. *I've looked.*'

If she was making some point with her remark, it was lost to him. 'If you find her, will you find me?'

Ida readied to depart. 'Yes, I will.'

She watched the light-headedness hit him in waves.

'I say . . .' said Samuel.

'Yes?' she paused at the door.

'I was just thinking of Marshall, I do believe I've seen little of her of late . . . almost as little as I've seen of you.'

'She's been very ill,' Ida told him, revealing nothing.

The dizziness seemed to depart in him again and with it came clarity. 'Do you know, Ida,' he told her, 'if I set my mind to it, and without making too much of a noise, I do think I might visit every room in this house, go to all of them, you see, one by one, and in one of the rooms I might find my wife.'

'Oh, yes?'

'No doubt with desire in her eyes.'

She betrayed nothing. 'No doubt, Mr Samuel.'

'I would be rid of her desire, Ida, if I could.'

He could see Ida, but not quite see her. His mind was dissolving with what he had unwittingly consumed.

'That's a very fine idea,' she told him. 'Why don't we look for her together?'

As they left the room they passed the body of Barker in the hallway, slumped where he had fallen, the remains of his own roast lamb and claret strewn across the floor.

The hallway seemed to expand and retract with each breath he took, swaying to the side and back again. 'It's almost like being at sea,' he remarked.

Following a short distance behind, Ida encouraged this. 'Perhaps you are at sea, Mr Samuel?'

'I say . . .' he said, struck by this. 'I believe you might be right there, Ida, I'm rounding Cape Hope en route to a New World!' He laughed uproariously, before confiding, 'Soiled my nest badly in the Old, don't you know.'

'Oh dear, that's unfortunate.' She knew that she needn't have gone to the library until well after Samuel had succumbed, but she'd been driven to see the results of her deed. She had wondered if she would find him slumped in his chair, just as Barker had been slumped, she hoped that she would, but that had not been so, and for a moment she had feared she had failed at first. Then it had become plain that success was just slow in arriving with Samuel. The effect of what she'd added to his claret hadn't been obvious at first, until, all at once, it was blinding.

Samuel struggled with his balance. 'Lucky I'm such a natural sailor, unfazed by the waves . . .'

'Very lucky,' Ida agreed.

'Bring a whiskey to my rooms, steward,' he ordered the crewman he imagined to be passing. 'And one for little Ida, too,' he indicated her, following in his steps. He leant on the wall for support in the swell. 'Nasty crossing for some, but not for a pair of old salts like us, eh, Ida?'

She made no reply and watched as Samuel found himself not at sea but at Summersby again.

'Good Lord.' He returned to his task at hand, flinging open another door. Again there was no sign of his wife. 'My love?' he called out. 'Why do you still hide from Ida and me?'

Ida continued to watch as the corridor expanded and retracted for him. More doors loomed ahead. Servants' rooms all of them, unused and unneeded.

'This house is ridiculously over-appointed,' Samuel declared.

Ida agreed with this, given that she'd grappled with cleaning them all.

'Now that I have committed myself to visiting each room, it occurs to me that there is simply so much purposeless space,' he said.

'Yes, Mr Samuel.'

'I will amend this in time. All rooms unable to justify themselves will be ruthlessly excised.'

Samuel leaned against the wall again as the ship he had previously imagined himself sailing returned once more, resuming its sway. 'I am not *really* onboard ship, am I, Ida?' he asked her, sounding worried now.

'Only if you wish to be,' she told him.

'I do not wish it,' he said, 'I fear this swaying is illusory. I am ill, perhaps, gravely ill, possibly – it has come on very suddenly.'

She studied him. 'Are you worried by it, Mr Samuel?'

He considered this. 'No, my purpose is all . . .'

Samuel looked to where his hand steadied him, pressed against the wallpaper, and he saw another door, different than the rest, the crack of its opening just inches from his palm. 'Is this really a door at all?'

Ida had already recognised it. It was a door disguised as a wall or perhaps vice versa. It was papered and dado-ed, and yet it also held a handle. It was the one locked door in all of Summersby. Ida knew without testing that it wouldn't be locked now. It was a door they were intended to open.

Samuel blinked, as the handle fell in and out of his focus. 'Like something from Lewis Carroll,' he said.

'Will you try it, sir?' she asked him.

Samuel did so and immediately fell down, striking his chin. His balance had failed him and with it his legs. Ida didn't help him get up again. He spat out a chip from a tooth. Had he bitten his tongue? Ida didn't care. 'Don't be put off, Mr Hackett,' she told him. 'Up you get now.'

With effort he righted himself and re-steadied against the wall, reaching for the handle once more. The small, brass knob seemed to lurch all over the surface for him, denying him grip. 'Stay still, damn you!' he commanded the thing. It obeyed. His fingers found purchase and he ordered them to twist.

The door opened without sound.

Inside was all gloom, yet from somewhere high above came hints of daylight. The room was not a room but a staircase.

The sensation of a draught upon her skin was something Ida had grown used to at Summersby; the little gusts of air, the breeze upon her face when she was inside the house and not out in the garden, where a person might be expected to feel air. Summersby was drafty, and yet it had struck her at once as strange that small wafts of air could start and then stop just as suddenly; draught felt just the once and then not felt again.

She felt the breeze now as it played along her arms, making the fine hairs stand on end. This time the draught didn't cease and Ida knew at last where it came from, where it had always come from: the tower. Whenever the locked door to the room with the spiral stairs had been open the breeze had blown through the house below. So, who had held the key to the door?

'Very good, Mr Samuel.'

The sound of a dog's hard little claws upon boards filled their ears.

He could barely see each step in front of him. His progress seemed glacial, as if the ascent was one of untold miles and not a spiral flight of stairs at all. Ida had to keep telling Samuel that this was all it was, a journey to the floor above, to Summersby's tower, a trip of no more than seconds. And yet the seconds ticked by and became minutes, then hours it seemed, and then time itself had fallen away for him, no longer measurable, and Samuel still climbed, step by single step to a tower that wouldn't come.

'Billy,' Samuel called. 'Good boy, Billy.'

The little dog was their escort, the dead little dog. Billy's strong, hard nails on the boards of the spiral stairs had announced his arrival first, the sound unexpectedly sharp, causing Ida to twist and look about until she had seen the dog in the flesh and used this as confirmation that everything was exactly as she had come to understand that it was.

But to Samuel the dog's reappearance was impossible; he, like Ida, had been told by Barker that Billy's corpse had been tossed onto the rubbish. 'Am I dead, too?' he joked with the animal. 'I must be, eh? I must be dead to be seeing you there.' Yet he knew that he was not dead, at least not yet. Grim purpose filled him to get to the top of the stairs. The little dog circled and ran about, barking and licking him, going up and then down, fluffy tail flailing like a whip, rustling Samuel along. 'Good boy, Billy,' Samuel told him, 'you're a good boy.'

And yet still the stairs seemed endless, an Everest of stairs, and Samuel was no longer upright but upon his hands and knees, crawling in ascent. 'One more step,' Ida told him, and with herculean effort he surmounted another only to find another again. 'One more step,' she sang.

And then all was quiet and still, and the sound of the little dog's nails was gone, and with it the barking and the circling, and there were no more steps at all and Samuel and Ida had arrived at a room that was open, it seemed, to the elements, being flooded with light and air. There was a bed in the room; a comfortable chair; a wardrobe of clothes Ida recognised – identical clothes. The breeze was cool upon their faces, good-humoured in their hair, teasing them, inviting them to join. Samuel felt fingers at his waistcoat buttons and looked to see that they were his own fingers, divesting himself of his clothing. His jacket was already upon the floor. 'When did I take this off?' he wondered. The waistcoat landed on top of it. He tore at his boots, the buttons there popped and spat, and the boots joined the clothes.

'How do you feel, Mr Hackett?' Ida asked him, her eyes already watching who it was that waited for them in the room.

'I feel freer now, lighter somehow.' He took deep breaths.

'You have found me then?'

Samuel's eyes were shut. He opened his lids to behold what Ida had already seen: his wife standing before an elegant, circular window, smiling at him, the breeze in the curls of her hair that fell loose like a shower of coal down her spine.

'Matilda . . .' He saw it again, the naked desire that was there for him and him alone when she would have him believe that she was the dead twin somehow made alive. Ida wondered if he knew her little tricks by now, whether he had guessed, as she had guessed, at how cleverly she had fooled him, had fooled everyone.

He could stand upright. His strength had returned, his balance, too.

'Samuel,' she purred, opening her arms to receive him, with one smiling eye upon Ida. 'Here I was all along . . . all you had to do was look.'

His mouth was on hers, his lips, her lips became one. She guided his hand as they loved, placing it upon her belly. 'Feel,' she whispered, pulling from his kiss. 'Do you feel our child there?'

He could feel it. The child they had made. She was swollen with it, ripe, more luscious than ever.

'You are an actress, my love.' He opened his eyes to regard her. She opened hers. 'An actress.'

'Samuel, don't be so cruel and unkind to me.'

'It is I who is cruel?'

She tossed her hair, still held fast in his arms. She was the coquette, the kitten, aflame with the thrill of entrapment.

'Acting upon a stage,' he told her, 'and I am your audience.'

'And me as well, Mr Samuel,' Ida came in. 'It's been a little show for both of us, don't forget – but I wonder if we've been watching the same show?' She was fascinated, not remotely shocked by any of it. Nothing shocked her now.

His wife laughed in delight, a sensual laugh; erotic. 'But when have I acted? What has been my part?'

'Oh, Matilda,' he said, admonishing. He tightened his grip, his hands on her arms, squeezing her, claiming her. 'What is your broken memory if not a play for my entertainment?'

She laughed again, squirming now, the captive. 'Nonsense.'

There was pressure in his loins. Ida looked away. He needed his wife to know how he would tame her. 'Your recall is total,' he told her. 'The memory loss was never real at all. I can see it now.'

Ida shook her head, and wondered if he could actually see anything, if he ever could. Matilda had been right to call him unintelligent.

'Do you?' his beloved taunted him. 'But what do you see?'

'I see a girl who never lost her mind – who only played that she did.'

'Played it? But why?'

'To confuse your father, to confuse the world – who knows? If you've forgotten anything, it would be that one thing: the original reason why. No doubt it made sense when you were just a little girl – when you pretended to be your sister, and behold there were two of you, both with broken memories, both having fun.'

She stopped squirming now, regarding him thoughtfully.

'But now your sister is dead, yet the play still remains and you would have me believe in it still,' Samuel told her.

Ida pitied him. He had misread the signs. She and Samuel had each seen a different show, where only the star was the same.

Her smile was gone. Her face was expressionless. 'But why would I persist with such a thing . . . when I love you?' Her hand slipped from his grip and went to her belly, stroking the child that was theirs. Then she went to his loins, resting there lighter than ether, testing him, owning him.

'To punish me.' He put a hand to his temple as it began to throb.

'But for what?' she breathed, her lips brushing his. 'Whatever would I punish you for?'

Samuel swallowed. The strain at his waist as exquisite as it was unbearable. 'To punish me for what I did to your sister . . .' She kissed him. 'For what I did to Margaret.'

'But what did you do?'

'I made you write messages – on scraps of paper – messages to play on her guilt.'

Her fingers found his fly buttons, released them one by one. *Matilda says you suffer the torture of guilt? Matilda says love's happiness is a lie?'* she quoted.

He nodded. 'Her guilt at confining you, imprisoning you in that place.'

'Yes?'

'Letting the world think she *was* you, while letting herself think that I was aiding her.'

Her hand was inside the fabric, pressing against his bare skin. 'Then you were not aiding her?'

'No.' He closed his eyes in ecstasy. 'I betrayed her. I used the scraps of messages you wrote to make her unstable. I hid them where she would find them one by one. They played on her guilt. I used them to make her take poison.'

'Matilda says drink it and you will know peace . . .' Her fingers seized the hidden parts of him, the points of her nails digging into the flesh. He groaned. 'And why did you do such a terrible thing? Drive my sister to kill herself?'

Ida saw the full extent of his shame at last, his mask was gone; the shame was glaring in his face. 'You were the better sister . . . better in your heart. Matilda was too dangerous, unstable. I feared what marriage to her might bring. But marriage to you, well . . .'

'Yes . . .?'

'It seemed the wiser option. I would still have Summersby, but with a bride I might control.' He looked to Ida. 'And perhaps somehow find happiness, too, where I had not expected it.'

Ida's mistress had contempt in her eyes. 'And you would murder for it?'

He blanched. 'I never touched her.'

'As good as murder, you drove her to it.'

He was paralysed by the pain; her fingers twisting him, exacting her claim.

'For that is how she left this world, isn't it?' she whispered. 'Driven to drink poison at your hands?'

He nodded, grimacing, tears pricking his eyes. *I had to have Summersby.*

'Yet did you do a thorough job?'

Ida sighed, sadly. She'd been waiting for it to come to this, knowing everything now as she did, knowing that it was inevitable.

Samuel stopped. His wife was smiling at him again, but no longer as the wanton, hers was the smile of someone else. Was it the victor's smile, Ida wondered?

'She is cold in her grave,' Samuel reminded her.

'Ah, but am I now?' She released her grip on him.

He stepped back from her, protecting himself. There was something in her face he had not seen before; something vile. There was a vicious thing that lived in her smile that Ida herself had only been allowed to see twice. Once on the night of the ball, and again when Aggie had been struck with the Remember Box. It was the thing that was wholly Matilda.

Billy's ears pricked up. Ida heard someone mounting the spiral stairs below.

'Am I really dead, Samuel?' The catlike smile was curling about his wife's lips.

'You are not *she*,' Samuel said. 'You are only *you* – Matilda Gregory – and the only lie was that of the broken memory you wore like a costume . . .'

'Ah, memory,' said Matilda. 'And what will we remember of today, I wonder?'

Ida listened to the tread on the stairs. She knew who was coming to find them all.

'I will remember a wife that was bettered, a wife that was cowed,' Samuel told her.

'Really?' She turned her attention to somewhere behind him, to the place in the floor where the spiral stairs were, from where he'd crawled to her panting and blinking only moments before. 'And what will *you* remember, sister?'

Ida stood respectfully aside for the new arrival.

'I will remember my hurt at this,' said Margaret from behind.

Samuel turned to see the mirror image of his wife staring at them both from the mouth of the stairs, hands held to her belly. He looked to the first wife, the one who had kissed him and held him and who regarded him now with mirth – Matilda Gregory. He looked to the second wife, the one who was identically dressed, but whose eyes held confusion and hurt – Margaret Gregory. No sister had died. The funeral was a fraud. What had been placed in the coffin, Ida wondered, rocks? There had been two sisters all along, which was exactly as Mr Skews had told Ida in his dying words. There was Matilda the mistress who had pretended to be her sister, and there was Margaret the mistress who had never pretended at all.

Samuel fell back. *'It's impossible . . . One of you is dead!'*

Ida was gentle with him. 'I tried to tell you. You thought you had helped send the wrong sister to the Hall, Mr Samuel, but *you* were wrong as it turned out. The right sister was in the Hall all along, safe and protected as her late father had hoped she would be.'

Samuel froze.

'By making everyone think that Margaret was actually she, the conditions of old Mr Gregory's will were still met,' Ida explained to him. 'Miss Margaret became the heiress because seemingly she *was* Matilda – the plan worked because of Miss Margaret's confusion . . .' She felt terrible saying this. 'It worked because of her damaged mind, you see, half the time she didn't know who she was anyway. For a while I thought she was one sister with both personalities. Then today I saw how I'd been wrong. The real Matilda has been with us the whole time, hiding away in this tower with Billy.'

'Husband,' pleaded Margaret near the stairwell. 'I love you . . . you must not listen to what Matilda says.'

Matilda laughed. 'But Samuel has listened to everything and believed it.'

'But I love him!' cried Margaret, coming closer. 'I am carrying his child!'

Matilda stroked her own belly. 'But we are both expectant mothers, dearest. Look, don't you see? Our husband has expressed his love with each of us.'

Ida shook her head, disgusted, having suspected this, too.

Margaret's eyes widened as she realised the apparent truth of this. Each of them *was* with child – Samuel's unborn children.

As Ida watched, the tower room began to tumble and spin for him. He was seeing double. 'What have you done to my mind?'

'What have *we* done?' Matilda laughed.

Margaret was stricken by his suffering. 'Oh sister, is he ill? Is he dying?'

Matilda shrugged, grinning at Ida, who held her gaze.

Margaret tried to go to him but he pushed her away, shaking with fear. 'What have you done! Tell me, for pity's sake!'

'But we are innocent,' said Matilda. 'The girl Ida is who you should blame now.'

Margaret paled.

'Yes,' said Matilda, enjoying her sister's shock. 'Ida put something on the lamb, something from inside that pretty blue vial. You would never have detected it, Samuel. Its properties were disguised by rosemary.'

'Not Ida.' Margaret was devastated. 'She never would do such a terrible thing.'

'Oh, but she would,' Matilda insisted, 'and she *did* . . . didn't you, Ida?'

Margaret saw Ida's face, her eyes filling with tears. 'Please, say it's not true.'

Ida said nothing.

'She can't,' Matilda crowed. 'She can't because she did it – and did it because I wanted her to. She did it because everything I'd let her see and hear and read and experience in this house led her to do it. Everything! She did it because Samuel needed to be punished for daring to think he could better me, and she was my means for punishing him!'

Ida stepped forward, ready. 'What I actually did, miss, long before I realised it, was let you manipulate me, yes, and let you make me your little pawn. What I did was let you lead me down the garden path and on a merry dance while I went there. What I did was let you make a fool of me, really.' Her voice caught in her throat. 'And then make me into something far worse than a fool.' She swallowed, thinking of what she had added not to Samuel's lamb, but to his glass of claret, and Barker's, too. 'A killer . . .'

Margaret rushed forward and grabbed her sister by the hair. 'What have you done to poor Ida – and to Samuel? You tell me!'

Matilda twisted in her grip. 'Sister, please . . .'

'You tell me!'

Ida saw that the room was now spinning in Samuel's eyes.

'It is not what *I* have done,' Matilda tried to calm her sister, 'my hands are clean, I have done nothing – it is all Barker!'

Margaret stared at her, releasing her hold.

'Barker is the most loyal of men,' Matilda went on, fingers patting at her scalp. 'There is nothing he wouldn't do to serve me.'

Samuel's eyes were tiny specks of darkness, lost in the drug.

'Barker has helped me in everything I have ever asked of him,' Matilda said. 'There is nothing he has not been willing to do for me – *nothing* – right from the very start.' She smiled at her sister.

Ida had already reached this conclusion herself. 'Mr Barker worked here at Summersby as a boy,' she told Margaret, 'before he'd ever met Mr Samuel. You remembered him from the stables. Mr Barker was the only one who'd never been fooled by the childish little games your sister made you play. He was the only one who always knew exactly who was who. He knew because he loved Matilda.'

'Yes, husband,' said Matilda, turning to Samuel, sympathetic. 'I'm afraid that any agreement that you had reached with Barker was already ruined by an agreement he had reached with me. No doubt you thought he was helping you – placing all those scraps of messages written in my sister's lovely hand around the house where I'd find them; coercing the poison from his own brother-in-law Skews and then placing it in the hope that I'd drink it – yes, he did all those things for you, but really it was for me – all of it. I knew you'd try to betray me. It was the very reason why I allowed you into my confidence at all. I had you believe I was really Margaret and that my father would have me locked away.'

Samuel's mouth had gone dry.

'But I am not Margaret,' she said. She nodded to the identically dressed woman who resembled her in every way. 'She is . . . and she is utterly mad,' Matilda said, simply. 'But she is also my twin, and there is no one I love more. Our father was very wrong thinking he could separate us, so I'm afraid I used you, Samuel, to ensure she was freed. Everyone needed to think that she was actually me and that Margaret the madwoman was dead.'

Samuel heard all this, Ida knew. He was willing himself to stay focused before the effects of the claret took his strength away entirely.

'Yet in a way I also love you, Samuel,' Matilda whispered. 'I hadn't planned upon it, but it happened. It made what I had to do so much harder.'

'Not love,' he whispered. 'That's not love.'

A tear slid down Ida's cheek for him.

'You hadn't factored your heart in this adventure, husband, and neither did I,' Matilda said, sadly, 'but it was insufficient for either of us to abandon our plans. After all, you hoped that whatever it was you had known with me would somehow be found in my sister.'

Transfixed, Margaret's eyes filled with tears, too.

Matilda looked to her twin. 'I will always love my sister more.' She looked back to him. 'And you will always love money.'

Matilda reached into a pocket of her dress, withdrawing a shiny gold guinea. 'Billy loves money, too,' she added. The little dog tensed at her feet. 'See, Billy,' she teased, 'see what I have here?'

The dog's eyes glowed.

'Don't you love it?' Matilda went on. 'Don't you want it, Billy?'

A bead of sweat dripped from Samuel's brow.

'Surely you want this pretty, shiny thing?'

She tossed the guinea and the little dog leapt to catch it. The sudden movement made Samuel snap. The coin was in front of him, spinning in the air. He reached out to snatch it before the dog could, leaping as if his legs were made of springs.

'No!' Margaret screamed.

His hands went for the coin as he fell in a single, balletic motion that saw him plunge into the yawning mouth of the stairwell.

Matilda laughed and clapped her hands. 'So clever, Samuel, so acrobatic!' She turned to her sister. 'Did you like it, dearest? Did you like what our husband did?'

She didn't see Billy until it was too late and the animal was beneath her foot. Billy yelped and Matilda twisted so as not to hurt him, but in doing so lost her balance. The mouth of the stairwell opened before her, just as it had for her husband. Matilda cried out, realising what was happening, unable to stop herself.

She tumbled into the void.

The white poodle shot down the spiral staircase ahead of them, the sound of his hard little claws on the boards magnified by the space. Ida followed, cautious, her ears tuning in to the sound of a whispered conversation in the gloomy room below. She held Margaret's hand in descent. The young woman was in shock, trembling, with all she had seen.

When they reached the lower floor they saw that Matilda was there, laid upon the floor where she had fallen and Samuel with her, her head somehow in his lap as he stroked her chestnut hair, whispering as he drifted into unconsciousness.

'Miss Matilda?' Ida said softly.

Matilda's eyes opened and for a moment she seemed to beam at them, pleased, never having known what it was to be confused about her own name, because it *was* her own name, the one she was christened with, and never for one moment the name of her memory-robbed sister.

'Are you all right, miss?' Ida saw that Matilda was not all right. Her back was twisted; her legs, her arms were unmoving. Samuel's eyes were unfocused, seeing but not seeing. His lips murmured sounds but not words.

'Samuel is . . . altered, I think,' Margaret whispered. 'Perhaps it is the poison?'

Ida shook her head. 'That new stuff in the blue vial, whatever it was this time – and I know that it *was* something different this time, and not the stuff from before – you wanted me to give it to them, didn't you, miss? Give it to Samuel and Barker. Everything that happened was leading to that. Those letters you wrote that you meant for me to read.'

Matilda smiled. 'You fell for Samuel, didn't you, Ida, just like I knew that you would? A simple girl like you, straight from the farm, how could you not fall for him?'

Samuel was oblivious.

Ida nodded. She had fallen for him. Fallen the first moment she saw him.

'I needed you to love him,' Matilda whispered, 'love him with all of your heart, until the moment when I needed you to see him for what he really is, so that you would feel betrayal, and love him no more.' Her eyes upon Ida were hard, cruel. 'And Barker – he, I needed you to *hate*.'

Ida said nothing.

'And you do hate him now, don't you, Ida,' Matilda went on, 'hate him for the terrible thing that he did?' Her eyes fell to Ida's belly. 'Oh, poor Ida.'

'You needed to be rid of them, didn't you, miss?' said Ida, unbowed, meeting her look. 'Samuel and Barker? You used both of them to get what you wanted, your sister made free, and then you needed them gone.'

Margaret was shaking her head. 'Oh, sister . . .'

'And for that I don't blame you,' Ida went on. 'Neither of them could ever be trusted, even Barker who loved you. But you wouldn't do it yourself, you wouldn't risk being exposed as their murderer, so that's why you needed me.'

'An inquisitive girl,' Matilda murmured. 'So simple and naïve.'

'Inquisitive enough to uncover things, things you meant for me to find. Young and silly enough not to listen to warning bells.'

'Not a very bright girl.'

Ida's expression was cold. 'Everyone always tells me I'm not bright,' she said, 'but I'm starting to wonder if perhaps I *am* bright, miss, at least just a bit, for working it all out.'

Matilda's grin was triumphant. 'Yet you worked it out too late.'

'Not *that* late,' said Ida. She leant closer. I didn't put that stuff from the vial in their meals, miss,' she replied. 'I put in sedative powders.'

Matilda blinked. 'What?'

'You were wrong to think you could make me kill them for you. You were wrong to think you could turn me into someone like you.'

'No!' Matilda tried to lift her head but could not. She could not move at all. Her smile fell away and Ida glimpsed the horror behind it. Matilda had done something very wicked that had once pleased her greatly, but had now made its consequences apparent. 'Help me.'

But there was nothing to help.

'It is her punishment due,' Margaret whispered from where she had listened to every word. 'She has caused this, caused all of it. I see everything now. *She* is the mad one . . . My only flaw is my memory.'

Ida nodded. 'I'm sorry for it, miss,' she whispered to her.

Matilda's dress had torn in her fall, rent at her abdomen. The curve at her belly had been ripped wide open, revealing not a growing child but cushion stuffing.

'She is not pregnant,' Margaret said.

Matilda looked shocked that her sister should say this. Then the horror reappeared.

'You're not, are you, miss?' Ida echoed. 'Did you pretend that you were with child to maintain the deception?'

'My sister . . .'

Samuel slumped at last in unconsciousness. Matilda's head slipped from his lap.

'Miss Margaret's pregnancy is real, though, isn't it?' Ida said, patting Margaret's hand by her side. 'That was why you had to pretend . . .'

'My sister . . .' Matilda's voice fell away to little more than air. 'For my sister . . .' She was looking away from Ida now, looking only at Margaret. Yet Margaret's eyes were straining to look at something that sat on the floor in the gloom.

Ida turned and saw what it was. The Remember Box.

'You must never forget this,' Margaret told Ida.

The light went from the sister's eyes.

Ida and Margaret left the room without a backward glance. There was a final letter inside the Remember Box.

Dear Margaret,

This is for your Remember Box.

When our father died and you were sent to the Hall, my true arrangement with Barker began. He was my first accomplice. Ever the opportunist, Barker had already returned to Summersby in a new guise, no longer the hateful stable boy, but as valet to unwitting Samuel Hackett. He had told Samuel so much about our family, and more importantly still, so much about our fortune. It was Barker who had suggested to Samuel that he try his luck with us; that he exploit his fine looks and gentleman's charm for profit – a great deal of profit. Samuel needed no persuading. But what he did not know was that Barker was never his man. He was always mine. Samuel was Barker's gift to me, and for that he was well rewarded.

My second accomplice was a Mr Skews, apothecary to Dr Foal in Castlemaine. It was from this Mr Skews that Samuel obtained the original blue vial and its contents. Mr Skews was not a naturally bad man, just a weak-willed one. Both his wife and his wife's sister had died, leaving him to care for two motherless boys – his own son, Jim, and his late wife's nephew, Lewis. He was Barker's brother-in-law.

Mr Skews was addicted to the substances that only an apothecary can find, and thus was positioned to be open to offers of an amoral nature: blackmail. Samuel believed that Barker was acting on his behalf when the vial and its contents were obtained, but here he stepped into a rabbit trap. Barker had come to his own arrangement with Skews – my arrangement.

The third accomplice was a woman called Haines, a servant who did nothing much wrong except hold her tongue when her conscience should have told her to do otherwise. Miss Haines was once lady's maid to both you and I at Summersby, but when you were sent to the Hall, Miss Haines went with you. Miss Haines was still there when Samuel visited to make you write all the message scraps. He induced Miss Haines to resign, buying her silence. Later, Barker got to her, giving her further inducement again – her silence suited everyone's purpose. Miss Haines was found employment as housekeeper for old Dr Foal. This meant Barker could keep an eye on her. Miss Haines' replacement was a decent and principled woman, Agatha Marshall, who knew nothing of the message scraps you had written, and indeed,

*you knew nothing of them either, because you quickly forgot
ever writing them.*

*Samuel's intention was that with me made unhinged by
the sinister messages from you – messages that were suggesting I should kill myself in guilt – I would attempt to do just
that and drink from the convenient vial. A sly scheme on
his part; his hands would have been stainless had I done so.
Still, I took no chances. The content of the deadly vial was a
wholly different substance to what Samuel imagined it to be:
it was chloroform. The day that I decided would be the day
of my demise, Skews himself attended me, apparently deliv-
ering medicines. In truth, he helped apply the chloroform in
sufficient quantity to render me unconscious – I was fearful
of doing it myself. The result was the appearance of death.
When Samuel was shown my body by complicit Barker and
Skews, he was allowed to view it just long enough to be convinced I was dead, and no longer. It fooled him.*

*A little sidenote was my poodle, Billy. I adore that dog
and couldn't bear to be parted from him. Billy was given
the chloroform, too, and rendered equally insensible. My
still unconscious body had been shown only briefly to the
undertakers upon their arrival and Barker insisted that my
remains stay at Summersby. It had been no great matter to
the men to leave a coffin and the rest of the work to Barker
to arrange. The thing was filled with stones for burial. The
inquest into my death was disgraceful in its laxness. No one
even opened the lid to look in. What a blessing it is to be
a Gregory.*

*There now began the next phase of my plan. First, Billy
and I took ourselves to Summersby's tower; a little used part
of the great house that Barker kept carefully locked. I had
my own key. We hid away from the household. Next, Barker
continued his apparent partnership with Samuel. With the
blackmailer's card only partially hidden, no doubt, behind
Barker's claims of friendship, the combination was enough*

to convince Samuel that the valet might be kept on side –
and made useful – with regular incentives of gold. What
it really enabled was Barker's manipulation of Samuel on
my behalf – for I had come to want more than your freedom.
I wanted Samuel to be punished for thinking he could better
me. I wanted him dead, and with him Barker, too. There was
room for neither untrustworthy man now that I had you with
me at Summersby.

What I needed next was a servant of reduced intelligence –
in short, a naïf – but not such a naïf that she would fail to
notice things. This person was duly obtained, a local girl of
small prospects but much inquisitiveness, one Ida Garfield.
Her gaining employment at Summersby was timed with most
of the other servants getting their notices. They were sacked
for gossiping – gossip that was essential for both Samuel's and
(if only he'd known it) my own respective plans to succeed.
From Samuel's point of view it was important that the local
people think I had killed myself. Better this scandal than the
far greater one that he had as good as murdered me. The
more servants sacked, the louder the gossip – the right gossip.
He wanted someone like Ida because she would fan the flames
further while lacking the brains to see through it.

The first strange thing I made happen to Ida was the
vial. She found it, she opened it – it smelled of rosemary.
Every nasty substance smelled of rosemary at Summersby –
Mr Skews used Hungary water to disguise what they were.
The appearances and disappearances of the vial were
arranged for Ida's benefit. Barker moved it sometimes and
I moved it others. Ida needed to know about the vial – and
know that someone was doing very odd things with it.

By this time you, the sister everyone wrongly thought of as
the real Matilda Gregory, had been released from Constantine
Hall and returned to Summersby. This not only brought a
mistress into Ida's life, it brought Agatha Marshall, too. It
also reunited us, sister. I had succeeded in freeing you. Now

all my attention was turned upon Samuel. Because you were so damaged in your mind, you only half knew what was going on. Certainly, you tried to tell the servants something of it, but because they had convinced themselves that you were really me, your claims that I wasn't dead at all were dismissed.

You did know something was wrong, sister, but your memory prevented you from acting on it. What Ida and Marshall – and Samuel, of course – did not realise was that they had two mistresses, each one answering to 'Matilda'. Most of the time, they served you, the false Matilda, because I kept myself hidden in the tower. But on some occasions it was me they served and they were none the wiser for doing it.

On the night of the return to Summersby Samuel found me in the hallway outside his room. I was teasing him from the start, testing him to see if he would fall for my ruse. He did. The girl Ida found me another day in the library. She fell for it then, too. Later Samuel took me, not you, to the ball, and Ida along with us, and I pushed deception to the limit. I let my true personality show that evening, yet still they believed I was you. The seed had been planted, however; they wondered at the state of my mind. On the day of Samuel's proposal it was I who struck Marshall in the face with your Remember Box. You, of course, would never have done such a thing.

It was at the ball that I truly began the campaign to manipulate Ida. I planted two letters to you that were really for her – one inside the old hut, another inside the Remember Box. With both she and Marshall suspicious that something was wrong at Summersby, I ensured that those flames of suspicion spread Samuel's way. Marshall took the bait far easier, Ida was reluctant – she was so in love with Samuel. Yet Ida had by now discovered to her cost that the vial contained something dreadful – chloroform, the substance I used to feign death. Forgive me, but it was the same substance Barker was using to repeatedly render you unconscious. On such occasions as the ball when I wished to change places,

Barker made you insensible and hid you away. The same thing happened on the night of the wedding. It was I that unwitting Samuel bedded first that evening, once Barker had spirited you from the room. It was you our husband bedded later when Barker had spirited you back again. Samuel was oblivious, the fool.

My actions were intended to bring Ida to a false conclusion that Samuel had driven me to kill myself with the blue vial. When Marshall fell ill at Barker's hands I wanted Ida to believe that Samuel or Barker, or both, were now using the contents on her. What mattered was that Ida's love for Samuel be killed by his apparent betrayal. Ida would imagine that Samuel was using Barker to complete his own ill deeds.

It was Samuel's misfortune to believe you were play-acting. In this he was correct, only wrong in whose performance it was. Having by now discerned that the differences in your behaviour from one occasion to the next suggested some subterfuge, Samuel believed you were trying to fool him into thinking I was reborn inside you. He never guessed the truth. Neither did Ida.

Samuel's misbelief led to his undoing. Ida's misbelief led to her undoing him. At the time that I write this the blue vial was emptied of chloroform, filled with a genuine poison, and placed by me in such a position that Ida would think Samuel was behind it. Ida emptied it in Samuel's dinner – and in Barker's, too. Ida will suffer for the crime.

As I complete this entry for your Remember Box, sister, I wait in the tower. Will you come and find me? I know that you will. Will you be angry? Perhaps, at least initially so, but I know that you love me above everything, just as I do love you, and I know that we will transcend this unpleasantness, take stock of its cost, and together plan new lives here at Summersby, made whole in our hearts by this adventure.

Your sister who loves you,
Matilda

Putting the letter down to let Margaret re-read it, Ida didn't know what a 'naïf' was, but she guessed it was unflattering. Matilda had fatefully underestimated her, and of that she was proud. Ida had been fooled and manipulated, yes, but she had learned from the experiences, growing cannier as she went, so that in the end she had not been fooled at all. Matilda had assumed she would remain a naïf.

Matilda had assumed wrong.

It was only when Ida put her hands in the dishwater that she realised how badly they were shaking. She took to the baking tray with a cupful of sand and the action of scrubbing and scouring at the burnt fat was calming. She felt her heart begin to slow, her thoughts becoming quieter again.

Ida felt no guilt at what she'd done. It was strange. No voices condemned her in her head, as they would have if she were some sensational novel's heroine. No dead weight dragged her beneath the waters of hell. She was made only lighter by it.

'When did you plan on telling me, cretin?'

She span around so fast a spray of dishwater shot along the flagstones. Barker slouched at the open baize door, picking at his hard, white teeth. 'Think I couldn't work it out?'

She'd been waiting for this, ready for it. She'd known he would come to, eventually, and then seek her out. She studied him to see if the powders were still affecting him, however slightly. If they were, then she knew she had a chance. 'Mr Barker . . .'

He made an unsteady step towards her. 'How stupid do you think I am? More stupid than you? More stupid than the mistress? I'm insulted by that, cretin.'

She let him think that she trembled in fear. 'It . . . it was an accident.'

Barker guffawed. 'You skirts are all the same!' He took another step towards her, grinning and wiping his eyes.

She looked around for where she might run. One wet hand clenched a fistful of scouring sand. 'I didn't mean it to happen,' she lied.

Barker's grin vanished. 'My arse, you didn't. You meant it from the start.'

'No . . . it just happened . . . I swear it.'

'You set your sights upon a man and don't get a moment's peace until it's done.'

Ida stared at him as he edged closer.

'Conniving, scheming piece, bringing a man to ruin. That's what you're out for – to bring a man to his doom.'

'Mr Barker, I'll make amends, I swear it . . . I'll go to the police.'

He stopped short. 'The Law?'

'I'll do it,' said Ida. 'I'll go to them; I don't care what happens now.'

He was on her at the sink before she could run, one hand gripped at her throat. 'You breathe a word to the Law and they'll hang you for the little slut you are.'

Ida choked, unable to draw air.

'Is that what you want?' He pressed her throat. 'Is that the idea? They'll hang you for trying to drag a good man down.'

She couldn't struggle, couldn't take her eyes from his pitch-black pupils.

Long, sharp fingers groped for her belly. 'They'll see *this*, and that's all they'll see – won't care how young you are, won't care for anything you say about me. All they'll see is *this*.' He clutched at her flesh, squeezing it, clawing at her unborn baby. 'The tell-tale sign of a slut.'

He was still affected by the powders, incapable of thinking straight. Somehow he'd awoken with no inkling that she'd drugged him at all. Instead, he'd guessed she was pregnant, seizing upon it as a focus for his malice.

Ida slammed the fistful of sand in his eyes and burst away from his grasp.

Barker howled. 'You little whore!'

She spat on the floor with contempt. 'Do you really think Matilda cares about you?' she taunted. 'Do you really think she'd do anything for you, just like you would do for her?'

He froze.

'Matilda wanted me to poison you!' She paused, savouring the worst of it. 'And if I were half the cretin you think I am, I would have done it, too.'

His mind took a moment to understand that she'd at last uncovered the truth of him. 'What?'

'That what's she wanted, not just Mr Samuel dead by my hands, but you, as well. She wanted you both gone. She despised you! You were just a servant in her eyes – worse than a servant, a slave!'

Barker clawed at his eyes. 'Stop it!'

Ida let herself laugh. 'Pathetic you are, in love with someone so above your station. What a fool you are, thinking you could have her! Well, it's all too late now, Mr Barker,' she said, relishing it, 'and do you know why?' She pointed to the ceiling. 'Matilda Gregory, the love of your life, is upstairs *dead*.'

'That's lies!'

'I'm sorry it's the truth. Matilda is dead, utterly dead.' Ida started backing out the room, hands clutched at her stomach, grinning at him.

He roared. 'You're not having that brat, do you hear me?' He lunged for her.

Ida bolted for the baize door. 'Help!' she screamed into the greater house for her mistress. 'Help me, miss! Please!'

She fled into the entrance hall and then made towards the stairs. Barker was behind her, stumbling half blind. 'You're not having that bastard – I'll bloody rip it from your guts.' His hand found a heavy brass oil lamp on a hall table, snatching it up. Ida slipped and skidded on the polished wooden boards. The lamp came down on her back, shattering the glass. Oil doused her head and hair. Barker raised the heavy base again and struck her across the neck. Ida shrieked, blood mingling with oil. She tried to reach the stairs, but lost her footing in the oil, falling onto her hands and elbows. Barker raised the lamp to strike her a third time but Ida turned and kicked him in a shin, sending him off balance, the oil lamp clattering from his hand.

'You filthy whore,' he spat at her. 'You'll not ruin me.'

She rolled on her belly from his grip, feeling her helpless child crushed beneath her. 'Miss!' She reached the bottom stair and then was scaling on her hands and knees. Barker had her by an ankle, just as he'd had her on the night she'd seen his evil for what it was. She kicked and kicked, screaming out her lungs.

A massive object flew from above, hurtling towards its target. She heard the shriek of agony from behind her and turned to see that the thing that had dropped was a marble bust; it had struck Barker on the leg, shattering it.

'Ida? Ida?' Margaret called from above. It was she who had saved her.

Ida's heel connected with the valet's face and he let go, writhing in misery.

She made it to the landing and was free of him.

BIDDY

FEBRUARY 1904

9

*M*iss Garfield had taken charge of their party, striding forth and securing two transports in the busy street outside Spencer Street Railway Station: an open, comfortable carriage for herself and Sybil and Biddy, and a dray for Jim, Lewis and the accompanying luggage. Once the young men had been extricated from the third class carriage she'd obliged them to travel in, Miss Garfield had left them to procure porters while she, Sybil and Biddy waited in sunshine outside, sipping lemonades.

Their carriage ride first took them along chaotic Flinders Street, choked with traffic and unpleasant odours from the river wharfs, passing sites of note, including St Paul's, which Miss Garfield endeavoured to use to engage with Sybil, extolling its fine architecture. Sybil would have had them believe she was more concerned with their luggage, although Biddy knew better. Several times Sybil turned to look for the dray that was following them. 'Our things will be perfectly safe,' Miss Garfield assured her, 'Jim and Lewis are taking good care.' Biddy placed a comforting hand around Sybil's own, guessing what was filling her thoughts: Jim. Sybil still didn't know that Biddy knew.

'I am attributing your quietude to awe at the great metropolis, Sybil,' Miss Garfield declared. 'Melbourne must be an astonishing sight for a girl who has seen very few views of the world. Our new nation's capital should rightly give you awe, why, I've been remembering my own response the very first time I was taken to visit the city – I was much the same age as you.' She laughed at the thought, and Sybil and Biddy, listening to her monologue, were attentive enough to smile at least.

'My Methodist aunts referred to Melbourne as Sodom,' the governess revealed. 'I had expected to encounter licentious writhing before golden calves as a consequence, and was most disappointed at uncovering neither.' She looked about her as she said it, as if such things might yet be found.

Biddy found Miss Garfield's pleasure in the whole adventure endearing. Sybil had been told no such falsehoods about Melbourne, she guessed. Rather, she'd been told very little at all. Still, she *was* very quiet, and of course Miss Garfield had noticed it. Sybil was also somewhat ill, an affliction Biddy accounted to nerves. Truth be told, Biddy's nerves were similarly jangled at the thought of the meeting ahead of them.

'Your own silence, Biddy, I can little account for, however,' Miss Garfield said, changing the focus of her attention.

'Sorry, Miss Garfield,' Biddy replied. She and Sybil met eyes.

Melbourne's business district receded, replaced by the parks that surrounded the Treasury, before East Melbourne was reached, the Cricket Ground, and shortly afterwards the less salubrious suburb of Richmond and the commencement of the Bridge Road.

Biddy unconsciously stiffened and the governess saw it. 'Do you know this locality, Biddy?'

'A little,' Biddy said, vaguely.

Miss Garfield was watching her. 'Did you live here before you came to Summersby?'

'Oh no, miss, never lived here . . .'

The look on Miss Garfield's face told Biddy that the governess was becoming better at seeing through her stories. She could rightly guess that Biddy had lived in Richmond, and Biddy saw that Miss Garfield also suspected she'd received ill treatment while doing so.

Several times the traffic fell to a halt due to a tramcar ahead of them. Biddy suddenly realised with alarm that their carriage had drawn level with Topp's General Store. To her mortification she recognised a pair of faces from among the crowd thronging the street: an older woman, severe in attire, accompanied by a girl of Biddy's age wearing a servant's uniform: Mrs Rattray and Queenie. The two of them stopped and stared in astonishment at the carriage, recognising Biddy immediately. Queenie was open-mouthed and pointing.

Wishing she could shrink in her seat, Biddy prayed they would not call out to her.

'How incredibly rude,' said Miss Garfield, seeing them.

The carriage began to move along again and soon the two unpleasant reminders of the past were lost.

'I can only assume they were struck by our fashionable millinery,' said Miss Garfield, adjusting her hat. 'Is fine attire rare in Richmond perhaps, Biddy?'

Biddy said that she thought it might be.

In time, the Yarra River was crossed and the driver turned around to inform them that they had now reached Hawthorn. Miss Garfield repeated the desired address again, relieved that the man seemed to hold a map of the metropolis's thoroughfares inside his head. Soon all thoughts of Richmond were behind Biddy as they clip-clopped through green and prosperous streets.

'Yes, this is one of the city's better situated environs indeed,' Miss Garfield emphasised again, in the hope, perhaps, of reassuring Sybil of the rightness of their destination. 'What a difference to where we have just been, Sybil, in the noisy Bridge Road. Why, the air is quite breathable here, almost as wholesome as home.' She took a deep lungful of air to prove the point, only to inhale a fly. A coughing fit ensued but no laughter came from either Sybil or Biddy. Biddy knew Miss Garfield took this as a sure sign that nerves were behind their uncharacteristic lack of pep.

'All will be well, Sybil,' Miss Garfield said, unprompted once recovered from the fly. Biddy met Sybil's eye again and caught a sudden glimpse of a terrible fear that was there and felt thrown by it. Her own emotions threatened, and Biddy realised that she had barely acknowledged them at all since Jim's phoney telegraph message had been received – a guilty secret that neither she nor Jim had shared with Sybil. Both of them wanted the Secret Heiress exposed, real or otherwise, and Sybil's relatives met, no matter how scandalous, so that Sybil's life proper could begin.

'Sybil,' Miss Garfield repeated, warmer now, 'you are truly an exemplary girl, a credit to Summersby. You have learned all I could teach you and could not have learned more. You are ready for this visit and you *will* do well.'

Sybil's fear remained palpable. She was ill with it. 'The Secret Heiress . . .' she began,

Miss Garfield anticipated what it was she imagined filled Sybil's thoughts. 'She is real,' she said, softly. 'That much I do know, but that is all that I know. Mrs Marshall knows everything, I am sure of it, but is bound somehow not to share it – not with you, not with me. She has chosen to remain in Summersby today and we must respect that she has her reasons. I don't know what these reasons might be, but they are because of some event from the past – an event of which you are wholly blameless, Sybil, but an event of great shame. Again, I do not know what this might be.'

Sybil looked to Biddy again, and if there was a flash of triumph in Biddy's eyes, Sybil lacked it. She was expressionless.

'And shortly, I hope, you will learn *why* you could not know of her before now,' said Miss Garfield. She allowed her deep and abiding love to show in her face. '. . . And why so many things were kept from you,' she went on, 'kept for a reason, a reason that was not of your making, I promise you.' She took Sybil's hand. 'You are a lovely girl, an ornament,' she insisted. 'Your family will see the great goodness at once in you, I know they will, and they will be so much gladdened by it.' She kissed Sybil on the cheek.

The open-topped carriage took them along an appealing, tree-lined avenue with large, elegant homes displayed on both sides of the road. The driver turned to tell them that Number One Hundred and Eight had been reached in Auburn Grove. The carriage pulled to a stop. All three of them looked to where a grand and imposing villa of some three storeys stood behind high stone walls amid a garden of claret ash and maple trees.

Biddy frowned, puzzled by where they'd arrived.

'Will she be inside there?' Sybil pressed.

Miss Garfield seemed to want no more paths left to them but that of total truthfulness now. 'I am sure of it . . .' She saw that Sybil still doubted her. 'Please believe me,' she pleaded, 'I have never met this person. I do not know who or what she is. I know only that she is of your family and that therefore your happiness and welfare must surely be at the very utmost of her mind.'

'Despite everything?'

Miss Garfield didn't know what she meant by those words, but Biddy did – the clandestine romance with Jim. The governess searched Sybil's face for any sign that the girl was in some way reassured. There was none. 'What is it, child? You are ready to meet your relatives and show that you are more than their equal.'

But Sybil shook her head, tears pricking her eyes. Miss Garfield was plainly at a loss.

The luggage dray came to a halt at the rear of their carriage. The governess turned to look behind them just as Sybil did, and for the briefest moment Biddy saw the yearning look of connection pass between Sybil and Jim, seated in the dray. The intensity of it stunned her before the connection was broken and both young people now looked as if nothing connected them at all. Biddy turned to realise that Miss Garfield had seen the look, too.

Sybil composed herself. 'I wish Biddy to accompany me,' she announced.

The governess nodded. 'Of course, child.'

'I would like you to remain in the carriage.'

Miss Garfield caught her breath.

Sybil saw the hurt astonishment in her governess's face and reached for her hand. 'Please. I mean no slight.' She drew herself up. 'This is my visit and mine alone. Biddy will accompany me inside, that is all. I will meet my family – and Margaret Gregory – alone.'

Miss Garfield nodded, with nothing left to say. Lewis and Jim had alighted from the dray and now were coming to assist them from the carriage. Lewis positioned himself to help Biddy to the ground, given she was nearest the door, and as he did so a look of great connection passed between them, too, open and unembarrassed.

Biddy realised what it meant. She and Lewis were in love.

The surprise of this was in no way shocking. Why shouldn't they seek happiness with each other, she thought? She was reminded of the brief and somehow fiercer look she had just seen pass between Sybil and Jim, and then it was Jim himself helping Sybil to alight and the same look was between them again, unmistakable, yet somehow lacking the joy that she and Lewis had shared.

Biddy turned and saw that Miss Garfield had seen everything. Sybil was in love with Jim Skews, and she, the governess, had only now realised it. How long had she been blind to this fact?

Sybil and Biddy were now thanking the young men and adjusting their hats and gloves, readying themselves to open the wrought iron gate. 'Wait . . .' said Miss Garfield, with apprehension. 'Wait, Sybil . . .'

Sybil turned. 'What is it, Miss Garfield?'

The governess could only stare at her pupil as if seeing Sybil for the first time in years, grown up without her guessing at it, living a secret life in which she, Miss Garfield, played not the slightest part at all. Sybil was no longer a girl but a woman. 'You will do well,' she managed to tell her. 'You will do very well.'

Sybil turned and faced the gate.

Biddy could see a plaque on the wall, a nameplate grown over and obscured by ivy. She brushed the tendrils away.

Constantine Hall.

She frowned, dismissing some half-formed thought from her mind.

Sybil stood with Biddy upon the entrance porch poised to ring the bell, and yet not doing so, unable to complete the simple action, her hand in mid-air.

'What is it?' Biddy wondered.

'I must tell you something,' Sybil whispered, and when Biddy turned to look at her she saw how ill Sybil really was, ill in a way that wasn't just physical but emotional; a terrible weight of guilt.

Biddy had been expecting this and was glad that her friend finally felt ready to confide. 'No you don't,' she whispered back, taking Sybil's hand. 'You see, I already know it.'

Sybil's mouth fell open and Biddy nodded, smiling naughtily.

'You *know*?' Sybil asked, incredulous. Both of them were all too aware of Miss Garfield watching through the gate from the street.

'Of course, I know,' said Biddy. 'I'd be a pretty dim companion if I didn't know by now, wouldn't I?'

Sybil was verging on tears. 'Oh, Biddy . . . but, but what must you think of me?' Humiliation was bleak in her face.

'Sybil,' Biddy said to her, firmly, 'it's not the old days anymore. Miserable Queen Victoria is cold in her grave and all the things she frowned upon are tossed in there with her. We're in the lovely new century now and this one belongs to girls like you and me. What's there to be ashamed of in having a nice boyfriend, for goodness sake?'

A tear rolled down Sybil's cheek and she shook her head. 'No . . . no . . .'

'Yes, yes.' Biddy was quick with a handkerchief, mindful of Miss Garfield. Biddy felt she'd best say every word of reassurance she could think of in order to get them both through the door.

'Jim's a very fine young man, adept with a trade – I was wrong to once say he had teeth like a hare – and it's obvious he cares for you, it's as plain as the nose on your face.'

'Oh, Biddy,' Sybil whispered. 'That's not it.'

'Don't worry,' she told her, 'I'll not breathe a word, as if I would. You and I might be sitting pretty in the lovely new twentieth century, but I'm not such a twit as to think that Margaret Gregory is.' She winked but Sybil just stared back, desolate. 'Come on, Syb,' Biddy pleaded with her, 'you and me are a couple of champion fibbers. We can make up stories with the best of 'em! Just keep your wits about you and you'll sail through this with all flags flying and no one'll be any the wiser that you've got a secret sweetheart.'

Sybil was trying to tell her, 'You don't understand.'

'What's to understand about a couple of stolen kisses in the long grass?' Biddy laughed. 'Sounds like heaven to me,' she said, thinking of Lewis on the other side of the garden wall, rolling cigarettes with his cousin.

'I'm with child.'

Biddy went still.

'I'm having a baby – Jim's baby,' Sybil told her. 'No one knows, no one's guessed at it yet – not Jim, not even you. But soon they all will know, most likely today, for how will I ever hide the truth of it from my face once I go inside? And when Margaret Gregory sees it.'

More shocked than she had ever been in her life, Biddy searched for words but couldn't find any. She had guessed nothing of this secret at all. It was beyond her experience.

'There's nothing more to be done, I must face it.' Sybil reached for the doorbell. 'You have been the truest friend I could ever have hoped for, Biddy. Far more than I deserve.'

Biddy's heart burst. 'Wait . . .'

She looked at Sybil with all the love and compassion that a true friend could feel. 'It is *not* the end,' she whispered, 'at least not today. All we have to do is get through whatever happens on the other side of that door, agreed? And think about tomorrow, *tomorrow.*'

She took Sybil's hands.

'Agreed?' Biddy repeated.

'Oh, Biddy,' Sybil whispered. But somehow she agreed.

'Good,' said Biddy. She reached for the doorbell herself and pressed it. 'I have an idea for a tiny little story.'

Mr Horace Clarkenwell had a gouty knee that evidently twinged as the housemaid, Polly, informed him of who had appeared at the door. He missed the name in the pain of it.

'She's a young woman, sir. With a travelling companion.'

Clarkenwell eyed Biddy waiting in the hallway outside his study, as she tried to look as if she hadn't been watching him through the door. He waved Polly away. 'Show her in, do.'

The housemaid returned to where Biddy waited. 'He'll see you now,' she said. She brought her into the room where Constantine Hall's obese proprietor eyed a half full decanter of port on his desk.

'This is the young lady, sir,' Polly said. Clarkenwell started pouring himself a liberal glass. Port slopped over the rim and onto the desk. The maid went to mop it up with a rag but Clarkenwell was feeling irritable.

'Enough. That will be all.' His knee clearly stabbed at him again. He rubbed it vigorously with his palm. The housemaid curtsied and was gone.

Clarkenwell allowed himself a sip of port before regarding Biddy. Now looking at her fully, Biddy hoped he saw a well-dressed, well-to-do young woman with strikingly attractive features.

'I did not hear your name, Miss—'

'Gregory,' said Biddy.

Clarkenwell blinked.

'I am Miss Sybil Gregory of Summersby,' Biddy smiled at him.

Clarkenwell had to steady himself in his chair. 'Gregory, you say?'

Biddy nodded.

'From Summersby?'

'From whence I journeyed today, sir, with my dear companion.' Biddy waited, still smiling as if she expected something. 'Your girl Polly is taking fine care of my Biddy, I'm sure.'

'But this . . . this is unprecedented,' said Clarkenwell.

'What is?'

'Your being here . . . a Gregory.'

Biddy shifted on her feet and hoped that Clarkenwell saw there was gumption within her and back-steel, too. 'I have been summoned,' she said, 'by telegraph message.' In the corner of Clarkenwell's office sat a telegraph machine almost identical to Summersby's own, with glass valves and tortoiseshell keys. 'A message sent from here.'

Clarkenwell looked at the machine. 'No message summoning you was sent from here, I assure you, Miss Gregory.'

She would have none of it. 'And I assure you one was.'

Clarkenwell made a move to stand but his gouty knee dissuaded him. 'Miss Gregory,' he started to say. He stopped and took another sip of port. 'A mistake has been made.'

'Perhaps,' said Biddy, knowing full well.

'Most assuredly,' said Clarkenwell. 'No one has summoned you. There is no purpose to you being here.' He indicated the door.

She made no move to leave. 'Take me to Margaret Gregory.'

The obese man blanched and Biddy noted it. 'This is her address, isn't it?'

His fingers crept towards the port glass again.

'Isn't it?'

'Miss Gregory, this is most irregular . . .'

'More irregular than a lifetime lived in ignorance?' She stepped forward and plucked the glass from his fingers before upending the contents onto the carpet. 'My apologies to Polly for the stain.'

Clarkenwell stood up from his chair, knee or no knee. 'How dare you!'

Biddy was pleased to see she was half a head taller than he was. 'Margaret Gregory is the ghost that haunts me, sir,' she said, unfazed by him. 'All my life she has been used to cower me. Today it ends. I wish to meet Margaret Gregory at once.'

Clarkenwell tried to hobble around from the desk, his knee now plainly screaming with the effort of it.

'Do you deny that Margaret Gregory is here?' Biddy demanded of him.

He stopped. He seemed to consider his answer. 'I do not,' he said, at last.

Biddy felt immensely satisfied. 'Then I will see her.'

He regarded her for a further minute in silence. 'All right.' He reached for a handbell that sat on his desk, ringing it. Biddy jumped at the discordant sound. The look Clarkenwell gave her was somewhat knowing, as if he was well aware of what he now suspected Biddy was not.

Polly returned in response to the bell and immediately noticed the spilled port. 'Our visitor would like to see Miss Margaret,' said Clarkenwell.

Biddy turned in time to see the housemaid's own look of surprise at this request. 'Mr Clarkenwell, that's not my place . . .'

He raised his hand. 'You will do as I order.'

'But sir,' she protested.

Clarkenwell seemed rather pleased to see the uncertainty now on Biddy's face.

'But Miss Margaret prefers her own maid,' Polly reminded him. 'She's particular.'

'I am well aware of what Miss Margaret likes,' he said, 'but on this instance you shall obey my request and conduct our visitor upstairs to meet her.'

Polly swallowed, casting a wary glance at Biddy. 'As you wish, sir.'

'Thank you,' said Biddy, more to Polly than the gouty proprietor. To Clarkenwell she nodded coolly.

Polly closed the door to Clarkenwell's office behind her as

she took Biddy into the hall. The young women stood assessing each other.

'I am sorry for the mess on the carpet,' said Biddy. 'You'll want to get some salt on it quick.'

Polly sniffed.

'I'm also sorry for any trouble my being here might cause.'

This seemed to soften Polly somewhat. 'I'm sorry if my reaction seemed rude in there before, miss.'

'I wasn't put out.'

Polly began to lead her towards the stairs. 'It's just that Miss Margaret has her own maid – a maid she holds very dear. She dislikes having to talk to other servants.'

'I see,' said Biddy, although she didn't quite.

'You know how she can be,' said Polly. They began mounting the stairs, Polly one step ahead. When Biddy didn't answer, Polly turned to her and the look on her face must have revealed she didn't know how Miss Margaret could be at all. 'You've never met her, miss?'

Biddy paused, and then shook her head. She suddenly felt very nervous again, despite the confidence with which she had breezed through the front door.

'You're related to her though?' Polly asked.

'I believe so, yes,' Biddy said. She guessed then that Polly herself had little knowledge of how things were either, at least as they pertained to Summersby.

'Well, she's really very nice,' Polly told her. 'You mustn't worry. I'm sure you'll enjoy a pleasant visit.' They reached the first floor and Polly directed Biddy along the hallway towards a closed door.

'In there?' Biddy feared her nerves were very apparent.

Polly opened the door for her. Inside was a comfortable parlour, quite empty. 'If you'll take a seat for a minute, miss.' She cast an uneasy glance downstairs towards Clarkenwell's office. 'Perhaps I might find Miss Margaret's maid after all . . . I really would hate to upset the way things are done. You don't mind, do you?'

Biddy shook her head. 'And my companion Miss MacBryde? Has she been made comfortable?'

'Oh yes,' Polly assured her. 'She's having tea in the Morning Room. Quite comfortable'

Biddy nodded and Polly took off along the hallway. Biddy tried to make herself at ease in the parlour, but found the task beyond her. Sitting down made her feel tenser still; it was better to stay standing. She was now regretting the reckless stupidity with which she had proposed the story to Sybil. It had seemed a fine idea on the doorstep. She and Sybil would only change places for as long as it took Biddy to gauge who and what Margaret Gregory really was. Biddy would pretend to be Sybil for the initial dialogue, putting on a fine imitation of her manner and voice, while Sybil gathered her wits as 'companion'. Then, if the famed Secret Heiress turned out to be perfectly pleasant, and what's more, sympathetic and humane in Biddy's view, then Biddy would retrieve Sybil, explain the little ruse, and somehow all would be well. But now that Biddy had been left alone to wait, the 'somehow' began to pose more possibilities for disaster than it did for redemption. What if Margaret Gregory was *not* perfectly pleasant or humane? What if the ill thought out scheme to hide the truth of Sybil's condition unravelled in an instant and the Summersby inheritance vanished? Biddy tried not to think about the dreadful possibilities. She was an accomplished teller of stories, and this latest fiction was just one in a long and profitable line. She would pull it off, just like she always did.

Biddy heard footsteps in the hallway outside and knew they would stop at the parlour. She looked about for the spot in the room in which she might best present herself when the door was opened. She decided it lay near the largest window. Biddy positioned herself there just as a hand gripped the doorknob. She straightened her back and smiled her brightest smile, expecting to see Polly come in with her fellow maid ready to broach the introduction.

It was not the two maids who entered the room but a man – a man Biddy had met before. He was rather old in her eyes, aged in his late-thirties, having been very handsome once, perhaps. He had extraordinary hair, the colour of honey, and beautiful hair for a man, but his face was creased and careworn. Most striking were his cornflower blue eyes, which gave him the appearance of seeming highly distracted, as if he were looking at something that could not be seen by anyone else and yet was blinding to him. The man's strange look disappeared for the moment it took him to realise that the parlour was occupied.

Samuel Hackett and Biddy MacBryde stood gaping at each other in surprise as the circumstances of their first meeting came back to each to them.

'You?' said Samuel.

Biddy pressed her back against the windowsill, shocked.

'You!' he stepped into the room. 'Biddy!'

She blanched. 'You are mistaken, sir. I . . . I am Miss Gregory waiting for the maid.'

Samuel blinked at this misinformation and Biddy formed the same impression she had formed when he had come to the house she shared with her mother in Carlton and he had made the claims that had exposed her life for the lie that it was. Samuel could barely control where his eyes were focused, she realised. He was not wholly right in his mind. 'No,' he said, forcing his gaze to remain upon her with effort, 'you *are* Biddy. I *know* you are Biddy. I found you before. Don't you remember me, girl?' He came into the room and held out his arms to embrace her. 'You have come to see me, you have come to see your papa.'

He was overjoyed but Biddy could only stare at him once more in dismay. How it could be that this very same man who had once appeared from nowhere and ruined her life and caused her to run away was now at the home of Margaret Gregory? It was almost beyond her comprehension, and yet it was not beyond it completely because somewhere in the depths of her reasoning, Biddy was starting to *see*. 'You are not my papa,' she told him defiantly. 'You are mistaken, sir. I am Miss Gregory.'

'You tell me you are not my girl Biddy?'

'No, sir,' she insisted, 'and I must ask you not to call me that again. I am Miss Sybil Gregory.'

'*Sybil?*' Samuel looked as if he was actually prepared to believe this unlikelihood. 'You are *Sybil?*'

'Yes, sir,' Biddy pressed, seeing that she might actually be believed. 'I've come all the way from Summersby.'

The name of that house seemed to stun him.

'I am the heiress of Summersby,' Biddy insisted, and Samuel's eyes lost the battle and took on their distracted air, seeing her but no longer seeing her. He stumbled, feeling for a chair, disoriented. 'Sybil Gregory,' he muttered, 'and yet I suppose it is right that you should look the same as Biddy.'

Biddy lost her nerve. It was a hopeless story she'd attempted and one she had known in her heart was beyond her. She would throw herself upon the real Sybil waiting anxiously downstairs in the Morning Room, she decided, and somehow they would construct a new story – a story that would save both of them.

'Wait,' said Samuel, realising she was on the point of leaving. 'Where is your sister?'

Biddy halted at the door, every nerve in her body telling her to run. 'I . . . I have no sister, sir.'

'But of course you do.' His eyes found their focus again, connecting with Biddy. 'You *know* you do.'

Biddy felt then as if she were poised on the cusp of extraordinary revelation. She didn't have a sister, *but perhaps Sybil did?* 'Do you mean the Secret Heiress?'

Samuel stared back at her, squinting, mouthing her words to himself, as if trying to decipher something lost in them. 'The Secret Heiress?'

'Yes. Is that Margaret Gregory?'

Samuel frowned, confused.

A voice from the hallway made her turn. 'Sybil!'

She looked to her right and saw that a woman had come from another room and was heading towards her, with Polly close behind. But it was the woman's face that struck Biddy with a shock equal to the one she had felt at re-meeting the man who had upturned her whole life. It was the woman from the photograph in Sybil's room. The woman named Matilda, older clearly, but still very beautiful. The woman that Sybil had believed was her dead mother.

The weight of the story could be borne no longer. Biddy knew she couldn't let herself tell this woman a lie. She ran for the stairs.

'Sybil!' The woman began to run, too.

Biddy reached the stairs first, panting, and practically threw herself down the first flight in her haste to get away. The woman reached the top and looked down just as Biddy reached the landing. 'Wait!'

Biddy looked up, her eyes filling with tears of disgrace at how she'd tried to deceive these people. 'I am so sorry, but I am not Sybil, miss.'

The woman processed this surprise for a second, before her eyes glistened with the emotion of a different realisation. 'Oh, heavens, I know who you are.'

'I am no one,' Biddy insisted, shaking her head. She began the hurried descent of the last flight of stairs.

'Yes you are – your name is Biddy.'

Biddy stopped.

'And I am Margaret Gregory,' the woman told her.

Biddy's mouth fell open. It was too much. She flew down the last steps and into the entrance hall, looking wildly about her to see where the Morning Room was. 'Sybil! Sybil, please come out!' Her tears were flowing. 'I'm so sorry, Sybil, I have ruined everything.'

A door began to open and she ran to it. 'Oh, my dear friend,' she sobbed, 'please forgive me for what I have done.'

Although Sybil was waiting inside the Morning Room, it was not she who came out the door. This was another woman, older than Sybil and dressed in a housemaid's uniform, but no less overwhelmed at the sight of Biddy's tears. This was the woman who loved Biddy more than any other person who walked upon the earth, and who would always love her until the day she went to her Maker.

'Mum—' Biddy cried, stopping dead in shock at the sight of her.

'Oh, my darling girl,' cried Ida, throwing her arms around her and kissing her cheeks. 'You've come back to me at last.'

IDA

APRIL 1887

10

*I*da dragged her mistress's dressing table behind her, gouging the floor, wrecking the collection of pretty things that lived on its top. Items rolled and dropped as she pulled the heavy dressing table to the door.

'Ida! Ida, stop!' Margaret cried.

But Ida wouldn't stop, and when she could move it no more, Ida went to the other side and pushed. The door was blocked by its bulk but Ida kept on pushing to be sure, willing herself to be numb to the pains in her belly. Good sense triumphed for a moment, making her stop and catch hold her breath just as another cramp stabbed at her and the fear of Barker returned.

'He can't get in,' Margaret pleaded, 'we're safe in here.'

But Ida could only look around for whatever else she could use to stop him from coming inside the Chinese Room and ripping her baby away. The bedside table offered something and Ida staggered to it, sweeping aside the ornaments and dragging it to join the furniture shifted already. She upended and hefted it on top of the dressing table and now looked to the Chinoiserie screen, folded and leant at an angle near the corner beyond the bed.

It would contribute little, she told herself; she would leave it where it was. She'd done enough.

Ida went to her mistress's bed and lay down on the thick, soft eiderdown. Cramps ripped at her guts. 'Safe and sound now,' she told the child inside her, 'safe and sound, my little dove.' But the child wouldn't listen, terrified still. 'Hush,' she begged of it, 'please hush.'

The baby answered with agony and very soon afterwards, blood.

Ida came to consciousness again to find her mistress crouched beside her at the bed.

'Ida,' Margaret said when she saw her eyelids flicker and open. 'Stay with me, Ida, I will get help.'

Ida glanced at the room and saw that some of the furniture she had heaved against the door had been moved. Her mistress had been moving them, she guessed. Then the pain came back.

'My baby . . . He hurt my baby . . .' She began to weep again and saw that her mistress was crying with her. Ida's housemaid's dress was sodden with blood and the bed cover with it. 'She's gone . . . I lost her, miss.'

Margaret pressed her hands protectively to her own belly on impulse, before she ran to the door again, trying to pull the dressing table aside, its legs scoring fresh marks in the floor. 'I will help you,' she promised. 'We've been misused, Ida, we've been deceived by Barker and my sister but now it is done.'

Ida heard this and shook her head, the pain terrible. 'He's still out there.'

Margaret succeeded in getting the dressing table out of the way enough for the door to be opened. Ida felt herself losing consciousness again.

'Ida!' Margaret ran and clutched her hand. 'Please don't die. I will help you, I promise it.' She placed Ida's hand on her own belly. 'See? I have a baby, too. It can be your baby now, Ida, if you like. Just please don't die.'

Someone began to push against the door from outside, twisting the handle, forcing it. Ida was terrified. 'Barker! You get away! No!'

The door came open, banging against the dressing table, but the face it revealed was a kindly face, a face to be trusted.

'Marshall?' said Margaret.

Aggie pushed her way inside, revealing another face behind her, also kind.

'Miss Haines?' Margaret was astonished.

'There, there, miss,' said Miss Haines, coming towards her. 'It's all right now.'

Aggie was at the bed, reeling at the sight of Ida's blood.

'She has miscarried a child,' said Miss Haines, white-faced.

Ashamed, Ida tried to cover herself. 'Oh, Aggie.'

Aggie clutched at her, bursting into tears. 'Just hold on, Ida. We'll get help for you.'

Margaret stood. 'But Ida has not lost her baby, so there is no cause for alarm. I have it here, see?' She stroked her belly. 'Do you see, Ida? I have it here.'

Aggie and Miss Haines passed a look between themselves, before Aggie stood and took hold of herself. 'I need towels, water.' She turned to Ida again. 'It will be all right, I swear it will.' She made for the door. 'Where is Mr Samuel now?' she asked Margaret, fearful. 'I have seen what has happened to Mr Barker.'

The question sparked something in Margaret's mind and she fumbled at the pocket of her dress. She withdrew a page torn from a book, on which she had written words to prompt herself. 'The tower,' she whispered, reading what was there. 'We left them in the tower.'

Aggie bit her lip, glancing upwards. Then she was gone from the room.

'Will Ida be all right?' Margaret asked Miss Haines.

The woman led her to a chair. 'It's in God's hands,' she told her. 'But we'll do what we can to help Him.'

Margaret shook Miss Haines' from her and returned to Ida's bedside. 'Please,' she begged her, 'please don't die. Fight for your little baby. Please . . .'

Ida clung to her last shred of consciousness. 'Is my baby not gone?'

Margaret shook her head, resolute, hands at her belly. 'She's here safe and sound, see? She's here with me.'

Ida felt a great weight lift from her. It was true. 'I am so happy, Margaret.'

She watched as Miss Haines took her mistress to the door. 'Best leave her now. Aggie and I will take charge.'

'But did you hear her, Haines? She called me Margaret, not Miss. It means I am her friend.'

Haines gave a little smile. 'She *is* your friend, miss.'

'Yes,' said her mistress, beaming.

BIDDY

FEBRUARY 1904

11

*L*eaning anxiously against the wall, it was Jim who saw the front door open first. 'Miss Garfield?'

She stirred from where she had been dozing in the comfort of the hired carriage.

'Miss Garfield.'

She looked up and saw that Jim was now at the gate, Lewis behind him, and coming down the path from the Hall was her charge. 'Sybil!' Miss Garfield made to let herself down to the ground before Lewis remembered himself and helped her descend the carriage step. Jim had opened the gate and Sybil was now coming into the street. 'Child!' Miss Garfield called in greeting, before perhaps remembering that she should no longer use this term. 'Sybil!'

Sybil stepped forward and embraced her. Her eyes were shining.

'Oh, Sybil.' She stepped back from her a little, so as to better see her face. 'Has all gone well within?'

Sybil paused before answering. 'It has.'

'Oh, Sybil!' Miss Garfield clapped her lace-gloved hands.

'But nothing was quite as I expected.'

She caught the strange tone to Sybil's voice.

'Nothing,' Sybil repeated. She looked behind her where Biddy waited by the front door, happily observing everything.

Miss Garfield was plainly unsure of what this might mean. 'Is that a pleasing result?'

Sybil considered this question. Then, to Miss Garfield's panic, she moved to Jim Skews and took him gently by the hand. Jim at first looked as thrown as Miss Garfield was, and Lewis with him, but Jim did not let go of Sybil's hand. Indeed, he soon looked empowered by it. Sybil smiled at him and Jim was soon smiling easily back.

'Stone the crows,' muttered Lewis, pushing his hat back from his brow. 'You're a dark one, Jim.' He cast a look to Biddy, still waiting at the entrance to the house.

He winked at her. She winked back.

'There is something I must tell you, Miss Garfield,' Sybil said.

Perhaps at another time Miss Garfield would have required a chair for such a forthcoming announcement and quite possibly some smelling salts, too, Biddy thought, watching on from the front door, but Miss Garfield seemed unusually sturdy in her constitution at this moment and clearly believed herself ready for news of which she had already partly guessed.

'Jim and I are in love.'

'Yes,' said Miss Garfield.

All of them waited for her reaction. Nothing came.

'Aren't you angry?' Sybil prompted.

Miss Garfield seemed to consider. 'No, Sybil, I don't believe I am.' She looked to Jim. 'You have chosen a very nice young man to give your heart to, a man we already know and like. I am pleased you are in love.'

Jim and Sybil stared at each other in amazement. Biddy just smiled.

'Have you been in love for very long?' Miss Garfield wondered.

'Yes,' said Jim, emphatically. He looked again to the beaming girl beside him. 'We hope to get married one day soon.'

'Stone the crows,' Lewis muttered again.

'Quite soon,' Sybil stressed. Her other hand brushed against her abdomen in a gesture Miss Garfield noted but clearly didn't yet comprehend.

Miss Garfield hesitated to frame a new question. 'And have you . . . informed those within this house of your happiness?' She glanced at Biddy and Constantine Hall.

'It is because I have informed those within and because they have reacted with such joy to it, that I am informing you now, Miss Garfield,' smiled Sybil.

Miss Garfield blinked. 'So you have met the Secret Heiress?'

Sybil opened her mouth to explain just as Biddy was joined by other people at the front door to the Hall and they all began to come outside.

'I have met my parents,' said Sybil. 'I have met my mother, Margaret Gregory and my father, Samuel Hackett. And I have met the Secret Heiress, too.'

'Who is she?'

But as Sybil was about to tell her, Miss Garfield's jaw fell. She saw a face she clearly recognised, the face from a photographic portrait she had no doubt once stumbled upon hidden among Sybil's things. This face was coming down the path towards them now, supporting a fair-haired man who walked less steadily, suffering from some malady in his eyes. 'Matilda,' Miss Garfield whispered, remembering the name on the back of the photograph.

'She is not Matilda,' Sybil told her. 'She is Margaret, her sister. And she is my mother.'

'I am confused,' Miss Garfield whispered, just as the new arrivals were about to come upon them. '*Who* is the Secret Heiress, then?'

Sybil slipped her arm through Miss Garfield's arm and kissed her tenderly on the cheek as she told her who it was that had been the extraordinary answer to the mystery all along. But the impact of the news was lost to Miss Garfield, for at this moment a final person came to the front door, linking arms with Biddy and beaming with joy. This was the person whose face Miss Garfield hadn't seen in many years, and yet she had never stopped thinking of fondly and missing dearly, and to whom she was profoundly grateful for all that this person had done.

'Ida!' she cried out, throwing her hands to her face. 'Oh, my heavens, it's Ida!'

She had the gate open then and was rushing into her sister's arms before anyone could even marvel at her uncharacteristic speed.

Some hours later Biddy took her seat in the kitchen of the little Carlton terrace house from which she had run away so long ago. She watched on warmly as Ida bustled at the stove, turned off the gas to the kettle and lifted it to fill a pot of tea.

'I didn't blame you,' Ida told her. 'I would have done the same. Well, I *did* do the same, or something like it, so I understood why you had to go.' She brought the pot to the table to let it sit for the required five minutes with a cosy on top to hold in the heat. 'Even if I didn't much like it.'

'Mum,' Biddy started to say, but Ida hushed her.

'I'm not your mum. It was lies,' said Ida, bringing the cups and sugar bowl.

Biddy felt tears prick her eyes again. 'You are my mum. You raised me,' she insisted. 'I don't care that you never gave birth to me, you're still my mum.'

'I should have told you the truth about it all,' said Ida, shaking her head, 'instead of letting you believe the wrong thing for so many years – and all for Samuel Hackett to turn up and tell you the truth himself.'

'You never let me know anything about that place you worked – the Hall.'

Ida nodded, ashamed. 'Because of the circumstances, the scandal of it, Biddy, that's why you couldn't know.' Then she said, 'There's something you should see.'

She went to the kitchen dresser and opened a drawer. She withdrew a beautiful wooden box, inlaid with ivory in a Moorish design. She laid it on the table. 'Open it.'

Biddy did. Inked under the lid were the words 'Remember Box'. Inside there were letters, dozens of them, in two different hands: one a perfect copperplate, the other less attractive. She had read a letter written in the latter hand before – the letter she had found in the hut; the letter that had felt somehow, but not quite, familiar, as if she had *almost* known of what it spoke.

'Who wrote all these?'

'The sisters,' said Ida, 'Margaret Gregory and her sister who died, Matilda.' She pointed to one where the words were uneven, spotted with ink. 'That's Matilda's hand. There's a lot more of those. They make better sense. Read them first.'

'I don't understand,' Biddy said.

Ida took a chair next to her. 'It's all in there, everything that happened before you were born. Matilda put it all down. Read it, love, while we have our tea.'

Biddy broke off to look up at Ida. 'That I even ended up in Summersby, Mum. It's just so incredible!'

'No incredible about it,' said Ida, folding her arms. She looked to the ceiling and – Biddy imagined – towards some nameless deity beyond. 'Some things are just meant to be and always were so.'

Biddy returned to the letters.

Biddy was hugging Ida tightly before she'd even put the last letter down. Ida clattered and spilled her teacup. Neither of them cared.

'I'm so sorry I ran away,' Biddy sobbed.

'I'm not,' said Ida, crying too, 'look what you went and found.'

'It's just so astonishing,' Biddy said. 'I went and ran away only to end up at the very place I was born.'

Ida looked to the ceiling again. 'That place is in your bones.'

'But *how* was I born?' Biddy asked. 'The letters stop before then.'

Ida took a long sip of tea. 'Three women found themselves with child at Summersby seventeen years ago, pet. The first was Matilda, her pregnancy being the fruit of her wedding night with Samuel Hackett. The second was Margaret, whose love for Samuel was given flower the same night. But it turned out that Matilda wasn't pregnant. Perhaps she thought she was at first, but time proved otherwise. That placed her in a spot because her sister was definitely expecting. In order to keep the lie going Matilda had to pad her own belly with cushion stuffing.'

Biddy boggled at the lengths Matilda had gone to. 'But who was the third woman?'

Ida took a deep breath. 'Me.'

After all that she'd read, Biddy didn't think she could know another shock, but she was wrong.

Ida shook her head before Biddy could get the question out. 'I'll never tell you who the father was. I can't bring myself to say it. You'll likely guess anyway, but I only ask you not to speak the name to me.'

'Oh, Mum.' Biddy's tears were returning.

'The man who forced his baby upon me took her away. He was violent. I miscarried. The baby was barely formed.' She sipped her tea again, composing herself before going on. 'Aggie found me in a bloodied bed the same day she found everything else. She found the two Matildas, one who was really Margaret, and one who was dead from a fall. She found Samuel Hackett, too, addled by powders I'd given him. She also found the man of whom I will not speak, who was never allowed to be a threat to us again.'

Biddy dabbed at her tears with the tablecloth.

'It fell to Aggie to fix everything,' said Ida, recovering. 'There was no one else to do it. What had come to matter most to her was Summersby. When she came to that house she gave herself over to it. She told herself she would never leave. She dedicated her life to making herself worthy of Summersby, but in my view, it was Summersby that wanted making itself worthy of her. But that was not what she thought. Aggie was too in awe of the great house and she wouldn't let the scandal of what had happened bring it down. But I just wanted to leave that place behind me. I'd been broken by it, you see.'

'Please go on, Mum,' said Biddy. She could only guess how long Ida had been keeping this story inside her.

Ida took the kettle to the water tap again and filled it before returning it to the stove. She struck a match and readied to make another brew. 'Samuel Hackett had known two wives,' she said. 'With one, Margaret, he fathered a child. The other, Matilda, was dead. Such a course of events had to be hidden away, let alone everything that had led to it. Aggie won an ally in Miss Haines and together they arranged things so that the truth about Summersby was never known outside. Matilda was buried in the same grave she was supposedly buried in when she faked her death. There was something very right about that.'

'But the baby?'

Ida nodded as she watched the kettle bring to boil. 'Margaret reached the end of her ninth month in the late spring of 1887. The birth was a surprise, and yet not a surprise, given the Gregory family history. She was delivered of twins – two girls, but not identical. The first born was named Sybil.'

Biddy looked at Ida in wonder, guessing what was coming. Ida smiled back at her, eyes shining. 'The second child, my precious Biddy, was you. Margaret is your mum.'

Biddy leapt from her chair and hugged her tight. But Ida wasn't done. 'There was never any question that Margaret – or Samuel – would remain in Summersby once the babies were born. Margaret was unable to live as a sane woman might. It wasn't her fault, but she was incapable of raising a child.'

'Oh, goodness,' Biddy said.

Ida stroked her hair. 'Samuel Hackett had been left in a damaged state by the fall down the stairs and by what I had put in his wine and by the weight of betrayal, I suspect, the realisation that he'd been so deceived. He was here but not quite here; seeing sometimes, blind at others. He was just as broken, really. The solution was Constantine Hall.'

'I understand now,' said Biddy.

'Margaret went back to the place that had played such an

important part in her story. This time she had Samuel with her, now a patient like her. The Hall's servants were well paid to stay silent. Margaret's first-born girl, Sybil, remained at Summersby in Aggie's good care. It was Aggie's hope to raise the girl in ignorance of her shocking beginnings, and for all I know she has been successful there – it seems you have come to know her well, Biddy? We knew you were at Summersby from the telegraph message.'

Biddy gasped in realisation. Her scribbled words to Sybil's relatives, tacked on the end of Mrs Marshall's letter, had ended up reaching her own family, because they were one and the same.

'When we got that message I was so relieved,' said Ida. 'I made them send in reply that you had been wronged by us all and that it was time for you to know everything. But it sounds like maybe they didn't do that – or not quite everything, anyway.'

Biddy didn't know how to answer. 'They didn't know who I really was . . . and neither did I.'

Ida shook her head. 'No child can remain in ignorance of the past. I learned this to my cost.'

Biddy hugged her again. 'But how did I end up here?'

'Aggie wanted to raise you as well,' Ida told her, 'raise you with Sybil as sisters. But Margaret did not want this. She wanted you to go to me. When I lost my baby it was Margaret's words that saved me, you see. She told me my baby had not died but was happy and safe in her womb. She meant it. She wanted me to be that baby's mother. I think it was because Margaret felt responsible for me. I felt responsible for her, too. When she returned to the Hall, I went with her. I became her lady's maid.'

The kettle boiled and Ida took it from the gas. The actions of making and drinking a fresh pot of tea seemed to help her in saying what she had never said before. 'I didn't tell my mum, my aunties, anyone what had happened to me at Summersby. For years, while you were still very small, I kept sending my wages as a means of keeping my family away. This money went to schooling my sister, Evangeline, who was always the bright spark. When

Evie finished her education, Aggie gave me the greatest gift she could. She hired Evie as governess for Sybil. This was when I took our little house in Carlton, and took for us both a new name, MacBryde, from a nice man I was friends with here.'

'He was nice,' said Biddy, remembering, even though his son Gordon had proved less so.

'I didn't want my family to find me,' Ida said. 'I didn't want you anywhere near the Hall. I kept the secret of your birth from you, and let you believe you were an ordinary girl and not an heiress; a girl with no knowledge of shame. I never told you about a twin sister. I know now how very wrong this was. So many times I came close to telling you the truth about yourself, Biddy, and so many times I failed. It was no one's fault but my own when the opportunity was stolen from me. The day Samuel Hackett came to this house, having followed me home, was almost the worst day of my life. But maybe I should think of it as the best day. In telling you he was your father, he ended the lies forever. There can only be truth with us now.'

When Biddy and Ida had each dried their eyes and sought out cake as a comfort, Biddy remembered with embarrassment that Lewis was still outside waiting for her in the street, no doubt rolling cigarettes.

'Gawd, I'd almost forgotten about him!'

Ida gave her a wry look. 'As if you'd forget about *him*.'

'What's that supposed to mean?' said Biddy, blushing, knowing that her feelings might be on show.

Ida waved the question away. 'I've known Lewis Fitzwater since he was tiny,' she said. 'He and Jim Skews were taken under Summersby's care. Aggie saw to that, although she was always more partial to Jim.'

Biddy brought some cake outside to Lewis, along with some tea.

'Thought you'd forgotten me,' he said, grinning, pleased to see her.

Ida was right. Looking at him in light of the late afternoon sun, Biddy knew she could never forget about Lewis. She was madly in love with him. Once he'd consumed the cake and tea and thanked her for them, she kissed him for the entire world to see. Peeking through the parlour curtains, Ida certainly saw it.

Biddy came back inside, holding smiling Lewis by the hand.

'Planning a double wedding with Sybil and Jim then, are you?' Ida asked, cheekily.

Mortified, Biddy was about to insist that they weren't when one look at Lewis told her he might have other ideas.

'He's taken a shine to you,' Ida declared in a stage whisper.

Talk turned to future plans and Ida made to excuse herself. 'The past has sorted itself out for me,' she said, 'the future can wait its turn.'

Biddy was insistent. 'You're part of our future, Mum, and don't think you're getting out of it. I'm an heiress now, remember, the one they always called the Secret Heiress. If I say there's a future then we're bloomin' well having one, and you can just lump it.'

'I know my future already,' said Ida, getting cross, 'it's the same as my present and the same as my past. I'll go on working as lady's maid to Miss Margaret up at the Hall.'

'No, you won't,' said Biddy, folding her arms.

'Oh, no?' said Ida, mirroring her. 'And how have you got that figured?'

'Because there'll be no more Hall,' said Biddy. 'The Hall is through.'

'What are you talking about?' said Ida, incredulous.

'What I'm talking about is going back to Summersby. All of us. We're a bloomin' family aren't we?'

Ida's eyes popped.

'We're *family*,' Biddy repeated. 'And Summersby, for all of it's dreadful draughts, and dogs in the night, and loonies and ghosties and crooks, is also a lovely place, a glorious place, and guess what, Mum, it's *home*.'

AGGIE

FEBRUARY 1904

12

The news was brought by telegraph. With Jim still in Melbourne and no one else at Summersby who could work the machine, the message had been sent to the village Railway Stores and there conveyed by a boy in a horse and trap to Mrs Marshall. She'd been contemplating baking something when he'd shown up. Once she'd read the long message and digested it, she made the Railway Stores boy stay for some dinner. Then she sent him on his way. She returned to her oven and made rhubarb crumble. It didn't take long.

Basket under her arm, and accompanied by Joey, Mrs Marshall moved along the kitchen garden path that led to the gate in the far wall. Pushing it aside, she surveyed the stretch of Summersby grounds for a moment, the stone cottage in the distance. The housekeeper made the short walk to her destination, displaying a tight smile. The dog ran around her in happy circles and Mrs Marshall dwelled on the joy he had brought her. It was Margaret who had sent Joey all the way from Melbourne, Joey being the fourth generation of offspring from the original pairing of Matilda's Billy, whom Margaret took with her to the Hall, and beloved Yip, whom Margaret found there, still devotedly waiting.

Mrs Marshall reached the cottage and saw again with dis-approval the evidence of those who lived there. Kicked off boots and cigarette ends among other unsightly debris. It was too much a male domain and Mrs Marshall made mental notes on how she would feminise it in future. Some potted pelargoniums could be bought and put in, she decided.

She went to rap her knuckles on the door before re-thinking it. Leaving the basket at the doorstop, she went around the side of the cottage, Joey at her heels, and looked for the candle box. It wasn't far from where she'd left it the last time, so she put it to its purpose again beneath the high window, standing on top to peer in. This time the bed and the room were empty.

Mrs Marshall climbed down and went to the rear of the dwelling. A rickety wire door hung half off its hinges. The wooden door behind it was shut. Mrs Marshall hesitated and then tried the handle. It was unlocked. Turning the knob as quietly as she could, the housekeeper looked in. Inside was an ill-kept kitchen, as empty as the other room. She heard a dull noise from somewhere further inside the house that sounded like an object being dragged along the floor. Joey's ears pricked up and he began a low growl.

'Hush, Joey,' Mrs Marshall told him.

The dog fell quiet.

A curtain divided the kitchen from the hallway beyond. Mrs Marshall lifted the fabric. There she found Barker shuffling along the floor on his crutches, making for the basket she'd left at the front door.

He fell upon the rhubarb crumble like a starving pig.

'I thought you might appreciate a little something nice,' said Aggie, watching him stuff his mouth with it. 'Especially with the boys away.'

In order to eat with something approaching decorum, Barker had heaved himself into his easy chair by the cold kitchen fire. Aggie suspected he'd have dined straight from the floor if there'd been no witnesses to it, and again she marvelled to herself at how easily he was able to get about, his battered pair of crutches being his preferred means of transport. His old injury had not much cowed him over the years, although it was true that he preferred to spend most of his days in bed.

'There now,' Aggie said when he had finished the rhubarb dessert, 'I bet you've been missing good cooking, Mr Barker?'

Barker's automatic response would have been to sneer at her and most likely fire off an insult, but the possibility of further meals was plainly his incentive to remain civil for the moment. 'It was passable,' he said. He managed a smirk.

The sight of those teeth, unfathomably hard and white as they ever were, was enough to make Aggie wish he'd kept them to himself. 'So then,' she said, regretting the lack of fire to boil a pot of tea. 'Let's have a chat about all that you've been up to, shall we?'

She waited for his affronted look to pass.

'Oh please, Mr Barker, let's not have games between us. I think we've known each other long enough for that, don't you?'

She waited again.

Barker's look evolved to one of almost pantomimic innocence. 'I don't know what you're talking about, woman.'

'Mr Barker, do you really wish to offend me?' Aggie wondered, with a chuckle in her voice.

The chuckle had its effect. The ghost of a smirk appeared on Barker's face beneath the fall of greying hair. Aggie tittered at seeing it. 'There, just as I thought.'

Barker snickered, too. 'You're a sharp one.'

'You are incorrigible, Mr Barker,' she told him, eyes twinkling. 'A very wicked man.'

'So what if I am?' he shot. But he was enjoying himself with her now.

'What confuses me is why you didn't exploit young Jim?'

He stroked his chin. 'Do what now?'

'Mr Barker.' She was stern. 'Didn't we say no more games? Your nephew holds a very trusted position in the Summersby household, sending and receiving telegraph messages for us as he does. We're almost at his mercy, really, with all that personal information that he sees. Yes, you could have done something there, surely, if you'd wished to, just to hurt us in some way.'

'But I didn't,' he countered. 'Yet you're right, I *could've.*'

'Indeed,' said Aggie, 'especially if Jim had done something *he* shouldn't have, perhaps? Something you found out about and thought you could use against him?'

There was a long minute's silence.

'Who says he hasn't then?' said Barker.

Aggie's eyes widened. 'Has he?'

Barker just smirked, leaning back against the cushion.

'Has he, Mr Barker?' Mrs Marshall pressed. 'Please tell me if he has. I would hate to think that our trust in Jim might have been misplaced in some way.'

He leant forward in his chair, toying with her. 'Give you such a nasty shock if ever you found out about it,' he taunted. 'A nasty shock indeed.'

Aggie patted his knee. 'Let me guess,' she said. 'Is it that Jim and Sybil are sweethearts?'

Barker's stubbled jaw set.

'I see that it is,' said Aggie, gratified. 'I've only recently found out about it myself as if happens.' She thought of the message the boy had brought. She'd had time to grow accustomed to the shock of it – and it *had* been a shock – but Barker wasn't to be allowed to know how badly it had hit her. 'I think they'll be very happy with each other,' she declared, as much to persuade herself as anything else.

'You were always a charmless liar,' said Barker, seeing right through her.

Aggie's mouth tightened. 'Unlike yourself, I suppose?'

'What's all your Secret Heiress palaver if not a half-cut fairytale from the start? You'd have done better to claim she just died at birth.'

'You know very well that Sybil's sister is real.'

'I know very well you made a bloody big bogey out of it,' said

Barker, enjoying the high moral ground with Aggie for once, 'and a rod for your own back now your lovely Sybil's old enough to think. It gives me hours of pleasure mulling on how it must be coming back to bite you now.'

Aggie drew a deep breath. 'It was her mother's wishes that the girls be separated. She was fearful of history repeating itself.'

'You were fearful of it, more like; fearful of everything and anything that threatened your precious house. The lengths you went to hide it all!' He laughed at the icy look on her face. 'Nothing stays hidden forever, you know,' he added.

But Aggie did know. 'You did try to exploit Jim, didn't you?' she asked. 'You tried to blackmail him in some way, get him to tell you little secrets about us, so that you could upset us all with them somehow, and upset me more than anyone I have no doubt.'

He watched her, expressionless.

'But Jim said no. He called your bluff. He's too decent a young man to be manipulated by you. Perhaps he guessed what really happened to his father all those years ago? Guessed you'd had more than a hand in it? That must have made you very cross to be refused by your nephew. Did he add insult to injury by laughing in your face? I can only imagine how angry that must have made you feel . . . so angry you wanted to hurt someone.'

His eyes twinkled. Despite everything, he was delighted with himself; thinking he'd scored another mark against her.

'Is that why you poured that nasty stuff into the bread?' Aggie wondered.

She saw him catch his breath.

'Was it inside that old blue perfume bottle?' she asked. 'I went and looked in the stillroom afterwards, you see, because of something Biddy said, and that's when I looked at the shelves. I found an old blue bottle up there from the late Mr Skews' apothecary – a bottle I recognised, as well I should. Someone put some very nasty stuff in my food once. Did it come from the same bottle?'

He was frozen, watching her.

'There was nothing left inside when I found it this time, sadly, but I guessed that there had been up until then. There was no dust on it, you see. Someone else had rubbed it off.' She looked at Barker's near-useless legs, skeletal beneath his filthy trousers. 'It beggars' belief that you got into my kitchen without me seeing, but you did somehow, didn't you, Mr Barker, and you have been coming in for some time. Late at night, perhaps, snooping about, stealing bits of food? That's how you found the blue bottle at all, isn't it? With you it's always been where there's a will there's a way.'

He put a hand to his temple as if the beginnings of a headache were coming on.

On an impulse she kicked him in the shin.

'Ow! Take a care, will you!? What's the matter with you?'

She leaned forward in the chair she was sitting in. 'You didn't give a damn who ate that bread, did you? No doubt you hoped that I would eat it or maybe Sybil, perhaps? It could even have been Jim who ended up with it as his dinner – would you have shed a tear then?' She sniffed at him in disgust. 'Probably not.'

Aggie got to her feet and began returning the things she had brought to her basket. 'I took some persuading not to bring the Law down on your head all those years ago when you did what you did to Mr Skews,' she told him.

'He was a drug fiend!' Barker sneered. 'I never got him hooked, that was all his own cretinism.'

'Let alone for what you did to poor Ida.'

He had no denial for that.

Aggie put away the baking dish. 'Such a vicious thing, rape. No matter how much you loved Miss Matilda, surely even *you* knew that that particular request was a step too far?'

He sank deeper into his chair, trying to tune her out.

'It was Ida who convinced me not to go to the Sergeant about it. She knew – and I knew, too, of course – that everything else that had happened would bring too big a scandal to Summersby, one we couldn't have survived.' She paused, thinking back on traumatic times. 'So, I didn't do anything to punish you back then. I suppose I thought being crippled was almost punishment enough.' She covered the top of her basket with a folded dish-cloth. 'But I see now that it wasn't.'

She waited for that comment to register with him. It took a moment, but when it did he looked up at her. She was pleased to see a sliver of fear in his hateful black eyes. 'Which is why I decided to punish you today.'

Barker's eyes bulged. The throbbing at his temple intensified.

'I held onto that bread when I realised it had been poisoned,' Aggie said, standing with her arms crossed protectively across her basket. 'I put it carefully away, sealed so that no one could get to it. And when I worked out that it must have been you who'd put that stuff inside it I resolved to make you eat it instead.'

She pulled the curtain aside, ready to make the short walk to the front door. Joey was already waiting there, eager to be gone. 'Not an easy thing to get a man to eat stale bread,' she said, 'no matter how hungry he gets. Then I thought of breadcrumbs. And then I thought of making a nice rhubarb crumble.' Aggie took one last look at the repellent man who had made so many lives a misery; the man who'd exploited her fear of scandal and lived off Summersby grace and favour for too long. Aggie took comfort from the thought that the next time she looked at him he'd be lying stone-cold dead. 'Do you know,' she asked, as she ducked through the hallway curtain, 'if you hadn't been in a hurry to make a pig of yourself, you might have savoured my crumble a little more, you might have appreciated the hint of rosemary there. Not every cook would think to add rosemary to rhubarb, but my experience has shown me that it complements things very nicely. Very nicely indeed.'

When Aggie pulled the front door closed behind her Summersby came into view. Retracing her steps towards the great house again, Joey by her side, Aggie found herself on the verge of a run. She made an effort to take hold of herself, conscious of her age and her standing. Then her mind wandered to the many tasks she would need to do if she was ever to prepare the house for the imminent return of the Gregorys. Before she knew it, Aggie was running fully, flying through the fresh autumn grass.

ACKNOWLEDGEMENTS

The Secret Heiress has been one of the longest creative roads I have ever hoed, and I have been humbled along the way by the patience and unceasing good humour shown to me by those who shared the trek at Simon & Schuster Australia, most especially Larissa Edwards, Roberta Ivers and Jody Lee. I also owe a debt of gratitude to my agent Lyn Tranter, who pulled no punches when reminding me of the differences between an intriguing mystery and a bewildering one. Andrew Brown, my partner of twenty-three years, experienced little joy in the creative journey, but this didn't stop him feeding me, thank heavens. He also drove our move to Castlemaine a decade ago, and for that he'll always be loved.

I'm a bowerbird when it comes to historical research, plucking nuggets of facts from sources and throwing them into the messy nest that somehow becomes a book. My earlier drafts had more evidence of this before the needs of plotting and pace forced me to be brutal. I hope enough of the glitter remains, however, for the reader to realise, as I did, that the Australian character was set in stone long before the modern age. Our insolent optimism in the face of adversity, our good-natured dismissal of authority figures, and our steadfast love of humour as the weapon of choice are all to be found in our past. These things aren't new, as any Aboriginal Australian will tell you without having to read any book. When the first Europeans found themselves beached here they simply sniffed the prevailing wind.

The works of two historians proved particularly gem laden for me: Michael Cannon's fascinating 'Australia in the Victorian Age' histories, *Life in the Cities* and *Life in the Country*; and Geoffrey Blainey's wonderfully eclectic *Black Kettle and Full Moon: Daily Life in a Vanished Australia*.

Luke Devenish

ABOUT THE
AUTHOR

*L*uke Devenish has written plays and historical fiction, and worked as a writer and script producer for much-loved, long running Australian television dramas. His first two novels, *Den of Wolves* and *Nest of Vipers*, about the women behind the men of Ancient Rome, were translated into five languages, earning him a passionate international readership. A film and television academic at the University of Melbourne's Victorian College of the Arts, Luke is as fervent about teaching as he is about writing, and is enjoyed for his lively, inspiring classes. Luke lives with his partner and pets in historic Castlemaine, Central Victoria.

Visit www.lukedevenish.com